THE SUN SETS IN SINGAPORE

THE SUN SETS IN SINGAPORE

A NOVEL

KEHINDE FADIPE

GRAND
CENTRAL

NEW YORK   BOSTON

Copyright © 2023 by Kehinde E. Fadipe

Cover design by Sarah Congdon
Cover illustration by Yehrin Tong
Cover copyright © 2023 by Hachette Book Group, Inc.

Grand Central Publishing
Hachette Book Group
1290 Avenue of the Americas, New York, NY 10104
grandcentralpublishing.com
twitter.com/grandcentralpub

Originally published in 2023 by Dialogue Books in Great Britain
First U.S. Edition: October 2023

Grand Central Publishing is a division of Hachette Book Group, Inc. The Grand Central Publishing name and logo is a trademark of Hachette Book Group, Inc.

The publisher is not responsible for websites (or their content) that are not owned by the publisher.

Grand Central Publishing books may be purchased in bulk for business, educational, or promotional use. For information, please contact your local bookseller or the Hachette Book Group Special Markets Department at special.markets@hbgusa.com.

Library of Congress Control Number: 2023940230

ISBN: 9781538741498 (hardcover), 9781538741511 (ebook)

Printed in the United States of America

LSC

Printing 1, 2023

To T and T, for cracking my heart open

THE SUN SETS IN SINGAPORE

Dara

Beneath the Singapore Cricket Club veranda, Dara watched two teams of lawyers sweat it out in the annual law rugby tournament held every January, and allowed herself a small, happy sigh. Under the cool shade, she felt some mild pity for the poor bastards playing under the sun's sticky glare, but suffering in the heat never lasted long in Singapore; discomfort was always reliably suspended in the blue or yellow taxis that swarmed the city, or through the icy gusts that rushed onto the streets from the malls. It was like a contract signed as a basic human right: *"You shall never perspire for long."*

Dara sat at the top of the stand beside Lucy, a junior associate on her team, and one of the new trainees. It was a good vantage point from which to keep an eye on her boss, Ian, as he entertained two of his most important Japanese clients at the bottom of the steps. She would be ready whenever he caught her eye and gave her the green light to approach. In the meantime, she tried to feign interest in the losing team in green, which was made up of amateur and semi-professional players from her firm, Morgan Corbett Shaw. She'd given up checking her phone to see if her best friend, Amaka, would make an appearance. Even though Amaka's bank was helping to sponsor the tournament, she somehow always found a way to avoid these work events, something Dara just couldn't afford to do.

Giving up a Sunday afternoon would be worth it, though. Dara felt as confident as Perseus with the Gorgon's head in his bag, being so close to the partnership she'd spent the past six years working for. Work was going so well that it didn't matter that she was experiencing caffeine withdrawals from missing her hourly fix, or that she was being forced to give up a much-needed day of rest. She usually wasn't in the city much at the weekend; she traveled every chance she got, taking advantage of Singapore's many public holidays, a welcome by-product of a country that officially celebrated three different religions. The past Christmas break had been spent cycling on her own in Laos, a wonderful change from the year before when she'd celebrated with friends of friends who, like her, were avoiding both the English winter and their difficult families, chugging bottomless glasses of champagne in a hotel lacking genuine festive spirit. Whenever her married friends started giving her dating advice (a grown woman of thirty-six!) or tried to fix her up at parties with men they would never have considered for themselves, she reminded herself that she'd been to ten out of twelve countries in Southeast Asia multiple times, and had seen and experienced things that would have been impossible with children in tow. So, whenever Amaka broke off in the middle of a conversation like a puppet, gawking at a nice butt and pulsing biceps (or shiny bag), or Lucy grieved over her latest failed date, it made the imminent payoff of Dara's investment in her career—at one of the largest law firms in the world, no less—even sweeter.

One of the green players—it was hard to recognize his face from this distance—tried to dash across the field; he was brought crashing down by three men in red.

"All the girls I've met here complain about the English guys catching yellow fever, but the guy I've been seeing has been here two years and he's never even *dated* an Asian girl," Lucy boasted, reminiscing about her recent date.

The trainee, who had only been in Singapore a month, looked confused at this bit of casual racism, but Dara stifled a smile, accustomed to the terrified insecurity of the English girls here. Most of the expats she knew were French, British or American; the women mostly dated other French, British or American expats, contracting their pool of dating options, while frustratingly (for them, at least), the men did not.

"He moved out here with his now-ex. They were engaged, but

he said she missed home too much, which I completely understand." Lucy tilted over the trainee, shaking her curls in earnest. "But nuking a relationship like that—madness. I'd pack all this the second there's a proposal. Are you kidding?"

"So she went back to the UK?" Dara asked, pressing two paracetamols into her palm. She'd worked for ten days straight and would have given anything to swap the warm cup of wine in her hand for an almond milk latte.

"Well, no actually. Yes and no. Total fluke—Andy said she met someone on the flight back and six months later they were married. They live in Sicily now, where the guy's from, and she's got one on the way," Lucy said ruefully.

"He told you all this?" Dara stared at her suspiciously.

"She invited him to the wedding. Anyway, I still say it was a risky move."

"Hmm." Dara couldn't hide a smile as she dug out a small, battery-operated fan from her bag and switched it on. "I see what you're saying. You've got your career and all she's got is a ball in her stomach, lemons everywhere and a bossy mother-in-law."

The trainee barked a short laugh and Lucy paused, unsure who the joke was on.

"Speaking of careers…" Lucy smiled conspiratorially. "Now that you've been given lead on the Nairobi case, it's only a matter of time, isn't it? As long as the case goes well, of course."

"Is that what everyone's been saying?" Dara shrugged and swapped the fan over to her left side, pretending her heart hadn't skipped a beat. Secretly, she was pleased it was so obvious to everyone in the firm. The one area of her life she was truly confident about was her ability to work longer and harder and smarter than everyone else. It was what had earned her a scholarship to a private girls school in St. Albans and got her through three lonely, uncomfortable years studying Classics at Oxford where she had never fitted in and couldn't afford the time and energy it took to try. Not for the first time, she wished she'd had some guidance along the way, someone to warn her that actual working life relied on so much more than intellect and being the smartest in the class.

She'd had to figure it out on her own, second-guessing whether she'd been given an opportunity for the right or wrong reason, if she was being too pushy or not pushy enough, if she'd stroked the right ego the right way, or how she would be judged for caring about partnership above everything else. Finally, it seemed, everyone around her was starting to see Dara the way she saw herself: as the best senior associate in the firm.

"Yes, Dara, *everyone*." Lucy lowered her voice, looking so excited they might as well have been talking about her. "The clients love you and it's a major arbitration. With the Kenyans so obviously in the wrong, it couldn't be more perfect. And with Ian so close to..."

Lucy made a noose gesture and dropped her head to one side.

"OK, let's not talk about that here, with everyone...*here*." Dara made a face. "How did the rest of the date go?"

"Well, after dinner—which was amazing, a little too rich but really nice—we went to a bar in Orchard Towers, just for a laugh." Lucy's voice carried a whiff of scandal. "Have you heard of it? I don't know, is that weird?"

Dara had to move—she couldn't take another second pretending to be interested or pretending it was normal for a date to take you to a building that was part of the country's Red Light Guide. It may have been smack bang in the middle of town, surrounded by malls and even a handful of preschools, but no amount of adjacent respectability could hide what took place on the top floors at night. The activities were (apparently) strictly government regulated, and the sex workers were regularly screened, but Dara was sure there were millions of other bars more appropriate. Lucy's date was yet more evidence of the rubbish on offer in Singapore's dating scene.

"Oh crap, sorry, Lucy." Dara rummaged in her bag until she found her phone and put it to her ear. "I've been waiting for this call."

Rising and shuffling to the edge of the bench, she turned her head away from the two women and pretended to speak to someone, relaxing only when she was out of earshot. As much as she found Lucy's lack of guile refreshing, her big mouth and unsophistication were the last things Dara wanted to be associated with, especially at this critical juncture. She also found Lucy's undisguised hunger to be married and spoken for truly disheartening, if not downright bizarre. No one droned on like this in London, but here, it was as if crossing an ocean made young, working women shed the tough skins they'd developed to conceal their desire for attachment in their home countries, revealing the raw, pink truth their ambition had been hiding all along. A haze of desperation was blowing from Lucy, and Dara needed to remove herself from its path.

Having bought some time, Dara checked her messages, tugging at the polyester T-shirt she'd been forced to wear. She missed the safe, predictable work clothes she relied on and felt most comfortable in. Even though some women found it suffocating, she was never more at ease than in an ironed shirt and pencil skirt. It made her feel connected to her grandparents, who were long gone now, but who had brought her up as their own child in Lagos. She'd been folded between them, safe within their unit, and had never had to question much about her life.

On Sundays at their Baptist Church, her grandmother's hat would always be pinned in place and her grandfather was always suited, a red silk flower blooming from his lapel, pipe tobacco tucked in his inside pocket. After escaping the tortuous Sunday school, Dara would sit between them, listening to the Yoruba sermon in what felt like an airless room. Her itchy dress would scratch her legs and the warm air would waft in her direction from the women's silk fans that fluttered like caged birds. The fans were often souvenirs from funerals and birthday parties, printed with the faces of the celebrants, and Dara always felt like they were leering at her. When the heat and her boredom would make her drowsy, Grandma would pinch her and stare pointedly, until she went back to clapping and mouthing the hymns she could barely understand. Grandad, unfairly, was able to hide his dozing behind his sunglasses.

At the end of the service, the adults would pour into the church compound, buzzing, blabbing and gisting, periodically reaching into their flowing *agbada* pockets and purses for dirty naira notes to drop into the hands of beggars jutting through the holes in the courtyard walls. No matter how hard Dara tried to sneak away, Grandma would always block her attempts to join the other children buying Wall's ice cream from the van by the gate. Dara was rarely allowed to taste the sweet, soggy blocks of ice cream wrapped in paper, since Grandma was convinced they were bearers of typhoid—she had always distrusted the hygiene standards of the factory where they were made. Grandad, Dara's partner in crime, lover of classical tales and ancient mythology and supplier of contrabanded sweets, would push his lips out behind his wife's back as she told Dara off, to show her not to mind the old woman. Dara would burst out laughing and inevitably get in even more trouble, setting off the lecture she'd heard countless times about "home training," "following bad company" and "carry-ing oneself like a lady." As members of that uncomfortable class of people who had enough money to buy a good life, but not *quite* enough to afford not to care what other people thought, they set high expectations for their granddaughter, which came with the understanding that she also look impeccable at all times. By the time they'd passed away, Grandad from sickle cell complications and Grandma in her sleep two years later, the foundation for their preferences had already been laid.

When they died, Dara was sent to England to live with her mother, Abigail, who worked in the office of her local Hertfordshire council in the daytime and tried to make it as a mixed-medium artist at night. At first, living with Abigail—who'd anglicized her name from Abisola—had been fun. What eleven-year-old wouldn't have been thrilled to have a mother who dressed in boob tubes and jeans like a Spice Girl, let her straighten her hair and was eager to share her makeup? The answer to anything Dara asked had been a shrugged *yes*, and the excitement of life with no rules had helped Dara push past her grief. Before long, though, she realized that Abigail's free-spirited liberalism came with never being able to hold down a job, never reading the school uniform list and not caring whether Dara fitted in at her new school. Dara would never be cool or keep up with the popular girls, but she learned quickly that the people who had the power to guarantee her future were not impressed by those things. It was *adults* who could give her As, make her a school prefect to award her academic brilliance and write her references for summer internships. In senior school, despite her mother's example, everything Dara's grandparents had taught her began to kick in. Now, it was completely ingrained in who she was.

So, it was a struggle to feel presentable yet relaxed in shorts and a fluorescent orange T-shirt with her firm's logo blazoned across her chest. It was a size too small for one thing, and, from the reflection in her phone, sweat was beginning to settle across her forehead like pellets of oil on a roast chicken. Her blow dry was beginning to revert in the heat and her foundation—the closest to her color she'd been able to find in Sephora—was two shades lighter than her natural hue. She put her phone away, reminding herself that her brains and not her beauty were what had brought her this far.

The Singapore Cricket Club was at least something to look at. Colonial, white-stoned and red-roofed, it sat on one edge of the Padang playing field, flanked on one side by traffic and by a river on the other. Its facilities were quaintly old-fashioned, and its members could enjoy a tennis court, two squash courts, billiards and snooker tables, a bowls green, a Men's bar and a reference library—when they weren't making millions tax-free and com-plaining about the high cost of living, of course.

An army of faceless skyscrapers watched on blankly as the men formed a circle on the field. Arms across shoulders, they grunted against each other, pushing in a scrum until a single player scram-bled away, the ball clenched under his arm.

The crowd roared and Dara's eyes turned from the field to the stand. When she'd first moved to Singapore six years before, she used to play a little game with herself, which involved counting how many black people there were at events like these and guessing how long they'd been in the city. If a black person bounced up to her, waved or introduced themselves immediately, she could tell they'd been here for years (or were probably American) and were a little lonely, missed home cooking or were curious about her backstory. They were also usually disappointed to find out that she didn't have kids—she always felt some sadness at the thought of black parents looking for *any* kid for their child to play with who looked like them. If said black person just made eye contact and smiled, then they'd been in Singapore a year and were not yet too fussed about building a community. And if they blanked you, then they'd either just arrived or had come straight from London or New York.

Today, at the match, she counted a total of one: her.

She looked over at Ian again, a little perplexed that he hadn't called her over yet to join him, Mr. Sano and Mr. Erikawa. They were executives at Hakida, a global construction firm currently in a dispute over a bridge they'd been contracted to build in Kenya. Dara had been working on the case for nearly a year and was practically running it on her own.

There was a burst of applause as a player on the red team kicked the ball, sending it soaring between a large white "H" on the field. She let the shift in energy pull her to her feet and down the steps to seek Ian out.

Once she'd set off, she wished she'd stayed put. In motion, she regressed from *"Dah-rah"* (tall, elegant, Oxford graduate) to "DA-ra" (gauche, clueless eleven-year-old fresh off the plane from Lagos's Murtala Muhammed Airport). All those years she'd spent refining a neutral, British accent, dropping the "l" in "salmon" and ironing out the pronunciation of words she'd only read but never heard before, dropped away. Never did she feel more out of place than when she was moving. She'd been unaffectionately nicknamed "Big Bird" at school, for always being at least a head taller than the other girls—nothing like the peacock or swan she'd always hoped to be. More like an ostrich or flamingo, a fowl capable of elegance, yet disappointingly clumsy.

She quickened her pace down the steps, trying to keep her still-full plastic cup of wine upright. Her flapping must have been eye-catching because Chris, one of her fellow senior associates, huddled down by the barrier with two others, raised his arm and waved her over. She pretended not to see him, but he waved again. Groaning inside, she approached the three men she liked to think of as The Sirens.

A look of bemusement crossed each man's face as they took in her outfit. Various-sized bellies protruded from their cotton polo shirts, and strips of hair bristled down their arms and calves. The obligatory pink cotton shorts were in full attendance.

"Did you hear about Imran?" Chris asked. "He got cut three days back from his secondment. Effective immediately. Three months loaned out to a client and had to be out of the office the next day. It's absolutely disgraceful the way he's been treated."

He made another sympathetic noise, in fitting with his role as all-around-good-guy. She liked Chris more than she should. The "Siren in a Sheep Suit" worked in shipping and seemed harmless on the surface but was ruthless underneath. She'd seen him be incredibly tender with his three boys, then use them to get into people's good books when it suited him.

Ben, "Baby Siren," a newly made-up senior associate in the finance group, pursed his lips. "Yeah, it's terrible."

With brown ringlets curling over his eyes and the back of his collar, Ben was the type of boy she'd spent the last twenty years running after who usually turned out to be gay. He was the kind of young lawyer the partners loved because he reminded them of their own sons—and their younger selves.

"Did you see his team's weeklies? They went below fifty percent at one point! Everyone saw that coming." Tim shook his head mercilessly.

Older, single and heavyset, "Chief Siren" Tim was too many years post-qualified in the general insurance team. One felt he was always on the verge of being cut, in danger of being thrown away, like a cup of milk left out too long. Everyone knew he'd never make partner; moving in-house to the legal department of some nondescript company (or, as Dara liked to think of it, the sixth circle of hell) was only a matter of time. Tim was the most dangerous of men: bitter and frustrated, with little left to lose.

"He never should have gone on leave," Tim pronounced. "What a mug. You're a target the minute your billables are down. You don't take a *holiday*."

"Colin stopped feeding him work." Dara leaned forward. "They fell out. That's why he got put on secondment in the first place."

She knew how to play this game. Sandwiched between the partners and the juniors, the senior associates were hyenas, dangerous pack animals that would turn on each other in a blood-curdling heartbeat. They did the actual work, drafting contracts and drawing up advice for the senior partner leading their team, but orbited close enough to the clients to make them a threat. She supposed she was a hyena, too, but she liked to think of herself more like one of those big cats in Milton's Garden of Eden, playing with a goat, claws retracted, aware of her powers but a vegan at heart.

"Really?" Chris looked put out. He worked for Colin. "I hadn't heard this. Why'd they fall out?"

"Sorry, my source runs dry," she smiled, sipping her wine.

"Partner's secrets?" Tim smirked, bitchily.

"I really don't...It's all hearsay at this point." Dara looked in Ian's direction, wary of this turn. A couple of yards away, Ian looked like he'd just swapped his usual uniform of white shirt, tie and trousers for a white shirt and slightly *less* formal trousers.

"Come off it. Any day now," Tim said. "We all know Ian's pushing retirement. If the firm doesn't want to lose its credibility, it has to stick to the rules, right?"

The three men stared at Dara, hungry for a reaction, their smiles doing a poor job of hiding real envy. So this was the real reason they'd called her over. They wanted to know if Ian Breen, a colossus in the firm and one of the founding partners, was really going to retire after his sixty-fifth birthday and leave his practice to a black girl. It didn't matter that she was Oxbridge and had completed her two-year training contract at Morgan Corbett Shaw's London office, qualifying and working at the firm ever since. Ticking a diversity box was one thing, but when it came to the face of the firm, she stuck out on the website like a beetle in a bag of rice.

"Ian's not going anywhere. He's got plenty of years left." Dara rolled out the party line, praying the opposite was true.

"Yeah..."

"Yeah..."

"Course..."

A pause settled, pregnant with questions, and in it she felt another tremor of excitement. She was so close, but still... you worked like a dog in your twenties and thirties, kissed ass, kept your mouth shut, traveled at the click of a finger, stopped exercising, stopped sleeping, forgot the feeling of a penis inside you, and... it actually paid off?

"Well, you've worked your arse off," Chris cut through the silence. "And it's great timing. You've been lucky the Asian investment into Africa has picked up in a big way—that more companies are willing to fight it out in arbitrations here instead of defaulting to London."

Luck. Of course.

"How do you get on with some of the... *Asian* clients though?" Ben lowered his voice. "Do you not find some of them... difficult?"

Do they like black people, you mean?

"I've got two of *them* standing behind us, so maybe..." Dara's voice said, *let's keep it down.* Her client relationships were fine, but you could never let The Sirens try to shipwreck you.

"Oops." Tim raised an eyebrow in mock apology.

Dara found Ian's eyes gazing over at her. At the small nod of his chin, she took her leave.

"Duty calls," she apologized before moving off.

"*Mata Oaidekiteureshidesi*—It's good to see you again." She bowed to Mr. Erikawa and then Mr. Sano, deliberately mispronouncing a syllable.

"Good, good," beamed Mr. Erikawa after repeating the phrase correctly.

"I've been practicing." She hoped she sounded humble enough. She'd considered getting more sounds wrong, but she didn't want to appear a complete halfwit.

"After our last Tokyo visit, I insisted she work on it—it was terrible," Ian said dryly.

The clients glanced at Ian, unsure if his comment was a criticism. They laughed a split second later, Mr. Erikawa the loudest. As the more junior of the two, Mr. Sano deferred to him on everything, letting the older man order for him in restaurants and enter and leave rooms first.

Mr. Sano was generous. "Your Japanese is better."

"Thank you. And we're really pleased with the progress we're making on the dispute. We've worked with the appointed arbitrator before and the contract is airtight," Dara said. In fact, she'd never seen a case so favorable, and still couldn't believe the Kenyan side had let things get this far. The case had been stalled due to a disagreement between the Kenyan authorities and some disgruntled chiefs, who claimed that the bridge was being built on ancestral land too close to a sacred river and was therefore protected by local law. Now, Hakida was suing the Kenyans for breach of contract on the basis that the chiefs were technically part of the government itself. The Japanese wanted the dispute settled or their investment returned.

"I was just explaining to the gentlemen that it's a fifty-fifty call whether the tribunal will rule in our favor or not. When dealing with unknown entities in Africa—however strong your case—you never know what to expect." Ian beckoned to a waiter. "Tonic water, please."

"We thought that the Kenyan government would settle before we even started this proceeding." Mr. Erikawa crossed his arms in frustration. "Our men have been in Nairobi for *three* months and do nothing. All the materials for the bridge—they sit there."

"We want to avoid arbitration, but we're concerned that the Kenyan government has not offered a deal," Mr. Sano explained more gently. "We just want the problem to go away so construction can continue. We want the bridge; the Kenyans want the bridge. The only ones who do not want the bridge…"

"The chiefs." Mr. Erikawa waved his hand in disgust. "They are the problem."

"They say the land is sacred, but there is an American hotel under construction there, so we are thinking this is not really the case. Maybe they want to change the terms; maybe they want more money. We are hoping this is an area Ms. Dara can be of service," Mr. Sano explained. "As an African woman, she can communicate with our local lawyer in Nairobi? This is just our idea."

Dara wondered if they thought being African was like carrying a member's card—you flashed it, racked up points and got email alerts when a private sale was on. It had already occurred to her that the Kenyan chiefs were grandstanding so they could be cut in on the construction deal, and she had just begun to form a suitably positive response when Ian beat her to it.

"Dara is an integral part of my team, and her work has been exemplary. I very much hope she will continue to cement her position—I have no doubt that her future is bright." Ian smiled at her.

Dara smiled back, but Ian's use of such a trite phrase was unlike him; it transformed her growing unease into full-blown dread.

"But you will be pleased to know that I am in the process of hiring another senior associate to join our team. I've been considering it for some time now and I've just made an offer. He's a great guy—Nigerian, like Dara actually, and based over in Geneva. He's got lots of experience in large-scale arbitrations and comes with fantastic Africa contacts, which will be very beneficial in our negotiations. Cambridge man, like myself."

Mr. Sano and Mr. Erikawa hummed with excitement.

"In fact, I've just got great news from our HR team that all his paperwork has been approved, and Lani—that's his name—should be with us in a matter of weeks." Ian made eye contact with each man but avoided Dara's gaze. "So, rest assured, you will have the very best talent working on your case, and we will do everything we can to settle and get the bridge up on its feet."

Dara's smile slid off her face. This had to be a joke. But Ian didn't tell jokes.

Another roar of applause. Someone must have scored. The men turned to the field and Dara was forgotten, lost in her confusion.

Nigerian...fantastic Africa contacts...Cambridge...

He'd found a male version of her.

Lani. He appeared to her with blinding clarity, sprawled out in his Premium Economy seat, flirting with the dainty, porcelain-as-teacups Singapore Airlines hostesses. She saw a Cheshire grin stretch across his face, numb from his third cup of whisky, and watched him kick back as the plane lights dimmed. She saw him journey across the ocean, a smug Odysseus, coming to steal everything she'd worked so hard to build.

Amaka

Amaka scrolled down the shopping app, her mouth moistening and heart rate quickening. The heels were six inches high and a rich shade of plum, with Roman cords that wove up the model's foot, tied around the ankle and dropped down in delicious tassels. They were exquisite, sexy and completely impractical, but she visualized herself in them anyway and loved what she saw.

She glanced up at Rohit, whose face was half-blocked by both their computers. He was immersed in his work, munching on a granola bar as he typed, depositing millions of microbes into the cracks of his keyboard. Many of the staff on the credit risk floor of the bank were doing the same.

She dropped the heels into her basket; with her credit card details already stored, the transaction was over in seconds. The climax came with the confirmation email and thumbnail of her purchase; delight coursed through her body as she enlarged the image with her thumb and forefinger. Below it, though, was the cold truth of the money she'd spent: *Charges will appear on your credit card statement.*

The quiver of pleasure ebbed away. Amaka closed all her phone tabs and deleted her search history, a pointless and unconvincing action. The "thirty percent," "forty percent" and "sixty percent" discounts below each item had initially beckoned her closer; now they looked like little stamps of failure.

Next, she batted away her mother's emails: an alarmist *Daily Mail* article about the cancer-causing ingredients hiding in most beauty products, a daily Catholic devotion and meditation, the details of their virtual Family Meeting in two weeks' time. Seeing

Ugo's name, who had brought her up to never waste anything, to use and reuse, and who kept the protective plastic wrapping on everything she bought, filled her with guilt. It threatened to bring back all those memories of scarcity, when the unpredictability of their lives depended completely on her father's money and whether it came through or not. One week, mother and daughter would squeeze into a cramped, doorless Danfo bus to get to school and work; the next, they could afford to collect Ugo's freshly serviced Volvo from the garage and inhale its pine-scented air freshener and foamy leather polish. One week, Amaka would be treated to pizza and ice cream on Victoria Island, the moneyed part of Lagos with beaches, shopping plazas, and British and American schools; the next, Ugo would have to fan a charcoal stove to make their pancakes in their Surulere building complex, opening the kitchen door to release the itchy fumes. She and Ugo had to ration luxuries carefully and always made sure they had a constant supply of candles and matchsticks kept in the exact same place so they could move easily in the dark when the electricity was cut off. They'd fill every bucket and spare container with water, ready for the moment when they turned on the tap and nothing came out.

Something white blurred between her eyes and bounced off her forehead. A scrunched-up paper ball dropped into her lap.

"Is your head OK?"

She glared at Rohit before following his eyeline to see their boss approaching.

"Morning." Amaka flashed a smile at Indira, tucking her phone away.

"Morning," Rohit echoed.

"Morning." Indira leaned on the partition, barely glancing at Rohit. "Have you got the numbers for the Toulouse report?"

"Nearly there. I'll get them to you today," Amaka replied.

"Good girl." Indira tapped the wall and crossed over to her office.

"*Good girl*," Rohit joked. "Are you her poodle now?"

"And why not? I bet her poodle eats very well," Amaka smirked. "And wears Louis Vuitton and gets regular manicures."

She clicked the file open for the French mining company she'd been researching. It had a poor track record and its credit rating had been slipping for years. It was true that, although she'd been working just over a year for Indira, she'd been given more responsibility and autonomy than was normal for a credit risk officer of her experience, especially moving from the bank's Lagos branch. Many of the other officers, including Rohit, had worked in banks in London, New York and Sydney before landing a coveted spot in Singapore, but on Indira's team, Amaka was rewarded for her aptitude with financial ratios and statistics, not to mention her borderline obsessive research of companies applying for bank loans.

Rohit rolled his eyes. "I'm not sure who loves who more: you or her. Do you think she knows that we've been...?"

"No, and it needs to stay that way, please," Amaka warned.

"Everybody knows..." He lowered his voice, teasing. "She's not blind."

"That's how they'll pass me up for a promotion, because I was distracted. I came to Singapore to make money, not to find a husband."

Rohit raised his eyebrows, amused. "Husband?"

"You know what I mean," Amaka said, suddenly flustered. "Husband, boyfriend. Same difference."

"So if I propose to you right now, you'll say no?"

"Can you stop? I need to work," she retorted.

"Everyone..." Rohit stood up, arms stretched wide as if to make an announcement.

"Sit down! Rohit!" Amaka hissed before doubling over in laughter.

He sat down, covering his mouth and pointing at her. "Your face!"

She kissed her teeth and tried to ignore him.

"It's OK," he said when he'd stopped laughing and could speak again. "We've been dating for six months—I'm not crazy. Besides, my parents would kill me if I proposed to someone they'd never met."

Amaka's smile wavered. Her nerves returned whenever Rohit mentioned his family. Added to her usual relationship hesitancy was her certainty that few Indian families would welcome her with open arms.

"That's the first time you've smiled today," Rohit said, not catching her dip in mood.

"Really?" She kept working.

"Thinking about your family call next week?" Rohit turned serious.

Amaka bristled. She regretted opening up about the family dispute over her father's estate since his heart attack two years before. During a vulnerable moment late at night, her head on his chest and their calves entwined, she'd let him coax some of the details out of her, but the next morning, she'd felt resentful and spiky, while he thought the conversation had brought them closer. It was as though she'd exposed a tender bruise and let him knead it; every time his hand reached for it now, she wanted to smack it away. Her yearning to be part of her father's family, to take his last name and be publicly recognized as the oldest of his four children, was a secret part of her no man before Rohit had ever been allowed to see.

"What are you talking about?" Amaka looked up. "I've been working."

"You just... don't look very happy today. I thought maybe..."

"I'm just tired, *chill*. And stop throwing stuff at me, it's so *Saved by the Bell*."

He laughed off her retort and wagged his finger. "Now you're showing your age. Shouldn't it be 'so *O.C.*'?"

"My friend, I have work to do," Amaka chuckled, sending a document to the printer and standing up. "I know you spent your time in New York wanking off to that stick-figure Marisa-what's-her-name..."

"Amaka, that is an inappropriate workplace comment..."

Smoothing her fitted knitted dress down, she went to collect her document from the printer. When she returned, Rohit was speaking into his headset and staring at his screen, so she was able to watch him undetected.

She had never expected to meet anyone in Asia, let alone a Thailand-born Indian man. When she'd first moved to Singapore, she'd immediately noticed the absence of male interest. She was the exact opposite of whatever Asian men were attracted to, and white men only seemed to notice her after they'd had a few drinks. The only real attention she'd received since moving was from a married Nigerian pastor on a business trip from Malaysia, and that interaction had been more entertaining than offensive, a source of laughter for her and Dara weeks later.

For the first few months in Singapore, she'd felt invisible—and it had been beautiful. She'd been desperate to escape the entitled idiots in Lagos, with their wandering hands and loose morals who saw any single girl as fair game, many of whom had been in their element during her short trip back to Lagos over Christmas. Worst of all, her mother's friends constantly judged her, warning her that there were five girls for every eligible man in Lagos, so she needed to conduct herself carefully to attract a good one. She'd left all that behind and stepped into... nothing. Zero. Bliss.

It hadn't taken long, though, for the anonymity to turn to insecurity. This was probably why she'd been open to Rohit in the first place.

When they'd first met, the only things they'd had in common were their jobs and the fact that they'd both been international students in the U.S. (public college for her, Columbia for him). Their work friendship had changed from easy banter to something more charged when she'd realized that his questions about her outfits, weave changes and Wendy Williams obsession were actually him flirting. They'd kept it playful until one night, in a taxi from a dinner Indira had held in her colonial black-and-white house, he'd kissed her and she'd kissed him back. He was easy to be with, gave her plenty of space and was a fantastic person to have something light and fun and obviously short-term with. He was a good listener, too, with his cute, American-tinged accent courtesy of the international school he'd attended in Bangkok. Her sharp barbs—which had turned off so many guys in Lagos—just seemed to amuse him.

Rohit had made it clear that he wanted to have a family and that he wanted children young. They were still in the early stages of their relationship, but was dating really this easy? Did men just say what they wanted? How could she be certain it was *her* he wanted and not just someone for the next stage in life? One thing Amaka knew for damn sure was that she'd make a terrible wife and mother: she was selfish and vain, and the more serious their situationship became, the worse it made her feel.

Her mother's voice was never far from her ear, pressuring her to settle down with "the right kind" of man—someone dependable and trustworthy and definitely *not like her father.* Though Ugo had never said a bad word about Chukwu, beneath her loyalty was the constant, subtle advice to make better decisions than she had, to not derail her life or bring shame on her family, like ending up a single mother in a tiny flat on the wrong side of town.

The real problem was not the unspoken fear of how Ugo would respond to Amaka getting serious with someone from India, but the warmth that had begun to spread in her when she was near him, the yearning to fold wordlessly into him, to blurt something stupid or reveal something intimate. More and more, she had to remind herself of who she was and who she wasn't. She wasn't a weak, lovesick twenty-year-old or a pathetic heroine from a mushy Hollywood movie, and she *definitely* wasn't about to give power over her emotions to a man. She was an Igbo girl; as her mother constantly reminded her, she may have grown up in Lagos surrounded by Yorubas, but she was from the East. She didn't have time for nonsense.

Rohit took off his headphones. "So it turns out I was right about K. W. Holding's mitigation risks. You remember the company in the Philippines?"

"I'm busy, Rohit." Amaka avoided his eyes.

The rest of the morning disappeared in phone calls and emails. The trading floor was manic; trade requests were coming in thick and fast. It was an adrenaline-filled job, requiring an in-depth knowledge of trading practices and banking laws, good judgment and the ability to multitask. One stupid mistake could cost the bank hundreds of thousands of dollars. Every time a trader on the floor pushed a button, a complex algorithm determined if they could make a trade or not. If the trader contested it, then it came to her, a credit risk officer, and she made the ultimate decision. She had the power to reject the trade or overwrite the computer's decision—and she loved it.

By eleven, she was buzzed and cheerful.

"Coffee?" She rose.

Rohit followed her to the office kitchen, which was empty except for two colleagues. They nodded hello before walking out with their mugs.

"Count your blessings one by one," Amaka grinned, lifting a half-full coffee pot.

"Nice." Rohit brought out two cups and she filled them. He took his black coffee to one of the wooden tables in the corner and she poured generously from someone's lactose-free milk in the fridge. She joined him, and a few seconds passed as they sipped their coffees.

"So that's it?" Amaka said. "We're not going to talk?"

"You're the one who doesn't want to talk!"

"Is it really the end of the world if I don't want to talk about my family? Can we *please* talk about something else?"

Rohit shrugged and nodded. "Did you know the record for the longest ever conversation is something like forty-six hours? It was this guy and girl talking on the phone and there was an audience braiding the two people's hair and playing poker and massaging their feet and all this shit."

"Are you for real?" Amaka laughed.

"They weren't allowed to be quiet for more than ten seconds. How long do you think we could talk for?"

"As long as you're the one paying the phone bill, you can talk to me for as long as you like."

Rohit smiled and took out his phone.

"I thought you said no devices while we're hanging out."

"Drawing app." He spun the phone so she could see the screen. "We're going to play hangman. If you win, I won't ask anything more about your family meeting. If I win, you have to tell me *one* thing. That's it."

Amaka's phone started to ring. Dara's name lit across the trembling screen.

"Ha! Saved by the bell." She grinned.

"Nope, we're playing. I'll even draw you a clue."

"Hey, Dara. Sorry, hold on one sec." Amaka pressed her phone to her chest and leaned over to stare at his sketch. "What the hell is that? It looks like a mountain and…is that a poo?"

"I'm personally offended by that." Rohit finished shading the oblong shape and drew six short lines under it. "And you've hurt the mountain's feelings too."

"Is that what it is? I'm right?" She grinned.

"No. Don't be ridiculous; it's not a turd," Rohit chuckled. "Oh, and if you lose, you *also* have to make me that spicy stew you brought in for Lunar New Year. With plantain."

"I told you that was a one-off. I don't cook and I *definitely* don't cook on demand," Amaka shot back.

"Those are my terms."

"Fine. But if I win…"

"You won't win."

"If *I* win—" she thought for a second "—you buy me some shoes."

"What? How does that even equate?"

"Shoes." She glanced at her phone to check that Dara was still there.

"What type of shoes?" Rohit looked amused.

"Who cares, motherfucker, you can afford it. So, what is this— and this?"

"A mountain and a jewel," Rohit grinned smugly. "Time starts now."

"A," Amaka sighed, putting her phone to her ear. "Sorry, Dara."

"It's fine," Dara replied, her voice heavy and slow. "It's not like I'm doing anything."

"Aren't you at work?" Amaka frowned at the long pole of the gallows Rohit drew. He got up from his chair and settled into the one next to her, stretching his arm over her shoulders.

"E," she whispered, and was satisfied to see him write the vowel on the penultimate dash.

"No, I took the day off," Dara sighed.

Amaka stiffened, then bit her lip as Rohit nuzzled her neck and planted a soft kiss behind her ear.

"Every time you get one right," he threatened.

"Are you busy?" Dara asked.

"No, it's fine," Amaka replied. "What's going on? Are you sick? I got Nana to add you to our book club WhatsApp group. Did you see it?"

"Mmm, I don't remember. I've pulled a sickie today. I just can't face going in. I think…I'm going to have to give my notice."

"What are you talking about? What happened?" Amaka sat up straight.

"I'm not getting promoted. He lied to me." Dara sounded close to tears.

Amaka listened closely as Dara explained. Every so often, she lobbed quick-fire questions to distinguish between what had actually been said and what she had inferred—and to distract Dara from wallowing in self-pity.

"But who is this guy?" Amaka griped. "*Ah-ahn*, your boss just plucked another Nigerian lawyer from thin air?"

"I've emailed you his profile from his old firm's website," Dara replied.

"OK, hold on." Amaka unlocked her screen.

"Hey. Letter." Rohit tapped the pen on the notepad.

"I, G and…C." Amaka opened her emails and scrolled down to Dara's, then clicked on the link.

She stared at Lani Idowu's headshot, biting back an expletive, and found herself angling her arm so Rohit couldn't see the screen.

A broad face of ebony smiled back at her, a chin shaped by a groomed goatee. His eyes were framed with black-rimmed glasses that did very little to hide the puddles of cocoa swimming in the whites of his eyes. He was delicious.

Putting the phone back to her ear, she did her best to modulate her tone.

"This is the guy?"

"Yup. Do you have time to read his CV?"

"Reading now." Amaka looked back at her screen.

"Next?" Rohit prodded then peered at her phone. "Who's that?"

"Someone Dara's firm has hired." Amaka swiped down to the words beneath.

"Next letters?"

"W, P, M, S." She really didn't care.

"What?! Who picks letters like that? You didn't even do all the vowels." Rohit made quick work of the stick figure. "I'll throw in a smiley face."

To get rid of him, Amaka glanced down at the remaining dashes and hazarded five more letters. All but one was wrong. She'd lost.

"Phuket? That's the answer? What does Phuket have to do with a mountain and a jewel?"

"That's what 'Phuket' means. Mountain jewel." Rohit laughed. He cleared their cups and put them in the dishwasher. "I very much look forward to our heart-to-heart after lunch."

He smiled broadly, tapping his watch as he pushed open the kitchen door and walked out.

Relieved to finally be on her own, Amaka read the rest of Lani's profile, then scrolled back to the top to tether the glowing work history to his face.

"OK, I'm not going to lie. This guy's CV is on point," she said. "I don't know any of the firms, but these are some serious awards. He's worked in Geneva, London and Paris. He's interned at the International Chamber of Commerce Lagos, and there are all these links to arbitration articles he's published. Plus, he went to Cambridge..."

Dara snapped. "So what? I went to Ox—"

"Calm down, I know. I'm just saying he's definitely qualified. So at least you know he actually deserves to be hired," Amaka reasoned.

"I don't care if he deserves it or not!" Dara hissed. "He doesn't have any Asia experience and Ian already has a senior associate. He hired me on false pretenses, worked me like a beast for six years and now he's screwed me over!"

She heard Dara take a deep breath. "Yes, he's qualified. He's assisted on disputes. Well, so have I. Fine, he's got the Africa experience, but I've worked with every single one of Ian's Japanese clients for *years*. I know the Japanese inside and out!"

"Your boss told you he was retiring and that he wanted you to take over his practice, right?"

"Well, he didn't use those words..."

"Yes, of course, no one says it like *that*, but you know what I mean. You told me he's been preparing you."

"Yes. *Yes.*" Dara was more definitive now. "He made it clear. Everyone knew. And he's two years past the normal age of retirement. But then, the day after the rugby match, he says the Hakida case is too big for one person to handle with the other disputes he still has going on, and that it looks good for his practice if he has enough work to keep two senior associates busy. It's a perfectly believable reason, but he's lying."

"How do you know?"

"Because he's scared. He's scared of retiring, so he's delaying it. He's spent his whole life building his practice and he's terrified of walking away. He's nothing without this place. Either that or he just doesn't think I'm good enough," Dara muttered.

"Wow, the mind games at your firm are on a different level," Amaka exhaled. "In Nigeria, the boss either never retires or brings in his niece or nephew to replace him, one 'I-just-got-back' who's supposed to have more common sense than locals because white people marked their book."

Amaka cringed, making a face at her own words. Dara was exactly the type of Nigerian who would have replaced her back home.

"Well, I wouldn't just take someone's job if they'd been promised it," Dara replied testily. "And I don't have a rich uncle 'back home' who can set me up like that. I've worked my arse off for this."

"No, I didn't mean you. I'm just saying—it's the same type of competition everywhere. Your boss is just being sneaky about it," Amaka backpedaled. "The problem, Dara, is you want to be a partner, but you want them to *like* you. You want respect but you want to be nice. You need to stop caring what these people think. I mean, how many black partners are there in your firm? In all the different branches, I mean?"

"Two."

"*Two?* In how many offices?"

"Nineteen. One on almost every continent."

"*Chineke*, these people…"

"I know. This whole situation is so embarrassing. Of course there are lots of qualified black lawyers Ian could have hired, but this is so suspicious," Dara complained. "At the law firm where I worked as a paralegal after law school, I hardly saw a black face, apart from the security guard and the law librarian. Now Ian, an equity partner who has *never* made anyone up in over thirty years of practice, hires two black lawyers and puts them on the same team, less than a year from retirement?"

"Very suspicious. And the fact that you're both Oxbridge… people like to lie to themselves about diversity, *sha*," Amaka mused. "Don't you think it's also a little fucked up, two Nigerian lawyers working in an English firm, helping Japanese clients beat an African government that's trying to screw over its own people?"

"I have a pounding headache," Dara sighed.

"When does this guy start?" Amaka asked.

"Two weeks," Dara replied.

"Two weeks?! How did they move so fast?"

"I know. I can't believe he got his employment pass so quickly," Dara griped. "Anything can happen between getting an offer and sorting out the paperwork here."

Amaka hesitated before speaking. "Unless your boss found him months ago."

There was silence on the other end.

"Look, forget this Ian-joker. You've got two options. You sharpen your game and do a better job than this new guy, or you find something on him. Do you get me?"

"Like what?"

"Anything. Mess him up. Pull some Machiavellian shit. Isn't that what lawyers do? Dig up some dirt."

"This isn't a Tyler Perry film, Amaka," Dara sighed.

"You need to get out there and annihilate the competition *o*, not hide at home like you've already lost the fight."

"I'm not hiding at home…"

"You know what?" Amaka interrupted. "We've got a book club meeting next week. Why don't you come? It'll take your mind off work, and we can strategize."

Dara made a very unenthusiastic noise. "Amaka, I read all day for a living. Reading a book is the last thing I want to do in my free time."

"You don't need to read it. Just come and hang out, and if you like it, you can join properly."

"What's the book?"

"*Purple Hibiscus.* And at the start of each meeting, we discuss what we want to read next, so you can add your own choice or, you know, just go with the flow."

"Fine. Where's it going to be?"

"This American girl's place. She just joined and it will be her first meeting, too. I'll send you the address."

They hung up and Amaka leaned back in her chair. She traced a finger on a half-circle coffee stain left on the table and listened to the rising din of the office on the brink of breaking for lunch, wishing she could fix her own problems as easily as she could fix her friend's. Despite being three years younger, Amaka knew she was more confident, pragmatic and single-minded than Dara, but there were some issues that required a softer, diplomatic touch.

Absent-mindedly, she picked up her phone to check how long her new shoes would take to arrive and found herself staring back into Lani's eyes. She minimized the window quickly, feeling both guilty and foolish at the rush of arousal that lingered long after she got back to her desk. She watched Rohit unwrap another bar.

Lillian

"How long have you lived in Singapore?" Lillian read slowly, her index finger trailing each word on her student's "About Me" worksheet.

"*How long have you lived in Singapore?*" The gum in Irina's mouth and her Russian accent thickened her words.

"You answer first and then you ask me." Lillian smiled tightly, trying to ignore the snap of the girl's jaws and the crackle of the bursting air bubbles. It was virtually impossible to buy gum in the country, so Irina must have smuggled it in.

One-to-one tuition lessons were her least favorite to teach because most of the students who could afford them were learning Business English, so the content was dry and the vocabulary tricky to explain, but Irina was an entertaining anomaly. This was their first session, and the contrast between teacher and student was heightened in the small, hot cubicle. Lillian was petite and bird-like, dwarfed by Irina's energy and height; her stone-colored linen dress was a blank wall next to Irina's denim playsuit with its exaggerated ruffles decorating the bosom. Lillian wore no jewelry except for a second-hand Omega wristwatch and her gold wedding ring; Irina's wrists were stacked with rows of chunky bracelets that matched her rings, and a clover-shaped pendant sat at her throat. Lillian's twists were pinned up; Irina's blanket of brown hair was continuously tossed over her shoulder, long strands shedding all over her chair.

"I live here just three months—I hate it," Irina huffed. "My boyfriend work all the time. It *so* boring. He tell me everyone speak English here, but no one speak English."

"Really? Most people speak English here."

"Not *English-English*. You American right? A-ju..." Irina squinted as she tried to recall Lillian's surname.

"Ajuwa. OK, let's get back to the present perfect—"

"It's so interesting...where it's from?"

NIGERIA.

"New Orleans. It's Creole." Lillian's well-rehearsed lie always made her wonder if her parents were turning in their weed-covered graves.

She changed the topic quickly. "What does your boyfriend do?"

"He's regional manager, so he travel all the time." Irina sounded bored. "When he tell me, I think *'wow.'* But I don't know what's 'region.' Now I know it's whole bloody Asia, so he travel, travel, travel."

"And how long have you been together?" Lillian interlaced her fingers to mime togetherness.

"More than one year, but I think I break up." Irina picked up her worksheet, then looked at Lillian with curiosity.

"How long you been marry?" She pointed an acrylic nail at Lillian's wedding ring.

"How long have you been marr*ied*?" Lillian corrected her, moving her hands under the table. "Just over three years."

After a short pause, in which Irina mouthed the new phrase "*just over*" and waited for more information, Lillian reluctantly continued.

"We got married just before we moved here."

Irina's eyes widened deliciously. "So you don't want marry? He have money?"

"No...I mean yes, he does, and I did want to get married." Lillian was starting to feel uncomfortable now. She'd only agreed to work a full shift on Saturdays to get out of the house and avoid having to take a tense taxi ride to her fortnightly marriage counseling with Warren. Now it felt like the therapy session had started early. She had a long day ahead, and it wouldn't end until late in the evening, when at least five strangers would descend on her home for the book club. Things with Warren had begun to get strained at Christmas, when Lillian had gone to the American Club's Winter Fair. There, she'd met LeToya, an animated African American woman with an impressive pineapple bun and way with words, who'd strongarmed her into joining a black women's book group. When she found out Lillian lived so centrally, she'd subsequently convinced her to host. It was too late to back out now, but it was a crappy day to have to rehash her life choices with a bored, nosy student, brave through another brutally honest counseling session and then chit-chat with women she didn't know.

"We moved quickly so we could get our paperwork done here. Let's get back to the questions. How long have you been learning English?"

Irina shrugged. "Long time. How long have you teach English for?"

"*Taught.*"

"Taught."

"A year." Lillian suppressed the urge to check the time on her watch.

"But before that…?" Irina grinned and mimed two hands playing an invisible piano.

Lillian stiffened. "How did you know that?"

"I google you! You very good. I hate this type classic music—it's for the old people, except when they mix with rap, you know? Me, I like trap. You like trap? My boyfriend so old, he have no idea…"

"Why don't we do a listening exercise?" Lillian reached for the old-fashioned stereo player and snapped in a CD.

The foyer was filled with students chatting on their phones, making plans for the rest of their weekends. Lillian slipped behind the reception desk into the large office where teachers and administrative staff were leaving for lunch. She took her Tupperware from the fridge and waited for her lunch of leftover noodle soup to warm in the school's tiny kitchen. She watched the lunchtime exodus, listening to smatterings of American slang, Mandarin and Malay, feeling, as always, like an outsider. The Mandarin teachers were young women in pinafore-style dresses and platform wedges, and the English teachers were a mix of Americans, Canadians and Brits—mostly young men who shared apartments, traveled around Asia by road and were not averse to dating the more liberal of their students. The one thing they had in common was that they were all broke. The language school paid so badly that everyone bought their lunch in greasy basement food courts where they could get hot meals for three dollars and local green vegetables like kai lan and bok choy for an extra, decadent dollar. There was a gulf between the full-time teachers and her fellow part-timers, who were all wives—or trailing spouses as they were derogatively known—looking for a reason to get out of the house and make some pocket money. Like her, they had paid the expensive tuition fees to qualify as English-as-a-foreign-language teachers in Singapore, but Lillian felt she had as little in common with them as she did the full-timers. Even though she had technically "trailed" behind Warren's career in coming to Singapore, nothing about the wives' budgets or lifestyles felt familiar to her. This, she realized, might have been different if she'd had children. They all did; she didn't.

All at once, it was still. Lillian carried her soup back through the quiet office, the peal of the phone at reception ringing then cutting off. Smiling at the tax accountant on the administration side of the office, she sat and ate her lunch, the only other person on the teacher side.

She scrolled through her messages before opening the book club WhatsApp group she'd just been invited to join. She was trying to lean into her old performance trick, reminding herself that anxiety and excitement affected her body in the same way, so all she had to do was trick her mind into thinking she was feeling anticipation rather than dread.

As she replied to a question about a parking space from a girl named Kike, who ended every sentence and question with an exclamation mark, she heard the unmistakable clomp of the principal's footsteps: Marigold. *Shit.*

"Hi, Lillian. How was this morning?" Both the question and her smile were benign, but Lillian had been working at SpeakNow! long enough to know when her words were being measured and assessed.

"Great. My classes were fine." Lillian let her phone rest face-down on her knee.

It was easy to be fooled by Marigold's softness—Lillian had been when she'd first started. In her early fifties, short, with a low hair-cut and faded sides, Marigold was always dressed in black trousers and a blouse that matched her dove-gray pearl studs. *Someone's grandma*, Lillian had thought the first day they'd met, but the ruthlessness with which Marigold let teachers go and stonewalled their requests for time off and flexible timetables made it clear that most of the unrest among the staff started and ended with her. The only thing the school was interested in was money: they crammed students into classes with overworked, underpaid teachers who had to purchase stationery once their quota was used up, and printing was strictly regulated. But what the staff hated most was the lack of quality control. It didn't matter how a student performed or if they were ready—they were all graduated to the next level at the end of each session, a decision that delighted their adult learners.

"There's a potential new student here interested in signing up for Japanese lessons. I know it's your lunch, but could you give him a little tour of the facilities? Answer his questions about the classes?" Marigold asked.

"I don't know anything about the Japanese course," Lillian answered. "The teachers will be back soon. Maybe he could wait?"

"He's interested in signing up for our twelve-week business course. I don't want to keep him waiting." Marigold's smile stayed in place, but her hands interlaced in expectation.

"I'm sorry," she squirmed. "But it's a really short break before my classes start again..."

Marigold blinked, her eyes and face widening a fraction.

"Of course, take your lunch." She nodded and angled her body away. "I'll take care of him."

There was a burst of laughter from reception—Alima, the receptionist, must have returned from lunch—and then a man's warm, low voice, catching the end of Alima's sentences.

Lillian's head cocked to one side, as though a high-wave frequency had been turned on.

"It's fine." She rose. Giving up ten minutes of her lunch break to stay on Marigold's good side was a small price to pay. "I can show him around."

"Thank you." Marigold stepped back with a smile, then leaned forward to whisper. "He's very handsome."

Lillian walked out from behind the reception desk and Alima, dressed in a pink hijab with a brooch pinned to her shoulder, waved her closer.

"This is one of our teachers, Ms. Lillian." Alima announced her with more enthusiasm than Lillian had ever experienced before.

A tall black man in a denim shirt over a white T-shirt and jeans stood on the other side of the reception desk, holding the school brochure.

"Hi. I'd like to sign up for the Japanese evening course, but I'm guessing you don't teach Japanese? I might be wrong." He smiled and his dimples pushed his cheeks back, turning the sharp angles soft, creasing the lines on either side of his nose so his glasses slid down.

Lillian swallowed, her mouth suddenly dry. She stared at his face, his eyes and beard, the impossibility of the resemblance— she was seeing the angles of her father's cheeks, the curve of his head, the wideness of his mouth. Even the man's voice, the deep, mineral timbre of it, carried traces of something she hadn't heard since she was a child.

"Do you...teach Japanese?" he asked, hesitantly.

British. He was British. The accent was wrong.

"Yes—I mean no." She had to snap herself out of it. "Sorry. We *do* teach Japanese, but I don't. Um, yes, I can show you around and...the structure of the courses are all the same, so I can help a little if you...are you going to be working in Japan?"

"I just moved to Singapore actually, but I think I'm going to need it for work. My law firm has quite a bit of business in Japan. There's no time pressure or anything. I just got here and I'm still jet-lagged!" he laughed. "But I'd like some conversational Japanese, maybe a business course at some point."

She watched his mouth move, catching every other word.

"I explained that the evening courses are twice a week—the business course, too—and that we also offer intensive courses," Alima said.

"Yes, the evening courses are twice a week, but we offer intensive courses, too," Lillian parroted, transfixed. "I'm Lillian."

She held out her hand. The man with her dead father's face took it.

"Lani. Lovely to meet you."

Lillian sat in her marriage counselor's office, oblivious to the soft carpet that swallowed her toes. A thick bouquet of cedar and jasmine lingered on her clothes, the worn desk, the framed pictures and abstract lamps and ornaments that looked like treasured pieces salvaged from around the world. Whenever Lillian arrived early, she would drift around the reception, hastily replacing a frame or candle when Dr. Geraldine Oh's door tinkled open behind her. But today, they were all invisible to her. She'd done the long, hot walk from Orchard to Dempsey, distracted and inattentive, barely noticing the field of schoolboys warming up for their football game, the Anglican Church guarding the roundabout or the parents dropping their children off at weekend tuition classes behind the Dempsey cafés. Normally she was glad there was never any music in Dr. Geraldine's reception—she'd stopped listening to music for pleasure when she'd moved to Singapore; the first thing she did when she entered a taxi was ask the driver to switch off the radio—but today she'd been desperate for something to take her mind off the man she'd just met. Now, she sat on the therapist's couch, biting a nail, trying to re-engage with the conversation happening around her.

This was only their third appointment, but she and Warren had been given homework to share their grievances and the causes of their resentments. Warren was going first.

"The first year we moved here, we agreed we'd have a settling-in period, you know? So she could find her feet." Warren's arms leaned on his knees.

Lillian realized that the shaking beneath her was him shifting his weight, jerking or tapping a limb with every other word.

"By the second year, I wanted her to explore the music scene here, try to see if she could play solo concerts or be a part of an orchestra, like she used to. I looked for music academies where she could teach, I—I tried to organize a venue for her to play at. I even asked friends if they had kids who wanted to learn the piano." Warren's frustration intensified his Southern accent.

"Then someone told us there were schools looking for native English teachers—that there was a high demand. So I paid for her to train up—it was pretty expensive, I might add—and we got lucky. She got a job and she's teaching now, which is great and everything, but I just don't understand why we shipped that damn piano ten thousand miles for no reason, and why we tune it so damn much when she doesn't play!"

"OK." Dr. Geraldine halted him. She sat a few feet away, hands in her lap, sitting so still even her horn-rimmed glasses seemed to be listening. "I can see it's been a frustrating journey, not without its obstacles, and what I'm hearing you say is that you've put a lot of time and energy and money into supporting Lillian and trying to find a way for her to make a life for herself here."

"Yes, that's what I'm saying." Warren stopped biting his bottom lip and sighed. "And I know how it sounds—me saying all this shit I did, I know how it comes off, but I did all that to help her. To take her mind off what we were trying to do."

"Which was have a baby?" Dr. Geraldine turned this question to Lillian.

"Yeah, have a baby," Warren answered, the barb in his voice so sharp that Lillian flinched. She blinked and Lani's face disappeared, allowing her to see her husband clearly.

"Most of our savings are gone," he exhaled heavily. "I mean, we'll be OK, but we have no real safety net right now. I've got a good job. Bought some stock when I first started working at Google, and our insurance paid for the first two rounds of IVF, but then we had to cover it. We've considered freezing her eggs, but we just can't afford it right now, and Lillian's thirty-seven. We should have done it years ago. If we'd known..."

Dr. Geraldine glanced at the notepad beside her. "And you've been on several IVF cycles."

"That's right." He folded his arms.

The seconds stretched into one of those pauses you were meant to interrupt to ease your discomfort. But silence wasn't hard for Lillian. Waiting used to be part of her job: waiting for the conductor's nod, waiting for the other musicians to finish warming up, waiting to hear if she'd got a spot on a tour. Waiting to get pregnant. Her life was really just a series of small pauses folded into a larger one.

"We've been trying ever since we got married." Warren exhaled like he still couldn't believe it. "Lil's had trouble ovulating since before I met her. I've come to accept..."

There was a catch in his voice as he struggled to speak. Lillian realized that something more raw was threatening to break free from his anger. She pushed her tongue into the gap between her bottom teeth, digging it in so hard that it began to sting, then finally looked at him, half hoping he'd look back, half hoping he wouldn't.

He stared at a corner of the ceiling. She saw him clench his jaw and swallow hard. "I've come round to adoption. Yeah, it took me a minute...but now I don't know if she really wants a kid at all. I don't know what the point is anymore. She's been so disconnected lately. I've started to wonder if she's checked out or moved on. I even thought there might be someone else. It would make a hell of a lot more sense. I don't know..."

He laughed darkly. Then—like a punctured ball collapsing in on itself—he deflated, his hands resting uselessly on his knees.

"Thank you for sharing, Warren. I'm sure that wasn't easy.

Before we move on to Lillian, is there any particular reason why you've been feeling this way? Wondering if Lillian may have met someone else?"

"She's been coming home later, working longer shifts. And we haven't had sex in six months, so..."

Dr. Geraldine nodded solemnly. "I see. Lillian, before you share what you wrote, do you want to talk about how the IVF has affected you? I think it's important for Warren to understand how it's impacted your ability to stay present in the relationship."

"It's been hard. It's tiring, the hormones and everything. My moods have been...a lot."

"How are you feeling right now?" Dr. Geraldine asked.

"I just...I don't know what to do. I don't know how we got here." She shook her head, trying to quash her rising panic.

Dr. Geraldine nodded. "You sound confused. Are you confused by things you've heard today?"

"No, not really, but I did everything I could. I thought I did everything I was supposed to do."

"What do you mean by that?"

"I moved here. I gave it *everything*." Her breath was short now.

She had to close her eyes to stay calm, to take the pressure off being watched as she struggled. If she focused on the jasmine and breathed it in deeply, she could take her mind off the furry sensation in her mouth.

"Take it easy." Warren's voice held no emotion, and he didn't move in her direction.

Nodding to show she'd heard, she opened her eyes and took a tissue from the box Dr. Geraldine was holding.

"Are you OK?" she asked.

"Yes. I'm sorry." Lillian rolled the tissue in her hands.

"Does that happen a lot?" Dr. Geraldine looked from wife to husband and both nodded. "It must make talking about things difficult."

When neither responded, she rose and took something from her desk, then crossed over to put it in Lillian's hand.

"It's a stress ball. I want you to squeeze it gently whenever you feel anxious and try to answer my questions without thinking. Just say the first thing that comes into your mind. Can you do that?"

Dr. Geraldine put her hand on Lillian's, patted it once, then returned to her chair.

"Do you like living in Singapore?"

"Yes." Lillian squeezed. "Yes."

"Did you want to move here?"

"I wanted to be with Warren. I loved him. I didn't want to hold him back."

"Is that something you're afraid of, 'holding him back'?"

Lillian squeezed hard and nodded.

"Was there any other reason why you wanted to move? I mean, if Singapore wasn't an option, would you have wanted to leave the U.S.? I ask because, from what Warren is suggesting, you're struggling to commit to life here. You don't seem to have made many friends, and you find it difficult to be clear about what you want to do. Would you agree with that?"

"I would have gone wherever he wanted. But yeah." She pumped the ball. "I wanted to leave the U.S."

"And in leaving the U.S., did you also want to leave your music career behind?"

"Yes," Lillian whispered.

"That was a chapter in your life you wanted to close?" Geraldine's eyes wrinkled in concentration.

"Then why'd you...!" Warren's outburst was ugly, like the slam of hands on a keyboard.

"You didn't feel safe enough to say this?" Dr. Geraldine let her words and the meaning behind them hang in the room.

Warren interjected. "And the piano? Why bring it all this way? Why care for it if music is no longer a part of your life...or is there something you're still holding onto? Something from your old life that you're not ready to let go of?" he demanded.

Lillian's fingers ached around the tight, hot ball in her hand, until finally the truth spilled out.

"I want a baby, but I don't know if I want it for the wrong reasons," she blurted, sick and tired of holding back. "I literally have no idea. I can't remember the last time I made a decision I was sure about. Every time the IVF failed, I was devastated, but I was also...relieved. I'm thirty-seven—that's what you're supposed to do in your prime—but I don't know how to be a mother. I moved here because Warren got a great job, I said yes when he proposed because he asked me, I trained to be a musician because everyone said I was good at it, and I brought my piano over because it's the only thing I have left of my parents.

"You keep asking me what I want like I'm supposed to know. It's just easier to say nothing than admit I don't fucking *know*. Since I was eleven, I've just put one foot in front of the other. The only people who ever really cared about me died because they put what I wanted before their own safety, so don't ask me these questions. *I don't know*. It was their job to help me figure this shit out."

When she opened her eyes again, Warren was staring at her, open-mouthed, like she was a stranger he'd just met.

The first two members to arrive broke off their conversation and looked up from their chairs. LeToya, the Atlanta native who had invited Lillian to join the book club, was dressed casually, and was sitting across from a British girl called Dara, who was almost double Lillian's height, with straight hair cut to her chin. Dara was dressed in a shirt and skirt that looked much too formal for a weekend outfit—she looked like she'd come straight from work.

"You have a beautiful home," LeToya said. "I just love this space. And the *view!*"

"Thank you." Lillian filled a glass of cold water for each woman from the jug she'd brought over. "Yeah, we took our time to do it up right."

She watched Dara take in the striped armchairs, pink divan, Balinese print cushions, canary-yellow sofa and huge blue rug. Dara's eyes ran over the reading lamps, two wire-mesh zebra heads hanging from the walls and a painting of a Vietnamese woman in a rice paddy, her face obscured by the white cone of her hat…color, color and more color. Even if guests were rarely impressed by Lillian's personality, her home more than made up for it. Although she'd tried to help when they were decorating, she'd been overwhelmed by all the choices, and had left most of the design decisions to Warren. Now she felt attached to the space, but not to the objects inside it. The only room she'd taken charge of was the nursery.

She was reassured that neither of the women had seen the piano tucked into a far corner of the room, concealed underneath a black padded quilt. They wouldn't ask questions or ask her to play. For Lillian, the piano was a black hole that pulsed no matter how much color surrounded it, but to everyone else, it was camouflaged.

"Incredible. Is it three-sixty?" Dara marveled at the open space and the backdrop of the salmon-pink sky.

"Almost," Lillian said, moving closer. "Can I get you a drink? Some wine?"

"Oh, no thank you. This is fine. Or tea, if you have some, but I can make it myself if you don't mind me in your kitchen. I don't want to put you out—I know Americans don't usually drink tea," Dara rambled.

"Tea is fine; I drink plenty." Lillian smiled. This girl was even more awkward than she was. "I'll boil some water and bring some teabags."

"Where in the U.S. are you from? I know you said Google moved you guys over from Cali, and you grew up on the East Coast, but I've been trying to place your accent." LeToya shook her wisteria of honey-colored curls away from her face and held out her glass.

"Philly."

"No way! You're from Philadelphia?" LeToya looked taken aback. "You don't sound like it at all. You grew up there?"

"Yeah. I haven't been back in years," Lillian mumbled, uncomfortable divulging even that much.

"Wow. I never would have guessed." LeToya turned her incredulous stare to Dara. "I used to date this guy who went to Penn

State—*lil'* office romance. He took me to his college reunion one time, and we spent a few days up there, drove around the city. My God. I thought we had it bad back home...I'd never seen anything like it."

A fierce anger seized Lillian. Caught between a need to defend her home town and her protective habit of giving little away, she kept her hostess smile in check, saying nothing as LeToya continued to describe the poverty she'd witnessed.

"You should join our Facebook group, 'Sisters in Singapore.' Just for Americans—no offense, dear." LeToya cracked up laughing.

"None taken," Dara replied.

"OK, good!" LeToya patted her knee. "We throw all kinds of events: barbecues, eighties nights, events we throw for the kids. Ooh, *my bad*, should we keep it down? You got kids sleeping?"

The question sliced through Lillian like a cold, hard knife.

"No, no kids. If you'll excuse me, I'll go get my copy of the book. Go ahead and get started." She rose quickly and walked down the dark hallway into her bedroom.

The dying sun threw small boxes of yellow and gold against the walls, diffusing the room in a gentle amber. Lillian shut the door, slipped down to the floor beside her bed, and smacked her head against the frame.

Dara

"This chick's place is insane *o*..." Amaka whistled as the kitchen door swung behind her and Dara. "Are you sure it's OK for us to help ourselves?"

"I don't think she'll mind." Dara was almost blinded by the whiteness of the curved room: the cupboards, fridge and floor, even the appliances were white. It was like being inside a coconut. "Can you see the kettle?"

"Oh! Here." Amaka put her glass of wine down and extracted something from the white wall. "Damn, this Google money must be good. I heard the Singapore office has its own train station."

"I have no idea, but can we not talk about this? She could walk in at any time." Dara hunted through the cupboards for the tea.

"How are you feeling? One week to go."

Dara blew out the sour frustration that had been building all day. The news couldn't have spread faster if Hermes had announced it himself. Some of the other lawyers had appeared sympathetic, though they were careful not to say too much. The Sirens had done a terrible job of hiding their delight; like the petty creatures they were, they were thrilled that an unexpected sea monster had wrapped its tentacles around her boat and slowed her progress.

"Ian's acting like nothing's changed. It's been the most crazy-making week, having to pretend everyone isn't gossiping behind my back. And the most galling part is that I still have to work just as hard. He's been piling even more on my plate, like he's trying to prove it's too much for me to handle."

"What have you found out about Lani?" Amaka filled the kettle.

"Nothing." Dara found some Earl Grey. "Absolutely nothing. His Instagram's private and he doesn't have a Facebook page. Some pictures popped up on an image search. I can't be completely sure it's him, but I think it is—holiday pics with some friends, a girlfriend maybe."

"White girl?"

"Of course." Dara sniffed a carton of milk from the fridge and poured some into her mug.

Amaka took an ice tray out of the freezer and turned two blocks into her glass. "So we wait and see."

Dara tidied everything away before turning back to the living room. "We wait and see."

Four other members of the book club were spread out across the armchairs and sofa. They were helping themselves to a tray of popcorn and tortilla chips, sharing photos from their Christmas holiday. A carrot cake in a cake keeper bided its time in the center of the table, and three half-empty wine bottles cooled in a bucket.

As Dara and Amaka settled onto the divan, Dara followed the threads of the group's different conversations, piecing together what she knew about them so far. Nana, a British Ghanaian child psychologist, sat with her knees hugged close to her chest so that she folded over herself like an abstract figurine. With a pashmina draped over her shoulders, she exuded a floaty calmness reminiscent of yoga and ginger oil. Yemisi was an older Nigerian mum whose large breasts bounced against the strained keyhole of her silk halterneck. Every other sentence was about her husband or sons. As the two women chatted, Dara realized they were the two sides of moneyed Africa that made their way across the ocean. Nana was dusty red roads and crumbling airports filtered through the glossy pages of architectural coffee table books; Yemisi was the Africa of excess: a bulky Celine bag and long Peruvian weave that hung like two curtains separated by the shiny railing of her faux scalp.

LeToya chatted with Kike Ibusun, the only other woman Dara had met before today. The daughter of a Nigerian state governor and former chairman of the national bank, Kike's wealth was rumored to be astronomical, but in her simple white polo shirt and white denim shorts, there was no evidence of this. She didn't even have a handbag tonight. In fact, the only tell-tale signs of her money were her cut-glass accent, and her long, straight ponytail (all her own?) and impeccable skin. A stay-at-home mum, Kike had always been friendly when they ran into each other at events, but Dara noticed that she was rarely with her husband, Bayo, and was never particularly eager to talk about her two young boys.

"Wait, you get your hair products delivered to Singapore for free?" Yemisi interrupted LeToya, overhearing her exchange with Kike.

"We pay postage, but it's U.S. prices, not international," LeToya said smugly. "Perks of the job."

"LeToya works for the U.S. Navy," Nana explained, catching Dara's eye.

"Oh cool." Dara cupped her mug. "How long have you lived here?"

"Five years. My kids are all grown—my son's in college and my daughter's finishing her final year of IB—so Singapore is awesome. I feel like I'm in my twenties again!"

Yemisi wrinkled her nose and shook her head. "I don't think I want my boys growing up here past ten. It's too disconnected from the real world. Last week we went to the cinema, and this kid—he couldn't have been more than thirteen—turned around to shush the woman behind him. If that had happened in some parts of London, he would have been slapped! Or worse!"

"Are you kidding me?" LeToya scoffed. "My kids have grown up without the weight of being black in America. They've had a childhood! It's worth it. Apart from the damn internet, you know they're safe here, and that is worth its price in gold. Back in Atlanta, we were up to no good as teenagers, drag racing every night. The worst they can get up to here is sniffing glue!"

"I don't know, I've heard some funny stories from the parents in our school—I think they're doing a lot more than glue," Kike said. "Now it's prescription, and they get it from their parents."

"You see!" Yemisi cried out. "I'm telling you!"

"Yemisi, this happens everywhere." Amaka rolled her eyes. "Or do people not take drugs to escape their problems in Nigeria?"

"What problems? What problems they got here?" LeToya protested.

"Are you serious? Everyone has problems," Amaka shot back.

"I mean, it's all relative..." Kike said to no one in particular.

"Just because you're cocooned in a bubble," Amaka teased.

"I've earned the right to my cocoon!" LeToya shouted, and the women laughed.

Nana held her hands up and leaned forward like a referee. "Ladies, we need to start, or we'll be here all night. Let's vote before we get too tipsy to know what we're doing. We get the vote out of the way before we start our discussion."

This last sentence was directed at Dara, who made an agreeable expression in response.

"What about Lillian?" Amaka said suddenly. "Isn't she coming?"

LeToya turned her head to look into the hallway. "She's been gone a long time. Should we check on her?"

The others shrugged or reached for another handful of chips. Kike uncovered the cake, revealing the cream frosting sprinkled with chopped pecans.

"We're going to need this." She started to slice. "My helper Annie's carrot cake is incredible."

Yemisi took the first plate. "I don't know how you stay so slim..."

"I need the bathroom. I could see if she's all right?" Dara offered, figuring she could plant the seed of an upset stomach to try and get an early night if discussions about the book proved to be too boring. Amaka had been no help with her Lani problem, and she'd worked three late nights in a row.

Amaka tapped her arm lightly. "Go after we vote."

"Mm-hmm." LeToya shot her a look. "I see you."

"What?" Amaka feigned.

"Girl, I know you're low-key sneaky the way you text everyone before a vote!" LeToya pointed a finger in Amaka's face.

Amaka looked like she was trying not to crumble into laughter. "What are you talking about? Are you telling me you're not happy we went with Adichie?"

"That's not the point."

"Can we please let this go?" Nana interrupted. "I can see the exact time everyone votes on the app, and no one has changed their mind after submitting their vote."

"You see? *Thank you*," Amaka gloated. "Just because you didn't get the outcome you wanted. I thought Americans invented democracy."

LeToya swung back, clearly enjoying the repartee. "At least we have elections."

"When I first started the book club, we were open to all genres." Nana took charge, speaking directly to Dara. "But the ladies hated my suggestions, so now we have two rules: no non-fiction and no books on slavery."

"Which is a *travesty*. I mean, *Homegoing*? Amazing." LeToya held her arms out dramatically.

Nana refused to be derailed. "That was our first book and we loved it, but we agreed. No more slavery—that's not what we want to be focusing on. And even though *Nothing to Envy* was an incredible portrayal of life in North Korea, no one bothered to finish it except me, so we're not doing non-fiction anymore. Anyway, each person nominates one book every meeting, tells us why we should read it, and then we vote anonymously online. The books we don't choose are added to a shortlist, and then every three months, we vote from that list. Oh, and the third rule is that it has to be a book no one has read before, so it's best to come with a few options."

"Why every three months?" Dara asked curiously.

"Because." Nana must have reached the end of her list of guidelines because she took an iPad from her bag and swiped it open. "All right, I'm nominating *The Sympathizer*, which I *know* none of you have read before. The writer won the Pulitzer. He's Vietnamese American and it's about a spy who defects from one side to the other during the Vietnam war. It's supposed to be incredible."

"War? Please no," Yemisi groaned.

"Kike?" Nana ignored her.

Kike spoke like a kid rushing around a sweet shop. "*The Seven*

Husbands of Evelyn Hugo. It's set in the fifties and it's about this actress who..."

"Read it," LeToya cut in. "It's *aight.*"

Deflated, Kike read from her phone. "I've got another one. *Love in Colour.* It's actually a collection of short stories retelling love myths from around the..."

"Read it. Loved it." LeToya wagged her fingers.

Kike took her copy of *Purple Hibiscus* and smacked LeToya's thigh. "Can you stop reading so much?"

"I told you, my kids are grown. Reading, drinking, and making love are all I do," LeToya cackled.

"I want to nominate Buchi Emecheta," Yemisi said solemnly. "I wasn't too sure which book at first, but I think *The Joys of Motherhood.* It was written in the seventies about a Nigerian woman who's ostracized by her family because she can't have a baby."

LeToya murmured into her glass as she sipped her wine. "That's original."

"But slavery isn't?" Amaka smirked.

"Seriously, this woman was a trailblazer, and we need to read more writers like her. I read online that her husband, who wasn't as educated as she was, burned her first book."

Each woman reacted visibly.

"Fucking men."

"Gosh, so insecure."

Nana nodded approvingly. "OK, good choice. LeToya?"

LeToya turned to Amaka. "Amaka?"

"No, please, go ahead," Amaka goaded.

Yemisi threw her head back. "Oh my goodness, can we please just vote?"

"Fine," LeToya gave in. "*The Bride Test.* Interestingly, also written by a Vietnamese American."

LeToya gave Nana a look of bemusement. Dara saw that this piece of information had landed well, and Amaka must have seen it, too, because she shifted in annoyance. Dara had to suppress a chuckle. She couldn't believe how seriously the women were taking this, or how much Amaka's competitive side was coming out. Even the way LeToya was canvassing the room like this was a general election was ridiculous.

"It's a romance about a woman who's brought to the U.S. to seduce an autistic guy. It sounds hilarious."

"It sounds offensive," Amaka said testily.

"It's not, though, because the guy's *mother* brings her over. And the writer's autistic, too, so you know it's sensitive." LeToya completed her slam dunk.

"Are you sure you haven't read it already?" Amaka accused.

Nana spoke before LeToya could answer. "Amaka, what's your selection?"

Amaka didn't waste time. *"Americanah."*

"The same writer two books in a row?" LeToya exclaimed.

"Ooh..." Kike inhaled, excited. "That's been on my to-read for years."

"Yes," Yemisi's head pounded up and down. "We should have read it first. I'll admit—I read the first chapter when it came out, but that's it."

LeToya could see she'd lost. "Nana, new members should not be able to vote unless they're fully signed up," she insisted, looking at Dara.

"What? Since when? OK, then Lillian can't vote either!" Amaka said quickly.

"That's fine with me," Nana said. "Let's do it, ladies."

The women took out their phones and opened the voting app.

"I'm going to find the loo." Dara got up before she could burst out laughing and went down the hallway.

There were two doors, separated by a tall bookcase. She tried the first. When there was no reply, she opened it, revealing a small room. With the glow of light behind the blinds, she could make out a baby's cot, a sofa bed, brown boxes on the floor and a train of cartoon characters stuck on the wall. She closed the door, then tapped lightly on the second. Realizing her need to pee was now very real, she pushed the door open without waiting for a reply and walked into what must have been the main bedroom.

Facing west, it was filled with the last light of the sun. It took her eyes a few seconds to adjust well enough to make out the girl sitting on the floor.

"Oh God, sorry! I'm looking for the loo!"

"Sure, just there." Lillian pointed at a door to Dara's left and began to stand. "I was just charging my phone."

"Thank you. I'm really sorry, I..." Dara hesitated, unsure if she should use the toilet or not. It was impossible to tell how long Lillian had been sitting there, and even harder to tell if she'd been crying. There was no phone near her.

"Are you OK?"

"I'm fine. Go ahead." Lillian pushed a handful of twists off her face and tucked it into her bun.

Hearing that, Dara's pelvic floor twitched and she hurried through the door, flicking a light switch on the wall.

Once she was done, she did her best not to stare at the personal toiletries neatly organized across the bathroom counters as she washed her hands. Reaching for the hand towel ring, her eyes fell on a small medicine box with an unopened syringe on top.

Feeling like she'd overstepped a boundary, she dried her hands quickly and re-entered the bedroom. The room was full of shadows and Lillian was gone.

Dara

A week later, Dara swiveled her chair away from her desk and pivoted to face the large window. The placid river below was serene without the tourist boat cruises that would clog it up by lunchtime. With the office to herself, she didn't have to hide her jitters. She'd arrived earlier than her usual 8 a.m. start, determined to have the upper hand on Lani's first day, but she still had no idea how she was going to work with someone sent to compete with her—and how to do so without making a total fool of herself.

She and Amaka had spent the evening after the book club at Dara's trying to hack into his social media, but it hadn't got them anywhere. None of the corporate acting workshops the firm had organized over the years had prepared her for dealing with this. She'd gone through her notes from those sessions and watched several YouTube videos on difficult relationships in the office. The most positive of them had concluded that a rival could actually make the quality of her work better. Although this made perfect sense, it hadn't stopped her hands from getting sweaty, or stopped her from changing her outfit three times this morning. If there was one module that was sorely lacking in law school, it was dealing with office politics.

Opposite her building, red cranes reflected against the glass of the other towers. It was less than three months until the Hakida preliminary hearing, when their appointed arbitrator would agree to a schedule for the exchange of documents with the Kenyan side. The arbitration itself was set for August. She had a full day's work ahead applying for disclosures from an opposing side that was experienced and uncompromising; obsessing over Lani was the last thing she should be doing.

She heard a faint swish of a door being unlocked and the ding of the air conditioning switching on. Cool air began to fill the room. The office she and Lucy shared was tucked in a corner, so none of the other hyenas—who she'd been avoiding since that humiliating day at the cricket club—would know she was in unless they checked. Thankfully, Lani would be sharing an office with Mabel, the fifth and only Singaporean member of their team, whose room looked onto the commercial hub of Shenton Way and vast swathes of undeveloped land. At the far end of their section, Ian's office overlooked the bay, taking almost the width of the entire firm. His secretary, Irene, sat just outside his door. Irene had been Ian's right-hand woman for the past twelve years; she'd been the only one in the office when Dara arrived. Dara had asked as nicely as she could to be told when Lani arrived.

She closed Lani's LinkedIn page—she could pass an exam on him with flying colors at this point—and managed to do some work for a couple of hours before stretching and looking over at the framed family photos on Lucy's desk. Lucy's Christmas in Bedford, her family's ski trip in Japan, her latest weekend with school friends in Phuket. Lucy had a never-ending rotation of visitors, and as a junior associate under less pressure, she actually got to enjoy her time off. Dara preferred traveling on her own, but a few photos with more than just her in them would have been nice. Unlike Lucy, Dara had only two photos on her desk. The first was a grainy print of a young Dara standing with her grandparents in front of their house; she could just make out the pink blossoms tumbling over the walls, and if she squinted, she could pretend to see the dragonflies half-blended into the paint. The second was a professional picture of her mother taken in a studio five years ago that had been paid for by Abigail's second husband. She was pouting into the camera, and the light on Abigail's cinnamon-brown skin and the sharpness of her widow's peak made her look much younger than her fifty-some years.

She sometimes considered calling her mother for advice but

stopped short each time. Abigail was no longer a broke artist; she'd become a pampered wife who lived in a predominantly white village in Surrey and designed textile prints, which she sold on a website that was always under construction. On the few occasions that they spoke, Abigail was usually outdoors, carrying on simultaneous conversations with other people while on the phone with Dara (often calling out to her neighbors as she took her small, yappy dog for a walk; giving instructions to her landscape gardener; or speaking over train platform announcements while catching the Eurostar to Paris with her current—and much older—third husband).

Dara knew better than to rely on her mother. The realization that she'd romanticized the young, hip sister-mother who'd rebelled by going to art school in London—who'd got pregnant but refused to reveal the identity of Dara's father, and who'd only visited Lagos twice a year when Dara had been young—had been painful and disorientating. Her mother shouldn't have been OK with her spending afternoons after school with their Cypriot neighbors, who had two teenage sons they barely supervised. Their younger son had been Dara's first sexual experience, at thirteen; their fumbled petting had sustained her through the winter but fizzled out by the New Year. It wasn't unusual for her mother to miss parents' evening and never sing her praises. She often dissuaded Dara from making too many black friends or trusting other Nigerians simply because they shared the same genetic history. Instead, Abigail let Dara watch inappropriate films like *Crash* and *Blue Velvet*, and was happy for her to stay at home and study, making no effort to encourage any real relationship between her daughter and whoever she was married to or dating. It suited everyone, including her partners, but no one thought to ask Dara what she wanted.

When Dara's Oxford acceptance letter came in the post, she'd been watching daytime soaps, alone as usual. She'd taken the letter to Mrs. Ojo's, who lived up the lane and was the mother of twin girls who'd been a year ahead of Dara at school. Mrs. Ojo had gasped and hugged her, even called the twins at university, and when Mr. Ojo returned, they'd opened one of his bottles of whisky. In her second year at Oxford, Abigail came to visit, got tipsy and complained that her parents had punished her for her mistakes by leaving money for Dara's school fees and nothing else. Even beyond the grave, Dara's grandparents were the reason she had got where she was.

In that moment, Dara knew her mother had nothing more to offer her. Abigail wanted Dara to do well and enjoy life but wasn't prepared to sacrifice anything to help her get there. Dara had framed Abigail's picture not to honor her mother, but to remind herself that she still had a living relative.

"Morning," Lucy sing-songed, swinging her enormous tote bag onto her desk.

Dara snapped back into the room. "Morning."

"Would you like a coffee? Or a cup of tea?" Lucy asked brightly.

"No, thank you. I had one after my run."

"You're so disciplined." Lucy settled into her chair and began to unpack her handbag. "I don't know how you do it in this heat, or how you find the time to go to the gym at lunch. That's why you look so amazing. I just keep getting fatter every month I'm here. I'm sure it must be something in the food...my friend was telling me about MSG—makes you totally huge, but tastes ah-*ma*zing. Or maybe it's the wheat. Maybe I'm gluten intolerant...I should really stop eating at food courts, but they're just so cheap and the food's so yummy!"

The honeymoon phase. Dara would give it three more months before complaints about the taste of Australian milk and the extortionate price of avocados started. For a junior associate, Lucy's work was surprisingly thorough, and she took feedback from Dara well. She just needed to calm the frisky puppy energy if she wanted to be taken seriously.

"...this lovely guy came up to us." Lucy blushed. "He works for a civil engineering company. I don't know, he was really nice. He's only been here a few months, too. I don't know—we'll see!"

Dara gave that a few months, too.

"Morning, ladies." Tim leaned against the open doorway. "Didn't see you at the monthly drinks last week, Dara."

Dara tried to think of a sharp retort that would put Tim in his place, something Amaka would say.

"You don't get weekly billables like hers by getting wasted and singing karaoke, Tim," Lucy said archly.

"Good thing you don't have to worry your pretty little head about weekly billables then, isn't it?" Tim smirked. "So, now your team's a little bigger, Dara, I expect you'll be wanting to sign up for the pub quiz? You know, now that you've evened out the 'gender equality' and all that with another *man*?" He exaggerated the word and made ironic quote marks in the air, which Dara thought made little sense.

"We *live* for the pub quiz, don't we Dara?" Lucy rolled her eyes.

Dara turned back to her report. She was touched by Lucy's allegiance, but office banter was exhausting. So was losing even more of her free time trying to keep everyone in the firm on side.

"Well, we know you don't, Dara," Tim said pointedly. "You literally never come out. Why is that?"

For once, Dara wished she had the balls to say something sarcastic, like *I didn't know you missed me so much, Tim*, or something that showed she really *was* one of them, deep down, like *Slip me a fiver and I'll text you the answers*.

Instead, she came up with a weak, "I'll definitely be there next time."

"Don't put yourself out for us. But speaking of your new associate, you know he's here now, don't you? Not very nice to keep him waiting."

Dara stared, unsure she'd heard correctly.

"Irene didn't tell you?" Tim was loving this. "He's been waiting in reception for quite a while. We had a nice chat—great guy."

He drummed his fingers on the door frame, sniggering as he walked away.

"Coming?" Dara rose, yanking down the silk, crêpe-like dress she'd chosen for its blend of soothing whites and blues. Now she thought it made her look like a giant teacup.

"Sure." Lucy reached under her desk and slipped on her black heels.

Was that hesitation she'd seen on Lucy's face? Were even the junior associates pitying her, too?

Walking through the U-shaped office, she passed Irene, who was gossiping on the desk of one of the other admin staff. Dara threw her a nasty look for not keeping to their agreement. Without pausing for air, Irene completely ignored her; Dara made a mental note to halve the budget for her Christmas gift this year.

The red sofas in the reception were bare, the morning's newspapers untouched.

"Where's the new senior associate?" Dara turned to Cecilia, the new receptionist.

"Oh, he just left," Cecilia said.

"Left where?"

"I think he just left for your office."

"My office? But I just…" Dara turned back, exasperated.

"Oops, sorry." Lucy moved out of her way.

"Chris took him through the side door," Cecilia explained, looking worried.

"Um, Lucy, could you give me five minutes before you come in?" Dara set off without waiting for a reply.

She made her way back to her office, aware of even more eyes on her. They were salivating for a reaction, any bit of gossip they could slobber over, but she wasn't going to give them the satisfaction.

She clocked Lani as she got closer. Dressed in a pinstriped suit, white shirt and silvery-blue tie, he sat on her chair, tapping on his phone. The physical, 3D manifestation of Lani Idowu was…taller, but infuriatingly exactly the same as his impressive LinkedIn headshot.

Two cups of steaming coffee sat on the desk. He was inches away from her computer screen. One tap on her keyboard would bring up several pages of internet searches on him.

He looked up from his phone and, smiling in recognition, stood and approached.

"Dara, lovely to meet you. I hope you don't mind me waiting in here."

"No, of course not. Hi. Welcome." They shook hands.

"One of the admin girls helped me make some coffee." He gestured to the cups. "I don't know if you drink coffee?"

"I don't. I drink tea but thank you. I'll have a cup." Her words made absolutely no sense to her ears. Did she drink coffee or not?

"Great. The beans are Kenyan—I brought them over myself. Hope I didn't make it too strong." Lani turned the tray around to reveal a tiny jug. "Splash of milk?"

"Yes, OK, yes. Thank you."

Lani handed her a cup.

To her relief, he moved away from her desk and pulled Lucy's chair into the middle of the room, letting Dara sit at her desk. She sipped the coffee. It was delicious. How annoying.

"I haven't met Ian yet." Lani turned in his chair, as if expecting the man to appear. "Not since my video interview. Kept calling me Leni the whole time. I heard he called you 'Daria' your first month."

How the hell did he know that?

"Did he? I don't remember. We can get up to speed on Hakida now, or I can show you the office you'll be sharing with Mabel," she offered.

"Hakida now would be great." Lani unbuttoned his jacket.

"It's too hot for a full suit here, by the way. Most people keep a tie and jacket just for meetings."

"Oh, thank God, it's boiling!" Lani laughed, but she noticed he kept his jacket on.

She cleared her throat and began. "I've been liaising with Patrick Ndoku, our local council in Nairobi, and Charles Summers, our London QC. The merits of our case are strong. Patrick claims to have a witness who saw a local registry document outlining a tax rebate given to the local Kenyan chiefs. This means that the chiefs were being treated as part of the Kenyan government. So the fact that they're obstructing construction of the Kenyatta bridge means the Kenyan government is obstructing construction—we can treat both entities as the same. Of course, the government is denying the existence of this rebate and insisting that the chiefs are acting of their own volition. So, obviously, our argument relies on finding this document. It's a major part of our submission, and right now it's the only real shot we have at proving they're in breach of the Hakida contract. Please let me know if you're a bit lost; it's a complicated one."

"No, that's clear. But the local chiefs have their own jurisdiction and feudal system, which is longstanding and can be easily proven," Lani considered. "And they're claiming to have evidence that proves they're a separate entity from the Kenyan government, aren't they? So the witness statement you're talking about might not be enough. It's still a risk for our clients and, I think, a good reason why Hakida should settle."

"You've read the full submission?" Dara couldn't hide her surprise. She'd deliberately delayed emailing Lani the thirty-page summary of the opposing side's dossier. He'd only got it yesterday.

"It's a long flight from Lagos." Lani grinned through a huge yawn. "This jet lag is a killer. It's been three days and I still feel like my head's on a different planet."

"You flew from Lagos? I thought you moved from Geneva."

"Yeah, I got put on gardening leave. I think my old boss was nervous I'd nick his clients," he laughed.

"Do you go back a lot?" She couldn't help herself.

"Couple of times a year. It'll always be home. You?"

"No, not really," she shrugged.

"No family out there?"

"No." She changed the subject before she could smell the sweet oak and peppermint notes of her grandfather's pipe.

"So, there are a few things we need to do asap. Mabel is arranging Charles's hotel for August, and we're waiting on Patrick's office, which has been researching previous land disputes with the Kenyan government. The opposing council has sent over their bundles, so I need you to start going through them. I've emailed you a list of the specific documents we're looking for."

"OK, great. Hey, did you know we have mutual friends?" Lani tipped his head to one side. "The Ibusuns. Bayo's been out here with Temasek for a few years, and I think you know his wife, Kike?"

He's friends with the Ibusuns. Of course. Dara felt like kicking herself for forgetting how small the Nigerian circle was in Singapore.

"Yes, I've just joined her book club. How funny. And Ian defended Temasek in a dispute a couple years ago."

Lani nodded earnestly. "I read that! And I read that they've been investing in countries like Rwanda. That intrigued me: the chance to work with companies with the global reach they have. Having friends here also influenced my decision to move."

Lani turned as Ian entered the office, Lucy and Mabel entering behind him. Mabel and Lucy's relationship was frosty, and the natural competition between the two junior associates was compounded by their lack of common interests. Mabel's usual pinched expression at being around Lucy had released into what Dara could only guess was a smile. The Chinese Singaporean was dressed in a tight white dress and was propped up in five-inch heels. Dara thought her outfit was more appropriate for a London Mayfair nightclub, but it was pretty standard dress in the Singapore financial district.

As Lani stood to greet them, Dara tried to process her thoughts. She'd been expecting Lani to be more guarded: friendly on the surface, yes, but more cautious, considering the position they were in. Instead, he was relaxed, even eager to come across well. In the few photos she'd found of him online, he'd been formally dressed, almost playing the part of a tall, dapper gentleman; none of them captured the boyish quality he had in person. She wondered if she should, for a few weeks at least, consider the possibility that they could actually work together.

"Lani, great to finally meet." Ian openly took Lani in, sizing him up.

Lani shook his hand enthusiastically. "It's great to meet you in person, Ian."

"Jet lag not too bad?"

"Terrible," Lani laughed. "But I love to travel, so I'm used to it."

"Ah, Dara's got the wanderlust too. And this is Mabel and Lucy, our two junior associates. Full suit, good. The firm's dress code is casual, but I prefer a full suit in my team." Ian nodded approvingly. "I always keep a jacket in my office. Irene can steam yours for you whenever you'd like."

"Brilliant, thank you." Lani turned to smile at Dara, his eyebrows raised. She turned away, guiltily.

"Let's have a team lunch this afternoon," Ian said. "Twelve-thirty? Raffles starts to heave if you wait any longer. Can you make a reservation, Lucy? The Fullerton."

"Of course." Lucy ignored the smirk on Mabel's face.

"You got my email about the witness statement? I'd like you on a plane to Nairobi as soon as possible. Ndoku's office is competent, but I want someone from our team to meet the witness—it's someone from a rival tribe, but that's all Ndoku's given us. Let's go through the details in my office." Ian gestured for Lani to follow. "Dara, can you make a start on the bundles?"

Without waiting for an answer, he led Lani away.

"Nowhere too close to the air conditioning, please," Mabel said as she swanned out of the room.

"I'm going to find a table so cold she breaks in two." Lucy gritted her teeth, phone to her ear. "Lani though... *hot*. Hi, can I book a table for lunch?"

Dara stared at the half-empty cups on her desk, their insides stained with the brown waves of coffee stains, all her fears confirmed. Not only should she be the one on the plane to Nairobi, she hadn't even known they needed the witness statement so soon. Ian had welcomed Lani with more warmth than he'd ever shown her, and in the space of five minutes had made him lead on her case. And, unlike her, Lani hadn't missed a beat.

She took the cups into the office kitchen and dumped them into the sink, ignoring two startled juniors piling chocolate digestives onto paper towels. It was impossible to tell how complicit Lani was in Ian's plans to push her out; regardless, step one was clear: dig up dirt.

Amaka

Amaka pulled down the blinds in the empty meeting room two floors down from her office, cutting out the evening light. She turned on a dimmer and logged on to her laptop, then in to Zoom, waiting for Uncle Emeka, her father's younger brother, to log on. As each minute passed in the dark, she grew more anxious about who, exactly, would be on the other side of her family video call. Ugo had done as much as she could to shield Amaka from her late father Chukwu's family, but she could no longer hide. Once again, she wrestled with the guilt of accepting this job in Singapore, leaving her mother alone in Nigeria.

Earlier that day, she'd acted completely out of character, reaching a hand to Rohit over the partition; without missing a beat, still talking on his headset, he'd squeezed it, pleasantly surprised. He had no idea the meeting was today. She'd opened up a little more about her family after losing that game of hangman, explaining that her father had remarried after abandoning her mother, and that she'd only met her half-siblings once; neither of those pieces of information were strictly true, but the story as a whole was too complicated to explain. So she'd lied about the call tonight, using dinner plans with Dara as an excuse to leave her desk early, and she'd lied to Indira about needing to use this room for a work meeting. The tight, gray, collared dress she'd been wearing for over twelve hours was beginning to chafe, as was her decision to take this personal call at work.

"Don't let them see where you live," her mother Ugo had warned her many times. After Chukwu's funeral, Ugo had met with his Lagos lawyer and presented a copy of his most up-to-date will, drawn up by solicitors in London; since then, she'd been terrified that Chukwu's family would use information about Amaka's personal life against her in some way. In the past, Amaka would have rolled her eyes and laughed at her mother's paranoia. Whenever a new hairdresser came round to braid Amaka's hair, Ugo would press her to flush her hair down a toilet rather than throw it in the bin, just in case the woman took some to do *juju*. Even now, Ugo still admonished her for wearing a black scarf over her head at night, as though the color of the scarf could block whatever blessings filtered in as she slept. But there was little to laugh at when it came to their family politics.

Amaka had started distracting herself by searching for reviews of a patent-leather Dior wallet she'd ordered when she noticed that her Uncle Emeka's account had changed from red to green. A photo of him in his *"Fly Emirates"* T-shirt appeared above the icon of an incoming call. She smoothed her wig down, took a breath and answered. The screen dissolved into a figure with a stomach poking through a red Arsenal jersey.

When her Uncle Emeka stepped back, she saw her father Chukwu's front room in his Ikoyi house, a room she'd only been in once, two years before at the funeral. At the time, the ostentatious room and house had been swarming with mourners, most of whom had ignored her and Ugo. It was still heavily carpeted with a black lacquered coffee table and an empty gold-plated fruit bowl in the center. The curtains were black satin with yellow swirls and velvet cords, and they were open, casting the two figures who were sitting on the sofa in shadow. She tried to make out their faces without being too obvious.

On one side of the room, Ugo sat on a gilded, throne-like chair, dressed in a long Ankara skirt and blouse. At fifty-seven, her mother's beauty was undeniable. Sitting away from the light, her full makeup was visible and battle ready: shaded eyebrows, lined lips, blushed cheeks, a long, curly wig. Behind the makeup, her face was tight and stony. For a woman who employed so many people—a woman who spent most of her time shouting and bossing people around—it must have felt unnatural to sit so quietly.

The humiliation of how her father's family had ignored them the last time they'd been in that room, refusing to let them see the coffin or make outfits in the same family fabric, still seared painfully.

"*Mgbede—Ututu oma*, Uncle," she corrected herself, remembering it was morning there.

"Amaka, how are you?" Uncle Emeka looked genuinely happy to see her. "Hold on."

He walked behind the sofa, tugging one end of the curtain and then the other, pulling the room into darkness. A second later, the brilliant glare of an unseen chandelier illuminated the faces of the two men on the sofa. Her father's older brother, Uncle Onyekachi, in his early seventies, was dressed in a dark-colored traditional tunic and he was sitting beside Amaka's younger half-brother, Chinyere. He looked nothing like their father; he was much fairer, his skin marred by adult acne. Neither of her half-sisters were there.

"Chiamaka," her mother's voice broke through. "How are you?"

Ugo spoke in Igbo, her words formal and contained, her usual affectionate "darling" and "my dear" carefully absent.

"Good evening, Mummy. Good evening, Uncles. Chinyere. I hope everyone is well," Amaka said. She knew Ugo was proud that she spoke Igbo fluently.

"We are well, my child. And how is Singapore?" Uncle Onyekachi asked her loudly, his voice cracked and hoarse from years of smoking. "Your mother says it's hot, but it cannot be as hot as Nigeria?"

"It's hot, Uncle, and more humid than Nigeria." Amaka smiled.

"Well, one day we must come and see you. There's no day we don't see something good about Singapore in the news."

"Yes, Uncle."

"So, let us start the meeting." He cleared his throat. "We are here to settle a family matter, a matter that has been in our family for many years, one that has caused so much unrest and unhappiness. We are here to settle it once and for all."

He spoke as though dictating a speech, his voice a mixture of his Umuahia accent and the Catholic school education he and her father had gone through. Whenever her mother talked about Uncle Onyekachi, which wasn't often, it was with a disparaging tone, always referring to him as the "civil servant" who had lorded his high government position over his brother until Chukwu's businesses began to flourish and overshadow him.

"As the most senior member of this family, I, Onyekachi Emmanuel Okafor, am the rightful nominee, being the representative of the Okafor family, to oversee this matter in my late brother Chukwu's stead." He cleared his throat again and nodded.

The more Uncle Onyekachi spoke, the more Amaka fought the urge to laugh. She prayed for self-control, but it was like kneeling down to pray at church; the pressure to appear holy and righteous only made her want to sin even more.

"First, let us introduce ourselves and make clear the concern at hand." He motioned at Amaka. "Amaka, of course, is the reason we are here. She is Chukwu's eldest child, and while she was not raised in her father's house, she was recognized by her father before his death, as was right." Uncle Onyekachi turned around to focus on Chinyere.

"Chini—Chinyere Okafor, my late brother Chukwu's only son and second child, born of Esther Adaeze Okafor, is the main claimant in this dispute and, according to our traditional customs, the rightful inheritor of Chukwu's estate."

Amaka and Chinyere were both thirty-three, only six months apart. If anyone in the room reacted to the reminder of this awkward family history, she didn't see it.

He continued. "*Chini's* younger sisters, Ngozi Okafor and Ifeoma Agu, née Okafor and recently married, are not present, as both reside in England."

Her youngest sister had got married. She'd had no idea.

"My junior brother, Emeka." Uncle Onyekachi raised a hand in Emeka's direction, giving him only the briefest of attention.

"And Ugomma Ezinulo, the mother of my late brother's daughter, Chiamaka," he gestured to Ugo.

Amaka had to hand it to him—the man had tact. The issue of

what to call her mother was a thorny one, yet he had managed to sidestep it neatly.

Uncle Onyekachi nodded, refocusing on Chinyere.

"Thank you all for attending this meeting today and for putting away past grievances. Thank you in particular to Chinyere, who has taken time from his brief holiday in Nigeria to attend today."

And no thanks, she supposed, for her presence, despite the seven-hour time difference.

"We all know that today's difficulty is owing to the fact that, while my late brother was at one time traditionally married to Chiamaka's mother, he was legally married to Chinyere, Ngozi, and Ifeoma's mother. *Chini*, I will not insult you by putting words into your mouth. I will let you speak on behalf of your mother and your sisters, who are absent today, and whose case we are here to hear. Please relate to us what you wish to be done."

"It's very simple." Chinyere's voice was crisp, shaped by years in an English boarding school. "My father's last will and testament is a forgery."

A spark of shock shot through Amaka.

"Chinyere, please." Uncle Onyekachi held his nephew's arm. "As we say, *Nwayo nwayo ka e ji eri ofe di oku*. I know you don't speak Igbo so I will translate, hmm? *Hot soup should be eaten slowly and carefully.* Please."

Chinyere shot his uncle an exasperated look but did not move his arm. Amaka saw that he had not learned, in spite of his *oyinbo* education in private schools, how to hold his tongue and hide his feelings.

"My father left a will, witnessed by his lawyer and best friend in Manchester," Chinyere began again, his emotions barely below the surface. "In it, he left the house we are currently sitting in to my mother, as well as the house he built in our village in Umuahia, the house in London, and the money from the sales of his snail farms in the Eastern Delta and his chicken farms in Anambra. All his stocks and shares he left to me, his only son. He also left significant sums of money to my sisters, Gozi and Ify."

It hurt for some reason, hearing her sisters' nicknames and

the familiarity with which he said them. Nicknames she had no right to use.

"This will was kept in a safety deposit box, and the key was held by his lawyer. But immediately after his death, a second will was..." He struggled to find the word, and Amaka could tell he was fighting against using a contemptuous one.

"...presented, by this lady." He pointed at Ugo, who looked squarely at him for the first time during the meeting. "A will that was witnessed by lawyers no one had ever heard of, bogus lawyers whose reputations are completely untrustworthy. In it, the London property was taken from us, as Amaka and Ugo's names were put on the deed, along with half of my shares."

"Onyekachi," Ugo snapped. "I will not be called a thief and a forger. If you allow this boy to speak of me this way, I will leave now."

The words were spoken in Igbo, not English. The meeting was doomed.

"Tell her to speak in English!" Chinyere demanded. "I won't sit here and be insulted!"

"Please, please." Onyekachi raised his arms.

Both Chinyere and Ugo continued to yell, one in English, the other in Igbo.

"Please! Fighting about this won't change anything!" Amaka cried out. The room fell silent.

She stared at Chinyere. She had no idea when he or his sisters had found out about her, if they had overheard some family gossip, witnessed conflict in their parents' marriage or—like she had with them—stumbled across her existence without any warning. She wished she could tell him she didn't blame him for his resentment, that she understood he was protecting his family. But to suggest even a word of that was to betray her mother, the person who had taken so many bullets for her, who even now was fighting a room full of men and an entire family that had been hostile to her for years.

"We're here to come to an agreement," she forced herself to continue. "Chinyere, Uncle Onyekachi said you have a proposal."

Something flickered on Chinyere's face. Surprise? Grudging respect for taking charge? He composed himself and looked directly into the camera.

"My family and I have agreed to recognize you, to allow you to use our father's family name," he said.

"She has always had the legal right to Okafor," Ugo shot back. "I am the one who chose to give her the name Ezinulo, my own father's name. That is our custom."

"If you choose to use it, we won't dispute it," Chinyere ignored Ugo. "We will accept you as an Okafor and we would be willing, if the appropriate respect is shown, to meet you at some point in the future. For the sake of peace in our family."

Amaka listened in, completely floored. This was the last thing she'd expected.

"Ugomma, Chiamaka." Uncle Onyekachi lifted his chin proudly, as though he were the one who had made the proposition.

"In exchange for what?" Ugo's delayed reaction caught up, and she spoke directly to Chinyere in English.

"The return of the shares my father left me." Chinyere stared at the screen. "And the proceeds from the sale of the London house."

The room held its breath.

"Chiamaka?" Uncle Onyekachi said. "You are of age and an equal partner in the shares left to you and in the house. As head of the Okafor family, and representing our family council, I cannot compel you to agree. Your papa's will was examined by an independent solicitor and, notwithstanding the concerns of many in the family, found to be legitimate. However, I must stress very strongly..."

He drew himself up to his age-diminished height, fixing Amaka with a warning look.

"...that your decision will have reverberations across the Okafor family, both here in Lagos, in the village in Umuahia and internationally. This will be..."

"Uncle, please." Chinyere waved for silence.

"Eh?" Uncle Onyekachi stared in disbelief at his nephew's disrespect.

"Chiamaka," Uncle Emeka said quietly, speaking for the first time. "What is your answer?"

What was she going to do? Her father had recognized her in his will, even though, in the eyes of the law, she was an illegitimate child and technically not entitled to the same inheritance as her half-siblings. Chukwu had spoken from the grave, giving her and her mother the respect and status he had denied them while he was alive.

She turned from her Uncle Emeka's face to her mother's. None of the men in the room could see it, but Amaka knew her mother was on the brink of tears.

It was so unfair that, after years of being in the shadows, Ugo was still being blamed for the fact Chukwu had had children with two different women at the same time. Past grievances had seeped into their current dilemma as if it were Ugo's fault that Chukwu had been sloppy with his estate, leaving two different wills. This Nigerian fixation on deifying the dead meant that Ugo was being attacked even more.

When Amaka had learned of her inheritance, she'd been determined to use it, to treat herself to all the luxuries her father had never given her. Ugo, however, had done what she could to reinvest what she'd been left. From share derivatives he had left her, Ugo had built successful businesses: a nail bar and salon and two juice bars in trendy malls on Lagos Island. She was doing well, even with the recession of the past few years slashing the value of Chukwu's shares. The London house was the real nest egg, worth nearly a million pounds. Even though it was heavily mortgaged, it had been split into two self-contained units for different tenants, and every month, the house brought in thousands in rent to Amaka's UK bank account. She resented every penny of it.

After she'd learned of her half-siblings' existence, she'd wanted to be part of Chukwu's family, to have brothers and sisters, be invited to birthdays and dance into family ceremonies with a procession of relatives. She'd never admit it, but she'd once dreamed of dancing into her own wedding with red coral beads adorning her head and shoulders as her sisters and female cousins waved white handkerchiefs beside her. She'd scoffed when her mother told her about the long list of items that both the bride and groom's side were expected to bring to a traditional Igbo wedding, but she'd made a mental note of both lists. It wasn't the money she'd wanted; it was the family that came with it.

Now they were opening a door, if she was willing to buy her way in.

"*Nne*," her mother's voice shook as she used the intimate but peculiar pet name that Igbo mothers used for their daughters, a term that actually meant "mother" but was used to mean "my dear." "We are waiting."

The look on Chinyere's face, the way he flinched when her mother spoke, left her with no choice. The offer was for her alone, but she could not separate herself from Ugo. Yes, Chukwu had recognized her and paid for her education, but it was Ugo who had pushed him to send her to the U.S., and it was Ugo who'd sent her money to live on when Chukwu had insisted he could afford the tuition but nothing more. She could not accept her siblings any more than they could stop taking sides against her mother.

"I'm sorry," she trembled. "I would love to meet you and your sisters, but—"

"Save it." Chinyere exploded out of his seat, startling everyone in the room.

He stormed out, Uncle Onyekachi calling after him. Uncle Emeka was on his feet, going after Chinyere when Amaka closed her laptop. Their voices cut away, returning Amaka back to the dark office.

Three heavy sobs broke out of her before she remembered she was still at work. She pressed her knuckles into her eyes.

Amaka sat slumped in the back of a dark taxi, but in her mind she saw herself springing into her father's arms. Ten-year-old Amaka buried her face into the long stretch of muscle that bridged his neck and arms and inhaled all the places he had been to. The places where she longed to be beside him. The London dry cleaners that laundered and pressed his wool suits, that British Airways sharpness, the watery lotion and gel hand wash he sometimes brought back in tiny containers. It was a smell Amaka loved, both familiar and exotic. It wrapped itself around her, drawing her closer to the foreign locations he had traveled to, filling her with pride at his worldly experience and confidence, and his ability to pronounce so many foreign words. It reconfigured who she was, pulling her out of her small apartment with its small, bland walls, net curtains and noisy traffic, to a vastness that she hoped to step into one day. A day would come when she would be old enough for Daddy to take her on one of his trips.

She remembered how much younger Ugo had looked when Chukwu was home. She smiled more, shrugged off Amaka's mistakes and, as long as Amaka kept her promise to give her parents time alone, Ugo let her stay up watching TV until the broadcasts were over. It was a running joke that Chukwu's homecoming breakfast of pancakes was more for Amaka than for him, since he was never hungry fresh off a flight. She loved every second of their family ritual, from the moment she woke, to the smell of oil and fried flour, to the fishing out of chocolate humbugs from Chukwu's suit pocket. By the time Ugo was dressed and ready for work, Chukwu would be snoring on the sofa, his favorite spot for the next few days. His weight would create a depression in the worn foam that would remain for several days after he and his suitcases had left. At the time, Amaka did not yet know that her home was not really his home—that his return was really just a quick stop, an extension of his trip, before he went home to his real wife and kids.

"Eight-fifty," the taxi driver grunted, switching on his overhead light.

Amaka wiped her damp cheek on her sleeve and took out her wallet. For a split second she ached for Rohit, and it took a superhuman effort not to call him.

"No NETS payment," he waved away her outstretched card. "Machine not working."

"It says NETS on your car." She gestured at the credit card sign on the passenger window, desperate to get away.

"No NETS. Cash only."

"I don't have cash," she shrugged, exhausted.

"Eh, you go ATM." The man pointed to a cash machine across the street.

"That's not my bank."

Opening her bag, she found three two-dollar notes and some change. She held the crumpled mess out.

"Here, Uncle, this is all I have." She used the respectful term expected when addressing an older Singaporean, but the word had a bitter taste tonight.

The man looked irritated but held out a gray coin tray.

She dropped her money in and opened the door.

"Eh!" He was lightning fast, counting the money quickly. "One more dollar! You give me seven only, *lah*!"

"I don't have any more, OK? Next time fix your stupid machine!" She slammed the door.

She headed into the 7-Eleven and walked straight to the cashier, who reduced the volume of sobbing from a historical Chinese period drama on her phone and looked up, unsmiling. Amaka pointed to the cheapest, pinkest bottle of rosé from the exorbitantly priced bottles behind the counter.

"And these." She snatched three chocolate bars and a packet of sour sweets from the stand beside her and tossed them down on the counter.

"NETS." She eyeballed the cashier, daring her to protest.

She pressed the six digits of her card security code and waited for her receipt.

The door jingled open and, out of nowhere, the taxi driver sprang out beside her.

"Eh, eh, eh—you run away!" he yelled. "I call police. Fare evasion!"

"Seriously? You're following me because of one dollar?" Amaka spluttered.

"You no pay fare, you go to jail!" The driver took out his phone and started pressing buttons.

"Go ahead! See how ridiculous you'll look." Amaka had reached her boiling point. It was unbelievable that today of all days, someone else was coming for her when she was just trying to do her best.

"Are you OK?" A male voice spoke behind her. "Do you need help?"

She half-turned to the man, gesturing at the driver. "I was short one dollar and he's trying to get me arrested!"

"It's just one dollar, right? Nothing to you," the driver defended himself. "I rejected two customers to pick you up because you say you're going in my direction, so why not pay the full fare? One dollar is nothing to you, right?"

As the driver was speaking, Amaka became aware that the guy had drawn closer and was reaching into his back pocket to bring out his wallet. She also realized that he was black and tall and... very familiar. And not in the way that there were so few black guys in Singapore that she must have seen him before. That profile and that chin and those glasses were *very* consciously and concretely impressed in her mind.

"Here." He held out a note to the driver. The sleeves of his white work shirt were rolled up and a laptop bag swung on one shoulder. "Does this cover it?"

"No change, *lah*." The driver eyed him, almost disappointed by the resolution.

"Keep the change." The man spoke in a British accent, his demeanor courteous but disapproving.

"I didn't need any help, but thank you." Amaka eyed the driver as he walked away. "It wasn't the money, it was the principle; his machine didn't work, and I don't see why I should put myself out for one dollar. I also don't appreciate being treated like a criminal—did he really have to humiliate me in front of everyone?"

She picked up her plastic bag from the counter, pissed at how easily people distrusted her with money in her personal life when in her professional life, she controlled bank loans only huge organizations could secure.

"To be fair, the place is pretty empty," the guy smiled, "but I'm surprised he'd flip out over a dollar like that. I thought Singapore was supposed to be one of the wealthiest nations in the world."

"Please. The gap between rich and poor is wider here than anywhere in the world." She turned to the cashier. "Do you have cashback?" The cashier was staring openly at them, less interested in the show on her phone now that a real-time drama had unfolded right in front of her.

The cashier shook her head.

Even though Amaka was desperate for a drink and her bed and possibly the sound of Rohit's voice, there was no way she was letting a strange man cover her debts and leave owing him something.

She pivoted round to face him squarely, her wallet out, ready to dismiss any objections.

"There's an ATM about five minutes from here. If you come with me, I'll pay you back."

"You don't have to do that. Please, it's my pleasure," he said warmly.

"Nope. I'm paying you back," Amaka said, touched but adamant. "I'm just round the corner. It's no trouble. How much did you—*oh*..."

The pieces of his face slotted together, pixels of an image coming to life. *Lani. The new lawyer from Dara's firm.*

He waited for the rest of the sentence. "Are you OK?"

A huge grin spread across Amaka's face. *How could she have been so dense?* "Yes, I...I'm fine. I just remembered something. OK, well, thanks for your help."

"That's it? I thought you were offering to pay me back?" he said wryly.

"You said I didn't have to."

He chuckled, a little confused. "Did I...have we met before?"

"No, we've never met, but thank you for doing the 'gentlemanly' thing." She had to get out of there and call Dara asap.

"Well, I don't need you to pay me back, but if you live round the corner...I'm staying in a serviced apartment on Gopeng Street, and I haven't been able to find my way back from work easily," he said. "You'd be helping *me*, actually. I'm terrible with maps."

Amaka hesitated. She may have been out of Lagos for a while, and maybe she was reading him all wrong with the whole British thing, but was he flirting with her?

"I have a boyfriend. He wouldn't be comfortable with that." She couldn't think of anything better to say.

Lani raised his hands good-humoredly. "Fair enough. Anyway, it was nice to meet you, and I'm glad I could help. I'm Lani."

She moved the plastic bag to her other hand, acutely aware of the rosé tugging it down.

"Amaka." She shook his hand.

"Ah, Igbo. My last girlfriend was Igbo." He grinned and raised his eyes to the ceiling, as if to suggest there was a story there.

Definitely flirting.

"Really? Poor thing," Amaka riffed, her family troubles all at once fading far away.

Surprised but clearly enjoying the repartee, he threw his head back and laughed. "Why do you say that?"

"You seem like the type of guy who dates, you know, *Sophias* and *Isabellas*. That one black guy on Instagram in a sea of white," she chuckled.

Lani stared back at her, and for an awkward moment she floundered, wondering if she'd gone too far. To her surprise, he reached for her hand and shook it again, an expression of delight and intense amusement across his face.

"It's very nice to meet you, Amaka," he grinned.

Lillian

Lillian clung to the edge of the sofa bed a second before hitting the floor. She rolled back and stared at the ceiling, the sounds from her dream lingering like the trailing tail of a bird. The old nightmare had resurfaced, twice now in the past week. She could still hear the knocking on the door, the jingle of the chewing gum advert that had played that day, its electric guitar and jaunty, grating drums. She could feel the cold station and the stiff cotton of the officer's uniform . . . it had to be linked to that British man—it had to be. Seeing him had brought the dreams back.

Abstractedly, she rubbed a sore, coin-shaped bump on her scalp, tugging at her roots until a long string of hair pulled free. The follicle smarted sweetly, and she lay like that, rubbing and pulling.

It was easy, lying there at dawn, to conjure her mother, Yahimba, whose presence had always been so strong when she was a child. It frightened her how few memories she had of her father, Bem. They all involved him coming home as the sun rose, the touch of his skin dried out by long East Coast winters and hospital disinfectant. Even when her father wasn't working a shift, he stayed late at the hospital studying for his medical licensing exams. She remembered Bem as a loving but empty space, a series of pats and kisses as she slept, a promise of a real father when he finally qualified as a doctor in the U.S. She could recall snatches of conversation, but it was mainly Yahimba's voice she heard, her mother's frustration at the unfairness of Bem having to retrain in the U.S. because he was an immigrant, at the absurdity of being penalized for being an experienced gynecologist because of the years he'd been out of medical school. While Yahimba, who had first moved to the U.S. with Lillian as a toddler, had been able to find a job as a nurse after passing one written test, Bem was forced to work as an orderly caring for patients, changing beds and throwing out the rubbish. Money was always, always tight. Yahimba's pay check covered rent and food while Bem saved for the cost of exams and endless residency applications.

She'd had many dreams about her mother, most vividly right after her parents had died and she'd been passed from relative to friend, finally landing at a distant aunt's house for most of high school. She'd moved to a different district of the city, started going to a new school and spent the next two years terrified that everyone around her would die. The dreams had started then. In them, Yahimba is always in constant motion: waking Lillian for school, locking the front door, pulling a wool hat over Lillian's braids, pushing her up from the curb into the school bus. Yahimba reads a medical textbook on an old, salvaged cabinet with no space to stretch her legs, directs Lillian with chopping and grating instructions, and helps her with her homework before taking over the cooking; they carry their bags of dirty clothes to a laundrette and cross unfamiliar neighborhoods to attend mass. Yahimba grips Lillian's arm, steering her far from the men and women openly slumped on the sidewalk, and says in Tiv: *"Look straight. Don't look at them."* The streets are so close that the trees form an archway, and children and dogs cross the narrow, one-way roads, forcing cars to use them as traffic lights. A lone figure folds over a sledge at the top of a hill, then shaves a path in the snow, as smooth and creamy as icing on a cake.

It was Yahimba who took the train with Lillian every Sunday to Dr. Cohn's house. A cardiologist at the hospital where Bem worked, he respected her father's medical expertise, and the two had become friends. When he'd heard about Lillian's gift for music and that she had to stay late at school to practice, he'd insisted they use his piano. Together, Lillian and her mother would leave the baseball hats, Viking sweatshirts and oil-stained Domino's boxes piled beside rubbish bins in their own neighborhood and venture into the green, so-rich-you-had-to-whisper Chestnut Hill, a mournful church bell tolling behind them. While Lillian practiced, Yahimba would read in a corner of a room that was larger than their entire apartment.

Yahimba was always in her dreams, but Bem—Bem had moved so far away in Lillian's mind that she thought she would never be able to picture him again.

She reached under the sofa for the air-con remote. She'd promised Warren she'd be more careful with the electricity bills, and even though they'd barely spoken over the past week, she hoped he'd notice this small gesture.

She'd moved into the would-be nursery the night of the book club, restarting the pattern they were stuck in, preferring the agony of being surrounded by evidence of their failure to being in a silent room with him. After each IVF attempt, she would move here and then eventually slip into their bedroom on a morning like this one. She'd press herself to his back, breathing in the damp, night-muskiness of his skin—like a country she was trying to find a passport to. In her tears, there would be guilt but also relief that the thick, red mass between her legs days before meant her inevitable failure at motherhood could again be delayed. Warren's own feelings unspoken, his knee would gently part her legs, and a feverish, fruitless desire would draw them close. They would make fresh plans, agree to try one more cycle and schedule virtual appointments with U.S.-based adoption agencies as a backup. They'd dress for work, moving in sync, and speak excitedly about the sex and age of their future child, whether he or she would be her biscuit-brown, the dark russet of his skin or a completely different shade.

It felt different this time. Her body had let her down and her marriage was close to dying, but the Universe had sent her a practical doppelganger of her father. It couldn't be a coincidence. How could she begin explaining this to Warren or Dr. Geraldine before she understood it herself? Not only would they think she was crazy, but there was no way it would improve things in her marriage. She'd never told Warren the details of how her parents had died or explained the feelings of responsibility that had dogged her ever since, and it was too late to admit the damage it had caused: if death was ruthless enough to take her parents, it was ruthless enough to take her child. In the solid reality of daylight, those fears seemed ridiculous and maybe even offensive to the thousands of women desperate to have children of their own, but to the eleven-year-old inside her, they were very real. Making a decision about her marriage and adopting a child terrified her, but the urge to find out more about Lani was an impulse that felt as natural as it was inexplicably strong.

She unplugged her laptop and sat at the dining table, opening her search results. *"Lani"* and *"lawyer"* were the only key words she had to go on, and so far, her digging had brought up mostly white, female attorneys in the U.S. When she added *"British"* and *"UK,"* she got a Croatian human rights lawyer based in London, but still no man and still no one black.

She scrolled fruitlessly through the results, sensitive to any movement from Warren's bedroom, then typed *"Reincarnation meeting a stranger you recognize."*

She spent the next hour reading.

Everything was about past life connections, recognizing a soul mate and how to know if you'd met someone before, but there were no articles about meeting someone who looked just like your father, who had the face she'd missed so much. When she searched specifically for that, every result had a sexual focus, and used some variation of a scientific theory called imprinting to explain why women were attracted to men who reminded them of their dads. But to Lani, she'd felt no sexual attraction—she was even starting to wonder if she'd imagined the resemblance.

Uneasily, Lillian closed her device and stood by a window, looking down at the swathes of trees, as dense and stiff as broccoli heads. Singapore was populated by lush greenery. Some of it was a relic from the ancient forest the city had carved its way through;

some of it was roadside trees and vegetation carefully planted by the first prime minister after independence was declared from the British.

She could stare for hours at the world below. On weekdays, teenage girls ran around a racetrack on the grounds of Raffles Girls' School, and school coaches heaved through the residential streets, picking up children too young to be awake that early; on the weekends, families on tandem bicycles navigated the busy roads to get to the botanic gardens. There was so much more to look at than she'd had as a child back in Philly, waiting for her parents to get back from their shifts. All she'd been able to see was the corner of the curb she wasn't allowed to play on, and a thin tree shedding its leaves. The silence of being an only child had followed her to Singapore. Sometimes, a yellow-legged sparrow would fly into the kitchen if she left the door open while cooking. After she'd shoo it back out, it would dawn on her that "Hey!" and "Out!" were the only words she'd spoken all day, her solitude becoming so thick and solid that the sound of her own voice was startling.

Never in a million years could her parents have imagined that she would end up in Asia, sitting in a three-thousand-square-foot apartment in such tremendous heat. America was the only name that had been on their lips, the only future they'd seen for her, and if the U.S. was anything to them, it was full of noise. Children would have been expected from her—a blessing. They would have wanted generations to spill out of her like a long piece of red thread knotting with another, and then another. They probably wouldn't even have minded her marrying an American. They would have embraced Warren, just as they'd embraced music as the path God had laid out for her. She'd been so young when they'd died that they were still caught up in their pride in her inexplicable gift. It was the reason she'd kept playing, the reason she'd applied to music school—the reason she had allowed her aunt to convince her that the piano arriving on their doorstep after her parents had died was a sign from heaven and not a cruel joke.

She'd learned how to stay quiet and do what she was told, to not take up too much space or draw too much attention to herself, spending most of her free time in school practicing the piano. Her aunt had five kids, so that suited everyone just fine. When she was in middle school, her new music teacher, Mrs. Walsh, had helped her get into a charter school music program; in high school, she'd won a full scholarship to the Curtis Institute. Her path and coping mechanisms were set in college—she could draw a straight line from the shy loner she'd been in university to the quiet musician Warren had been drawn to years later.

She could understand Warren's confusion—he'd fallen in love with an artist, and she'd barely touched her piano since they'd moved here. As they'd unpacked their boxes three years ago, both excited at their new start, she'd found her envelope of family photos. Doing the math in her head, she'd realized she was now past the age her parents had been when they died. There seemed to be no place for her grief in her new life with Warren, so she'd pushed it down, not realizing it was slowly eating away her drive and desire and purpose.

Across the open space, her copy of *Purple Hibiscus* on the coffee table caught her eye. She gazed at the image of a girl's full lips floating above the pink petals and a yellow stamen of a flower.

The book club.

What did she have to lose? She didn't really know of any these women and hadn't spoken much on the night she'd hosted, but at least they'd been kind enough not to ask questions about why she'd disappeared for so long. Dara in particular had gone out of her way to include her in the conversation, though Lillian had struggled to maintain eye contact with her after their embarrassing exchange in her bedroom. It was a long shot, but they were the only black community she knew in Singapore, and it would be worth reaching out to see if they had any information about Lani; even if none of them had met him yet, they might meet him down the line and remember she'd asked.

She hurried to get her phone from the guest room, moving stealthily when she passed Warren's door.

She opened the book club WhatsApp group and drafted a message to send at a more decent hour.

Hi, ladies. This is a random one but I'm trying to find someone. His name's Lani, he's a lawyer, and he just moved to Sing. Anyone know him? Tnx.

A bout of coughing. She looked up and scanned the room. Her Elementary 2B students were deep in concentration. They scratched at their workbooks on the white desks attached to their chairs, and one of the Japanese men drank from a flask. Irina slipped some chewing gum into her mouth.

Reassured that they would be occupied for some time, Lillian returned to her phone. It was under the table, hidden from view.

The first response had come at the start of the lesson, her last of the day. It had sent a frisson through her, seeing the message appear on her screen as the students filed in. A spontaneous smile had lit across her face. She hadn't been able to read it properly until now.

Kike: Lani Idowu? Is that who you're talking about?

Idowu. Lillian's heart flipped. She had a full name.

Lillian: Yes, I think that's him.

Kike: He and my husband grew up together. Did something happen?

Thinking fast, Lillian replied.

Lillian: Not at all. He left something behind where I work and we're trying to get it to him. Our receptionist doesn't have his details.

Kike: Oh OK. I can send him your number?

Before she could reply, another message came through, bringing more intel.

> Amaka: Isn't this the new guy that just joined Dara's firm?
>
> Kike: **@DarasimiCoker** I didn't know you and Lani were at the same firm!
>
> Amaka: Dara never reads group chats.
>
> Kike: Why not?
>
> Amaka: Because she has a job.

Another person joined the chat.

> LeToya: He Nigerian too? Y'all just taking over. We should start calling ourselves the "Nigerians in Singapore Book Club"!
>
> Nana: Ladies, I think it might be wise to start suggesting book titles before the next meeting. Then everyone can do some research and make a more informed decision. There's a novel recently translated from Korean everyone's been talking about. It looks really good. It's called The Vegetarian.
>
> LeToya: Aww, hell no. I hate translated books.
>
> Nana: Why is it a problem if it's translated? We should be reading widely. It's about a woman who protests against her misogynistic culture by not eating meat.

Amaka: 🏩

Yemisi: **@Nana** Send us the link, but no promises.
Voting at the meetings is getting too heated, ladies!

The messages went back and forth with very little else being said about Lani until Lillian noticed that the energy in the room had shifted. Some of the students started peering at each other's work, exchanging quiet comments in their native tongues.

"OK." Lillian spoke loudly, dragging herself from her screen and tucking her phone inside her laptop sleeve.

She gestured for everyone to rise and raised three fingers. "Find three people and practice: *'Have you eaten here before?' 'Yes, I have.' 'No, I haven't.'*"

The students began to mingle. The three Japanese students from an auditing company were shy and polite, easily frustrated when they made mistakes, but respectfully ignored their partners' errors. Irina was overly confident, tossing her long brown hair over her shoulder as she moved from partner to partner, questioning each person when they tried to point out her errors. Then there was a Japanese woman, Miki, who was being sponsored to learn English by her cosmetics company, and Even, a Chinese exchange student who was proud of the English name she'd chosen for herself.

At the screech of the final bell, they handed their workbooks back, collected their things and valiantly tried to keep the English going as they left.

Lillian was back at her desk before the last of them had filtered out. Above the book club chat, there was a message from an unidentified number.

Kike: Hi Lillian, it's Kike here. Do you want me to give Lani your number?

Things were moving too fast—the last thing Lillian wanted to do was spook him.

Lillian: We can find him easily now that we have his name—thanks!

> Kike: Np. Actually, I know Bayo's helping Lani meet more new people here (not that he needs help, if you ask me), so if you and your husband are free on the first of February, we've just moved apartments and are throwing a Lunar New Year housewarming party. We're keeping numbers small and I'm not sure if I can invite all the book club ladies yet, which is why I haven't shared this on the group chat. Send me a message if you can make it.

Lillian bunched her fingers up to her mouth and breathed in slowly. It was like the universe was slotting everything into place. There was no way this was a coincidence. Plus, he was Nigerian, too, something she rarely divulged about herself. On the few occasions she'd revealed this to other Nigerians, they knew so little about the Tiv ethnic group that it compounded her insecurities about her own lack of knowledge. When people usually spoke about Nigerians, they unknowingly referred to Yorubas and Igbos, the two tribes that migrated from the south of the country to the rest of the world. From time to time, Hausas and Fulanis from Northern Nigeria were mentioned in negative news reports about murderous herdsmen destabilizing the region and killing nomadic farmers and their families, but the only time she saw her own people was when she went digging in blogs and on YouTube. She'd found out that Benue State, her father's state, was in East Nigeria, and that the Tiv people spread out into Cameroon but could be traced as far as Congo. She'd read about the fried yams they loved to roast and eat with red palm and salt, had watched videos of the traditional Girinya dance and watched ceremonies with both men and women dressed in a black-and-white dress pattern they loved. She'd been fascinated and eager to learn more, but what she'd learned felt as foreign to her as learning about the Innuits in high school.

She let a safe amount of time pass before she replied to Kike's message.

> Lillian: The 1st should be fine. Looking
> forward to it.

A few seconds later, a group invite appeared below the words "Kike and Bayo's Housewarming." She accepted and scanned through the attendees. There, among a few of the girls from the book club, was Lani's name, number and a profile picture of his back on top of a mountain, arms outstretched, face hidden.

The lift took her to the building's back entrance, her exit startling two pigeons sleeping behind bins and a smoking waiter squatting nearby. She followed the alley, avoiding the hot breath of fried potato that was being expelled from the back of a kitchen restaurant. This was the less glamorous end of Orchard Road, full of aging plazas and chipped tiled steps leading to basement food courts. A large poster for Korean skincare promised results in just six days from the side of a mall, and red lanterns hung down from lampposts. Opposite, a large red dragon clung onto another building, the early signs of the coming Lunar New Year.

The queue at a nearby taxi rank was full but moved quickly. She spied a taxi with its green lights on and raised her hand before letting it fall, remembering that she was meant to be cutting down on her spending. As she waited at the nearest bus stop, mulling over how to mend things with Warren so that she could propose this barbecue invite, a young Japanese mother in a wide-brimmed hat pushed a pram past her, both she and the baby's faces hidden from the sun. On the other side of the road, two white women in workout clothes jogged in step, one hand each on a three-wheeled stroller.

She saw an image of herself carrying a newborn in a sling,

spooning pureed fruit into an apricot mouth, holding a toddler's hands as they staggered along the path. She and the baby would draw smiles from passing cyclists and from the mothers of older children now confident on scooters, and would wave to the familiar faces of restaurant owners and waiters along the quay. Finally, she'd scoop her child up, dirty, tired and happy, and they'd walk back up the hill, racing the setting sun and evening mosquitoes. Her daydreams used to be almost as real as the world around her; they'd kept her warm and safe, patiently waiting, and more importantly, kept the memories she did not want to remember at bay.

A candle burned on Dr. Geraldine's desk. "It doesn't look like he's coming." She looked away from the clock on the wall and gave Lillian a sympathetic look. "I know today is your time to express your past hurts. We could have a personal session, if you want to proceed? I'm happy to refund the difference."

Lillian nodded, rubbing the sole of one foot over the other. She wasn't looking forward to delving into her marital grievances, not while she was just starting to tug at the thread of who Lani was. "Thank you. That'd be good."

"How have you been? How are things at home?" Dr. Geraldine's palms crossed on her knee, a sign that they'd officially begun.

"Um...the same in some ways, worse in others."

"What do you mean?"

Lillian played with her wedding ring, the finger suddenly itchy. "I moved into the guest room again. The baby's room."

"Why?"

"I need some space. Things have changed, and I'm tired of pretending they're still the same, or that they're not as bad." Her mouth went dry, and she scratched at the skin beneath her ring. "And I met someone who...made me start thinking about..."

She laughed her discomfort away before a thought struck her. "Is this confidential? When it's just me and you?"

"Yes, it is. Nothing we say here will be mentioned in our marriage sessions unless you bring it up, but if you prefer, I could recommend someone for you to see privately?"

Lillian shook her head and cleared her throat, which had started to tighten. "I can talk to you."

"You said you met someone?"

"Not like *that*, just someone who reminded me of someone." She laughed again, as if laughing could somehow lighten the pressure of talking about it.

She rushed on before Dr. Geraldine could probe. "But I've been having these dreams ever since."

"OK. Have you told Warren about this? I think it would really help if you could open up about this with him."

"I don't want to talk to him about it," Lillian said testily. "He already has a long list of things to complain about. How am I going to add 'I've been having nightmares' to the list? He treats me like I'm a child, like I'm this . . . *ward* he needs to take care of. It's obvious what he thinks—he said it last time. I'm not what he signed up for and I'm dragging him down. I get it. I don't fit in with all the other wives who are either career-driven or take care of their families—I'm somewhere in between, and I'm no longer the eccentric artist he can wheel out to impress his friends."

When she inhaled, she was surprised to find that the narrowing in her throat had relaxed.

"You're angry."

"Am I? No, not really, I'm just . . . tired."

Dr. Geraldine waited, listening. "Tell me about how you met."

Lillian shifted, crossed her arms. "He was working for a medium-sized start-up in California. I was there for work, on tour with an orchestra. His company hired some musicians to play at a function. I was one of them. I was burnt out from touring so much."

"When was this?"

"Long after I graduated from Curtis. That's the music school I went to."

"And you got married quite soon after, didn't you?"

"Yes. We dated for less than a year. Moved out here six months later."

"How did he make you feel? Why did things move so quickly?"

It took Lillian a few seconds to remember, but much longer to say it out loud. "He felt safe."

Dr. Geraldine let the words land.

"When was the last time you both did something together? Just one night where you didn't talk about IVF or his work or your music?"

As if in response, there was a knock on the door, and it opened a crack.

"I'm sorry I'm late," Warren said hesitantly, his breath short as if he'd been running.

"Hi, come in." Dr. Geraldine rose, reassuring him, and he entered and sat on the divan.

"Sorry." He spoke in Lillian's direction.

"I'm glad you're here. I was just asking Lillian how often you two spend time doing nothing. Just having fun?"

"Actually," Lillian answered before Warren could say something negative. "There's a New Year barbecue at the end of the month. I was going to mention it before..."

They locked eyes, and she kept her face blank as he read her expression and she read his. He looked surprised and a little skeptical, but not as opposed to the suggestion as she'd expected. She knew she was being a little dishonest, talking bluntly about him one second then pretending the barbecue was for them, but maybe it was time to be a little calculated and stop waiting for him to come up with every solution. Maybe everything didn't have to be about Warren all the time.

"I think that's a great idea," Dr. Geraldine said brightly. "Warren? What do you think?"

Dara

Dara watched Kike Ibusun weave through the gardens of her new apartment, avoiding the thick smoke rising from the barbecue pits. For over an hour she'd observed Kike, her off-the-shoulder linen dress and nude espadrilles melding into the colors around her, wondering how willing a source of information the hostess would be. Most of their interactions to date had been superficial, but Dara hoped that being on Kike's home turf would make her more likely to open up.

Amaka was running late but pretending to be closer than she really was, so Dara was left to navigate the barbecue on her own. She'd chatted with a Malaysian colleague of Bayo's, who picked politely at a plate of pork sausages; an Indonesian heiress with a transatlantic twang, who talked for fifteen minutes straight without drawing a breath; an ex-professional Nigerian football player, whose easy smile and expanded midriff confirmed the eighteen years he'd enjoyed in the city with his Malay Singaporean wife; and had a stilted conversation with the Nigerian High Commissioner's wife, an overdressed, over-powdered woman who looked like the party was a total inconvenience.

The food was catered by a Michelin-starred Australian barbecue restaurant on the 50 Best Asian Restaurants List that Dara didn't even know did home catering. Although it was still being cooked, guests could scan a QR code to see the menu, and it looked orgasmic: garlic crab; quail eggs and oysters; mini-steaks in hazelnut and butter; peri-peri duck; fennel, orange and burrata.

Exhausted by all the interaction, and needing to distract herself from her hunger, Dara retreated to a garden loveseat on the west side of the grounds, the perfect vantage point not only to look for an opportunity to get Kike alone, but also to keep her eyes trained on Lani, who was swimming in the pool with Bayo and his sons. She was determined to watch him in a more natural habitat, where, at ease with his friends, his true personality would surely reveal itself. Whatever tiny bit of goodwill she'd felt for Lani on his first day—whatever doubts she'd had about giving him a chance—had disappeared over the past two weeks. Lani had made it abundantly clear how much of a political operator he was in his willingness to develop relationships with *literally everyone* at the firm.

He'd been to "Ye Old English" pub almost every night that first week with Lucy and Mabel and had had nights out with lawyers from other teams, including The Sirens. She'd noticed, too, the way everyone warmed to him, reveling in the salty slick of his compliments and cheerful banter. It was more than bonhomie, more than being friendly to the new guy. These were Brits, after all; after the customary "have some office drinks to welcome the new hire," they usually retreated to their own cliques where they could bitch freely and not be judged. But with Lani, it was different. Everyone genuinely liked him, and the one part of the job she hated the most—the socializing—he actually seemed to enjoy. No one had invited her out this much when she'd first arrived (or since), no one had added her to any WhatsApp groups and no one had put her name down to represent the firm in a touch-rugby match in Hong Kong in the autumn. And therein lay the problem: the firm was predominantly white and male, which meant that, unless she liked golf or followed Premiership football, the odds of creating any meaningful bonds with the decision-makers were stacked against her. Lani had even started sharing in-jokes with some of the girls about the latest *Love Island* results, and by the time he'd flown back from Nairobi, he'd had Irene eating out of the palm of his hand by ordering her birthday flowers while he was away. This must have contributed to Irene opening up about Ian's calendar because Lani had gone out to lunch with Ian twice, something Dara had never done.

She was left with no choice: the first step of warfare was knowing your opponent. Lani, on the surface, had continued to be friendly to her, asking for travel recommendations and pretending he wasn't already a favorite, when he must have known that being asked to fly to Kenya to take the witness statement for the Hakida case was hugely symbolic. Finding out who he was underneath his performance was crucial.

The pounding, percussive Afro-beats reverberating through the garden made it impossible to hear them, but Kike looked furious by the pool as Bayo and Lani flipped the giant unicorn the boys were sitting on and burst out laughing. They seemed to be ignoring her. Kike's rigidity was abnormal; the girl was usually so chill.

Kike began wrapping one of her sons in a striped towel, gesturing to her Filipina helper carrying a large beach bag nearby. Dara decided to seize her chance and drained her glass. As she'd anticipated, Kike began ushering the children inside the building's lobby, her hands on one boy's shoulders, her helper's on the other. In a few bounds, Dara had caught up with them, converging at the steps of their lobby.

The boys giggled at the squelchy sounds their flip-flops made on the ground as Kike and her helper shooed them like a pair of geese.

"Hurry up! It's getting late!" Kike took the younger boy's arm to hoist him up the front steps, but he lost his balance and slipped sideways. Even though his leg barely made contact with the ground, he howled and grabbed his knee.

"You pushed me!" he cried, and Kike immediately scooped him up into her arms.

"Sorry, sorry," she soothed against his ear, the plea of a mother trying not to bring more attention to herself.

He ignored her, wailing and trembling, his little legs knocking against Kike's lean thighs.

"Let me help you." Dara darted round her and over to the door that Kike's helper was struggling to keep open with the heavy bag and older boy in her arms.

"Thank you. Annie, go through." Kike puffed, pressing her back against the door.

"Dara!" Her eyebrows raised in surprise when she looked up. "Thanks, dear. The kids are literally five minutes from a meltdown."

"Oh no...Do you want me to help you upstairs?"

"That's so nice of you." Kike looked hesitant. The e-invite had been very clear that the party was strictly outdoors. "Actually, yes. It'll be easier for me to slip out if you're there. Come on up."

They walked through the lobby, which was gray and bronze and full of *l'objets* so abstract that Dara couldn't immediately tell what was furniture and what was art. She followed Kike to a single glass lift.

"Hello, ma'am." Annie smiled and nodded at Dara.

"This is Tife and Timini and this is Annie." Kike touched her wallet against a panel, and the doors sealed soundlessly. "Boys, say hello to Aunty Dara."

"Hello." Dara's smile froze when Kike's youngest stuck his hand into his mother's bra and began massaging her breast.

"Ah, *Tee-feh*, you a baby? You still want milk?" Annie teased good-naturedly, her arms crossed over Timini's shoulders.

"Don't mind them, Tife." Kike pressed her lips against his forehead.

"Baby!" the older brother laughed, rocking against Annie.

"I'm *not* a baby!" Tife yelled back.

"Oh, I brought some *hóng bāo*." Dara took two red envelopes of money out of her bag after Kike shushed the boys again. "Happy New Year."

"Thanks, dear, you didn't have to. What do you say?" Kike took the *hóng bāo* and gave one to each boy, who thanked Dara shyly.

Kike started giving Annie instructions about their bath time, what snacks they were allowed to have and how many YouTube videos they could watch before bed. Dara lost the thread with so many complicated steps, especially with the boys interjecting whenever they disagreed with the threat of something being taken away. As the lift rose, Dara retied the long bow at the bottom of the pink crêpe blouse that hung over her high-waisted shorts. She really liked her outfit but felt like she was trying too hard standing next to Kike, whose frayed, off-the-shoulder linen dress threaded with pink-and-yellow stripes conjured visions of white sandy beaches and frothy sea foam.

The lift was suddenly filled with light and Kike, the children and Annie spilled out into a private foyer, the lift doors opening directly into their apartment.

Dara needed a few seconds to take in the leafy, city landscape and sweeping stretch of sky. Finally, she turned into the penthouse, which extended into a huge lounge and open-plan kitchen, glass orbs dangling over the dining table. A spiral staircase rose up to the next floor. There were floor-to-ceiling windows on all sides, and through the glass, a garden roof terrace rimmed the length of the apartment, decorated with potted ferns and shrubs, backlit with orange light. The apartment was like a tropical cathedral. Napier Road was the perfect location: walking distance to Orchard Road, yet quietly tucked away among old embassies and long boulevards. Her Grab taxi driver on the way here had enjoyed pointing out all the historical buildings on Kike's street; Dara had no idea what an apartment with this much square footage in the center of town must be costing.

The furniture was sparse and neutral, so as Dara stood by the lift, her eyes had no choice but to pull away from the vastness to a large painting hanging on the wall. On it floated the upper torso of a brown girl with an unnaturally large head, a thin neck and round, gold-rimmed spectacles that magnified her eyes. Her lips were tiny, bubble-gum pink and pursed shut, and her hair was threaded into seven loops that crowned her head. The subject stood against a wet-clay canvas, with peacock colors wound around her neck. She was ageless—at once shrewd, innocent and knowing.

"This is an incredible painting...this is an incredible *apartment*." Dara exhaled, not caring how she came across. She stepped down a small flight of stairs to soak in the pure opulence of the place.

Kike let Tife down. "Thank you."

"Come, come." Annie gathered the boys together. "If you listen and you brush properly, you can have the iPad thirty minutes!"

"*Annie*." Kike's displeasure with Annie's decision was drowned out by her sons' whoops of joy. "Fine, only thirty minutes."

"I'll put the alarm on, ma'am," Annie reassured her.

A second woman appeared at the top of the staircase and the boys ran up to her.

"Can you warm them some milk, please?" Kike asked as Annie followed the children.

"Yes, ma'am." Annie called out to the second helper, speaking in another language before handing her the beach bag.

"You have two nannies?" Dara asked, fascinated.

"Maria is part time, only when we need extra help." Kike sat on one of the kitchen stools and Dara joined her.

"You want tea too, ma'am?" Annie was walking around the kitchen island.

"Yes, please." Kike turned to Dara. "Do you want some of Annie's lemon drizzle cake?"

Dara laughed, incredulous. "But you've got so much food downstairs!"

"I like feeding people," Kike shrugged, grinning. "I can't actually cook, but feeding people is my love language. I nursed both my boys for over two years. Haven't used my marketing degree, but I can break down the way breast milk adapts to a baby's body."

Dara laughed again, loudly. Kike's sense of humor was a surprise.

"Annie's a great cook, and she can bake everything. She wants to open her own bakery when she moves back home," Kike continued.

"That's amazing." Dara took a porcelain teacup and saucer from the tray Annie had placed on the island. "Thank you. Where in the Philippines are you from, Annie?"

"Calaguas, ma'am." Annie cut two slices of cake and placed dessert forks beside each one. "It's in the south."

"Oh, I've been there before." Dara took the cake. "It was incredible. Completely secluded."

"Oh, you went there?" Annie beamed. "It's not very common for people to visit. I think ma'am Kike gonna come with me this Christmas."

Kike ate a piece of her cake. "I really want to. I've only been to Manila."

Annie rested her hands on the island, more at ease now. "But if I open my cake shop, I won't open in Calaguas. It's too quiet!"

"Annie's kids are all grown up now," Kike explained. "Can you believe she's a grandmother?"

Annie giggled at the shock on Dara's face. "Yes, ma'am. Actually, it's my youngest who has a baby. My son is nineteen and he have a baby girl now. I haven't seen her yet."

"Nineteen. Wow." Dara hoped her face didn't look too judgmental. If she got her sums right, Annie couldn't be much older than she was.

"That's how we are in the Philippines. We have kids young."

Kike put her fork down. "I'm going to change, Annie, and then I'll try and slip out before they see me."

"Yes, ma'am." Annie took Kike's plate. It looked like Kike had taken just one bite, and her piece had been significantly smaller than Dara's.

"Do you want to come up?" Kike offered. "I'm changing, so I can't really give you a proper tour..."

"Are you sure?" Dara asked. "I can wait down here."

"No, it's fine. Come up. You'll make me move faster."

"OK, sure." She finished her cake and tried to hide her glee; Amaka would froth at the mouth when she heard Dara had been upstairs.

They followed Annie, who carried two cups of warm milk for the boys. The second level was, disappointingly, much less impressive, although the corridor led to a large window seat and view that was undoubtedly breathtaking. Dara caught up to Kike, who had already opened her bedroom door and was waiting by it.

"Thanks, dear." Dara stepped through the open door. She tried not to stare at the security alarm blinking on the wall by Kike's hand.

She sat on a chaise longue, averting her eyes as Kike stripped off her dress and opened her walk-in cupboard. The carpet looked so thick and soft it made her want to unstrap her shoes and dig her toes into it.

"How are you enjoying the new place?" she asked.

"Mmm, it's nice. I've had my eye on this building since we moved to Singapore, but you literally have to wait until someone *dies* before a unit frees up." Kike rustled through a rack of black dresses.

"Amaka told me the prime minister's sister lives here," Dara said.

"Yup. I'm sure Bayo told her that," Kike scoffed, moving to a rack of white clothes. "He wanted a smaller place closer to the kids' school, but now that we're here, he just loves showing it off."

"It's stunning." Dara knew she'd have to stop saying that word eventually.

Kike chose a white lace dress with spaghetti straps and moved into the bathroom, leaving the door open.

"Isn't Amaka coming? I didn't see her down there," Kike asked. "You know, you two are so different. Apart from being Nigerian, you're like night and day."

Dara tried not to let it annoy her how often people made that lazy comment.

"So, I had no idea you guys knew Lani." She thought she'd segued quite smoothly.

"Of course, I know him. He's one of Bayo's oldest friends." Kike sounded like she had something between her teeth: Dara pictured hairpins. "I think it's nuts that you guys are working in the same firm. But I guess there can't be many English firms out here?"

"Erm, there are a few," Dara replied, amused by how disconnected Kike was from the corporate world Singapore was built on.

Kike poked her head around the door, her forehead scrunched up mid-thought. Foundation was dotted in an oval around her face and her long, straight hair was twisted up. Her dress had tiny cut-outs along the arms, waist and neckline, and turquoise and gold earrings hung from her ears. All at once, Dara understood Amaka's fixation with and revulsion for this girl: even half-dressed, she was perfect. And she had the money, time and taste to iron away any flaws a lesser beauty would have struggled to conceal.

"So, you practice the same type of law?" Kike blended her make-up with a brush.

"Yes, disputes and arbitration, and we work for the same partner on the same cases," Dara replied. To her annoyance, she realized she was rounding out her own vowels to match Kike's Cheltenham

Lady inflections. She prayed she hadn't been doing that unthinkingly with Lani, too.

"Gosh. I think Bayo might have mentioned something about that, but my brain is like a sieve these days—I can barely remember anything. Nigerians, *sha*...we're bloody everywhere." Kike went back into the bathroom.

Dara laughed, but her mind was moving fast.

That Kike Ibusun was not the sharpest tool in the box was what Dara suspected she wanted you to believe. Dara had spent too long as an outsider at school and at Oxford not to recognize the sharpness behind that public-schoolgirl insouciance. Pretending to be thick was a privilege only girls whose parents had spent half a million pounds on their education could afford. Somewhere between the Bluebird nightclub in Chelsea and being whacked on the head on a lacrosse field, they happened to forget their eleven A* GCSEs and the cut-throat survivalism they'd honed in the boarding schools they'd been registered at since birth.

"You said they went to prep school together?" Dara tried to sound offhand.

"Yup, their mothers are best friends—practically identical. You can't tell them apart. Dress the same and everything; it's a little silly. The boys have been chums since anyone can remember—where one is the other is sure to follow. We're thrilled to have him here."

Dara straightened up. Her mother's constant absence after school had forced her to watch hours of *Dynasty* and *The Bold and the Beautiful*. She could pick up a bitchy undertone with the sound on mute.

"You two don't get on?" Dara dared, glancing almost guiltily at the bedroom door as though she were expecting Bayo to walk in at any moment.

"What? Of course we do!" Kike laughed. "Technically, I met him before I met Bayo—we met when we were in nappies. Anyway, Lani's your typical Nigerian: went to boarding school, loves rugby, loves football, plays polo, goes back to Lagos once a year." She paused. "Dull as shit. What else is there to say?" she rounded off dryly, entering the bedroom to get something and then walking back into the bathroom.

Dara digested this, thinking how unlike the "typical" British Nigerian he sounded, and how this said as much about Kike as it did about Lani.

She decided to try a different approach.

"Well, he comes with a stellar record. One of our associates, Lucy, heard from a friend at another firm that his boss in Geneva didn't want to let him go. And he's been really lovely so far—very friendly, super helpful." She winced at joining in on the murder of the English language. When had "super" become an adverb?

"He joined less than a month ago, but he's already made such a massive contribution to the team. He just got back from Kenya. He had to fly down there to get a witness statement that's crucial to the case we're working on, and he did an excellent job."

"Hmm…"

"What?"

"Nothing." The flash of a camera beamed against the bathroom door.

"*What?*"

"It's just, this is how it starts." Kike emitted a long, weary sigh. "He has every girl doing this. Lani-this, Lani-that, like he's some type of wonder man-boy. He did this when we were at uni, he does it in Lagos and now he's doing it here."

"What do you mean, 'doing this'?" Dara asked plainly.

Kike's face appeared.

"I can't count the number of my girlfriends he's messed up. Don't get me wrong—it was entertaining when we were younger, and he was stringing along someone you didn't particularly know— but somehow he always walks away from a disaster that's shat itself around him. He's always sorry and he's somehow always the good guy. I'd hate to see you fall for his act."

"I'm not falling for any act, don't worry," Dara said.

"Good." Kike disappeared back into the bathroom.

It felt so good to know someone else disliked the wanker, even if Kike wasn't openly saying it.

"Look, I'm not saying Lani's not good at his job, but I'm pretty sure he had help getting his role in Geneva. He has connections to all sorts of people." Now Kike was on a roll.

It was laughable, really, for Kike of all people to look down on Lani for using his connections. Maybe when you stood on a mountain for so long, the ground started to feel flat.

"What type of connections?"

"Well, his grandfather set up one of the first law firms in Nigeria. It's defunct now, but the family has all sorts of relationships with English firms. Also, his uncle's a SAN—one of those senior advocates who run the courts in Nigeria—so even if he didn't have help getting the job, he definitely threw some Nigeria business their way. That's how he brought so much oil business to his old firm."

When Kike reappeared, her outfit was complete, and her energy signaled to Dara that it was time to head back down. She sprayed some perfume at her vanity table before rubbing lotion onto her hands.

A notification dinged on Kike's phone, and she tutted a second later.

"Great, the lion dancers are here—an hour later than they were meant to come. The boys will never stop complaining if I don't let them watch..."

Dara had stopped listening. She was too deeply buried in her thoughts now she understood a crucial part of who Lani was. Neither Kike, Bayo nor Lani had got where they were on their own, but unlike them, she didn't have an uncle or parents to put in a good word for her or pass her some business; no one to even pass on useful advice. Her granny and grandad were long gone, and with her mother's complete lack of interest in Nigeria, any link to someone who could have helped benefit her career in any way was gone. Maybe being confident in your own skin came from the knowledge that someone would catch you if you fell, of having an entire lineage of people vested in your success.

It was down to her to tip the scales these nepotistic bastards had rigged.

Amaka

As Amaka slugged her third glass of prosecco, the late afternoon sun warming her bare legs, she felt more like herself than she had in weeks. Sitting on a wide raffia mat with the book club women, she could almost forget the angry humiliation that had been bristling in her since her family meeting. Feeling light, bubbly and as loose as the cool liquid slipping down her throat, with the music slowing into a jazzy bossa nova, it was easier to relegate her family to the backstage of her life and turn them into minor antagonists. She didn't have to pick up her mother's calls or answer Uncle Emeka's cloying texts or give her uppity siblings a moment's thought. She could focus on the positives: she lived in a country most people would kill to move to, she made an excellent amount of money for a young woman with no dependents, and possibly the finest man she'd met in Singapore was sprawled across a deck chair on the other side of the pool.

Sitting near Bayo and a small group of friends, Lani glanced over at her every few minutes. Their eyes would meet and then he would break eye contact, nodding and laughing at something someone was saying.

A surge of energy rippled through the garden as small groups of people began to get up at the same time.

"I think the Lion Dance's here!" LeToya rose from the mat excitedly with the other ladies. As Amaka stood, she rearranged the pleats of the leather pinafore dress that was zipped over her plain white T-shirt. She'd chosen her outfit carefully; the dress straps pushed her breasts high and the ankle boots elongated her short legs. The fringes of the dress just covered her bottom.

She was proud of herself for not buying something new. She'd wanted to, but a few days ago, she'd received a larger tax bill than expected, forcing her to dip into her savings. It shocked her to see how little she had left in that account, until she'd remembered the three indulgent purchases she'd made since Christmas: red-patent Gucci boots; a fringed Chloe crossbody bag; and second-hand Van Cleef clover earrings that were a quarter of her rent. She'd started to wonder if she should transfer some money from Lagos as a safety measure. The more she thought about it, the more selling some of her father's shares seemed like a ready-made solution.

She followed the women and the river of guests into the Ibusuns' open car park. As they funneled down the way of the footpaths, someone turned the music off. The energy was infectious; for some, seeing a Lion Dance up close was a rare novelty; for others, it was an unexpected surprise.

The guests trickled in and split into two streams; the space filled up quickly. There must have been over sixty guests, a fact that was easy to miss when they were spread out on the grass. Three members of condo management stood by the gate, laughing and glancing down the street.

"I thought the cars would be much more impressive." Amaka looked around, disappointed.

"The good ones ain't up here," LeToya chuckled. "They're down in the basement. There's always an underground car park."

"Hey. Excuse me."

And just like that, Lani was in her space. Bare-chested, with a towel round his neck, he waited for the women to take a small step back before squeezing past Amaka. She dropped her eyes to the ground, and he didn't look at her, but it was impossible not to breathe in his skin. Water droplets were dotted on his neck, and his sun-kissed face was so smooth and hewn it looked like a sculpted bust. His arm almost brushed against her, he was that close.

He walked past LeToya and Yemisi and ended up on the other side of Nana, who he struck up an easy conversation with.

"Fuck. Me," LeToya stuttered.

"LeToya, you're married," Yemisi said under her breath. "Calm down."

"*Child!*" LeToya threw her an incredulous look. "Is this what we working with now? I mean, *damn.*"

"Stop. Please stop," Yemisi whispered, not looking in Lani's direction. "He's right there."

LeToya grinned at Amaka cheekily. "You better hop on that, girl. Nana's all up in his ear, and you sure are dressed for it."

Amaka kissed her teeth. Seeing him up close was a big shock she had to hide. "Looks aren't everything, especially in men."

"Oh, I see, you don't want to look too thirsty. I remember the game," LeToya smirked. "If it was me, I would...*mmm.*"

She let out a satisfied moan.

"He's young enough to be your son!" The effort of Yemisi keeping a straight face was suddenly too much. She and LeToya burst out howling, clasping hands and wiping their eyes in a way that made it obvious they were talking about something taboo. Nana and Lani's conversation stalled, and Lani's eyes met hers. And held them. Amaka's skin tingled at the directness of his gaze, but she refused to break eye contact first. One, two seconds passed, her nipples hardening painfully against her bra.

Nana said something and Lani looked away.

In the distance, the clang of sticks on a gong and the shake of hard, metal beads grew louder and closer until a small, open-air van arrived at the gate. The crowd cheered as the van drove in, and five men in red shirts and black trousers jumped out. Two giant white-and-yellow costume lion heads were pulled off the roof of the van and placed onto the heads of two of the men. Two more men slipped nimbly into the lions' backsides. The fifth clenched a drum between his knees. It was done so quickly that the moment the men vanished and the lions appeared was almost missed.

The dance began. The first lion trembled and shook, rotating its head and bobbing its tail to the rhythm of the drums. It blinked its huge eyes, spread and crossed its legs, jigged around in circles and shuddered its red jaw. Bursting into the air, the man at the front was briefly seen; in an acrobatic leap, he landed on the shoulders of the man behind him, and the lion loomed over the guests. As the second lion trotted beside it, two brown boys in matching pajamas raced in front of Amaka, followed by Bayo. Lani hoisted the younger boy up, letting him climb onto his neck. The two lions crouched in front of two trays of lettuce and orange peel before spitting everything out over the crowd. Kike's children squealed, scared and delighted in equal measure. Bayo led his older son to the lions, egging him on all the way. The crowd laughed at the boy's apprehension as he threw some of the peel into the mouth, then ran before the lion could spray him with the New Year's "blessings."

Over the lions, Amaka caught sight of Dara and gave her a wave, but Dara, whose arms were folded, was glaring at Lani.

When the party started up again, the mood was more charged. People began to swim, and the music seemed louder than before. After a little chit-chat, the conversation on the raffia mat turned to *Americanah*, which Amaka was delighted the women had chosen at their last meeting.

LeToya took some popcorn from a bowl on the mat. To her credit, she hadn't let their tussle over the next book get in the way of enjoying it. "Ooh, I haven't finished it yet. Don't spoil the ending for me. Why we even talking about this before the next meeting—that's cheating."

"Hey," Dara's voice came from behind Amaka. "How long have you been here?"

"Not that long. I looked for you when I got here." Amaka tried to sound convincing. "Sit down."

She folded her legs to make space.

"I was upstairs. Kike gave me a tour." Dara sat down.

"Really? I thought the party was strictly outdoors. The invite wasn't very subtle," Amaka griped as Dara shrugged and reached forward for the snacks.

She was dying to ask questions about the Ibusuns' place, but the shut-down expression on Dara's face suggested this wasn't the right time. She was also a little peeved that Dara was one step ahead; Dara was never a step ahead of anything.

"You look nice." Amaka tried to be gracious. And it was true—a little stiff and prim, maybe, but nice.

Dara munched on some nuts. "Thanks."

"Come now, I said I was sorry I was late." Amaka thumped Dara with her elbow. "We were trying not to talk about *Americanah*, which I finished in a week. Are you coming to the next book club?"

"Doubt it." Dara avoided eye contact.

"What did you think of *Purple Hibiscus*? You didn't say much in the meeting," Nana grilled, looking at Dara.

"I still haven't read it. I just went to see Amaka," Dara replied, scooping some more nuts.

Nana, Yemisi and LeToya all traded a look, but Dara seemed oblivious to it.

"Dara is more into classics," Amaka explained, feeling the need to defend her friend. "What's all that stuff, Greek and Latin? Ovid or something? That's what she studied before she became a lawyer."

"Oh, I always wanted my boys to get into that," LeToya said eagerly, but Nana didn't look impressed.

"It's a little strange not to read any of the great books coming out by contemporary African writers: Teju Cole, Helen Oyeyemi, NoViolet Bulawayo," Nana chided.

"*I* haven't heard of any of those people." Yemisi made a face. "Wole Soyinka and Chinua Achebe—those were all the writers I knew before I joined the book club."

Nana pressed on, acutely disappointed.

"You're basically reading a bunch of books by dead white men and leaving no space to discover your own writers," she criticized.

Seeing the conversation had taken a turn, Amaka reached for the oversized beach bag behind her. "There's plenty of space for everyone, ladies. We'll survive if we let one dead white man in."

She unfolded herself up from the ground and spoke to Dara. "I'm going to change into my swimsuit. Coming?"

The pool changing rooms were empty and smelled faintly of chlorine. With their heavy, wooden doors and dirt-colored tiles, they contrasted sharply with the overall elegance of Kike's party.

"*Eurgh*, so good," Amaka sighed, peeling off her wig. With a grunt of pleasure, she took off her hairband and let her natural hair fall out of its bun so she could give her scalp a good scratch.

"I didn't know you were going to swim." Dara sat down on the slats beside Amaka's leather basket bag.

"Me? Swim?" Amaka fluffed her Afro with both hands, enjoying how stretched out it was. The alcohol was wearing off, but she could still feel some of its delicious buzz. "I've got a new bikini. There's no way I'm getting it wet."

As she pulled out her two-piece and towel, she saw that Dara was lost in her thoughts, a frown etched across her face. Amaka couldn't help feeling exasperated: why did Dara always have to get so weird when they were around other people? Staying up late watching movies, hanging out one-on-one: this, Dara was perfect for. But put her in a social situation and the girl turned into Issa Rae minus the jokes.

"What's the matter?" She sat beside Dara, praying her friend would give her the short version so they wouldn't spend half the night in the changing room. Her armpits were already beginning to reek in her leather dress.

"You didn't have to tell them I like Greek mythology," Dara complained.

"But you do," Amaka teased.

Dara shook her head in a way that either meant *I give up* or *there's no point* or both.

"I never feel less like myself than when I'm around other black women. At least at work, I *know* I don't fit in, and I can decide how much I want to try."

"But that's how we all feel," Amaka shrugged. "Nobody really fits in—that's why people try to oppress everyone else. Why do you think I was ready to get the hell out of Lagos? *'Ah-ahn, you're putting on weight. Hope you're not trying to be a fat somebody.'*... *'Don't be too skinny, o. Don't lie to yourself—that's not what men want'* ...*'Working, working, working, stay there and be doing career woman while your mates are raising children...'* I mean, it just never bloody stops. At least here, there's a seven-hour time difference all that nonsense has to jump through. Why do you think Kike gets on my nerves so much? She's the type of girl who gets away with the most: pretty, rich, had all her kids before thirty, but she swans around like we're all the same, like she goes through what we go through."

Kike's only real achievement, as far as Amaka could see, was holding multiple wedding ceremonies seven years ago, including a three-thousand-guest "extravaganza" in Lagos and an "intimate" white wedding for three hundred friends and family on the Amalfi coast. At least her husband Bayo had an impressive profile. He'd been featured in the top ten of Forbes Africa's 30 Under 30 for setting up a successful start-up, helping middle-class Nigerians secure affordable loans to rent in the overpriced Lagos housing market. Now he worked for Temasek, Singapore's largest investment holding company, and was the owner of several government-owned subsidiaries.

"I don't know." Dara looked unconvinced. "Out of all of them, Kike seems like the one person who just is what she is, and she's never laughed *at* me. At least she's not pretending. Not like Lani. God, I can't stand that guy."

Dara made claw-shapes with her hands and feigned strangling someone.

"The way he plays down how good he is when I'm around, like he feels *sorry* for me. I should have gone to Nairobi—God, I would have killed to have an all-expenses-paid trip anywhere in Africa, but it just came to him like *that*. He knows what he's doing. He knows he's taken over my case, he knows what it means to have two lawyers on the same team, but he walks around with this sheepish look on his face. He knows he didn't *earn* it, and he doesn't care. He knows he has an advantage but acts like we got here the same way."

Hearing Lani's name, Amaka tried not to fidget, which only made her squirm even more. The more time passed, the harder it became to bring up the 7-Eleven meeting; she'd had to listen to Dara's vents, wondering if Lani would say something first, but knowing, somehow, that he wouldn't.

"At least he's good with kids." She couldn't help herself.

Dara grunted but didn't reply.

Feeling uneasy, Amaka decided it was best to show clear solidarity. "Did you read the book club group chat?"

"No, why?"

"I thought the American girl's text was weird, trying to find out information about Lani."

Dara stared at her for a second, then yanked her bag open. "What are you talking about?"

Amaka let Dara find the message herself.

"Lillian? The girl who hosted the last meeting?" Dara drank the screen in. "How does she know him?"

"I have no idea." Amaka had actually been hoping Dara would know.

"This is bloody weird. Isn't she married?" Dara squinted.

"*Abeg*, I don't know. She said he forgot something at her work. I just thought it was strange."

"Something about this guy is so off," Dara grumbled.

Amaka picked up her bag before she could make things worse and walked past the cubicles until she found a changing stall. She hung her new Pucci bikini carefully on a hook and began to strip; as she changed, a sadness weighed on her and she felt an unexpected flood of emotion. Sniffing as quietly as she could, she adjusted her straps and fastened a slinky gold Y-chain around her neck. The pleasure of her new purchases was already ebbing away. Even if she bought a million outfits, spending her father's money could never compensate for what his actions had robbed her of.

"Why didn't Rohit come with you?" Dara broke the silence, her timing at its worst.

Amaka wiped her nose, then wrapped the sarong around her waist.

"He had a stag do in Bangkok. A school friend." She sat down on a changing bench and took out her make-up bag.

Rohit…the dry humor they used to enjoy had turned more earnest lately. No matter how much she tried to separate him from her family problems, he seemed intent on getting her to open up. She was starting to get tired of it; she needed a distraction, and an attractive new face like Lani (who, let's face it, would probably never have looked twice at her in Lagos) was a very pleasant distraction.

"That's a shame. I like him. I know I've only met him once," Dara said after a pause.

"It's not going to work. He's just not my type," she said, dully. The words sharpened something inside her, giving a focus to the pain.

"Are you serious?" Dara's feet approached until her weight pressed against the cubicle door. "But he's so funny and cute and *nice*."

"There's a difference between having fun and spending your time and energy on someone with serious prospects," Amaka snapped. "And dating a co-worker is the dumbest decision you can make."

"Amaka, he really likes you. He's smart, he makes good money… when we all had dinner, you could see how much he was—"

"Seriously, Dara, can you stop being so green? In what universe am I going to marry an Indian guy from Thailand? What is it about me that screams 'alternative'?" Amaka huffed. "The problem is you didn't grow up in Nigeria, so you don't understand. You think everyone thinks like you and everyone has a mother who gives them total independence and wouldn't care if they brought home a five-foot penguin. Most Nigerian mums are nothing like that."

Unzipping her make-up bag, she began to touch up her face. It was just like Dara to play up how tough she had it without any real understanding of what things were like for Amaka. Dara, who had enjoyed the comfort of growing up in the UK and was trapped in a ridiculous, romanticized fantasy about Nigeria, who had never had to endure the humiliation of applying for visas to almost every country she had ever visited and the constant worry of being rejected, who had never had to question whether her dreams were too big or impractical, who was so focused on her goals that she couldn't see the young, sexy black guy in her firm as anything more than a threat.

The bathroom door opened, letting in a sliver of noise.

"I'm heading back out." Dara's voice and her footsteps faded away.

Amaka stopped powdering her face, then continued. Feeling relief at Dara's departure and refusing to feel guilty about it, Amaka decided that the best thing would be to meet Lani away from Dara's overly critical gaze. She sent Bayo a text asking if she could keep her bulky beach bag upstairs and chewed on the corner of a gel nail, waiting for his response. Finally it came, full of exclamation marks, elated she'd arrived with instructions to head over to the lobby of the West tower.

"*Makstarr!*" Bayo descended a spiral staircase, his arms out-stretched but his voice sotto voce. "This Nigerian time is too much, even for you. You should be ashamed."

"Hey, Bayo. Thanks for letting me keep my stuff up here. Your place is...insane." She took in the space extended before her but kept her admiration in check. With rich people, you had to be indifferent—overreacting could spook them—and you couldn't act like you were impressed by their wealth.

"Yeah. It's a great space at night. Kike didn't see you, did she?" Bayo hugged her carefully, and she made sure not to press too closely to his bare chest—the usual married man choreography.

"Nope. Why?" Amaka was trying to keep her irritation in

check. Why would Kike be sensitive about her seeing the place when Dara had been let up? She didn't know what Kike's problem was, or why she was so sensitive about her being friends with her husband. Bayo had been nothing less than a gentleman, and it helped that he was short and not in any way attractive to Amaka. They'd seen each other several times at busy lunchtime spots in the city, but had only spoken properly for the first time when an ex-Nigerian president was invited for a talk at a Singapore business school. They'd sat next to each other, and in the intervals when they could speak, he'd mentioned his wife at least three times. It had been sweet and funny, and it was obvious he couldn't separate himself from Kike even when she wasn't around.

"Good, good. I promised her I'd keep guests downstairs. She doesn't want people upstairs till we've finished decorating, but I'm definitely planning a small thing soon. This place was made for throwing parties." Bayo led her to the kitchen and pointed at a baby monitor on the island. "The boys are going to be a nightmare sleeping off all that adrenaline, so if you don't mind..."

He made a *keep it down* gesture.

"No problem. Where can I keep this?" She held up her beach bag.

"Sit, chill. You can put it away in a minute." Bayo waved at one of the stools. "I was just about to rustle up some drinks. My guy's in the guest room changing. I can make cocktails: rosé or prosecco?"

"Prosecco, please. Had too much rosé recently." Goosebumps prickled over Amaka's arms as she sat and put her bag on another stool. 'Your guy'?"

"Yeah, he just moved here. He works with your friend, Dara." Bayo kneeled to open what she assumed was a small fridge.

"Oh *riiiight*, Lani. Yeah, we don't like him. He's competition." She spoke as nonchalantly as she could.

"Is that so?" Bayo cackled, twisting the neck of a bottle. "Speak of the devil!"

Lani appeared out of a corridor beside the kitchen, dressed in a fresh T-shirt.

"*Lanstarr,* this is Amaka, workaholic and banker extraordinaire. Amaka, Lani: general douchebag and ultimate loser."

"Nice to meet you." Amaka stuck out her hand before he could say anything. "I've heard a lot about you."

"Nice to meet you, too." He shook it, and she noted with a thrill that he was pleased to see her. "Ignore him. You know how guys get when they're threatened by an idol they can never be. Have we met before? You look familiar."

For a second, she was stumped. Was he really going to put her on the spot?

"Ah, yes," he continued. "You remind me of a friend of mine: *Sophia.* Or maybe *Isabella,*" he said.

She couldn't help smiling. He must have been practicing that line since that night.

"*Sophia...Isabella...*what's wrong with you?" Bayo took out a packet of raspberries, a lemon and a chopping board, reaching behind Lani for a sharp knife. "Amaka was just saying how she hates your guts because you've come to take her friend's job."

"Easy with that thing!" Lani jerked forward, laughing. "I assure you I'm doing no such thing. A little competition never hurt anyone, but take her job? I'm not all bad."

"Spoken like a true Disney villain." Bayo started crushing raspberries into a marble mortar.

Lani chuckled, sitting on the stool beside Amaka.

Being so close to him, she felt the warmth from his body, which left her feeling charged, fidgety, tense.

"So, Bayo, you cook or is it just cocktails? Isn't Kike a very lucky girl." Her words came out much bitchier than she'd intended.

"She *is* the lucky one, but not for his food," Lani answered. "I will never, ever be able to remove the taste of some of the crap you've made over the years."

"What? I've made some good stuff," Bayo blasted back, pouring the pink mass into glasses and topping it with lemon juice.

"I distinctly remember one dish that comprised overcooked sausages, pasta and mushroom sauce. He had the audacity to call it carbonara!" Lani ribbed.

"Mate, that was in *uni*! No one knew what they were doing!"

"Bruv, speak for yourself!"

Amaka laughed, mockingly. "Why are you speaking in Cockney accents? It's so weird."

"Voilà." Bayo slid the flutes over and they clinked glasses. "Cheers."

It was bitingly cold, tangy and delicious. The alcohol punched back into her and all hovering doubts about Rohit, her family and the bill for the printed Pucci two-piece she was wearing disappeared.

Bayo laughed at the blissful smile on her face and topped up her glass. "Here."

His phone began to ring.

"Yup...yup...coming." His face changed. "No, just wait. Chill out, I'll be there!"

Face glowering, he pressed his phone to his shoulder and mouthed something about Kike, fireworks and heading downstairs first.

Lani must have understood because Bayo tossed a set of keys and Lani caught them.

"Better make a run for it," Lani said quietly, holding an arm out for Amaka to go ahead. When they got to the lift, he pressed the ground-floor button.

"Nice bikini," he said, and she saw for the first time, underneath his wisecracks and teasing, real desire. Desire that matched hers. He let her see it and she held his gaze, relishing the way he looked at her.

He let her through, and the doors shut noiselessly.

"No glasses today?" she teased.

"No boyfriend today?" he murmured.

She never got to answer. His mouth was on hers, and his raspberry-flavored tongue flicked between her lips.

Lillian

Lillian slipped her arm around Warren's, overwhelmed by the noisy swell of guests. She tried to manage her wired, keyed-up energy, but she still couldn't believe her husband was spending time with her for the first time this year. She didn't know if it was because he wanted to get out of the tomb their apartment had turned into or if he was trying to prove he could follow Dr. Geraldine's advice from their last session, but she was grateful she had company. She needed to squash the anxiety that squeezed her insides every time she wondered if Lani had already left the party.

It was comforting to feel the press of Warren's arm after so long. An arm link felt safe—not as symbolic or intimate as hand holding, but close enough that she could see the countless parts of him she'd missed up-close. This brown, geometric collared shirt against his lean, sinewy arm, for instance, which made him look like somebody's dapper grandaddy, depending on how he styled it. She'd missed his small earlobes, especially the right one, which still had a hole from the stud he never wore anymore; his bottom lip that folded into his top when twitchy; the hands stuck into his front pockets—the simple repetitive confirmations of who you were that only a partner could see.

"This ain't like any black party I've ever been to," Warren muttered, facing the open patio where three women danced to a backing track, twirling flaming batons in circles.

Lillian giggled and twisted into him. "Kike said she was keeping the numbers small. She's tripping!"

She touched the corner of her eye to stop a happy tear from ruining her liner. As impressive as the performers were, she couldn't help but check out the other people around her. It was definitely a strange mix of guests: some more reserved and relaxed, others more playful and skittish. They gathered in clusters under the fairy lights decorating gazebos and the patio, their voices buzzing against both the long, square sheets of water that plunged over the pool and the relentless blare of sonic bass that emitted from a surround-sound station. The light had dimmed since they'd arrived, leaving the sky a powdery gray with what looked like yellow-gold pawprints in the distance. Smoky fumes of dry, peppered ribs wafted over from the queue, and waiters in white dashed between the guests. A row of stone dolphins jetted a steady curtain of water from their beaks into the blue-pebbled swimming pool, creating a waterfall, and at the far end of the pool, people swam and hung out.

So wasteful. She winced at a waiter carrying a trayful of half-eaten plates, and she knew Warren—who'd grown up with a little more money than she had—was thinking the same. She would never be comfortable spending the way Kike and Bayo clearly did, and all just because they'd moved house? Even though she and Warren lived in an apartment that firmly put them in the "financially stable" bracket, they would never be one of them.

"Give it up for Helios! Thank you, you've been a great audience!" A man cheered into a microphone as the guests whooped and clapped. "Please avail yourself of our cards, which are spread around. 'Helios Fire Fighters!' Thank you!"

The fire women bowed and began to pack up their gear. Low chatter filled the brief lull.

"It was *aight*. I was hoping they'd eat the flames," Warren said dryly.

"Speaking of food, I'm starving." Lillian pressed a hand to her belly.

"Hmm, I smell food—good food. If we're lucky, they'll have an English pig with an apple in its mouth turning over one of those barbecue pits."

They walked down a stone path, low-hanging creepers brushing over them.

"You look nice. Haven't seen this before…" He glanced at her, chewing his bottom lip.

"Yes, you have." She smoothed her hair up from the nape of her neck, careful not to disturb the defined curls that spilled over her right ear. She wore a red linen jumpsuit that complimented her brown shoulders, much bolder than anything she would have normally worn.

"Really?"

"I got it on our trip to Hong Kong." She swapped her clutch to her other hand so her figure could be seen.

"Right…I remember now." His cheek muscles tightened at the thought of the trip they'd taken right after their first loss.

A woman crooned over the thrum of a jazz bass, heating up an old memory.

"Do you remember that concert I played in New Orleans?" She grinned.

"*Girl*, please, not that," he groaned.

"You remember we played under a bandstand, and in the middle of every piece, I'd hear this chair scraping against the ground? Every piece—I was so pissed!"

"It wasn't *every* piece." Warren's forehead creased in mock indignation. "I only stood up, like, two or three times."

"I only played like five pieces, so that was every other song!"

"Please. So I had to use the bathroom a couple times, so what?"

"I couldn't even be that mad at you. It was so funny."

"What? You were *hella* mad. '*Oh, you messed up my show. I can't take you no place!*'"

She held up a finger, giggling. "I never said that!"

"It's good to see you laugh," he said. "It's good to hear you talk about playing, too. Would be even better if you'd play again…"

He must have seen her face shut down, her body tighten, because he stopped short.

"I know you get nervous at these parties. Let's just try and have a good time. Like we used to. We don't have to think about… all the other stuff."

They stared at each other. He looked like he wanted to say

something else but held back. The music doubled in volume, breaking the spell.

"How hard do you think it'll be to get a drink?" Warren bellowed over the music.

"Impossible," Lillian yelled back.

"Should have brought our own," Warren joked, one finger in his ear.

Like an answered prayer, a waiter took a sharp turn past them and almost disappeared behind a wooden beam.

"Hey, hey, excuse me!" Lillian and Warren both called out.

"Sorry, man." Warren laughed at the waiter's surprise and took the last two highballs from his tray. He handed one to Lillian. "Why don't you join the queue and I'll go hunt down a couple more of these?"

"Yeah, sure." Lillian looked at the barbecue pits, even though separating was the last thing she felt like doing. "They look pretty long..."

"I'll come find you. You probably won't get to the front before I get back, and I'll be able to find a waiter faster on my own."

"No problem. I'll be over there."

"Back in a minute." He touched her arm.

She watched him leave, still amazed that he had come. With a shiver of excitement, she sipped the gin-based drink and walked over to the line, doing a quick check for Lani in the queue. The flames of the chef's pans flared and smoked over her.

"Excuse me." Lillian edged closer to the tall woman directly in front of her who was staring down at her phone.

"Sorry," the woman mumbled, taking a few steps forward.

"Dara, right?" Lillian blurted after a blank second of wondering why the girl looked so familiar.

Dara turned around. "Oh, yes—hi!"

"Lillian. She grinned, thrilled to see someone from the book club.

Dara looked surprised. *"Lillian.* Sorry, you look so different. You look great!"

"Thank you!" Lillian's hand went to her neck again. "I scrub up good when I want to."

"You look amazing." Dara moved with the queue and picked up a plate. Lillian took one, too, laughing self-consciously and, like Dara, balancing it with her glass in her other hand.

"Are you here by yourself…shit!" Dara nearly dropped the plate.

"You're OK—close call." Lillian moved closer but couldn't do much to help with her hands full.

"Crap, stained my shorts," Dara slurred. Lillian realized she must be tipsy.

"Do you want to put the drink down?" Lillian asked gently.

"Yes. I hate drinking. I never drink," Dara said tonelessly. "And I hate parties. All parties."

"I'm not a fan of them myself." Lillian picked up a prong and began helping herself to some lamb chops and mint sauce.

"I know, I remember." Dara stared at her for a long time, like she was trying to work something out.

Lillian began to feel self-conscious again and wondered if her make-up had smudged. But then the Brit blinked slowly—a controlled, deliberate blink—and Lillian could see that Dara was definitely drunk.

"Do you want me to help with your plate? Do you need to sit down?" Lillian asked, concerned.

Dara shook her head but didn't speak.

The people behind Lillian were beginning to look impatient.

"Can you move on?" Lillian nudged Dara.

Dara nodded and continued down the queue, staring at the food but taking very little.

When they got to the grilled asparagus, Dara sprang back to life, her words forming full sentences again.

"I never thought I would say this in Singapore, but there are too many Nigerians at this party. They all have their little clubs." She made an exasperated face and slid a generous heap of vegetables onto her plate. "It was the same back in London. '*Coker? Which Coker is that? Oh, do you know so-and-so?*' When they realize you're just an ordinary person who doesn't rely on their last name, they completely lose interest."

"Are there many Nigerians here? It seems pretty mixed to me." Lillian looked around.

"One too many," Dara muttered and moved forward.

Lillian tried change the subject. "You're a lawyer, right?"

"Trying to be." Dara made a sour smile. "I work for a British firm that's currently making it very clear it doesn't want me, but they know I'm too many years post-qualified to be a cheap hire somewhere else, so they're banking on the fact that I'll stay until they're done using me and funnel me out like a stool in a cramped intestine while they replace me with the ultimate wanker from Wankerdom."

Lillian turned her face away from the pulled crab meat and stared at Dara. "Wow."

"Sorry, I don't usually . . . it's not been a great day. Shit, actually." Dara looked once again like the girl from the book club.

"No, it's fine," Lillian said earnestly. "It's so OK. It's refreshing. No one ever talks about their jobs honestly here. Everything just seems so *easy* for people, vacationing all the time, spa treatments, massages, pedicures and *eating, eating, eating*. It doesn't feel like real life. And then people just leave and you never see them again."

"That never used to be my life—well, in between work, anyway. I used to travel all the time and it was bloody brilliant," Dara said ruefully, helping herself to five satay sticks.

"Well, I'm sorry about your job. I hope it works out for you."

"Thank you," Dara shrugged.

She turned around again when they got to the salads.

"Please ignore what I said about Nigerians. I'm just . . . in danger of getting bitter," she laughed.

"That's all right. I'm Nigerian too, but I don't have any friends from there." The words slipped out as easily as a knife in butter, and to her surprise, there was only a slight sting attached to them.

"*You're* Nigerian?"

"Yeah." Lillian felt sheepish, like she'd revealed the underside of her dress. "I'm Tiv. We're an ethnic group from the East. You might not have heard of us before . . . Anyway, I've never been to Nigeria. I grew up in the U.S. and my husband's American, so . . ."

Dara gaped. "I can't believe you're Nigerian. You don't look Nigerian at all! You're like a cross between Alicia Keys and Esperanza Spalding."

"What? I've never heard that before!" Lillian laughed, brushing away how eerie it was that Dara had inadvertently compared her to two musicians.

Dara laughed with her. "You really do."

"You're Nigerian, too?" Lillian asked shyly.

Dara nodded. "I left when I was ten and haven't been back since. I miss it sometimes, but then I'm not sure if it's really the place I miss or what I've imagined over the years. According to Amaka, it's all in my head."

"I hear you," Lillian responded, because it was easier than explaining that no memories of Nigeria had been passed down to *her*.

They got to the end of the food line where glasses of non-alcoholic drinks were set out.

"Oh shit!" Lillian raised her hand to her mouth. "I forgot to get Warren a plate. Warren's my husband. I was supposed to get food and he was meant to get drinks, but he never actually came back."

Dara looked at the queue. "I think he's going to be hungry for a while."

"It's OK, he can have mine." Lillian frowned. "Actually, I don't know what's taking him so long."

Placing her glass and plate on a nearby ledge, she opened her clutch and checked her phone. No messages or missed calls.

She stepped away from Dara and dialed Warren's number. He picked up on the third ring.

"Hey, where you at?" His voice was loud over the music.

"I'm...by the food, like we said. What do you mean?" The effort it took to control her annoyance made her stutter.

"I didn't think you'd be so quick." He apologized, then broke off to speak to someone she couldn't hear. "I'm by the pool with some guys. You want to come over?"

"Sure. OK, I'll find you." She ended the call and reminded herself that this was a good night. A step forward. She had to ignore what sounded like apathy in his voice and focus on the reasons she was here, and not make things worse when they were finally looking up. If not for the chance to see Lani and figure out if the resemblance was in her head, she'd have booked a taxi home.

Dara, who had been hovering a few feet away, smiled as Lillian approached. Ironically, they had both switched moods.

"My husband's near the pool." Lillian tried to mirror Dara's expression. "It was nice to see you again, but I'd better go find him."

"That's OK, I'll come with you."

"Oh, you don't have to. Try to enjoy the party." Lillian hoped she'd get the hint.

"We hate parties, remember? We have to stick together." Dara drew closer and made a face. "And I haven't seen Amaka for an hour. It's either follow you or head home."

Dara fell in step and Lillian let her. They wove through clusters of people, and Lillian tried to ignore her racing heart. The more she moved, the more she panicked. It all felt wrong: Warren disappearing, Lani nowhere to be seen, Dara glued to her elbow. Everything was heightened: the weight of the plate in her hands, her heels against the ground, the loud music.

When they got to the swimming pool, she still couldn't see Warren. Large groups huddled around the rectangular pool. She did a full circuit, trying to scan the guests inconspicuously, questioning whether to call him again or not, until she came to a standstill by the dolphin water feature. Three women sat fully clothed behind a screen of water, their feet submerged. They giggled at a guy who climbed out of the pool, fully clothed, and shook out his hair. Hard beads of water flung against Lillian and Dara.

"Great! Now he's in my food." Dara glared at her plate and wiped her arm with a napkin.

The jet of water from the dolphin fountain cut off, leaving—to Lillian's relief—one fewer layer of sound. Now she could hear the voices coming from the direction of a garden alcove about thirty feet away, beside a thick, leafy hedge. There were fewer guests there and the grounds were not as brightly lit, but almost immediately, she recognized Warren's shape and the pattern of his shirt.

She made a beeline for him. He was talking to a man she'd never met before, and both had beers in their hand.

"Hey. Here," she interrupted them, flashing the guy a smile and giving Warren a look underneath it.

"Thanks. Didn't you get something?" He took the plate sheepishly.

"We can share," she said breezily. "Where are the drinks?"

"I couldn't find any, and then I met Bayo and we got to talking. Bayo, this is my wife, Lillian. This is Bayo's place." Warren drew her closer. "But you knew that already."

"Nice to meet you," Bayo said. "You're friends with my wife?"

"We know each other from the book club," Lillian said nervously as she shook his hand.

"Ah, right. Of course. Well, let me get you a drink." Bayo started to move off. "It might have to be non-alcoholic, I'm afraid. We underestimated our numbers quite a bit!"

"Aww, no, it's fine," Lillian said.

"Please, let me. Kike will be pissed if she found out one of her friends didn't have a good time," Bayo joked. "I'll be back. Don't move. Seriously man, don't move; I want your barber's number."

"No problem," Warren chuckled as Bayo left. "Lil look, I'm sorry. I was having a good time, saw a friend from the office and his girl, and they introduced me to the host. Just felt like I should, you know, converse a little. Lil?"

Lillian had stopped listening. The alcove went in deeper and longer than she'd initially realized, and there were people there who'd been concealed by the design. One of them, Lani, had stood up from his seat, and was trailing three or four people heading for the main party. An overhead lamp illuminated him clearly and their eyelines crossed.

He raised his hand in greeting, smiling in recognition. Never had she been seized by two more conflicting emotions: a yearning to speak to him and alarm at doing so in front of Warren.

"Who's that?" Warren's voice darkened.

"I'm not sure. He looks like a student from SpeakNow!" Lillian turned to Warren but couldn't resist another look back.

Lani must have picked up on her hesitation because he nodded a *goodbye* and caught up with the people he'd been with.

"A student?" Warren repeated incredulously. "At SpeakNow!?"

"He's taking Japanese," Lillian said. "At least, I think that's him."

"Well, is it him or not?" Warren watched her closely.

"Hey, hi, there you are." Dara appeared beside them, her plate half-eaten and now without a drink. "I'm Dara. You must be Warren."

"Hi." Warren's eyes stayed glued to Lillian, his body only half-turned to Dara. "Sorry, who are you?"

"Dara. Lillian and I met at book club." Dara enunciated each word, as if speaking a different language. She seemed to have sobered up a bit.

"Right. The book club." Warren shook her hand briefly, his mouth tight. "Nice to meet you."

"Speaking of book club…" Dara took on the tone of a spy conspiring with an ally. "Wanker. Wanker alert."

"What?" Lillian snapped, her frayed nerves stretching under the tension.

"The guy we were talking about—the one you texted us about?" Dara stared at her like she was the crazy one. "Oh, wait. You met already."

"No, not really…" Lillian's stomach twisted.

"Who is this?" Warren's words were less a question and more a warning.

"No one," Lillian stammered. "A new student at the school."

"Taking Japanese lessons?" Warren repeated.

"Lani's taking Japanese lessons?" Dara made a disgusted face. "Of course…"

Warren looked at Dara, then back at Lillian. "Why are you texting people about him?"

"He forgot something at the school."

"*Why* are you texting him?" Warren didn't take his eyes off Lillian.

"I wasn't texting him!"

To Lillian's disbelief, Dara drew closer. "Trust me, he's a

complete twat. She was trying to help, which was really nice of her. He doesn't deserve it."

Warren grabbed Lillian's elbow and pulled her a few feet away.

"What is this?" he hissed. "Is this why you've been working overtime?"

"Stop! You know why I've been working overtime. I wanted to replenish our savings..."

"That's what you said."

"It's nothing, Warren! He's a student, for Christ's sake. She doesn't know what she's saying. She's drunk!" Lillian tried to keep her voice down, but she was trembling.

"Is this why you're in the guest room? Is this why you've been sneaking around, working strange hours? Is this your exit? Is this how you fucking—" Warren's anger matched his disbelief.

"Oh my God," he exhaled when she struggled to reply.

He shook his head, swallowed, turned away. When he looked back at her, his eyes were cold. "I saw your search history. On your Mac. I saw him."

Lillian's mouth went dry and the skin on her arms chilled.

She would never be able to understand how quickly things escalated after that. It was as if an old recording had jumped ahead, cutting from one moment to the next, making no sense of the seconds in between. The plate in Warren's hand must have been flung to the ground. She must have chased after him, and he must have shaken her off—the red welt on her cheek must have come from his elbow jabbing behind him. He must have called out—he couldn't have known Lani's name at that point—and it must have been loud enough to cut through the noise and halt Lani by the pool.

Warren slammed into him and they barrelled headfirst into the pool, creating a deep crater in the water. Lillian watched in horror as the two men roiled, limbs intertwined, flailing like a faceless beast.

And then she was in the pool, too, her hands beating at them. A kick to her stomach propelled her backward. Her body slammed against a wall. She gasped for air but was answered with a mouthful of choking water.

Coughing and panting, she wiped at her eyes until they could focus again. When she could finally breathe and see clearly, a sea of blurred faces stared down at her. A woman's voice screamed as Warren lunged for Lani and two men jumped into the pool, pulling them apart.

"Warren, please! Let me explain!" she cried, fighting against the waves to get to him.

She almost lost her balance as he pushed her away and dragged himself out.

The other men climbed out of the pool, and one of them helped her up. People at the edge stepped back from the puddles forming around them, gaping at the drenched bodies and plastered clothes. Some covered their mouths in disbelief; one or two had phones out and were filming. Ashamed, Lillian hid her face.

"What the hell is wrong with you?" Lani yelled at Warren.

"Are you out of your mind?" Bayo, who was next to Lani, said angrily. "This is my house! What are you *doing?*"

Warren pointed at Lani, his chest rising fast. "Ask him. Piece of shit."

Kike appeared at Bayo's side and gripped his arm. "Bayo, he needs to go. There are cameras."

"I'm gone," Warren snapped.

The throng parted as he walked away. He didn't look back. Feeling everyone's eyes on her, Lillian followed, her wet feet slapping against the ground.

Amaka

The beach tapered off until it stuck out into the ocean like a long, sandy toe. The water surrounding it was blue-green, and a thin line of carefully placed palm trees forked through the ombre sky. A cinema screen several meters high flickered images over hundreds of people in white deck chairs, a light beaming from a projector behind them. On two of those deck chairs, Amaka and Lani sipped beers and waited for the film to start.

"I wasn't sure you'd say yes," he admitted, a playful grin on his face.

"Why not? They have raspberry fruit beer," she quipped.

"Yes, you like raspberries...that's the only reason you came?"

"Why else?"

"I don't know. It took you two days to reply to my text. We're lucky we could still get tickets."

"You're lucky I was free."

"And your boyfriend? Is he 'comfortable' with this?" He looked at her fixedly.

"It's not serious. We're just dating, but I wasn't going to say that to a total stranger in a 7-Eleven now, was I?"

"So I'm not a total stranger anymore?" he flirted.

The vision of the drenched, shivering American girl staring at her husband as he stumbled away from her at Kike's party stopped Amaka from speaking. Lani must have read her mind because his expression changed.

"I had nothing to do with that. Seriously, is everyone going to keep thinking that I did? I met the woman once before that night, I swear."

Amaka stared at him for signs he was lying and noticed the purple welt on his cheekbone. The disastrous end to the party the week before had driven out most of the guests, none of whom wanted to risk their names being input into the "system" when the police arrived. The fact that Lani had been involved was shocking, particularly since Amaka had been sitting by the pool seconds before he'd been shoved into the water. She and Dara had shared a taxi home that night, dissecting what had happened, piecing their two narratives together. The next day, the book club created a new WhatsApp group without Lillian in which they salivated over the details of the attack, but no one had any new information.

Of course, Amaka had also withheld details of their kiss. She now knew that the attacker had been Lillian's husband. What she couldn't figure out was whether something had happened between Lani and Lillian. Bayo believed his best friend and had cooperated willingly with the police—and there *was* something about Lani being with the American that didn't make sense. He'd only been in Singapore a month; when would he have found the time to get enmeshed in marital discord so quickly? Still, Dara was now even more certain that he was untrustworthy, and Lillian's husband had certainly been convinced.

Instead of taking a giant step back, Amaka found herself even more intrigued by Lani, yielding to the deep attraction he had ignited within her in the elevator. She'd tracked him through Bayo's Instagram and sent him a message. They'd exchanged numbers, texted back and forth over the past week, and he'd finally asked her out. So far, they'd kept the conversation tonight to his search for a new apartment. She was glad Lillian was finally being addressed, but she didn't want the mood to turn heavy.

"Let's drop it," she said finally. "Lillian's obviously going through a lot."

Lani cleared his throat and gulped some beer. "And what does Dara think?"

Amaka held up a hand. "If the barbecue's off limits, then Dara's off limits, too."

He scratched his chin, his nails crackling against his goatee. "OK, fine. Fair enough."

The cinema screen went dark and the lights on the headphones attached to their chairs began to glow.

"You look nice by the way." Lani picked up his headset and grinned down at her dress: strapless, sheer and the same shade of brown as her skin.

"Goes without saying."

She put on her headphones and cut off his laugh.

As they watched a trailer for a new superhero film, she saw a reply email from her mother's broker in Lagos.

The sale is complete, Ms. Ezinulo, it read. *The funds should reach you within 48 hours. Please see the attached statement and today's selling price.*

She silenced her phone. It was a joint account. Her father's shares were as much hers as they were Ugo's. She was doing nothing wrong.

A rush of air blew into Amaka's apartment. It whistled through gaps in the panes, shaking her windows and pounding against her door. The loud rattling forced her to get up. Dazed and fighting her instinct to stay in bed, she moved through the dark and into the bathroom where the noise was erratic and frenzied.

She found the cause—a blind cord sticking out of a window was being flung against the glass—and fixed it. Returning to bed, she saw that her phone had lit up. Even before she looked at the screen, she knew it was him.

Sitting on her bed, cold suddenly, she swiped her phone open and found three messages. Above them were the ones they'd sent since their date.

> Lani: You awake?

Amaka: No.

> Lani: ☺ Sorry I woke you.

Amaka: You didn't. It's Friday night, I'm out
with friends.

> Lani: ?…It's impossible to get a straight
> answer from you.

Amaka: At 11:30 at night? Yes.

> Lani: With your boyfriend?

Amaka: No…Drinks with the girls, but we're
wrapping up soon.

There was no response. Amaka turned over and folded a pillow
between her legs.

> Lani: Found a new place. Would love you to see
> it…and I got you a gift.

She chewed on a nail.

Amaka: I didn't ask for a gift.

> Lani: I know. That's usually how gifts work.

Amaka: Thank you. Give it to me when you
see me next.

> Lani: Come over.

With the excitement of a child going to an amusement park, she dressed in half-darkness, wearing a shredded T-shirt, skinny jeans and heels. She dabbed perfume everywhere she could think of. Stepping into the blustery night air, she walked down to her MRT train station. A taxi would get her there in less than five minutes, but she wanted him to wait. A part of her was also hoping that the journey, filled with glaring, phosphorescent lights and bleary-eyed midnight commuters, would kill the fantasy, and bring her back to her senses.

She arrived at Tiong Bahru station just before it closed and walked along the main road before turning down a side street. Swings in an empty children's park swayed like shadowy specters in the wind. Most of the bohemian restaurants and coffee shops located in colorful shophouses were closed, the tables and chairs cleared away, though one or two still emitted an orange glow. Above them, wooden window shutters waved lazily. The walls were printed with black and red Chinese characters, a design characteristic of this quaint neighborhood. A community cat meowed invitingly and rubbed its heavy belly against a beam.

Amaka crossed the road, continuing past a waiter throwing rubbish into a side-alley until she came to a low, white condo on top of a wine merchant and dry cleaner. On both sides of the building, curved balconies looked out on to the street. Potted plants and ferns created a flimsy curtain that protected the inhabitants from view.

She dialed Lani's unit, her heart pounding. The entryway clicked open, and the security guard stirred as she moved past his desk and up the four flights of stairs. The building was old, each step wide and high, so by the time she reached the top, she was breathless, and her skin was prickling with heat. This was a good thing—it meant she'd be convincing as someone who'd been out all night.

Lani's door was ajar, and the sight of it made her mouth dry. The door widened just before she touched it, and there he was, smiling and angling closer to peck her on the cheek.

She let him. "Hey," she said.

"Hey." He brushed his lips against her face. The strength of his aftershave and a whiff of minty toothpaste were tell-tale signs that his nonchalance was also a facade.

He directed her through an arched doorway. "Mi casa."

The kitchen was divided from an open-plan living room by a narrow, white tabletop. There was a worn-looking dining set and two long bookcases skirting the bottom of the walls, close to the wooden floors. Apart from the table, a white cloth sofa and two chairs on the balcony, there was no other furniture; the white walls were bare. It was dimly lit.

"What do you think?" he asked behind her.

"You need some plants." She put her bag on the kitchen table.

He chuckled, coming round to stand by her. "I'm rarely here—they wouldn't last a month. Something to drink? Or are you merry enough?"

"I'll have a drink." She found herself with nowhere to sit. She felt unmoored. She didn't know if the tabletop was meant to be a type of bar or for chopping food, so she didn't know how to use it without looking clumsy.

"Just beer. That all right?" He opened the fridge.

She shrugged OK.

"Cheers." He held the beer out. "Oh—wait."

He tore off a paper towel and wiped the inside rim of the bottle mouth.

"I used to work in a bar in London. I've seen too many rats on top of crates of beer."

"You used to work in a bar? *You?*" Amaka took the bottle.

"Yes! In law school," he said indignantly. "OK, I lasted a month, but still."

"I knew it," she scoffed, taking a sip. The iciness helped her manage the beer's tartness, but she would have preferred something sweeter.

He tapped her bottle with his, grinning. "And you've worked with your hands? With those nails?"

Amaka thought of all the crappy jobs she'd had to take while studying in the U.S., cash-in-hand jobs because of the restrictions on her student visa. It was ironic that she was playing the part so well—Lani thought she was like him.

"No, but that's only because people in Nigeria never want their children to look like they're struggling," she smarted. "They would rather you be broke but not look it than actually let someone see you get your hands dirty."

Lani eyed her handbag on the counter playfully. "I'm trying to picture you broke, but it's a stretch, I'll tell you. Girls always say they've got no money, but what they really mean is they have to shop in the sales until they get paid."

"Which *girls* are you talking about?"

"I'm not walking into that one." He shook his head and stepped closer, pulling something out of his back pocket. "For you."

He let the orange box lie flat in his palm.

Amaka felt her body go slack and the blood run from her face. She put the beer down and wiped her hands on her jeans.

"I feel like you already know what this is," he teased.

She couldn't trust herself to speak. She let the brown ribbon drop to the floor, lifted the lid and unfolded the white tissue.

"I thought this color would work with the bag you had at the beach."

It was a gorgeous little horse, green as the ocean, with white wings and a brown fringe. She would die before pairing it with the black Lady Dior she'd carried that night, but she gave him an A+ for trying.

"Pegasus," he murmured, drawing closer. "You know, the winged horse in Greek mythology?"

She had no idea what he was talking about—that was Dara's nerdy area of expertise. The charm was so heavenly she could eat it.

Lani took it out of the box and stretched behind her to get her bag. His arms grazed her waist until his pelvis, waist and chest were only a fraction away. She turned her face to one side as he looped the charm over her bag handle.

"Do you like it?" He spoke in her ear, his voice thick and gruff.

She nodded and touched the lingering bruise on his cheekbone, pressing against the constellation of broken vessels. He winced, and it aroused her.

He responded by pulling her zipper down and tugging her jeans off.

"Tell me what you want me to do." He pressed closer again and groaned in her ear.

"*Don't* lick me there," she muttered, shuddering.

"What about here?" He slipped a finger through the side of her knickers.

She made a short sound: *fine*. He mimicked it, and she heard his thinly masked laugh.

"Turn around," he said after pulling her knickers off.

Their eyes were inches apart; she saw this was his favorite part, making her wait, reading her face, seeing her trapped, how no amount of sharp-tongued bluster could erase how hooked she was.

He kissed her, at the exact moment piercing his finger inside her so that both parts of her were soft *and* hard, pained and shivering. She tore her face from his, but he covered her mouth again and turned her cry into a moan.

When the first light of dawn tinged his bedroom, Amaka stirred, having been in a light, restless sleep for most of the night. Realizing she was alone, she reached for her clothes on the floor before remembering they were still in the kitchen. Taking a T-shirt from his wardrobe—and praying he didn't read too much into it—she pulled it over her naked body and went into the sitting room.

It was empty, too, and the balcony doors were closed. Her handbag had been placed on the sofa and leaning against it was a guitar she hadn't seen before.

She could let herself out. Her message would be crystal clear: whatever this was, it was an arrangement that required no follow-up. And yet, she was curious. He'd left no note, and her phone, which had messages from Dara, Rohit and her mother, had none from him. Seeing all three names together made her stomach churn.

Rohit was coming over tonight. The feeling of transgression that had pressed against her as she'd edged closer to this line with Lani felt different now. Flatter. She'd done it, and now she had to figure out what to do. Or not do... Maybe all sleeping with Lani had achieved was widening her pool of options, and was that so bad? She was young and unmarried—would she feel this guilty if she were a man? All she had to do was navigate Rohit's feelings, and hers, too, while she worked out who was the best fit.

Dara was only a matter of coming clean. Despite the slightly simplistic and puritanical way in which her best friend looked at the world, one night of lust with a friend's work rival was unflattering, but hardly insurmountable.

Ugo was the most complicated of the three. Not only was she pushing for another video call—this time just with Uncle Emeka—but she had also started texting Amaka random bits of information about her father's family. *Had she heard that this aunty's business was struggling,* and *did she know that so-and-so cousin was finding it hard to have a baby?* It was baffling. These were people who had never had the time of day for Amaka and her mother. Although Ugo hadn't mentioned Chinyere by name (she'd sworn never to speak of him until he apologized for his disrespectful behavior), Amaka was just as surprised to see Ugo showing interest in Chukwu's family. She was tired with the lot of them.

She responded only to Rohit to confirm their plans. She got dressed, played with her new charm for a while, then rifled through Lani's book collection. His shelves were filled with memoirs of past presidents, philosophy and psychology books, and large glossy tomes on African architecture. The glass and wooden balcony doors were easy to fold open, and the early morning breeze spun the pull-switch ceiling fan into its gust. As she leaned on the ledge and looked out onto the street, the front door clacked and creaked open behind her.

"Hey," Lani called out a little too loudly, removing his earphones. He was dressed in light running clothes and was completely drenched in sweat.

"Who leaves a practical stranger in their home?" She came off the balcony and re-entered the room's cool shade. "It usually takes people a while before they start leaving their bag open or their door unlocked in Singapore."

"Are you saying I shouldn't trust you?" He smiled, peeling off the phone strapped to his arm.

"It's just a little strange..."

"Most girls would be thrilled that I'd be comfortable enough to let them stay over," Lani chuckled.

Amaka opened her mouth to reply archly but he beat her to it.

"It's seven in the morning. How can we already be fighting?"

"That's so cute. You think this is a fight." She picked up her bag and stood at the kitchen table across from him.

Taking out a jug of water from the fridge and two glasses, he looked bemused. "You know, you're like the opposite of a were-wolf. Hot at night but really mean in the daytime. Or maybe not a werewolf, more like... the opposite of a gremlin."

He laughed at his own joke: a full belly laugh. Before she could stop herself, her mouth curled into a small smile.

"Bloody hell, a smile." He stopped mid-pour, smiling that lazy, maddening grin of his. "What are you up to today? I don't have to work until this afternoon. I can make smoothies and... we can do other things."

"Mmm." She drank some water, feeling self-conscious over the warmth stirring in her at his gaze. "I've got to go. I only stayed to make sure you hadn't been kidnapped."

"So, wait, you hung out with Dara last night?"

She was immediately on the defensive. "Yes, why?"

"No, never mind, forget I said anything."

"No, ask me," she pushed back, unconvinced by his casualness.

"I know we agreed it's off limits, but she's been really difficult since the barbecue. I just want to make sure she's not spreading anything about me that isn't true."

"She's not spreading anything," Amaka responded, watching him closely. "But she thinks there's no smoke without fire."

"That makes no sense," he snapped. "God. Ever since I moved here, she's had it in for me. I don't know what her problem is. She must be the most immature, unenlightened person I've met, and I'm a lawyer—I've met a few."

He was really venting now. "She's been an absolute nightmare to work with. The most irrational co-workers are the ones who are so resolute in their convictions about you that they refuse to use their common sense. We work in a pyramid structure with the sole purpose of funneling you out the closer you get to the top—everyone knows this. So why make me the villain? We make the *perfect* team. I don't know why she doesn't see that."

"Maybe because she feels replaceable and disposable. Maybe because she's spent six years building a practice, being constantly told her time is coming, only for you to dance your way in and make it look easy," Amaka spelled out. "You can't relate to that? Because I can."

She was starting to see why Lani's selective blindness was rubbing Dara the wrong way.

"She thinks I make it look easy?" A quizzical look replaced Lani's frown.

"Please, I'm not stroking your ego."

"I don't need you to stroke my ego," he said, exasperated. "I'm just baffled. You know she's the reason I'm going into work today? On a Saturday. She's been so secretive when we're supposed to be working on a client presentation together. She won't share her slides with me, just keeps making excuses. It's ridiculous."

Amaka slung her bag across her body. "I don't really want to know about work stuff—just don't mention anything about *us* to her. I want to keep everything and everyone separate."

Amaka's kitchen smoked as Rohit fried onions, garlic and pepper on her tiny stove. He poured her a glass of ice water when she began to cough and took the tin of coconut milk she'd been trying to open away from her. The small amount of table space she had was covered with Hokkien noodles, beansprouts, tofu, chili paste and a carpet of vegetable peelings.

"Why don't you open the window?" he asked, pouring the coconut milk into the pot and adding some fish sauce.

She made a face into her glass of water. "It's stuck."

Wiping his hands on a dish cloth, Rohit crossed the small space and forced the window open. He didn't look at her on the way there or back.

"Everything cool?" Amaka couldn't take the tension anymore, even if it was of her own making.

"You tell me." Rohit sliced a lime in half and began squeezing it into the pot. "Ever since I got back from the stag do, you've been cold as hell. And don't say that you haven't because you have."

He put the pot lid on and turned to face her, crossing his arms. "Look, I'm not trying to force this. Ever since I got back from Bangkok, you've made excuses when I try to make plans, but then you post pictures and it's clear you've been out, just not with me. I feel weird even saying that... I'm not keeping tabs on you, but I like you, and I thought you liked me, and I thought we were having fun. I'm fine with things happening naturally, but... if you don't want this, just tell me. I can take it."

This was her chance—served up and handed to her. They could return to just being colleagues who'd dated and then fizzled out. It might be awkward at first, but no one would be blamed, and both their prides could stay intact.

The second the thought formed, however, she knew she couldn't do it. It wasn't solitude she was afraid of; it was returning to it after knowing this care and consistency: cooking for her, checking up on her, having someone who understood her job who she could click with inside the office and out. How easy would it be to find someone else who worked as hard as she did, then forced her to take a break and try out a new late-night burger shack before booking her a yoga class to help fix her neck ache? Ending their relationship would mean the end of re-watching cheesy nineties romcoms they preferred to argue over than concentrate on. It would be like shivering in the shade after basking in the sun. She wasn't a fool;

as someone obsessed with luxury goods, she understood Rohit's intrinsic value, especially in a market like Singapore where men had so many different types of single working women to choose from. Her struggle was believing that value was also hers.

Words wouldn't work—what she felt for him was too strong to joke about. She walked over and buried her face into his chest, breathing in his aftershave with its soothing undertones of lemon oil and burnt leaves.

"I'm a bitch," she mumbled into his shirt.

"No, you're not." He pulled her into a hug and kissed her temple.

The urge to cry rose with the mist of the hot, sweet coconut milk on the stove.

"Listen." He stretched behind her, taking something out of his laptop bag. "My sister's getting married in the summer. In Thailand. I want you to come."

He held out a red book, and she took it slowly. It was covered in soft silk and embroidered with gold thread. There were three sections inside: turquoise green, burnt orange and purple. Each section had slits for pockets and little gold envelopes were slotted into each one.

"We've taken over most of the Marriott—the rooms are covered, so you only have to take care of your flight. Three nights at the end of November. Make a weekend of it. And you don't have to worry about visas. Thailand should be easy, and you have plenty of time, but if you have any problems, we've got a guy my family uses. He's the best," he continued nervously. "I sat on my sister until she gave me an extra invitation. Look, I can try and get you another one if you want to invite one of your friends—Dara, maybe."

"Are you sure? You want me to meet your family?" Amaka said, terrified and surprised and excited all at once.

"Yes, and Sanaa will be here soon, doing some wedding shopping, so you can meet her and get the vetting process out of the way—joking, joking." He laughed and pulled her into a tight squeeze.

Dara

A knock on the door raised Dara and Lucy's heads, breaking an hour of silent work. Lani stood at the door, holding his laptop. The smell of roasted coffee beans wafted in with him.

"Bundle 106—are you working on that now?" he asked. His tone was annoyingly chipper, despite it being past dinner.

"Yup." Dara made a tight, horizontal line with her mouth that theoretically passed for a smile at this hour.

"I'm working on 107. I was thinking—it makes sense if Mabel and Lucy finish prepping the Erwin case in my office and I come in here so we can work on Hakida." He looked down at Lucy. "If that's OK with you, Lucy."

"There's nothing I'd love more." Lucy made an innocent face. "Me, Mabel and Erwin—the Thursday night of my dreams."

"Thank you." Lani touched Lucy's shoulder as she slipped out.

"They *really* don't like each other." He shook his head as he sat in Lucy's chair. "Not a day goes by without Mabel complaining about her, though I can't really put my finger on what the issue is exactly."

"Hmm. Lucy never says a word." Dara kept her eyes on her screen.

Ever since Lani joined the team, Lucy had found ways of showing Dara her solidarity. Seeing how much The Sirens were enjoying the rivalry between Lani and Dara, Lucy had kept them at arm's length, despite the fact that a recent rumor suggested Ben may not, in fact, be gay and could be a prospective love interest for her. Lucy had also done her best to rein in the constant chit-chat, picking up on the increased stress Dara was under. The last thing Dara was going to do was throw a possible ally under the bus.

They worked in silence until an email from Lani appeared on her screen.

"Small amendment to page sixty-three," he said, almost to himself.

"Sure." She swiped the email away.

"Did we hear back from Patrick Ndoku's office?"

"Regarding what?" She refused to look up but could feel his eyes on her.

"The chiefs' tax rebates. His investigators still haven't come back with anything?"

"You've got the same emails I have."

"I know. I just thought that since you started corresponding with him before I got here..."

"That I'm hiding emails and keeping information to myself?" She couldn't help but stick the needle back.

He faced her squarely. "That's not what I meant." The space between them felt like it'd shrunk in size. "Look, do you want to talk about this? What the issue is?"

She was impressed he was able to ask the question with a straight face.

"I have absolutely no issue." She squinted her "smile" back at him and tried to get back to work.

"Really? Because it doesn't seem that way." He stretched back in Lucy's chair and let his hands drop into his lap. "Ever since I got here, you've made a concerted effort to either avoid me, snap at me or shut me out.

"I'm not talking about emailing Ndoku." He raised his hand in a conciliatory gesture before she could speak. "But you've left me off of some emails, and if you're not trying to get information out of Irene or Lucy or Ben or Chris, you're giving them these looks..."

"OK, stop." She'd had enough. *Was he kidding?*

"I've just been doing my job," he said sharply.

"Yes, the job I was doing *just fine* before you got here and split it in two." Her words were barbed and she immediately regretted them. She sounded bitter and childish and she'd given too much away.

She stuck her pen in her notebook and closed it. "I'm going to call it a night."

"And the presentation? We need to make sure the slides—"

"I think it's best we give them to Irene. She can upload them to the projector." She gathered her things. "It's a digital SMARTboard, so it saves a copy."

A few days later, Dara leaped up the brick steps of Fort Canning Park, taking them two at a time. The wind pushed against her like a hand holding her back, making the ascent even harder. She kept her head down; one ill-timed glimpse of the endless, red staircase ribboning up before her and she would lose the will to keep going. Chipped steps, dust, the leaves under her feet: these were the only things she could allow herself to focus on or she'd collapse. Not her breathing, or the burn radiating in her solar plexus, or Amaka struggling behind her. Attacking the last five steps with a furious intensity, she finally emerged onto a smooth footpath and leaned on the wooden battlements, relishing the sudden and welcome cool weather.

She enjoyed the aerial view of the city, staring down at the long terraces that wound round the park, and smiled as she watched her friend's uphill slog dwindle to a snail's pace. Her smile waned when she remembered the way Amaka had spoken to her at the barbecue, how ruthlessly dismissive she'd been about Dara's naivety and lack of African identity. The worst part—and Amaka couldn't have known that she'd pressed the most painful nerve— was the comment she'd made about Dara's mother. She'd told Amaka about growing up with her grandparents and how un- orthodox her mother was. That Amaka could interpret Abigail's neglectful disinterest as a form of healthy adult parenting was one of the reasons Dara rarely spoke of her mother. It was impossible to explain how someone who came across so well to others could be completely different in private. She knew, on some deeper level, that this was the reason she was so suspicious of Lani, but she couldn't understand why no one else saw it.

Dara moved off to a shaded bench and started her stretches, working from her quads to her calves, trying not to fixate on the hurt from Amaka's snub. She'd always been aware of the sharpness of Amaka's tongue—Dara had just never expected to be on the receiving end of it. In the five years she'd lived in Singapore before Amaka arrived, Dara had befriended girls from all sorts of backgrounds, but they'd been friendships of convenience, easy and surface-level. When she'd met Amaka, she'd been drawn to her like a Velcro strap finding its other half.

Dara had been playing beach volleyball at Tanjong Beach Club. The game, organized by Australians in a Meetup group she'd joined, had been vicious. Whether she reached for the ball or tried to get out of someone's way, it smacked into Dara, each hit a loud, humiliating slap. It was obvious she was just getting in the way, and she'd grown tired of being covered in sand, so she'd used the excuse of a toilet break to sub.

The beach beds lining the pool were crammed, every inch of the water packed with swimmers, children, floats and families. It was impossible for anyone in the pool to do a full length. Even the decking was full of people in their bikinis and shorts, drinking, snapping, waiting for a table or chair to free up; a short distance away, beachgoers wandered along the pristine shore. Tanjong Beach Club was the worst place to have a relaxing Sunday brunch, yet it was packed every time she came.

Hovering by the club's reception desk, it only took a few minutes of indecision for her to get a taxi back to the mainland. Ten minutes of trying to find a cab passed—it was always harder to get off Sentosa island than get on—and she was starting to accept that she'd have to wait for the volleyball match to finish and share a ride back with a teammate when she heard someone call her name.

Confused, Dara had looked around, trying to place the woman's unfamiliar voice, or see if someone sitting nearby would respond. Her confusion doubled as a black girl in a hot-pink bikini hurtled at her, a sarong tied around her waist and white sunglasses pushed over an impeccable Diana Ross weave. The girl brought her waving hand down and greeted her with the spirited warmth of a decades-old friendship, gabbling at full speed: she recognized Dara from her LinkedIn profile, she'd literally just moved to Singapore and was still getting used to it, she saw Dara had been here for a couple of years, did she like it and was she here with friends, did she want to join Amaka who had a beach bed, it was impossible to get service you had to wait so long, actually they were trying to take the bed back, there was a long queue of people giving her the evil eye but she sure as hell wasn't giving it up after waiting so long, so she'd lied that she had friends coming, wasn't it so lucky Dara was here, why didn't she join her, Amaka had a tab going, she was still getting used to earning in Singapore dollars, she had to stop converting to naira in her head, and wasn't it amazing how low the taxes were here, she should come join!

Swept along by the force of her infectious energy, and recognizing, even then, the rarity of meeting another Nigerian girl this open and friendly, brunch turned into lunch, which turned into cocktails and the exchange of phone numbers.

They'd been each other's plus-one ever since, quickly becoming comfortable enough to rely on the other to fill any free pockets of time together. But this was the first time there had ever been any tension between them. It was possible the tension was only in her head...so far, neither of them had mentioned their last conversation.

"Chineke!" Amaka swore at the top of the stairs then bent forward, hands on her hips.

By this point, Dara was doing tricep dips, her palms on the bench.

"Why are you making me walk all the way there?" Amaka wheezed. Each step she took looked so unstable that Dara envisioned her legs crumbling underneath her, like a sack of potatoes sliced open.

"If you're already complaining, you're not going to make it through the whole workout." Dara gritted her teeth as she pushed herself up.

"The 'whole workout'? This is it for me!" Amaka collapsed onto the bench.

"I've still got the outdoor bars to do."

"You go ahead, don't worry about me. I've got my phone." Amaka patted her belt bag.

"You're ridiculous," Dara laughed, cutting her set to fifteen reps instead of twenty.

"See your legs." Amaka eyed Dara enviously. "You do this every Sunday?"

"Mostly. Sometimes I swim or I run in MacRitchie, if I've had an early night," Dara grunted, squatting.

"That place with the monkeys?" Amaka shivered. "I went there a few months ago and this monkey climbed down from a tree and started jumping at me—I was terrified. It was only when Rohit said it wanted the drink in my hands that I dropped the bottle. The nasty animal caught it before it even hit the ground. Never again."

"You went with Rohit?" Dara straightened up.

"This was months ago; we went with some of his friends." Amaka shook her head. The gesture seemed part dismissal, part warning.

"Oh, OK." Dara took the hint.

"I only went so I could say I'd seen the famous reservoir, which was completely overrated. No cafés, hardly any toilets and it was only when we got there that people started speaking up about the snakes."

"It's nature, Amaka," Dara said, restarting her squats. "It's one of the few places in Singapore where you can really experience the jungle."

"Botanic gardens is jungle enough for me."

Dara said nothing, moving on to lunges. On the other side of the path, a rooster crept out of the undergrowth then disappeared again, its inky-black feathers trailing behind it. Amaka took out her phone and crossed her legs.

"Those are unusual." Dara squinted at Amaka's feet. "Are they new?"

Obviously flattered, Amaka grinned, turning round and lifting a foot. "They're so hot; I love them."

"They're so dressy. Why are you wearing them to run?"

"They're Yeezys." Amaka looked at her like she had tentacles growing out of her head.

Dara must have looked blank because Amaka began to shriek. "Dara, you're too much!"

"Are they really expensive?" Dara shrugged, smiling. This type of teasing she didn't mind.

"Oh my God, you're clueless. They're impossible to find. I had to use a personal shopper in Hong Kong to get them."

"But why did you have to get this particular pair?" Dara was puzzled.

Amaka tutted good-naturedly, as if Dara were a little sister or cousin who had to be schooled.

"Not everything is about functionality. Clothes aren't just about rules and codes," Amaka said.

"I know that," Dara replied, but her grandmother's rules about dressing couldn't be shaken off that easily.

"So come on, update me." Amaka must have read her mind. "What's the latest with the American girl, Lillian?"

"Can we stop calling her 'the American'?" Dara swapped feet and began pulsing her back leg. "I don't think being American has anything to do with what happened."

Amaka snorted derisively, but drew her knees in and kept quiet, which Dara took as a sign that she was listening.

"I called Kike and she said Lillian texted her to apologize for ruining her party. When I explained what I knew about her problems with her husband, Kike was really understanding."

They'd actually had lunch in person, at Shisen Hanten, a two Michelin–starred Sichuan restaurant that had been Kike's treat, but Dara thought it best to play that down.

"Apparently, the police have been in touch. They'll be interviewing Lillian and her husband soon." Dara veered to one side to let a shirtless jogger pass.

"And your nemesis? Was it definitely a mistake with him and Lillian?" Amaka hung on to every word.

A frown darkened Dara's face. "That's what everyone says. I

didn't tell you before, but...I feel a little responsible. I said something that night that I think triggered the whole thing."

"What are you talking about?" Amaka stared at her.

Dara grimaced as she sat beside Amaka. "I was the one who told her husband that Lillian had texted the book club about Lani. I didn't realize I wasn't supposed to. Warren said something about her laptop...I have no idea—I was pretty tipsy by that point.

"Even if something is going on, I don't want to jump to conclusions," she continued. "What her husband did was violent and irrational. No one should have to live with that."

"My God." Amaka shook her head. "How humiliating. That is literally my worst nightmare, being disgraced in public."

"Anyway, I got Lillian's number from Kike," Dara exhaled. "I just feel like I should apologize. Maybe meet up with her for coffee."

"Absolutely not. One hundred percent no," Amaka commanded. "Stay away from all maritals, trust me."

"I feel sorry for her, Amaka." Dara thought about the hormone therapy she'd seen in Lillian's bathroom. She knew from a Google search that it was preparation for a type of IVF treatment, but it wasn't her place to tell Amaka this. There was a line you didn't cross, and it was an extension of the etiquette she'd inherited from Granee, which included being on time, never eating while standing up and not getting involved in public spats.

"Married people are messy. She'll suck you into her chaos and then probably turn around and bite you," Amaka warned. "They've probably made up by now. Who knows, maybe they're the type of couple who get off on this shit. You have no idea what's really going on there. The fantasies women have about marriage are complete bullshit. I'm serious—it can be really warped."

"I'm not talking about the institution of marriage. I'm talking about one marriage—no, one girl. Who I dumped in it. All I want to do is make sure she's OK." Dara couldn't figure out if Amaka had always been this cynical or if she'd deliberately blinded herself to it. "Why should Lillian be the one treated like a pariah while everyone rallies around Lani, and he goes back to business, scot-free?"

"Because her husband charged him like a linebacker! Look, do what you want. Just don't go over there on your own."

"I won't." Dara wiped her forehead with her wristband. The conversation had almost sapped her will to hit the bars when she remembered the main reason she'd invited Amaka out today.

"Speaking of he-who-shall-not-be-named..." she continued.

"You named him already," Amaka quipped.

"Shut up and listen to the second step of my plan." Dara elbowed her. "We've got a client presentation next week, which I was working on last night. We were the only two people in the office, and we barely said a word to one another."

She thought back to his stony-faced expression as he'd walked past the office kitchen.

"It's a little risky, and it could definitely backfire, but I think I've got an idea. We're supposed to submit our slides to Irene, Ian's secretary, who then uploads them to the SMARTboard. If I can get into his file—"

"Wait, wait, wait," Amaka interrupted. "Are you sure this is the best idea? Sabotage? You don't want to put your job at risk. Maybe you can figure out a way to just manage to work together...he doesn't seem that bad."

"Are you joking? 'Doesn't seem that bad'? What happened to 'Pull some Machiavellian shit'? 'Annihilate the competition'?"

Had her friend been replaced by a clone? Dara's work and everything she was trying to achieve as a lawyer was the most important thing to her. She thought Amaka understood this and shared the same drive.

"Would you say the same thing if he'd come for your job?" Dara said sharply.

Surprisingly, Amaka backed down.

"Fine. Don't bite my head off. Just be careful, and don't get yourself arrested." Amaka shrugged, but her nonchalance seemed forced. Dara felt uneasy—they hadn't found a single subject to agree on today.

"Thank you all for taking time out of your busy schedules." Ian was addressing a room full of clients. The walls of the boardrooms in Morgan Corbett Shaw had been collapsed to create a larger space. Dara and Lani stood beside him, watching everyone move away from the refreshments.

"We know your lunchtimes are precious, so we'll get straight to it. Lani Idowu, senior associate and the newest member of our team, will get the ball rolling, and then he'll pass the mic over to Dara Coker, who most of you know. I'll be back to finish. Thank you." He stepped away from the lectern and took his seat in the front row.

There was a smattering of applause—mostly one-handed, as the other held a sandwich, phone or business card—as the fifty or so people in attendance took their seats. On the rolldown screen behind them beamed a map of Africa, the firm's name and the title of their speech. The digital lectern showed the same image.

"Good afternoon, and thank you, Ian," Lani began. "'Investing in Africa: Merits, Risks and the Potential for Success.' Today, we will focus on how Asian entities can make inroads into the African economy and explore the legal frameworks that can protect those investments. My associate, Dara, will then focus on two arbitration case studies here in Singapore that have set a precedent, resulting in favorable outcomes for outside companies. Afterward, there will be a short Q&A, and detailed notes will be handed out. We hope this lunchtime talk is helpful for you—it should hopefully save you a few thousand in future billing." He let the joke land. "Sorry, Ian."

An enthusiastic ripple of laughter moved through the room. Ian, pleased to have the attention brought back to him, laughed the loudest.

Lani nodded at Dara, his signal for her to take her seat and allow him the limelight.

"The first thing to remember is the disparate states and economies within Africa," he began, rolling the screen clicker in his hand. "For the purpose of expediency, this talk will focus on emerging markets in African states with a gross GDP of more than four billion dollars. With an eye to the interests of the parties in this room, we've selected six states."

He pointed the clicker at the screen. It stayed the same; the map of Africa didn't change.

"My apologies." He clicked again. Nothing happened.

"Excuse me." He threw a quick smile at the room, stepping to the side to tap on the laptop on the table.

Dara sat completely still, letting step two of her plan unfold. She let the muscles in her face completely relax, resembling, she hoped, an innocent child, and watched Lani's long torso bend over the table.

Just a glitch—happens all the time, she imagined him thinking, as he swiped his mouse vigorously.

Seconds turned into a minute. He tapped and scrolled but nothing changed. Dara could feel Ian's growing irritation and the room's restlessness. It was delicious, this knowing, this childish power at watching a cool, collected man flounder in his excellently tailored trousers. She was ready to spring forward. All she needed was one look—one plea—for help.

He was wondering whether to call her over, whether to trust her. Was he considering if she was behind this? Or had his mind not leaped that far? Was he simply weighing his options? Should he call IT? Make a joke? Wing it without slides? Ask Dara to take his place while he figured something out?

The USB stick with a copy of his slides weighed down her pocket. She only had to feign surprise and save the day. Ian would see her quick thinking under fire, the level of her preparation. She was a scorpion, ready to sting cocky Orion to death. Like a glowing star, Lani would *Pssht!* and disappear into corporate oblivion.

She almost sprang up as he stepped away from the screen, but instead of approaching her, he walked to his laptop bag on the other side of the room.

"My apologies, we seem to have a minor technical glitch." He pulled out a mini tablet, unlocked it, and connected it to the screen before he'd finished speaking. "Please excuse the inconvenience."

The screen behind him went blank and then an image

appeared: six small map outlines with the names of the countries above them.

Dara stared at the screen, dismay leaking onto her face.

"There we go," Lani smiled. "All wired up and ready. Burundi, Rwanda, Zanzibar, South Africa, Ghana and Nigeria...all nation states that have enjoyed a surge of Southeast Asian investment, and whose relationships with Japan, China and Singapore look set to strengthen."

For the next twenty minutes, he held the room captive, adding nuggets of information from recently published research that were not in the original talk.

He knew. The thought played through her mind on a constant loop. How?

As his presentation wound down, Dara tried to pull herself together. She had to admit he was a brilliant speaker, confident and natural, crafting his argument clearly and tying the seams of each country's fact file to the next. Whatever Kike had said about his nepotistic advantages, there was no doubt he had the oracy to back it up. She'd been stupid enough to underestimate him. Now she had to make sure her talk was even better.

The room applauded warmly as Lani thanked everyone. He hung back for Dara to step forward and take his place.

"All yours." His eyes bored into hers.

She took the clicker from him, her mouth suddenly dry.

"Good afternoon," she smiled at the room. "Thank you, Lani, for that in-depth analysis, which leads us now to our two arbitration case studies. Both had very different outcomes and judgments, which serve as a warning for parties with ambiguous risk thresholds looking to invest in Africa."

She pressed her clicker.

Her slides were blank.

Lillian

The heel of Lillian's foot tapped against the wooden floor, the only perceptible sound in the police station. Panic ballooned in her chest. She took deep, quiet breaths to try to calm herself. She focused on all the things that were not the same as the police station in her dreams: it was warm, not cold; it was quiet, and this space was open plan—nothing like the rowdy Philadelphia district department she'd been taken to that day. She clenched and unclenched her hands.

On the other side of the room, Warren sat with his back to her as another, more senior officer interviewed him. They were too far away for her to hear, but she could see Warren in his work clothes, nodding to the officer; the rest of his body was stiff. A patch of sweat mushroomed across his back.

The cop opposite her glanced over, and she stopped moving her foot. He looked like he was about to speak but turned back to his computer screen. Though he was of Chinese descent, and at least ten years younger than any white cop back in Philly, just his presence made her nervous. She hadn't actually seen that many cops before the day her parents died, but she'd definitely heard them as they'd swooped into the neighborhood at night, their sirens blazing down the street, the clunk of their boots hitting the pavement as they stormed abandoned buildings on her block.

"Don't run, don't run, don't—run!" The breathlessness in their yells had always made it clear they were in motion. Their voices would sound so close that she would have to turn the TV as loud as it could go. She would fall asleep like that, scared, waiting for the end of her parents' shifts, listening for the sound of keys turning in the lock, oblivious to how close she would one day come into contact with the police.

Her handbag vibrated. She quickly dug out her phone and switched it off, cutting the call. Although she never answered the unending buzz of texts and phone calls, she knew they were from the book club. Their messages of sympathy and solidarity made her skin crawl, and triggered memories of Lani's face, the rush of falling water and Warren shouting. Most of them were from Dara.

Footsteps reverberated through the quiet station as the officer speaking to Warren stood up and approached her, carrying a brown folder. Warren rose and followed behind.

The officer gestured for Warren to sit in the empty chair next to her. With thin-rimmed glasses, and more flesh on him than the younger man, he was unsmiling but not hostile. He looked like an office manager or bureaucrat. There was none of the lined hardness she'd been expecting. Like the younger man, he wore a dark-blue tunic with silver buttons; shiny badges were affixed to his shoulders and collars.

He sat across from her, and the younger policeman came to stand just behind him, bringing a piece of paper from his desk. Both men had the same short, dark hair, parted on their left temple.

"I am the station inspector here, Mrs. Parsons." The station inspector took the paper being held out.

"The allegations made by Mr. Lani Idowu have been investigated. We've taken witness statements and collected CCTV evidence. The footage does indeed show an altercation between Mr. Parsons and Mr. Idowu, but due to the angle of the camera, it is not clear who instigated the assault.

"As you were informed by the arriving officer, Mr. Parsons, you have been charged with voluntarily causing harm based on eyewitness accounts. This is a letter of warning, which we are issuing since this is a first-time offense." He placed a sheet of paper on the table, turning it upside down so they could read it. "There will be no formal charge today."

Lillian bit her bottom lip and leaned over to scan the document.

Warren read slowly, a slight tremble in his hands, so she had time to read the top.

"Letter of warning…Warren Parsons, NRIC number G7834982K…voluntarily causing hurt…a stern warning… administered in lieu of prosecution…hereby warned to refrain from such conduct or criminal conduct…any offense in future, the same leniency may not be shown…does not amount to a conviction…does not amount to any of your legal rights being…"

"Thank you." Warren's relief was palpable.

She let out the breath she'd been holding. "Thank you."

"Mr. Lani Idowu has requested a condition be placed on the warning, to prevent future altercations." The station inspector took out a thicker piece of paper from his folder.

"Mr. Idowu has requested that you do not approach his place of work. This has been granted and will be enforced for a period of twelve months. Failure to comply can lead to the warning being revoked and you may be prosecuted for the offense. You will be granted a discharge once a certain amount of time has passed. Do you understand, Mr. Parsons?" His gaze turned icy as he held out a pen to Warren.

"Yes, I understand." Warren took the pen and signed, gripping it tightly.

"He, Mr. Idowu," Lillian stammered, trying to couch her words in apology for asking. "He takes lessons where I teach. That's the only reason I know him. Will I have to leave my job?"

The station inspector considered her, warning deepening the furrow of his brows.

"The conditions of the warning apply to Mr. Parsons alone," he replied.

The inspector gathered the papers, putting two of them in an envelope before sliding them forward.

"You're free to go."

The dark road outside the station was on a curve, secluded enough to make finding a taxi difficult. The street lamps stared down like phantoms, and stiff palm fronds swayed in the force of a gale. Their leaves were stiff and long, an eerie score of hands waving across the pavement. This, plus the sound they made, a shush that grew then fell, magnified the surrealness of the night. She might have been the last human on earth, so pointed and unwavering was Warren's turned back.

"Are you going to speak to me?" she called out, battling against the wind.

He raised his hand as a taxi approached and entered it without a word. The car drove away.

Her palms began to sweat, and her body ran cold, but instead of the rejection she'd been afraid of, she felt an anger as sudden and consuming as a blaze of fire. How could he leave her again? Unlike the night of the barbecue, she wasn't going to run from this fight.

Why had she been the one to take the blame for not having a baby? Why had that guilt been hers to shoulder alone? What happened to "for better and for worse, in sickness and in health"? Or did that only apply if you were fertile? She was sick of feeling like the weak link in their marriage, the reason they weren't able to enjoy everything Singapore had to offer, with its indoor baby gyms and cute nursing rooms in every mall. She was so mad at herself for needing her worth to be determined by him and a non-existent child for so long.

A second taxi finally arrived, and she set off. Fuming, she sprang out before it stopped outside her lobby, ignoring the blare of a car's horn as she cut across to her tower. She jabbed her bag against the card access system and let herself into her apartment, slamming the door shut.

"Hey!" She burst into their bedroom. "What are you doing?"

An open duffle bag lay on the bed, its sides flattening with every item Warren tossed into it.

"I want you gone tonight. I don't want you here." He took another item out of her closet and hurled it into the bag.

"You're crazy. You're actually fucked up, and you act like I'm the one who needs help!" Lillian yelled. "No one cheated on you, Warren! You humiliated us and put your job at risk and now you want me to leave? You leave, dumbass—you on some nut-shit!"

"In case you've forgotten, it's my name on the lease, and I pay the rent," Warren spat.

"Oh, here we go! It took you what, fifteen seconds? What you going to do, Warren, cancel my dependant's pass? Get me deported?" Lillian replied, outraged. "Is that really what you need to feel like a man?"

"I didn't say that!"

"But it's next, isn't it? You're so comfortable controlling every aspect of my life, you think you have a right to me even being here!"

"I control you? I gave you everything and now you're saying I control you?" Warren's voice dropped to a harsh, incredulous whisper. "Your actions brought the police into my life, Lillian! Police!"

"My actions? No, you did that! You broke into my laptop! You made a fool of yourself at that party!" Lillian balked. "I gave up everything for you! I moved across the world, I—"

Warren flung the duffle bag across the room. It clipped her shoulder, stunning her into silence.

"For me? For me, Lil?" he roared, close to breaking down. "You were running away! You wanted me to fix you! But I can't fix you—I can't fix you!"

He pointed at her as he cried the words, gesturing at her abdomen.

Wailing, she charged at him, slapping and kicking and screaming. He grabbed her wrists and pushed her onto the bed, twisting them painfully before moving away. When he was out of view, she collapsed into herself and began to sob.

She didn't fully hear him the first time he spoke again.

"Tell me the truth. Please."

When he begged her a third time, she heard the change in his voice, a strained plea that was unrecognizable to her. She was unrecognizable to herself, lying there clutching the sheets, her face and the linen below her soaked as she sniffed miserably.

How could she confide in him now? How could she verbalize her compulsion to be close to a man she'd barely had a conversation with—that her mind was starting to go wild with theories about why Lani was her father's spitting image, that she was starting to wonder if it wasn't just a genetic fluke but a spiritual connection? It would be irrefutable proof of her mental instability, and she no longer trusted him not to use it against her.

Understanding revealed itself like a slow rip in a piece of cloth, a hole that widened and gaped until the truth slid out. Lillian Parsons was gone. The children she and Warren were meant to have would never be born. The slow death of their marriage was killing her. She needed to face her past, and she couldn't do that holding on to him.

"I don't want you anymore." She stared at the wall, hammering the final nail in. "I don't want this."

When he left and the apartment was noiseless again, Lillian dragged herself off the bed and picked the duffle bag up from the floor. She filled it and started shoving things into another backpack, forcing herself to think methodically. Work clothes, underwear, toothbrush, toothpaste, pajamas, jeans, laptop, chargers: commonplace items for a life in survival mode. The final thing she packed was her envelope of family Polaroids which she grabbed from the shoebox under her bed.

Collecting her handbag from the entrance, she placed all three bags on the sofa and sank down. She had no plan and no idea what to do next, but she couldn't stay here another night. Stretched out before her was the familiar skyline of condos. Their square pockets of light and the fluorescent sign of a hotel filled the nearly 360-degree view she'd once been so proud of, making the black space around her feel even more gloomy. Just a few feet away stood her Steinway piano. It had followed her nearly ten thousand miles and was worth thousands more. It had become a child she resented and loved in equal measure, a step sibling committed to her trust, the only tie left to her parents. Sometimes she wished she could be rid of it for good and with it the weight to make something of her life that her parents would have been proud of. There was so little they'd be proud of now.

Pulling on the backpack, she walked over to the piano and reached between the instrument and the wall. After a few seconds of groping, she felt the plastic sleeve crinkle and took out the deed of ownership, shaking off a years'-old coating of dust.

Outside, she sat on the condo steps and breathed deeply, exhausted. The adrenaline had started to drain away. The fight had been like bursting a pus-filled wound; releasing years of repression had felt satisfying and intoxicating, but now that the numbness was wearing off, all she would be left with soon would be pain.

She took out her phone and toyed with it anxiously. She couldn't sit here forever, and she had no idea when he'd be back. She needed to book a taxi but had no idea where to go. While she was in the center of the city, there were only so many hotels around her, and they would all be expensive, especially the ones closest to her. She could go further afield, but how would she start to choose? Come morning, then what? Her teaching shift started at one in the afternoon, and she'd have to check out of a hotel before that; would she cart her things to work? Did she have the strength to pretend her life hadn't fallen apart? And then where would she go when work was over?

Head in her hands, elbows on her knees, she made herself think clearly, one step at a time. She needed help. Options. Space.

She went into her phone history and returned the last call. Dara picked up on the fourth ring.

"Hi! Lillian?"

"Hi."

"Thanks for calling me back. I hope you don't think I was pestering you."

Lillian said nothing, waiting for more. She needed to feel the girl out before she asked for help.

"Are you OK? When I didn't get a reply...I was just checking you were OK?"

"Why you calling me? You've been hitting up my phone—what do you want?" Lillian demanded.

There was a short silence.

"I wanted to apologize properly. If I hadn't opened my big mouth that night, things wouldn't have escalated."

"What are you talking about?" Lillian frowned, confused.

"What I said about Lani and the book club. I feel responsible for what happened."

"You feel responsible?" Lillian laughed darkly. "Jeez, and I thought I had a guilt complex. Nah. You're not responsible. It was kicking off before you turned up, and it was a long time coming."

"Are you sure? I feel really bad. I wasn't myself that night. I'd been drinking, and I never drink. If anything I said about Lani made things worse..."

"You work with him, don't you?" Lillian remembered suddenly.

"Yes. We work in the same firm."

What had been a vague possibility now became clear.

"I didn't want to intrude," Dara continued. "I just wanted to say I'm sorry and ask if there's anything you need. I can imagine things must be tough. I've never been in—"

"Thank you. Thank you for offering. Actually, I do need some help. I need somewhere to stay."

"Oh..." Dara replied a few seconds later. "Erm, yes. I have a spare room. Tonight?"

"The Crown" had grand aspirations, but instead resembled a crumbling Spanish resort. It was an old building with blue-tinted windows and red-tiled roofs behind the popular Robertson Quay, and Lillian's taxi dropped her beside a busy restaurant.

When Lillian came out of the lift, Dara was waiting by her front door, dressed in loose tie-dye pants and a gray vest. As Lillian lifted an awkward hand hello, she was taken by surprise when Dara reached her arm around her and patted her back.

It was the first gentle human contact she'd had in weeks. Choked up, she struggled to speak.

"I'll show you to your room," Dara said sheepishly, taking one of Lillian's bags.

They walked through the living space. It was small and filled with street noises from the open window.

"It's simple but comfortable." Dara opened the door on the right and switched on the light.

Lillian followed her in and shrugged off her backpack. The room was simple only if Dara meant it was tastefully and impeccably furnished. The bed, which filled most of it, was four-poster, and both bedside tables had glass vases with faux lavender sprigs and reading lamps. There was a suar wood bench with light-brown rivulets running down it by the window, and propped against the wall was an antique flower-patterned mirror.

"Thank you," Lillian said, and she meant it. Dara's room was the answer to a prayer she hadn't dared make.

"You're welcome. It's just sitting here. There's a clean towel in the bathroom. Have you eaten?"

Lillian shook her head. She'd gone to the police station after work and her nerves leading up to it had destroyed her appetite.

"I'll warm something up." Dara closed the door quietly.

The shower was hot and consoling—a comforting end to the night—but the longer Lillian lingered in it, the more she feared her grief would unleash itself. She changed into cotton shorts and a T-shirt, avoiding sitting on the bed. She needed to talk to someone before she could sleep. It was frightening to admit, but she was scared of the nightmares that would inevitably visit her tonight. Just thinking about them was enough to make her queasy.

Dara was waiting at the round dining table, which Lillian now saw was glass and bamboo. There was a table mat, and on it were a banana, a glass of juice and a covered plate.

"Sorry," Dara said, her hands folded around a cup of tea. "I only had leftovers."

The smell was heavenly: flour, cheese and oil. Lillian uncovered the plate and began eating the two slices of pizza before she'd even registered them.

"It's delicious. Thank you." She chewed.

Mercifully, Dara let her eat in peace, rising after a few minutes to reheat her tea in the kitchen. She'd closed the window, so it was quieter than when Lillian first arrived, and she was impressed with the perfect balance Dara had manged to strike between beauty and utility in the room. There was an asymmetrical marble bookcase full of books, a teak sideboard, a small purple sofa. There was no showiness, but the furniture looked well made and had a purpose, as if each piece had ticked a box on her list.

"You like tea, don't you?" Dara asked, returning.

"Yes. Any type is good." Lillian managed to smile and began peeling the banana.

Dara sat down with two steaming mugs of mint tea.

"You must be shattered," she said. "We don't have to talk, you know."

"I don't mind. I feel like I owe you more of an explanation, just turning up like this."

"You don't. You've explained enough."

Lillian drank her tea, glad that she didn't have to relive the police station and the fight.

"Do you have any idea of what you're going to do?" Dara asked tentatively. "Do you just need some space?"

Lillian shook her head. "It's over. There's nothing to go back to. I've got to figure out a plan. Maybe talk to my boss at work tomorrow, see if I can go full-time. And I'll need to look for my own place. Don't worry—I'll be out of here whenever you want. I can go tomorrow, even."

"No, no, I didn't mean that," Dara reassured her. "I'm a lawyer. I thought I might be able to help. You can stay as long as you want."

"Really?" Lillian scrutinized her. "I was hoping just a few days…"

"My room is free. I don't need it. I'm up early and I usually get back late, so you won't be in the way," Dara said. "I can't cook to save my life, so if you want to use the kitchen, it's all yours, and I have a spare key card. It might take a while to find your own apartment."

"You don't need it?"

"Not really. I thought I'd have more guests when I moved in, but no. It's just me."

"OK...I can cook," Lillian offered brightly.

"There you go. You cook and I'll bring home the bacon," Dara cracked.

To her amazement, Lillian found herself laughing, albeit briefly.

"God, I used to think I was so different from the other teachers at my school, especially the full-timers." She pulled her mug closer. "Now, I'm exactly the same, sleeping in someone's spare room, trying to figure out how I'm going to make things work here."

"Is going home an option? Back to the U.S.?"

"I don't know where home is anymore," Lillian replied. "Philly has never truly felt like home, and even if I wanted to, the flight back would cost everything I have right now. I have no idea what to do. I haven't even been teaching that long. I'd probably have to sell my piano if I wanted to go back."

She used a palm to cover her hot tears as they spilled out. Something warm picked up her other hand and squeezed.

Heavy sleep pulled her under and into a dream she knew all too well. She stood on a long, dusty road. She could see the cabin, and even from this far, she could hear the invisible baby crying: hungry, thirsty. Begging to be held.

You're dreaming, she repeated in her head, as if an incantation could ward off the inevitable. Don't run, don't run, don't—run!

The moment she took a step, the road stretched, unending.

Desperation or obligation or instinct—she could never tell—fired her up and she began to run, the crying louder, her tongue so dry she couldn't cry out. She ran until her footsteps and her heartbeat merged into a pounding knock on the door and the nightmarish howl of a tuneless guitar.

Then she was in a boat, the ocean around her, the water the same gray as the sky. The air felt thick enough to touch.

In the blink of an eye, she was drowning. The water shrouding her until it was everywhere. It shot up her nose and surged into her mouth, choking her as she struggled to breathe.

Amaka

Amaka meandered through the grounds of Kike's condo, her mother's voice in her ear. The enclosure was quiet now that the fountains had been switched off, the stillness of this March evening a far cry from the commotion at the party the month before.

"Nne, I expected to hear from you before now. It's been almost one month since you've picked up the phone to call me," Ugo chided gently, using her favorite term of endearment. "If I hadn't called, would I have heard from you?"

"Mummy, I've been texting you." Amaka sat on one of the deck chairs, her phone resting in her palm. "And I responded to your voice notes."

"Is that the same? Don't you know we have many things to discuss? And we agreed when you moved there that you'd call me regularly and let me know you're safe."

"Mummy, I'm safe, it's very safe here," Amaka replied in Igbo.

"Mm-mm, don't tell me that," Ugo shot her down. "Wait until your own child moves to another part of the world and you don't see them, don't hear from them... even now, where are you? Why is it windy?"

"I'm at a friend's place, Mummy, and I'm outside. We have a book club meeting tonight."

"A friend? Nigerian?"

"Yes," Amaka sighed, looking down at the new Hermès "H" slippers she'd bought to match her bag charm. She shuffled them out of view.

Amaka waited as her mother called out to someone in broken English.

"Every morning I have to remind him to switch on the gen. If I text his phone, he'll say he didn't have credit, so he didn't see the message," Ugo tutted. "I don't have the energy to keep walking downstairs to tell him."

"How are your knees?" Amaka listened, concerned.

"Eh, the arthritis is getting better. I found one company making shea butter with ginger."

"Have you been going to your doctor?"

"That one." Ugo blew her lips out derisively. "What can they do? Once the medicine finishes the pain comes back."

"Maybe we can meet in London this summer and try and see someone there."

"*Ada m nwanyi oma*, my beautiful daughter." Ugo's voice brightened. "I know God is speaking to you! That's exactly what was in my mind."

"OK, perfect." Amaka grinned, happy to make her mother smile. "And if we plan early, we could get visas for Dubai, too."

"Ah, there's no need. Really, it's London I want to do. This is what I wanted to talk to you about, and God is confirming it is right."

Amaka laughed. "Confirming what?"

"The house in London." Ugo grew serious. "The Lord has been putting it in my heart to put it on the market. We haven't spoken since the family meeting, Nne, but I've been praying seriously about this."

"Why would we sell the house, Mummy? That makes no sense."

"Chiamaka, you know I would not suggest this lightly, and you know, if it's up to me, I will never give them one kobo, especially that rude and disrespectful boy. But God has called on us to be an example, and Uncle Emeka has confided in me that their mother...Nne, she's very sick. Ovarian cancer. They need the money."

"Uncle Emeka said this?" Amaka spoke after a long silence. "Is he sure?"

"What do you mean?"

"How can he know for sure?"

Ugo drew in a shocked breath. *"Kedu ihe na-ekwu?* What are you saying? You think they will pretend and put a curse on their mother's head just to get the house?"

"I don't know, Mummy, but we shouldn't just take what they say at face value," Amaka said defensively.

"I can't believe what I'm hearing."

"Mummy, you told me not to trust them—I don't trust them. We should do our own investigations."

Ugo made a throaty sound, reluctantly agreeing but disappointed, too.

"I will look into it. If it's true, then we will sell the house and share it with them," her mother decided. "You've been investing the money from the rent, right?"

"I . . . yes, but—" Amaka stammered. The lies were tying her tighter and tighter; at the end of every relationship, a knot of lies cut her off.

"And we have the shares that your father left us. This is what your father would want."

"We know what he wanted," Amaka growled, tears stinging her eyes. "He gave us the house because he owes us!"

Ugo's voice dropped to a whisper. "Chiamaka, where is your compassion?"

"What about them?" Amaka struggled to contain herself. "Where was their compassion when he was alive? They knew I existed at some point before he died. Did any of them ever reach out to us?"

She got up. "I'm sorry, Mummy, I've got to go. I'm already late."

Ugo sniffed, irritated. "You must call me back immediately when you finish."

Amaka locked her phone and crossed her arms, completely thrown by her mother's sudden grace for her half-siblings and confused by the heat bubbling inside her. She'd never been this angry with her mother before. How dare her mother completely change her position when Ugo was one of the main reasons why Amaka had never been able to have a relationship with Chinyere, Ngozi and Ifeoma? Their loyalty to one another was the only absolute they had ever counted on, so much so that Amaka had never been brave enough to push for an explanation as to why Ugo and Chukwu had continued their affair after he'd legally married someone else. It had always been easier to direct anger at Chukwu. If she shared some of her fury between both parents, then she would have to blame Ugo for creating a family with an absent father. Ugo would have to take responsibility for all the times Chukwu was absent, all the times her local government school fees were paid late while Chinyere, Ngozi and Ifeoma went to a British school with the children of politicians and ambassadors. Or was this all Amaka's fault? Was she the reason neither she nor Ugo had been permitted to see Chukwu's body before the casket was closed, or allowed to follow the family procession to the church?

She dried her eyes with a tissue from her bag and resolved not to be swayed by her mother and her inconvenient Christian charity. In a few weeks, some inauspicious sign or disquieting sermon—being gentle as a dove, but wise as a serpent or something—would change Ugo's mind. The best thing Amaka could do was forget the conversation and try to replenish the accounts her mother was circling around as quickly as she could.

The meeting was held on Kike's roof garden. It was the smallest turnout so far, but that hadn't stopped Kike from providing a large spread, the women's favorite item being the candy-colored Janice Wong chocolates that were nestled in paint-splattered boxes. Each woman got a box; only Lillian's sat untouched as she'd cancelled at the last minute. Yemisi and LeToya made a couple of attempts to rekindle some gossip about the American, but gathered in person, there was less enthusiasm for the subject, and Amaka had too much on her mind to care. Voting for their next book went more smoothly this time—*The Bride Test* by Helen Hoang won hands down—and they immediately began to dissect

Americanah. The food, cool breeze and city lights twinkling below kept the meeting going well past midnight.

"I love that Adichie writes about the injustice that's so commonplace in Africa. You really feel for Ifemelu." Nana was on a roll. "Her father losing his job because he wouldn't call his new boss Mummy. I mean, how screwed up is that? People are so narcissistic...and Obinze's mother losing her job because her boss was a total idiot!"

"Ifemelu." Amaka had had to correct the women on the right pronunciation of the Igbo name so many times it had become a running joke.

"That's just the way it is," Yemisi shrugged. "Nigeria has always been that way. The power imbalance goes to people's heads."

"I get that," Nana nodded. "But it's wrong, and I'm glad Adichie shows you that it's wrong. It's not just something we should accept."

"Well, I just think it's sad that Obinze has to suck up to the very kind of people his mother stood up to in order to become successful." Nana tried to draw a line under the debate.

"Yeah, that was shit. But what was even more shit was how her aunt totally depended on that disgusting general who wouldn't give her any money." Kike downed her glass. "And then she settled for that horrible African guy in the U.S. Just so desperate!"

"Why are we so quick to judge her?" Amaka argued. "Why don't we judge the system that eradicated all her choices?"

"Hmm, she made her choice. Did it turn out well?" Kike said sarcastically. "For her or her son?"

"Hunny, it's hard out there!" LeToya boomed. "The woman was a hustler—I liked her. She couldn't find any good men, so she had to take what she could find. Shoot, I get it!"

"What do you mean 'you get it,'" Yemisi teased. "You're happily married!"

"Look, I love Dexter, but hell, men ain't worth shit sometimes. You think, surely each generation gets better, but...Ifemelu had the right idea with that white boy. She should have stuck with him!"

Dara had to say something. "That's a really outdated stereotype.

I've dated more white guys than I have black, and you're not missing anything."

LeToya elbowed Dara. "Don't give me that, girl. I know there's things them white boys do that our brothers don't!"

"Like what? Paint your toenails? You've watched too many films," Yemisi cracked.

"Anyway, I liked the American scenes more than all the African ones and all that religious stuff." LeToya moved things on. "I loved the parts with Curtis—she one hundred percent should-a stuck with him."

"Curtis was fucking boring. Take his money away and he's wallpaper. And are you telling me she couldn't have had that life with a black guy?" Nana protested.

"In the U.S.? Nah!" LeToya rejected. "Not like that. Not without the baggage."

"I didn't like the blog posts..." Yemisi added. "They were too much hard work. I don't want to read essays about racial identity in a novel, ah-ah! Books shouldn't make you have to work that hard."

"Really? I loved them," Dara remarked. "They kept me going."

Amaka teased her quietly. "Oh, you read the book?"

"Yes." Dara looked in Amaka's direction, not quite meeting her eye.

"LeToya, please tell me you don't believe that Curtis and Ifemelu traveling round the world, and him buying her nice things, is a privilege that only comes with dating white men." Nana completely ignored Yemisi and kept her eyes on LeToya.

"I'm just saying it's never that straightforward with brothers. It always comes with something," LeToya argued. "Black guys always got to prove they got it, even when they do got it. There's baggage."

"That is so..." Nana struggled for the word. "Internalized!"

"It's the truth!"

"I'm married to a black guy," Yemisi sniffed. "And luxury really isn't a big deal. Nigerians have always sent their kids to the best schools, traveled widely...it's no biggie."

"Oh, OK, right," LeToya jibed.

"It's true," Yemisi shrugged. "We have."

"Well, I have to say, Nigerians always come off a little arrogant to me, but never mind." LeToya made a face. "You always like, 'My uncle is a prince. My father is a chief.'"

"Maybe they really are royalty!" Yemisi fired back. "We've got lots of royal families."

"Why you got to have lots of royal families? Shouldn't you just have one?" LeToya raised an eyebrow in suspicion. "And why am I always the only American in our meetings? Where's Lillian at when you need her?"

"Lillian's Nigerian, actually." Dara smiled. "She grew up in the U.S., but her parents were Nigerian."

LeToya threw her arms up in surrender and the women laughed.

"Stop fighting it, LeToya—trace your ancestors' roots back and join us!" Yemisi shrieked.

Nana silenced them after a few seconds, her expression serious. "Look, there are a lot of differences between Africans and African Americans that Adichie points out, but most of them are things *other* people use to divide us, like that taxi driver thinking Ifemelu was American because her blouse was tight, and that Bartholomew guy complaining about Nigerian women being 'wild' after being in the U.S. too long. It's really just African men not being able to control you as much over there. But the thing is, there are some really important bonds, too, and not just the bond of struggle. You don't have to scratch that far beneath the surface to see how connected we are through music, art and dance. Even the way we express ourselves.

"The more we stay blind to our connections, the easier it is for us as *women* to allow ourselves to be oppressed and to oppress each other. Adichie calls the way women hold each other back the 'Oppression Olympics,' and she's right. We judge each other, we compete with one another as if black men are the last dodos on earth. Our mothers raise sons to think they're gods and we accept everything men do but question everything *we* do! If we released one another from these impossible standards, we wouldn't put up with half the shit we take from men."

One by one, each woman left, taking her copy of the now-dissected *Americanah*, like rings unlocking from a chain. Dara and Amaka moved down to Kike's kitchen, taking her up on her offer of coffee. Dara, who took Lillian's chocolates, had been cool with Amaka all night, rarely responding directly to her opinions on the novel. It was starting to make Amaka paranoid.

"The tea bags are over here. Coffee pods are in there. Milk, sugar, syrups." Kike cheerfully opened a drawer, then switched on an espresso machine. She took out two glass cups and laid them out. "None for me. I'll just go check on the boys and be right back!"

Amaka turned to Dara. "I'm surprised you found time to read the book." Amaka's comment failed to get a smile out of her friend.

"The library had a copy," Dara said, taking out the bottles of syrup and two spoons. "It's the best thing I've read in a long time. Homer included."

Dara's sarcastic tone cautioned Amaka from joining in on the joke.

"Someone needs to get a social life," Amaka cracked when she was sure Kike was out of earshot. "She's obviously desperate for company."

Dara stuck a pod into the machine and switched it on, standing as Amaka sat down. "I'm sure she could go out every night if she wanted. I think it's great that she cares more about being with her boys than being afraid of missing out. And it must be lonely, raising kids without any family around."

"Can't she just fly them in? Isn't it normal for rich kids like her to have a jet on standby, especially since her father's been sticking his fingers into the state?" Amaka said spikily. "Her father was governor for like eight years. You know he bought them this apartment, right? And do you know how much paintings by that artist go for?"

Dara ignored the canvas of the enormous head. "Amaka, I don't want to bitch about the woman in her own home," Dara said stiffly. "Every governor can't be corrupt."

Dara pressed a button, and the grating noise of the espresso machine cut off the possibility of Amaka replying.

How naive, Amaka thought, as she watched the steady stream of coffee pool in the glass cup. Everyone knew that the children of the rich rationalized their parents' dealings but were quick to condemn others less sophisticated in their schemes. If she heard one hypocritical word come out of Kike's or Bayo's mouths, she wouldn't hold back from giving them a tongue-lashing.

"Kike doesn't hide her father's money," Dara continued after the second cup was done. "I prefer her to people who pretend they've got where they are because of their hard work and act like we're all on the same, level playing field."

"Yeah, I hear you." Amaka squeezed a generous dollop of caramel syrup into her cup and stirred slowly. "So I'm guessing your diabolical plan for the presentation didn't go well?"

"How did you know?" Dara looked appalled. "Did Lani tell Bayo?"

"No, no, I can see it on your face. You wouldn't be so down if it had gone well. I just had a hunch."

"God." Dara sat on a stool. "It was terrible. Totally backfired. Somehow he figured out what I'd planned and deleted my slides, too. I have no idea how he got the password for the interactive screen settings, but I've changed the code on all my devices, just in case. Now he has lunch with Ian every week, and *he* passes information on to *me*, not the other way around! And you don't have to say 'I told you so.'"

"I won't," Amaka assured her, relieved that Lani had stayed true to his word and not said anything about them having sex.

"Amaka, if you had a 'hunch,' why didn't you call? I've barely heard from you the past few weeks, and if you're not biting my head off, you're going dead. It's not on," Dara grumbled. "Things are shit at work and you haven't even sent a text."

"OK, I should have called, but—" Amaka wrestled with conflicting feelings. In all the time they'd been friends, Dara had only asked a few questions about Rohit, and barely any about Amaka's work or family. True, Amaka wasn't the most emotionally expressive or open to intimate conversations, but she knew more about Dara's childhood in Lagos, the mother who'd had her as a teenager and rejected her Nigerian heritage, Dara's years at university and every step of her career struggles than Dara knew about her own background. No matter how Amaka said this, it would come off as defensive and petty. Deep down, she was scared that if she opened up and got a shallow response—which was very possible, given how little Dara really understood about Nigeria—she would flip out and their friendship would never recover.

"I didn't think it was a good idea to focus on the guy too much. It feels like every time we talk, it's all about Lani and work, and I didn't want us to get too obsessed with him," she lied. "I should have called. Anyway, Rohit and I are back together." She pretended to pick dirt from under an acrylic nail.

Dara's face transformed and a genuine smile spread across it. "OK, that *is* good news. You came to your senses. Amaka, the guy is so good for you."

"Yeah, yeah, we'll see," Amaka said coyly, wondering why she felt both shy and a sense of pride at Dara's reaction. In that moment, she couldn't hide the fondness she felt for Rohit. She felt like a schoolgirl admitting her crush was bigger than a crush.

In a recent meeting with Indira, Rohit and the head of their trading desk, Amaka's Toulouse report had been torn apart, and her decision to deny several of the bank's requests to trade with the mining company heavily criticized. Amaka hadn't really needed Rohit to vouch for her, but the way he'd stood up for her made it clear that her problems were his. She'd been unable to keep her hands off him for days and had even let him stay over a few nights. Since then, she'd seen so clearly the solid friendship they'd built— their bond was more than sex and jokes. She'd let herself ease into their sweet playfulness more and had started ignoring Lani's texts. The anticipation of sex with Lani was like a bomb waiting to detonate: an intense, raw and explosive fever. He was the type of cocky bastard she used to lust over from afar: Nigerian boy-men, resplendent in their foreignness with the entitlement that comes with being a well-connected, multiple passport-holder. They descended on the world she'd had to struggle through, lazily consuming the best it had to offer, including its women. Even the way he'd started buying her gifts—three gifts for each time she'd come over—was starting to feel condescending and transactional. Juggling two men was hard work.

"So, what's happening? Is it serious? Wait, is this a little love gift?" Dara touched the little horse charm coyly.

"Um, no, I got that myself." Amaka smoothed her hand over it. "He'd never splash out like that. He's invited me to his sister's wedding in November. I'm actually supposed to be meeting her in a few weeks. She's visiting and we're all meant to hang out."

"She'll love you," Dara nodded, smiling. "If he loves you, she'll love you."

"We'll see." Amaka wanted to believe her and not the cynicism that had become her default. Dara's encouragement was exactly what she needed to open up more. "The other thing is that I may have to start looking for a new job."

"What? You love your job! You're literally the only person I know who does."

"I don't want to, but I need to earn more money," Amaka revealed. "I've been a little heavy with my spending. I need to rein it in, but I also need to make more."

"Is it that bad?"

Amaka made a face and shrugged, not comfortable saying more. "Don't tell anyone."

"Who would I tell? Don't worry. If you ever need help, you know you can just ask."

"No, never. I never mix friends and money. Do you even have money like that?" Amaka quizzed, intrigued.

Dara ticked off a list on her fingers. "I don't have dependents, I don't have a mortgage and I have no sense of style. My money's just sitting in the bank."

"Then you're definitely paying for our taxi home tonight."

There was the sound of a door closing above them.

"Oh yeah, another thing," Dara whispered, rushing her words. "Before you got here, Kike mentioned a Bali trip. She's got some friends visiting and found a great deal on two villas. She said even with her friends, Bayo, her boys and her helper, there'd still be lots of space. We could share a room, or if it's not too expensive and you can afford it, you could have your own, maybe?"

"Bali?" Amaka breathed excitedly. "When?"

"In July," Dara replied, animated. "She said I could have a plus-one, so just be nice to her. Keep the whole 'your father is a thief' thing to a minimum and it should be fine. I've never been away with a big group before. I wouldn't mind trying it once. Now, the downside is he-who-shall-not-be-named will be coming too, but we can just ignore him."

Dara leaned forward. "And I was thinking—it's a long story and I know you'll have lots to say—Lillian's been staying with me for a few weeks, and if she's still around in the summer, we should try and get her to come. I know we all need a holiday, and she's actually really nice, violent husband aside. A little tightly strung, but…"

"Dara, those are two very good reasons to leave the girl in peace," Amaka balked.

"It's fine. She's lovely. She's been really careful not to be a bother. She cooks almost every night and she's just trying to keep her life together. Did you know she was a professional pianist? I googled her and her profile is amazing. Just give her a chance. She's gone through a lot, but she's genuine and real. We could have a great time with her in Bali."

"She sounds like a professional troublemaker, but fine," Amaka said reluctantly.

"Then you'll get on perfectly," Dara teased.

A girls' trip was exactly what Amaka needed to take her mind off her family. She would keep her distance from Lani, and it would give her a chance to observe him and Lillian for herself. And, if she could get through the trip without giving in to him, she would know she'd kicked the habit.

Just as she began to mentally pack her wardrobe, she remembered how hard it was for Nigerians to get visas to Indonesia.

The Westin Hotel was the perfect location to meet Rohit and Sanaa, not just because of its high tea seafood menu (which his older sister apparently loved) or quaint lobby with tartan rugs and over-the-top chandeliers, but because the incredible view from the fortieth floor was an incontestable hit in online reviews. And so Amaka had recommended it and made Saturday brunch reservations. She'd agonized over what to wear, veering between a white sleeveless halterneck, jeans and a vintage Chanel bouclé jacket or a sand-colored double-breasted shift dress that pinned in her waist and would prevent her from eating too much. In the end, she went with Chanel because she knew Sanaa would be operating as their family's eyes and ears. Chanel wasn't even her style—she would always view it as a brand for older, unimaginative aunties—but the second-hand retail price had been too good. She made sure to take the new horse charm off her bag.

By the time Rohit and Sanaa arrived, Amaka had admitted to herself that she cared very deeply about how this meeting went.

"The view is totally ruined by those god-awful ocean liners." Sanaa craned her neck to stare through the glass.

She was dressed down in a black hoodie with the sleeves pushed up, face free of make-up, hair pulled into a ponytail. As she turned, Amaka spied the Alexander Wang initials embossed on the side of her sweatshirt and her Cartier bracelets and smiled. Sanaa wasn't a complete tomboy after all.

"Without those liners, Singapore would be stranded with no supplies." Rohit topped up Amaka's glass with champagne.

"This is the thing about Singapore," Sanaa tutted, selecting her third macaron from the sandwich stand, not looking like she cared about squeezing into wedding outfits in a few months. "It lacks real character. Even when they try to give you this vision of perfection, the commercialism always gets in the way."

Rohit leaned into Amaka. "She does this all the time. When she's home, she complains about Bangkok, and when she's here, she misses home. In India she just bitches all the time."

Amaka laughed, pleased that Rohit was making her feel

included. She also thought it was cute how his accent got stronger around his sister.

"Why did you decide to hold the wedding in Phuket?" Amaka asked.

"Mountain jewel," Rohit winked at her.

"You mean mountain poop," Amaka smirked.

Sanaa raised an eyebrow. "In-jokes already? Have I been usurped?"

"It's just a stupid thing," Amaka said sheepishly. "A silly game."

"And that's not how you pronounce 'usurped,' you mare." Rohit reached over and tugged at the skin of one of Sanaa's elbows.

"Ugh, *Baccha*, you're so annoying!" Sanaa slapped his hand away and they dissolved into giggles, their laughter infecting Amaka too.

Warmth spread across her chest as she watched their playful dynamic. Not only was it sweet and childish, but it also didn't make her feel like an outsider. She started to understand why Rohit had been attracted to her dry humor.

Saana turned back to Amaka. "To answer your question, I have zero control over this wedding. We have family in India but, thankfully, both our families have lived in Thailand for years, so our relatives will come to us. The traditional religious part might be a little stressful..."

"Don't worry, we can just text each other lots of *judgey* stuff about everyone else in the room. Oh wait, you'll be indisposed," Rohit teased.

Sanaa ignored him. "But the Mehndi and Sangeet should be fun."

"So much fun," Rohit reassured his sister, then turned to Amaka. "The women paint their hands with henna at the Mehndi—it's all very nice and proper—but the Sangeet is my favorite. We're all doing dances: the guys, the girls, parents, both sides of the family— it'll be great. My parents hired a professional choreographer."

Glee spread across his face. "Hey, you should learn one of the dances! Sanaa, why doesn't she join the bridesmaids' dance? Ask Chachi to send her the choreography. Chachi is my mother's sister."

Horrified, Amaka grabbed and squeezed his hand. "No, no, no. I don't think so."

"Don't you think it's a great idea?" Rohit asked Sanaa.

His sister looked skeptical. "Maybe she should meet Baba and Ma first."

"Exactly! Chill, Rohit," Amaka spoke lightly, but she hoped he could read the seriousness in her eyes.

"You'll be staying in one of the sea villas, sharing with Rohit's friends," Sanaa said, finishing off the tier of sandwiches.

"So, you've hired the whole of the Marriott? For how many guests?"

"Two hundred and fifty. The entire clan and their dog," Sanaa quipped. "Our grandparents, aunts, uncles, their children, partners and nannies."

The wheels in Amaka's brain turned as she processed two things: Rohit's family was loaded, and it wouldn't be just his parents judging her. It would be his entire family. No matter how well she got on with his sister and friends, could she handle three days of being stared at and evaluated by conservative relatives? There were too many twists and turns in her own messy family to take on Rohit's as well. Plus, with the state of her finances, she shouldn't be paying for flights and the traditional Indian clothes Rohit would want her to wear. Admitting this would mean coming clean about how tight things were with her finances.

"Have you booked your flight?" Rohit interlaced her fingers with his.

"Not yet, but I will." She tried to stay present. "I don't need a visa, so it's very straightforward. But I was going to ask if I could use your visa company to process an Indonesian visa. I've got a Bali trip coming up."

"Bali? Am I invited?" Rohit smiled, squeezing her fingers.

"Um, it's a girls' trip," Amaka lied. Rohit and Lani on the same trip would be a nightmare. "But if I can get the visa, we can definitely go another time."

"Rohit could be a girl," Sanaa offered as she flagged a waiter, "if you asked nicely."

"Ha," Rohit said drolly, but he disentangled his hand from Amaka's to take a sip of champagne.

Although the mood remained light, she noticed that Rohit mostly focused on Sanaa for the rest of brunch.

Dara

Dara strode toward the conference room at the same time as Lani came out of his office. Simultaneously, they made their way down parallel aisles running alongside the secretaries' desks, ignoring each other but headed in the same direction. She picked up her speed, almost losing her balance as she swerved around one of the partitions into the reception area.

"Mr. Erikawa, Mr. Sano." She greeted them warmly as she pushed the glass door open. "It's great to see you again."

Both men bowed and she reciprocated before shaking their hands.

"Ian will be a little late," she explained. "He's just wrapping up a meeting with one of our global heads."

"Ah." Mr. Erikawa brightened, looking over her shoulder. "Mr. Lani."

Dara watched with a tight smile as Lani bowed and greeted them in Japanese.

"It's a pleasure to finally meet you," Lani grinned.

"The pleasure is ours," Mr. Sano replied. "We have been looking forward to discussing the case since you arrived. Your emails have been very illuminating."

"Shall we begin?" Dara was eager to start their final meeting before the preliminary hearing next week, but nobody heard her because Lani spoke at the same time, a long stream of Japanese rolling off his tongue.

"Eh!" Mr. Sano voiced the amazement on Mr. Erikawa's face.

Lani laughed and spoke more Japanese, more confidently this time as he gestured in the direction of the sideboard where a large, steaming French press sat brewing.

"Excellent! This is excellent!" Mr. Erikawa actually clapped, reaching out to shake Lani's hand again.

"*Arigato.*" Lani beamed, looking like he would blush if he could. "I've been taking lessons."

"Amazing," Dara said, deadpan.

"I took a couple of classes in Geneva, then found a place here. So, gentlemen." Lani repeated the long sentence that had so impressed them.

Tickled, the men responded in Japanese, giving what Dara guessed correctly was their drinks preference.

"Two coffees—one black with sugar, one with milk, but no sugar?" Lani repeated carefully.

"Yes, yes, this is correct!"

The men tittered like a couple of geishas.

"I'll get them," Dara offered stiffly. "You make a start."

She ignored his show of modest surprise and overturned the coffee cups. Letting him make the coffees while she steered the meeting wouldn't come across well to the two men, no matter how modern clients liked to pretend they were.

"We thank you for your successful acquisition of the witness statement from Mr. Wachira, the clerk from the Local Housing Office in Nairobi. Do you think this will be a strong piece of evidence for the arbitrator?" Mr. Sano clasped his hands together, while his boss crossed one arm and held the other to his mouth.

"Thank you," Lani replied. "It was a team effort, and it's an excellent result. Mr. Wachira has agreed to testify that the chiefs in Kiambu enjoyed tax benefits only groups affiliated with an arm of the Kenyan government would enjoy, so the next stage is to prep him thoroughly for the tribunal. As a government official, a sworn affidavit from him will go a long way in convincing the panel that there has been a breach of contract, especially since he's taking the risk of losing his job."

Dara offered the clients their coffee and held Mr. Erikawa's gaze. "We need to manage our expectations, though. We still haven't found any paperwork that shows a chain of command connecting the chiefs to the district governor. Until we have that, we can't prove that the chiefs and government are working as one entity to block the bridge construction."

"So, our case does not..." Mr. Erikawa turned to Mr. Sano and said something short in Japanese.

"*Rely,*" Mr. Sano translated.

"Rely on the clerk?"

Lani shot Dara a look, barely disguising his irritation. "The clerk works in the Nairobi Local Housing Office. He's very senior and has been personally vetted by Mr. Ndoku, our lawyer on the ground. His statement is a damning indictment of the government—I wouldn't be surprised if we received a counteroffer after we disclose our documents in the preliminary next week. Ian will go through strategy when he gets here, and we still have four months before the arbitration in August."

"Good." Mr. Erikawa nodded, assuaged. "And then, of course, the hourly rate will increase."

The three men chuckled at the joke and moved to the conference table. Lani glanced back at her, taking in the coffee in her hand and the absence of one for him.

She ignored him and sat down. She still couldn't figure out how he'd logged onto the SMARTboard with her details and fiddled with her slides—the only theory she'd come up with was that Irene had helped him without realizing what he was up to—but she should have anticipated he'd do everything he could to ingratiate himself with Hakida today.

"I know you have lots of questions about the arbitration," she began. "I'd be happy to outline what usually happens over the five days, as well as the two-to-three-month waiting time before an award—the decision—is made—"

"Sorry to interrupt." Irene, Ian's secretary, knocked on the door and poked her head around. "Dara, could I have a quick word?"

"Of course," Dara said after a split-second of going blank. "Excuse me."

She followed Irene into the reception.

"It's the Hakida meeting, Irene," Dara said when they were far away enough for their body language not to be read. "It's been in the diary for weeks. What is it?"

"Ian would like you to do a conflict check on a new case."

"A conflict check? Now?"

"It just came through and he wants you to run it."

"Lucy's in the office. Ask her to do it."

"I'm simply passing on Ian's message." Irene shrugged, bored.

Dara turned to one side, bewildered, and tried to think on her feet without giving too much away. Why was she, a senior associate, being asked to run a basic procedure to see if another lawyer within the firm had already worked with a prospective new client? Even the juniors were trained on this, and there was a conflict team that generated a report that any associate could read. And since when had Ian started giving her orders through his secretary? He had been irritated at the messiness of her last presentation, but she'd convinced him that it had been a technical glitch, so why on earth would he want such an important meeting to go ahead without her?

Without another look at Irene, Dara walked back to her office and shut the door. She stood by the window and stared down at the river, blinking back tears. For months she'd been railing against Lani's hire, his closeness to Ian, his seamless integration into the firm and unacknowledged privileges, but all the time she'd been smarting, a part of her had hung on to the belief that this was a fair race, that despite Ian's obvious preference and Lani's charm, her abilities and skill would speak for themselves in the end.

If this was really happening, then she knew the process well— she'd watched it happen many times, and she'd seen many lawyers burn out, get pushed out or just get cut, some handed terminations in the middle of performance reviews, their stupefied faces later described in detail and added to Morgan Corbett Shaw folklore. First, she'd get cases taken away from her. Then, Lani would be made lead on new ones, and she'd be assigned more menial administrative paperwork below her paygrade. Then out of the blue, one of their clients would express an interest in her coming to work for them on a temporary secondment, which meant that, while you were still technically employed by the firm, the clients were considering making you an offer to join them. Ian would pretend to consider the offer before supporting it fully. Even if she put in minimal effort, the feedback would be positive. When she returned to the firm, there would be a conversation about her low billable hours, and it would be made clear that she now had two options: go in-house with the client or find a new job. Singapore's employment laws were ruthlessly in favor of the employer, so she'd have no choice but to agree.

She would be the new Imran, and her fate would be dissected as entertainment at the next corporate event. It would be a battle she'd already lost.

"Hey." Lucy entered behind her. "Aren't you meant to be with Hakida now?"

Dara honed in on a river boat cutting a white trail in the murky water. Like the characters in the fables and fairy tales her grandfather had loved to read to her, she'd come to the point where she had nothing more to lose; she had to risk the very thing she loved to save it.

"Are you OK?"

Dara sat back at her desk and logged onto her computer. She had no choice but to go to step three: steal another lawyer's client. Burn a bridge to build a new one. The question was who was worth making a new enemy out of?

She opened the firm's online drive of monthly billables for partners and senior associates and picked up a pad and pen. She scrolled through last month's billables and began to make a list.

"Dara," Lucy said warily, standing by her shoulder. "What are you doing? Why are you—"

"Stop!" Dara seethed. "Just stop. Turn around and turn your eyes away."

Lucy recoiled but didn't move. "You know you can't touch those clients. Even if it's a different sector, you're not allowed. Dara, I know the system is skewed against us—the same unspoken inequalities that affect black people affect women too, but—"

Dara swung her chair around. "Honestly, Lucy, shut up. I'm sick of pretending like we're the same. We both know you'll be a senior associate in a year, tops. As long as you play the game, partnership will be a shoo-in for you one day. Hell, you'll probably even make the board if you stick around long enough. Yes, you have to put up with some stupid comments once in a while, but you have no idea what it's like for me, so if you really want to help, back off."

She turned back, ignoring Lucy and what she knew was the hurtful impact of her words, and continued adding names to her list. A few moments later, Lucy went to her desk and began shuffling papers, and Dara began circling the names she could start with.

"If we were sticking together," Lucy's voice was thick with emotion and her face was turned away. "I might tell you to start with Jan at Interscope. I *might* tell you that I overheard him tell Chris at the rugby game that they're looking to expand their shipping operations to Africa, and that he mentioned he grew up in Nigeria. I might also tell you that I have a good guess where they're meeting for lunch next week."

Dara groaned inwardly and sprang up a second before Lucy walked out. "Lucy—"

She hesitated, torn between apologizing for words she'd meant or apologizing for underestimating Lucy's friendship.

"We're not the same, Lucy," she said gently. "We're not."

Lucy nodded, the pinks of her cheeks brick red. "I know that. You're a good lawyer, but you're just as bad as them."

Chico Loco on Amoy Street was heaving. All the plain, square tables and stools inside and on the street were taken with lunchtime eaters. Delivery guys loitered outside, helmets in their hands.

Dara lurked around the corner, trying to stay out of sight. When she got a text alerting her that her order was ready, she took a deep breath and made her way to the front desk. She refused to give in to her nerves; if this backfired, The Sirens would shred her reputation within the firm, so she only had one shot.

"Hi. Number sixty-two." She gave her order number to the guy at the desk.

"Here you go." He held out a brown paper bag with the rotisserie chicken she'd ordered.

"Erm, do you have a toilet I can use?" She grimaced, lowering her voice.

"Yeah, sure. At the back, to the left. I can hold on to this."

She walked into the small restaurant. Above her, fairy lights and thick foliage hung beneath a glass ceiling, and the chefs worked in a gap between a brown tiled wall directly ahead.

Toilet? she mouthed to a waitress, who pointed at the back of the restaurant.

She inched out, scanning the room to confirm which side Chris was sitting on. As she passed his table, she made sure to catch his eye.

Dara raised a hand and nodded *hello*, and although he'd been taken by surprise, he raised a hand back. He was mid-sentence, so the change was enough to make Jan Müller, who was sitting opposite him, turn his head. She smiled, and Jan, a middle-aged white man with sunspots and a receding hairline, smiled back. Taking his friendly, intrigued expression as encouragement, she approached their table.

"How did you get a table?" she quipped incredulously. "I've been waiting for ages. I had to order out in the end."

"Oh, you have to order well in advance," Jan grinned. "Are you new to Singapore?"

"No, Dara's been here quite a few years," Chris practically snarled. "Jan, this is my colleague, Dara."

He gave her a pointed stare: *Go away. Now.*

"Darasimi Coker. Dara for short." She shook Jan's hand. "I work in disputes, and I think I saw you at the rugby match earlier this year."

"Jan Müller, Interscope. Darasimi?" Jan took the bait of her full first name. "Naija?"

"Yes, how did you know?" Dara felt like she was putting on the performance of a lifetime.

"I grew up in Lagos! Moved there when I was five and stayed until two years before university," Jan said. "Best years of my life."

This time Dara's surprise was genuine; the Nigerian tinge in his German accent was more obvious now. "Really? I grew up in Lagos for a bit too."

"My sister, come and sit down, *jor*! Do you know how hard it is to find another Nigerian in Singapore?" Jan cast a look around, but all the stools were taken.

"That's OK, I don't want to interrupt your lunch." Dara backed away. "My order is ready; it was lovely to meet you."

A group of four got up from a nearby table at that exact moment.

"Ah, let's see if we can grab one of the chairs." Jan wriggled round and stopped a young waiter heading to the table with a dishcloth. "Hey man, do you need all those stools? We've got one more joining us."

"Let me check." The waiter caught the eye of the man at the front desk, who held out three fingers. "I think it's OK…yes, it's fine."

"Thanks, man." Jan made room for the waiter to squeeze the stool beside him.

"Thank you." Dara took her place.

"Thanks." Chris managed a stiff smile.

"I think I did see you at the cricket club during the Rugby Sevens," Jan said. "I brought my wife, Kitty, and son, Ayo."

"Kitty's Singaporean, isn't she?" Chris tried to take back some control of the conversation. "I wish I'd known we could bring kids—my boys are crazy about rugby."

"You should bring them to hang out with Ayo—he plays in a touch rugby team at the weekends. We normally spend Sundays with Kitty's parents, so it took forever to get down to the match that day, but Ayo's a rugby nut, so we had to go. You know I gave him a Yoruba name?" Jan turned to Dara, his gray eyes shining. "Ayodele. It's always very entertaining to see people try and guess where it's from."

"I've definitely never met a German with a Nigerian name

before." Dara arched to one side as the waiter set a place for her, clearing Jan and Chris's empty plates.

"Actually, he's Singaporean like his mother, 'officially.' I've got his German passport hidden in a secret cupboard—you know Singaporeans can't be dual citizens. I tried to get him a green one, too, but the Nigerian consulate here just looked at me like I was mad." Jan beamed. "So, Naija for real, eh? Time pass plenty since you see Naija?"

Dara froze. She had some idea of what he'd just said but no idea how to reply.

"*Ah-ahn!*" Jan laughed, incredulously. "You no dey talk pidgin?"

"You mean slang, right?" Chris looked very confused.

Dara tried to think of some excuse, but the truth was that, even living in Lagos as a child, she'd never uttered a word of broken English. Her grandparents would have flogged her if they'd heard pidgin pass her lips.

"You've not been back for a while?" Jan translated.

"No, I haven't been back for...over twenty-five years," Dara calculated. "I used to dream about going back, but most of my close family's gone and I'm not in touch with any extended family over there. I moved to the UK when I was ten. I've spent more of my life there, so it's all I really know. But my grandfather was a lawyer. He's the reason I became one, too."

The words slipped out easily—she was just so comfortable with him.

"Your parents must be proud," Jan joked, turning to Chris to explain. "Nigerians love their children to follow in their footsteps."

"Ah, no lawyers in my family," Chris cracked weakly. "I hope at least one of my boys follows in my footsteps, though."

"But your accent, *dey small, sha,*" Jan smiled at her.

"My accent?"

"You still have a little bit of the accent."

"Really?" she laughed, bemused.

"Listen, anytime you *wan* taste rice and stew, it *dey,*" Jan replied heartily. "My wife cooks *well-well,* but when it comes to Nigerian food, there's no competition in our house."

He brought out his business card.

"Your timing is perfect. Interscope is expanding, mainly to West Africa. It might be right up your alley."

Lightheaded and euphoric, Dara opened her front door to the aroma of tomatoes, onion and garlic, and the sound of tinkering in the kitchen.

"Hi. You cooked!" Dara opened the kitchen door, making Lillian jump, a steaming colander of spaghetti nearly slipping out of her hands.

"*Jeez!* You scared me. Sorry." Lillian looked embarrassed.

"No, I'm sorry—I'm not used to someone else in the kitchen. I should have knocked."

"Please, don't knock in your own house. I'm just naturally jumpy; don't even worry about it."

"OK, no more apologizing," Dara chuckled.

"Done." Lillian smiled back.

"This smells amazing." Dara peered closer. "When you texted about pasta for dinner, I thought you meant opening a jar of sauce. You really didn't have to do all this. Not that I'm complaining," she added quickly. "I'm actually starving, so this is perfect."

As successful as lunch had been, keeping up with Jan's banter while trying to ignore Chris's sulky scowls had left her with very little appetite, and had led to the rotisserie chicken she'd ordered congealing.

"It'll be ready in a few minutes." Lillian tossed the spaghetti into a pot of creamy sauce bubbling on the stove.

"Great. I'll just…freshen up." Dara lingered by the door, feeling clumsy in her own house.

She looked on as Lillian, in a gray T-shirt and running shorts, turned down the heat and began washing up. The question that had been nagging at her for the past week could wait until they were seated.

As she showered and dressed, the elation of the day's success began to wane, and the reality sunk in that she was now hedged between two bona fide enemies in Chris and Lani.

Toughen up. She pulled a T-shirt over her head. *You can't get ahead without making some enemies, so it's either Odysseus or The Sirens. Don't be a pussy.*

And wasn't it ironic, she thought, that her Nigerian heritage, the part of herself she was the least comfortable with, was the very thing that had helped her today?

When she got to the dining table, two places were set, and a serving bowl of creamy mushroom and herb fettuccini waited in the center. Lillian also sat, waiting.

"This looks delicious. Thank you." Dara draped a napkin on her lap.

"Thank you," Lillian replied. "You're in a good mood. Things going well at work?"

Dara smiled and started to twirl some pasta round her fork. "You could say that. I did something a little unorthodox today. I went after another lawyer's client...it's not technically allowed, but I think I've found a way to get around that."

"Right." Lillian looked taken aback. "Is your job very competitive?"

"My God—is the sky blue? Lawyers are like gladiators trying to convince you their hands are empty while they stab you."

Lillian laughed and began to eat. Dara considered telling her about deleting Lani's slides but decided to wait until she got to know her better. Lillian looked markedly more at ease, but as Dara poured water into their glasses, she noticed the American scratching at her left hand. Her wedding ring was gone, taken off a few days after she'd moved in, and the skin from that finger to her wrist was angry and red.

"Is the cream not working?" Dara started eating, trying not to be put off by what she was seeing.

"The doctor changed it to a higher dosage." Lillian switched from scratching to rubbing. "Feel like it's making it worse."

"Do they know what's causing the eczema?"

Lillian put her hand on her lap and picked up her fork. "Maybe the constant change from heat to aircon. Maybe stress."

They ate for a few minutes.

"You taught today, right?" Dara asked.

"Just a few hours in the morning. I'll feel a lot less stressed once my employment pass comes through. I could have continued working on my dependant's pass as Warren's spouse, but I can't sign a lease with that, and if things keep getting nasty...I don't know. I'm just worried I'll wake up one morning and find out he's cancelled my right to stay."

"Of course, that's definitely wise. And the lawyer you found? Did they get back to you?"

Lillian's good humor dipped slightly. She reached for one of Dara's yellow legal pads, which had scribblings all over it, and passed it over for Dara to read.

"I can file here because we've been married more than three years and have lived here just as long. But filing in Singapore means proving unreasonable behavior or adultery, which feels like something from the fifties, and is *not* going to go over well. The only other option is for couples to separate for three years before filing. On the one hand, it would mean putting my life on a giant pause, but on the other it gives me time."

She spoke more firmly. "I know I want to be free, but I don't know if I'm prepared for a full-blown divorce."

"Wouldn't it be easier to file in the U.S.? Then you could rebuild and maybe play music over there?" Dara chose her words carefully, twirling a forkful of pasta. She'd made a point of not prying into Lillian's affairs too much, but now that things were starting to look up for her, she wanted to understand why Lillian was so stuck. "Your options wouldn't be as limited—you could work several jobs if you needed to, or retrain?"

There was the smallest flicker of annoyance on Lillian's face.

"I know you don't get it. I'm sure it's different in England, but Singapore is the first place—really, the only place—where I'm not constantly reminded that I'm black. Yeah, we're expats and we're foreign and everyone assumes I'm American just by looking at me, but no one cares. I'm not one of them, but I'm not anything else, either. I don't know what to do next, but I'm not running back to the U.S. Not without any real family there.

"Plus, this is the first time I haven't had to explain why I'm not playing. Piano was my whole life. When I stopped playing, I had to constantly justify why I didn't want to keep doing this one thing I was so good at, the *only* thing I was ever good at. God, I used to feel guilty if a day passed without practicing. I literally couldn't relax until I played. Now, I'm sleeping in someone else's room, there are zero expectations and it feels amazing. Sorry, I'm ranting."

"No, it's fascinating," Dara reassured her. "I can't imagine being so gifted so young. Most of the time, you hear about pushy parents forcing their kids to do these kinds of things, telling them how 'special' they are, but it sounds like music was a...compulsion for you?"

Lillian nodded and cleared her throat. "Yes. It was. For a time. When I was younger, there was no pressure to perform. None at all. After I graduated, I played for ten years: toured Europe and North America, had art residences all over the U.S. There were some shitty years playing corporate gigs and stuff—that's how I met Warren—but just before we got married, I had interest from an international music agency that tried to sign me. I got that close...but I felt like I was doing it for all the wrong reasons, like I would have been signing away any chance of exploring a life that hadn't already been mapped out for me since childhood.

"I never told Warren that." She laughed mirthlessly and sipped some water.

So many questions hung in the air, but a few too many seconds passed for Dara to feel comfortable probing further.

"If you're worried about me staying here too long, please don't be. You've already been so generous, and I've started looking for flat-shares." Lillian's energy had changed.

"Honestly, Lillian, it's fine. It's not that."

Lillian stared at her questioningly. "But there's something?"

Dara put her fork down—she felt surprisingly nervous bringing this up. She'd begun to enjoy the ease of Lillian's company and the comfortable silences that settled between them. Unlike Amaka, who was usually glued to her phone or hijacking their discussions, barrelling into a tunnel of reality-TV-show references that Dara had no knowledge of, Lillian was always fully present, always listening, always attuned to the sounds around her. With Lillian, Dara didn't feel inferior like she did with Kike, or uptight and boring next to Amaka, or just plain clueless like she did around other black girls.

"We haven't mentioned Lani once, or the fact that he's been taking Japanese lessons at your school." Dara observed her carefully. "Why was your husband so convinced there was something going on?"

Lillian went very still. "Are you asking me if I slept with him?"

"I'm not asking that. I'm asking why you've never mentioned him. I've spent weeks ranting about the guy—you know I can't stand him, you know he's going after my job—so why haven't you said something?"

"I'm sorry, I don't...I was going to, but I didn't want you to think..." Lillian wrestled with her words, then bounded from the table. "Look, it's easier if I just show you."

"What—Lillian." Dara rose, wondering what to do.

Lillian returned and sat back down, her face shining with excitement. She had an envelope in her hands.

"I wanted to be sure," Lillian breathed feverishly. "I've been trying to find a link, something to explain the resemblance. I couldn't tell Warren—I was afraid he'd have me committed or something—but I want to tell you."

She opened the envelope and took out a bundle of Polaroids, choosing one.

"My parents," Lillian stammered, as Dara accepted the photo from her.

It was a prepubescent Lillian, lean and soft-eyed as a fawn, a black couple standing behind her. In the background was a small auditorium, a stage and a piano. From their clothes and the lack of light, it was clearly winter.

"I don't understand. What am I looking at?" Dara searched Lillian's face for a clue.

Lillian had unlocked her phone and was holding up the screen. Lani's corporate headshot, magnified, gloated back at Dara.

"Do you see it? Isn't it nuts? I couldn't believe it when I first met him, but each time I see him, it becomes clearer. Look at my dad. Can you see it?"

Dara stared from photo to phone, trying to find the resemblance, unnerved by the intensity of Lillian's emotions. She wondered for the first time if Amaka might have been right about her underestimating Lillian's true frame of mind.

"Yes, I see it," she lied, mirroring some of Lillian's amazement.

Lillian

"I couldn't believe it the first time he came to SpeakNow! I've been going through every photo I own, and in all of them—especially the ones of my dad when he was young—he looks just like Lani! Or Lani looks just like him."

Dara put the photo down, resting her fingers on the edges. "They look...similar, yes. Do you think you might be related?"

"We might be," Lillian giggled nervously. The idea that she and Lani might share the same genes—that his family's red thread might be tied to hers—was delicious and fantastical and wonderful to hear said out loud, but it wasn't where her mind had gone first.

Dara looked thoughtful. "I once read that sub-Saharan Africa has the widest gene pool in the world. Is it possible that somewhere, hundreds of years ago, you might have been distantly related?"

"Maybe...The only other thing I can think of—and I know this is going to sound completely crazy—is reincarnation. Do you believe in reincarnation? That people you've lost can...*find* you again, somehow?"

From Dara's reaction—two rapid blinks and raised eyebrows—Lillian was sure she'd gone too far. She was officially nuts.

To her surprise, the lawyer's skeptical expression morphed into contemplation.

"Maybe," Dara mused. "My grandfather once told me that he was given his name because he was born not long after *his* father died, and his name means 'Father has returned.' So I know they believed in reincarnation on some level, but I thought people were reincarnated as someone completely different, not as a lookalike."

"But you think it's possible," said Lillian. "And in a different time and place, who would know if they looked the same?"

"I guess so, but in Yoruba culture—and I think in all reincarnation theories—one person has to die before the other person is born. How old…how old were you when your parents died?"

"Eleven." Lillian did the math quickly, trying not to feel deflated.

"And you're thirty-seven, right? The same age as Lani."

"Right…but there has to be—I don't know. I have to look into it some more." Lillian blew her lips out.

"Even if there is a link, Lillian, what difference would it make?" Dara asked, gently. "How is it going to change things? It's not going to fix your problems or help you figure out your next step."

"Maybe it will. Maybe he's the sign I've needed. I can't shake this feeling that this is all happening for a reason—that there's something I'm meant to do, or there's a reason why he's come into my life right now." Lillian's voice dropped to a husky whisper. It was so difficult to get the words out.

"Have you spoken to him at all? Has he said anything?" Dara asked.

Lillian shook her head. She gulped some more water, her hand shaking. After a moment, she felt able to continue.

"I've always been alone. Even when I wasn't alone, I felt alone. I don't need a shrink to tell me why. My parents died when I was a kid. It was a car accident, and it happened so quickly. I went to bed and they were alive; I woke up and they were gone. I still have crazy dreams about what happened to them, but mostly I don't think about it. I try not to think about them."

"I'm so sorry." She could feel Dara's eyes on her.

She had so many doubts about what to do with Warren, with her life, whether to keep trying for a baby or not. If she could *just* find some proof of the link between Lani and Bem, she'd know she was on the right path.

She so desperately wanted to believe there was some way to ask Bem what she was supposed to do.

"So much has changed since I met Lani. I can't explain it—I just see things so differently now. I'm questioning things I used to accept: why I married Warren, why I moved here, why I gave up music. Even the decisions I thought I was making for myself I'm now unsure about. I thought I loved Warren. I wanted a baby so badly. But what if I'm just using them to fill something empty inside? Or is having a baby just what I'm 'supposed' to do? Each time my body failed me, I convinced myself I was being punished for my parents dying, for them going over there that day for me."

She laughed sourly.

"Don't do that," Dara said. "Don't laugh at yourself. Going over where?"

Lillian shook her head. It was too much to get into now.

"But how does Lani help?" Dara looked like she was losing patience. "I mean, no offense, but the guy's a twat. He's a pompous, egotistical shark. I work with him; I know. I'm not saying he doesn't have good qualities, deep, deep, *deep* down somewhere, but you don't really know him. On top of that, he was the catalyst behind your marriage ending. How could he have made such a difference without even trying?"

"When I look at his face, I feel...good," Lillian confessed guiltily. "I can't explain it. I see my dad, and I feel...whole."

Dara exhaled. "That guy is one lucky bastard, I swear."

"Is this going to be a problem?" Lillian put the photos back in the envelope. "With you two at work?"

Dara looked unsure. "I still want to help, and I like having you here...but I'll be honest. I get enough of the guy at the office."

"I promise I won't get stuck on this. I just want to understand the link. If he's family, I want to know without embarrassing myself any more."

"Family's important. I understand that." Dara still looked apprehensive. "But I'm not going to hold back at work. It's me or him for partnership, and I'm going to make sure it's me. As long as you're fine with that, I can help you find out more about him. I can talk to Kike again. I'll try to help, but only if you promise to stay away from him. He's not good for you, and if he knows we're friends, he'll use you to get information about me. I know he will."

Lillian knew it was wrong of her to agree when everything

inside her compelled her to get closer to Lani. She also felt it was wrong of Dara to ask this of her, but she nodded and promised, fearful of losing her one friend and sole source of security.

"Short of doing a DNA test or checking his family tree, how do we look for a link?" Lillian asked shyly.

"Kike will know more about his family," Dara answered. "If he's your father's spirit reincarnated, I have no idea how to verify that, but if you come to Bali this summer..."

Dara drew her words out, teasing Lillian for the answer she'd been waiting on.

"I would love to, Dara, I really would, but I have to start saving..."

Dara interrupted her, holding up a hand. "If you can cover the flight, we can share a room. I'm sure we can get two single beds, and Kike's taken care of all the meals and transfers. There's nothing like getting on a plane and getting away from your problems to give you a fresh perspective. Granted, my fucking problem's coming *with* me, but we can do our own thing while we're there. Your problems will still be waiting for you when you get back."

Lillian put a thumb in her mouth, grinning slowly. "Are you sure? I know you love traveling alone."

"I do, and I've never been one of those girls with a big group of friends. I see pictures of people I know going on all these girls' trips, and on the one hand, it looks like hell, but a part of me has always been curious. I know, if you come, I'll always have someone to disappear with when Amaka doesn't stop talking or Kike makes us all feel like shit about our lives."

Lillian laughed and joined Dara in clearing the table. "OK, thank you. But can I pay you back when I..."

Dara touched her elbow to Lillian's. "No. Shush."

A few weeks later, Lillian met a property agent in the car park of a prospective condo early one Saturday morning. Although she hadn't yet been paid her first full month's salary, and the joint account she shared with Warren was almost empty, she'd decided to explore her options and gauge what her money could get her. Neither she nor Dara had mentioned Lani since—Lillian had to trust that her friend was keeping her word and looking into things. After a few days, his looming shadow had faded somewhat, allowing them to enjoy each other's company more. They'd gone to art exhibitions, started running together and had eaten out several times, including once with Amaka, who Lillian had found crude and a little stuck up. Lillian noticed how much more reserved Dara became in Amaka's presence. She could also see how much Dara liked having Lillian stay, and they both enjoyed unwinding after work with cold bottles of Tiger beer. And yet, Lani was always there, his name unspoken. Lillian felt like some distance from Dara soon might be healthy—hiding her thoughts about him was starting to feel too similar to living with Warren.

"*Aiyoh*, so early," Tan the property agent grumbled as she got out of her car and led the way to the basement lift.

As they made their way up, Lillian paid close attention to her surroundings.

It was a huge condo in the northern province of Yishun, in Singapore's heartland; it was on the border of Malaysia and the furthest she had ever been from the city center. The condo was a mini-village, complete with a supermarket, childcare center, dog grooming service and Indian takeaway. In the online photos, there was a swimming pool so gargantuan it looked like a dinosaur's watery footprint. On the plus side, Yishun was on the same train line as Orchard, and judging by the short bus journey that morning, it would only take her half an hour to get into work every day. The train station looked nothing like the futuristic glass and Perspex porthole in Orchard. It was a throwback to old Singapore: open air, the walls a sickly, classroom green, with red metal frames on the roof criss-crossed overhead. The downside was how many people had stared at her, making her aware of her otherness in a way she hadn't previously felt in Singapore.

"I already have two more viewings scheduled today, so you

better sign now. With your budget, I don't have many properties for you." The agent had the keys ready and headed for the middle unit when the lift doors opened.

The apartment door had a metal, gate-like frame in front of it, but no shoes or doormat outside. The unit on the left was decorated with Chinese urns, a Persian rug, and a weathered chest, presumably for the owners to sit on when taking off their shoes. The unit on the right was a tornado of rubber shoes, kids' bicycles and scooters.

"The tenants are probably still sleeping." Agent Tan let them in to the narrow entranceway.

"Sure," Lillian whispered, closing the door quietly.

As she entered the apartment, she recoiled in horror. The living room floor was covered in boxes, plastic trays and rolled-up carpets. The boxes were piled on top of one another, stacked on wooden stools, and underneath were large bags and bursting bin liners. A ladder had been propped against the wall and a plywood bookcase was crammed with crap that looked like it'd come from a second-hand shop: porcelain figurines, tarnished bronze figures, glasses of all sizes.

"The landlady lives in Malaysia. She'll be clearing out her things soon," Agent Tan said in response to Lillian's reaction.

The only cleared space was a black sofa, which had a T-shirt tossed over it, a widescreen TV mounted on the wall and the dining table, where there were two empty plates streaked with dried, yellow sauce, a cold cup of herbal tea and a side plate with cigarette ends. A rancid whiff of rubbish left out too long curled under Lillian's nose.

"The other people living here never clean up." The agent sniffed and cleared some space on the table. "Maybe no time."

"Even if they didn't know I was coming, they shouldn't leave the place like this." Lillian was shocked at how unconcerned the agent was.

"You talk to them—I'm sure they'll agree to house rules. Let me show you the room. It's currently empty."

Reluctantly, Lillian followed her. She thought she could handle living in a shared accommodation, but the reality of rooming with strangers on her tiny budget was beginning to dawn on her. Before she'd got married, she'd lived with other musicians over the years and had slept on friends' sofas a couple of times, but this was different. This was a one-year lease, and once she handed over the rent and deposit, most of her first month's teaching salary would be gone.

The room was tiny and devoid of character. Bed, wardrobe, desk, chair, window. There was a "brand-new" smell of rubber and plastic.

"North-facing, very lucky. You get good breeze because you're high up. Not too much sun."

The agent drew the curtains open and unhooked the window latch, but the damage was already done. The gloominess of the stark room took her back to the silence of her childhood bedroom in Philadelphia, resembled too closely the gray void of her dreams. The thought of waking up here every morning, shaking off visions of water and howling babies...

"I'm sorry, no." She stumbled for the door. "This isn't what I'm looking for at all. This isn't... no. Sorry."

"*Aiyoh*," the agent said, peeved. "At least take a look at the facilities. I can show you on the way to the car park."

"OK, but I know it's not right for me," Lillian said firmly.

She let herself be led back down to the ground floor and out of the building, following the agent up a small flight of steps along the side of a smaller annex. As they reached the top, they walked into a chorus of sound she could only call childhood.

On a flat, tiled playground, children jumped and flipped on a trampoline, zipped and weaved around on scooters; in little pockets, they skipped and twirled inside hula hoops; some played football, others raced down slides; smaller toddlers pushed dolls in mini strollers. Their parents and helpers watched on from the sides. Lillian stared too at the little babies in their strollers, mouths half-open and frozen in sleep.

Over the next week, Lillian felt a dark cloud spread over her. The realization that she was stuck, broke and unable to afford even the most basic level of living ate at her until it sapped all her energy. Returning to Dara's from work, she started to go straight to bed, sleeping through dinner and struggling to sit up despite sleeping nearly ten hours straight. The eczema on her ring finger had worsened, and it was impossible to get out of bed without rubbing and tugging on her scalp.

The following Saturday, she woke, gripped by a palpable thirst and a sadness as deep and visceral as it was unseen. Before she'd got out of bed, she knew she would break her promise to Dara about staying away from Lani. Her morning had started with a dream. She was in a church hall, her parents' hands resting on her shoulders. A camera flashed, blinding her, and when she blinked the lights away, she looked up at her mother. Yahimba smiled down. She refused to look at Bem, feeling and knowing that something was wrong. Bem crouched down beside her. Wherever she turned, fingers covering her eyes, his face followed her. Finally, she peeked and cried out at his eyeless, mouthless face.

She walked to work from Dara's place in Robertson Quay. As she crossed at the traffic lights, her eyes fell on the migrant workers in a makeshift building zone in the middle of the road. Red and white piping lined the area, like bunting in a fairground. In jeans, T-shirts and protective yellow helmets, they clasped their fingers together in rows and stretched down to touch their toes. They moved in unison, following the lead of the foreman at the front. They continued their stretching routine, the giant excavators and loaders waiting patiently behind them. Like her, they were far from home and on borrowed time, welcome only so long as they served a purpose. She thought of the families they'd sacrificed time with to make a living in Singapore dollars, thought of the hostels she'd read they were crammed in, and how tightly their lives were controlled. With shame, she remembered the way she used to recoil when the open vans they sat in the back of drove by.

When she got to work, her mood sank into full gloom. In

the staffroom, tensions between Marigold and Joe, one of the Canadian teachers, had erupted.

A short white guy with a buzz cut, Joe drew the room's attention as he stuffed his things into a canvas bag and slung it across his body.

"Un-fucking believable!" he seethed, his movements swift and hard.

"Kindly vacate the premises in a calm manner, Joe, or I will call security." Marigold stood to his left, her hands clasped in front of her.

"Vacate, my ass!" Joe shot her the middle finger. "This school is a joke. Everyone—get out while you can."

He stomped out of the room and, as if responding to a punchline, Marigold opened her arms and smiled at the watching room.

"My apologies, everyone. Please get ready for your next class. Break is over." Like a traffic warden, she waved the teachers away.

"Did you know they're letting teachers go?" one of the Mandarin teachers whispered to Lillian as she took a stereo player from the box of equipment. "They didn't get enough students for the summer school. I've started looking for a new job already."

With each ticking hour of her shift, Lani's Japanese lesson grew closer. All she wanted to do was to speak to him and apologize for the barbecue. If she could make it clear that she'd wholeheartedly denied any wrongdoing on his part, and explain that she and Warren had separated, maybe it would put them on a good footing, and she could start asking questions about his family and background, questions that could help her solve this puzzle.

She paced around her classroom, deserting one resting place after a few minutes and scratching absent-mindedly at her now-bare wedding finger. Her Elementary 4A class worked in groups of three, their chairs bunched together, creating rules for an imaginary company using the words *should, must* and *need to*. She paused by three of the girls and forced herself to pay attention.

"You must have nice dress," Irina dictated, tossing her long curtain of hair over her bare shoulder. Today's outfit was a flamenco number, and her stack of tennis bracelets had doubled.

Miki, in her usual black lace cardigan and white pearls, giggled, but Even, tomboyish in khaki-green dungarees, wrote down the sentence seriously on their group worksheet. Lillian noticed she spelled the word "nice" with an "s," but couldn't care enough today to correct her.

"In my company, we must..." Miki struggled to complete the sentence.

"Work hard?" Even enunciated carefully.

"Yah, of course." Irina was unimpressed with such a boring rule.

"We must make-up," Miki tried again, miming a mascara tube near her eyes.

"Ah yes, yes." Irina now nodded enthusiastically.

"Must or should?" Even looked up from the sheet.

"What's difference?" Irina asked Lillian.

"Hmm?" Lillian brought her mind back to the room.

"'Must and should.' You should wear make-up work...you must wear make-up?" Irina's manicured hands lifted each phrase.

"No difference," Lillian answered. "You can choose."

The bell shrieked to signal the end of the lesson and the end of the day.

"Eh? But we don't practice!" Irina looked indignantly at the clock before frowning at Lillian.

"Next time." Lillian closed the laptop on her desk. "Can you put the chairs back, please?"

The rest of the class began collecting their things. A few of the Japanese men tittered nervously at Irina's outburst.

"But next time we do something new," Irina confronted Lillian, moving closer. "We don't practice today."

"We'll practice more next time, don't worry." Lillian switched off the interactive white board.

When she turned back, Irina was still standing there, her whole being charged with disgruntlement.

"We pay money for this class, but we don't do all the English," she complained. "We practice very small and then the class finished?"

"It takes time to learn a new language. Sometimes you work more on writing, sometimes more on speaking." Lillian parroted her usual excuse.

Irina huffed and grabbed her things. Lillian realized the girl had real grounds for complaint and could endanger her job, especially if she flounced out of there and caught Marigold on a bad day.

"You know what, Irina, you're right. You need more speaking practice, but there's no time in the lesson. Would you be interested in one-to-one lessons outside of school?" The words rushed out before she could censor them.

Irina's face transformed. "Yes! Yes, I want this!"

"OK, great! Let me give you my number and we can arrange it. But we have to meet in a café because I'm not really supposed to…"

"Thank you! I'm telling my boyfriend I need this. He need to stop be so cheap." Irina was playful now, tapping and sliding open her mobile in its fluffy-pink case.

Fuck it. She entered her number into Irina's contacts. Working outside the school was breaking the terms of her contract, but she was done following everyone's rules, making herself small and quiet and *good*. Where had that got her?

"And if you know anyone else who wants private lessons…"

This time, she would make as much as she could, take as much as she could and figure out the next step *her* way.

Emerald Hill, a short, narrow road feeding into Orchard Road, was full of street bars. A stone's throw away from the school, it was perfect for an unplanned, coincidental meeting. It was the shortest route from the school to the main road, but the establishments were too expensive for most of the SpeakNow! teachers, which meant Lillian could hide in plain sight waiting for Lani's lesson to end. Most of the bar stools and wooden barrel tables were taken, so she'd been lucky to get one outdoors on a Saturday night.

She took her time drinking her second Singapore Sling, chosen chiefly so the cherries would stave off her hunger. One of the bartenders, seeing how much she liked the drink, had given her a brief history of the pink cocktail, and Lillian had chuckled when she learned it was created in 1914 to help Englishwomen conceal how much gin they were drinking—but her mirth had dried up when she spotted Lani at the top of the hill.

She put the exact amount for the bill on the counter and leaped out of her seat. The words she'd planned vanished.

Just as Lani strolled past her, his eyes on his phone, she reached out to touch his arm, gently grazing the sleeve of his shirt. Oblivious, he carried on.

The street was teeming, thick with night-time tourists. In front of the malls, sales assistants tried to give her flyers for discount designer sales and nearby jewelry boutiques. She ignored them and cut between people as quickly as she could without crashing into them. Her heart beat hard as she searched for him. Giant billboards lasered adverts of beaming girls dancing on a beach in fringed bikinis, and the clamorous clatter of a legion of birds rained down from the trees; a wiry old man with skin as hard and tanned as dried leather hula-hooped a rope of heavy wooden beads around his neck and waist, the rest of the beads a family of sleeping snakes at his feet.

A mass of people split off to cross the road—and then suddenly there he was, crossing with them.

She made it just before the lights changed, then slowed down, keeping him in view but at a safe distance. She followed him down into Dhoby Ghaut MRT station.

They changed trains once, resurfacing in Tiong Bahru. She hung back as his pace slowed and he approached a low, white building.

When he entered the winery next to it, she waited in the shadow of a closed-up shop across the road.

After about five minutes, he came out again with a bottle of wine, a girl walking beside him.

Amaka.

Lillian stepped into the street, pulled forward by a feverish loathing for the girl as she watched Lani buzz them into the building. Through the glass door, she watched Lani go up the stairs, Amaka behind him.

A car horn blared to her right and shot past, just missing her. As she pulled herself upright, heart racing, she locked eyes with Amaka.

Dara

White foam bubbled on the powdered sand as waves tumbled down. Near the shore, hundreds of swimmers bobbed in the green ocean while, in the distance, a concertina of boats and jet skis droned; paddlers and surfers braved the choppy waters. Against the lush, leafy canvas of mountain and dense jungle, families walked barefoot, their children on their backs, mouths sticky and dry. Suspended hang-gliders swooped and rustled, coloring the sky; distant bells jingled against the flank of tourist-bearing horses. The latest pop songs from beachfront restaurants swallowed-up snippets of sound. It was day two of the four-day Bali weekend, and Dara lounged on a deck chair, listening to the audio version of *The Bride Test*, enjoying a blissful hour of solitude.

Eyes closed, stretched out lazily in a bikini, she chuckled at the scene playing out in the novel as Khai, an attractive but emotionally numb techie, became frustrated at the earnest, sexy young woman who had moved into his house. From the first scene, when Khai's mother had enlisted Esme, a single mother and bathroom attendant in Ho Chi Minh, to marry her autistic son, to the scenes of Esme besieging him with fruit and inducing early-morning boners, Dara had found herself crying with laughter one minute and becoming aroused the next. She couldn't wait to dissect this one with the book club. Even though she'd been to Vietnam twice before, she immediately began to plan her next trip, dreaming of egg coffee with condensed milk, hot Bahn Mi bread rolls with pâté, and steaming bowls of rice noodles and beef broth. There was nothing like landing a great deal in a boutique hotel in the center of town, renting a bike and exploring local spots recommended for solo female travelers. The fact that she and Lani had been put in the same bloody villa made her itch for real time off even more.

She glanced behind the row of deck chairs, satisfied that Kike's children and nanny would be in the hotel's kids club a while longer. Their party of seven adults and two kids had booked the three chairs to her left and the two to her right, and Dara, who was intent to do as little as possible on this holiday, had been left with the job of watching everyone's stuff. Somewhere on the horizon, Lani, Bayo and Bayo's friend, Tokunbo, were on jet skis, while Tokunbo's wife, Saffy and Kike were having a surf lesson at a calmer end of the beach. So far, Dara had failed to get Kike on her own long enough to ask more questions about Lani's family. She felt awkward asking about him after the warning Kike had given her, but nonetheless, she was armed with more facts from Lillian's history; she now knew the dates her parents had moved to the U.S., her mother's maiden name and the year her parents had died. Accessing this knowledge had not come without strain— Lillian still couldn't speak about her parents without difficulty and talking about how they died was completely off limits. Sometimes the American was completely closed off; at other times, Dara saw the real Lillian—humming a piece of music as she cooked, her twist-outs framing her slender head, making her appear freer and looser. They'd play a game where Lillian had to guess the composers of different movie scores and she'd got every single one right, some after only three notes. Dara kept finding sheet music scribbled on the back of envelopes, as though Lillian was trying to recall something playing in her mind.

Feeling sleepy, Dara took her earphones out. She considered ordering another lychee martini but decided against it. There was no telling how expensive this four-day break would be, and it was still only day two. She was naturally frugal, and on past trips to Bali, she'd usually eaten at local, family-run *warungs* and hired local taxis, especially when she'd traveled around the lesser-known islands, but as soon as she'd arrived last night, heading straight to the airport from work, it was clear this would be a costly trip. Despite Kike's assurance that the two three-bedroom luxury villas were a "great deal," Dara's share for rooming alone in July's high season was more than she'd paid on her last trip to Seminyak. She was still waiting to hear if Amaka's visa had come through, but if not, then she and Lani would have to split the cost of the villa two ways instead of three.

She dozed off against the blend of wind, waves and engines, and was gently summoned back to consciousness by a shadow blocking the sun.

"Hey, sorry to bother you." A white guy in his thirties stood nearby. He was dressed in shorts, with sunglasses tucked into the front of his black T-shirt.

"They're all taken, sorry." Dara sat up.

"I was going to ask if you needed help guarding all this, actually." He gestured at the heap of bags, towels, hats and flip-flops. "Bali's pretty safe, but you never know."

"Thank you," she said, surprised. "But I'll be fine."

"I'm Adam." He held out his hand.

"Lucy." She shook it, accustomed to over-friendly strangers when traveling on her own.

"That's not your real name, is it?" He grinned.

"Nope," she chuckled.

"OK, Lucy. You're British?"

"Yes. You're Australian?"

"Kiwi. Common mistake. We're over from Wellington on our winter break. We teach at the same school. It's a long way from England. Is this a special occasion?" he asked.

She raised her eyebrows. "You're very inquisitive."

"Sorry, just making small talk."

"Too bad. I thought you were flirting with me."

Was she actually enjoying herself?

"Trying to." His face had started to turn pink.

She had to give the guy a break. "I live in Singapore. I'm here with friends."

"Ah, cool. And you're a...?"

"Lawyer."

A waiter approached, a tray in hand.

"Lychee martini?" The waiter replaced the empty glass on the little table next to Dara.

"He was meant to bring that after I left," Adam laughed, scratching the back of his neck.

"Oh. Thank you." She laughed too. Whatever the opposite of smooth was, this guy was it.

"My friends and I are staying here at the hotel. If you and your friends are interested, they play really great music in the evenings, if you like to dance."

"I'm a terrible dancer."

"Great, me too. Anyway, if you and your friends are around..." He took a step back. "Enjoy your martini."

"You, too. I mean, thank you." Dara cringed. He didn't have a martini.

"Nice to meet you, Lucy."

"Dara."

"Dara," Adam repeated, to make sure he'd got it right. He nodded and smiled goodbye.

He walked back to his table of friends, who had been watching and looked extremely amused. Dara turned her face away to hide her smile. Bloody hell, she thought *she* was awkward. Not only was he sweet and cute, he was completely rubbish at chatting her up, which made it even more endearing that he'd tried.

She heard the approaching racket of Kike's boys and gathered her things as quickly as she could. She pulled her kaftan over her head, flung her beach bag over her shoulder and put on her floppy hat. The boys had been noisy, brattish monsters this morning, melting down over every rule Kike had tried to set. Dara had heard them late last night from across the villa, and it was apparent that Annie was struggling without a clear routine, caught between Kike and Bayo's inability to agree on anything.

Traffic crawled down the streets of Seminyak, two lanes of slow-moving cars vying for space, competitively tooting their horns. Dara walked along the street, navigating the narrow curbs and the motorcycles parked outside spas, cafés, clinics, supermarkets, pharmacies, banks and money changers. The road widened into a busy crossroad, each intersection crisscrossed with overhead power lines, nightclubs and bars on every corner. She loved walking down these dirt paths, dropping into whichever shop took her fancy to pick up snacks, artwork and magazines, but most of all she loved how manageable the dry heat was compared to Singapore's clammy humidity. Without the pressure of going into the office, her long limbs felt looser and more at ease.

She had no idea what time it was; it might have been two o'clock or it might have been five. Another day in Seminyak and she'd forget the date. For the first time in months, she felt like her old self. Things were starting to look up at work; a few weeks after the meeting with Jan Müller, Interscope had instructed her on a new case. Of course, Ian, as senior partner, was taking lead, but not only did the Interscope work help distract her from the sting of being demoted on Hakida, but a second German client, recommended by Jan, had emailed needing urgent work done on a case that was sure to go to arbitration. In the space of a week, she'd brought in two solid cases with legs—more than Lani had, despite his shiny credentials. Miraculously, her gamble had paid off, and the tide had begun to turn in her favor. It hadn't solved the problem of how to get rid of Lani, but it had helped increase the value of her stock. The only backlash so far was being iced out by The Sirens. Ultimately, she'd got away with bending the rules because she was helping Interscope with a different area of law than that practiced by Chris's team, and they were all, supposedly, meant to be on the same side. The old Dara would have been content to focus on bringing her A-game, but she knew better now. Her best chance was bringing in new clients *and* keeping an eagle eye out for a chance to exploit any flaws in Lani's work. With the end of the year approaching, the senior partners would be finalizing their promotion candidates by the following April, the start of the new tax year, and Ian would be coming up on another birthday. Time was running out, but for the first time, she felt like she could park things to one side and take a well-deserved rest.

Dara toyed with her phone as she turned off the main road. She was torn between texting Amaka and letting things be. Getting a visa had always been a longshot, but the news that the Indonesian embassy still hadn't confirmed was disappointing. The last thing she wanted to do was rub Bali in Amaka's face, especially since the excitement of the trip had helped smooth over some of the friction between them, but the planner in her wanted to prepare herself if Amaka *was* coming. Now that things were improving, there was so much she wanted to share with Amaka, and this trip would have been the perfect time to get closer again. They'd both taken today—Friday—off, and she'd been looking forward to a full day of bitching and ribbing before Lillian arrived tomorrow night. Now, it was just her and Lani avoiding each other. With a twinge of sadness, Dara had to admit that the past few months had been much calmer, since she and Amaka had been interacting less. She missed her friend, but not how Amaka had been making her feel lately.

A short while later, Two Tree Villas came into view. The bamboo gate rolled open and she walked through, placing her palms together and bowing in greeting to Kadek, their Indonesian hostess. Dara walked down the stone slab path, past the gym and Villa One, where the Ibusuns were staying, to her residence, Villa Two. Beside the villa was a rectangular pool surrounded by lotus ponds and trimmed trees, with a large water feature running down the side of the compound wall. Cushioned chairs faced the pool, looking on to an open-air living space with wicker chairs. A larger, longer path led to a shaded breakfast patio. It was designed as an island to adjoin both villas, and it housed not only a long wooden dining table, but also a grand piano, placed there, Dara guessed, for party performances. A scattering of stone buddhas and giant urns completed the effect of an Elysium of tranquility.

The doors of the two ground-floor bedrooms—Lani's and the room being held for Amaka—were wide open, both being aired.

Between the two rooms, short stairs led to the single bedroom on the top floor; Dara skipped up the stairs and entered the bedroom. She showered and took a nap, enjoying a sweet, energizing sleep until Kadek's gentle but persistent knock woke her. She tied a sarong around her neck and went down to the pool deck, where a Javanese masseur had a massage table, oils and batik cloths set up in a shaded corner. The smell of the frangipani oil and the rhythmic swish of the water feature knocked her out again, so she experienced a trance-like nothingness that only lifted with the masseur's firm, final tap of her shoulder.

"Thank you," Dara smiled lazily, sitting up to touch her palms. She made the decision there and then to go back to the hotel the Kiwi had mentioned when Lillian arrived. Flirting on holiday with complete strangers was exactly what her friend needed, especially since she'd been working almost as much as Dara recently. All the girls, married or not, needed a little fun.

She retied her sarong and paid the masseur in rupees, half-listening to the sounds of Villa One stirring.

Thank God they have their own pool. She looped around to the villa and stopped short. Her heart sank.

Sitting on a wicker chair, legs crossed on top of the low table, was Lani. He was staring at a laptop on his knees, dressed in a Rolling Stones T-shirt and linen trousers. The intense vision she'd had of him six months ago at the rugby game returned, but now, the smug triumph had been replaced with a frown and air of exasperation that she had begun to see more and more in the office. He looked up before she could back away.

"Hey." His frown was swiftly replaced with a smile. "Good massage?"

"Yes, thanks." She slowed down.

"Just trying to catch up on a few things." He closed the laptop and put it aside. "I've been meaning to say congratulations, properly, about the Interscope case. Looks like it's really going to turn into something."

"Thank you," she replied archly, her hand resting on the chair opposite him. She hated to admit it, but the man was not unpleasant to look at. He was like a real-life Ken doll. As he shifted, his shirt slipped to one side, revealing the skin above his groin. It was all a bit much.

"Congratulations to you on the recent Lagos case. I guess some connections came through." The massage was making her feel uncharacteristically generous.

"You could say that." He looked a little bemused. "I've worked with the firm in the past."

"Really? Not some pals of yours?"

He took her in, picking up on the spikiness in her tone.

"What are you talking about?"

"Just, you know, you seem to have really good connections." She smirked, then looked around. "It's a beautiful place, isn't it? Have you been to Bali before?"

"First time."

"I love it here. The office feels a million miles away, if you can leave it behind." She nodded at his laptop.

"Sit." He waved at the chair.

It was inevitable, she supposed, that they would face each other without all the polite bullshit they'd been using at the office to dance around the truth. At least, by *really* speaking to him once, she could tell Lillian that she'd tried and it would be the truth.

So she sat.

"You know, you're not what I expected." He broke the silence first. "When I looked you up and saw your CV and the cases you'd worked on, I thought you'd be just like the girls I went to Cambridge with. Or at least someone like Kike."

Spoilt and entitled?

She must have unknowingly used sign language because he chuckled at her expression.

"No, I don't mean that. I mean...capable of saying one thing and doing another. Someone who smiles to your face but really hates your guts."

"Well, Kike *does* hate your guts, so she's probably had lots of practice."

Lani threw his head back and three deep rumbles of laughter

burst out. To her annoyance, she found herself struggling not to smile—it was that type of laugh.

"This is what I mean," he said. "You say what you mean, or you don't say anything at all. Working here is very different from my last firm, that's for sure."

Isn't Geneva full of pretentious twats? You should feel right at home.

"Geneva was ice-cold," he continued, "and I'm not just talking about the weather. Here, no one pretends they're not ambitious or competitive or threatened by you. Maybe you're all just too busy coping with the heat to pretend."

"I'm not threatened by you, for the record."

"Noted. So why don't *you* just do your best work, *I'll* do my best work, and we'll let the work speak for itself?"

She wanted to boil a thousand cups of his Kenyan coffee and throw them in his face. If doing her best work was enough, he wouldn't be here with his stupid African contacts and his back-scratching uncles in high places. He was like those Nigerian men in *Americanah*: the charming face of a rotten system. Somewhere along the chain holding him up was a corrupt general and a megalomaniac who insisted he call her *Mummy*.

"What?" His smile waned when she didn't respond.

"I *have* been doing my best work. For six years. Work I was doing before you got here and my job was split in two. What did you expect? That I would welcome you with open arms? That I'd be happy my entire future had been knocked off course because you were black?"

"What did you expect from *me?*" Lani folded his arms. "Was I supposed to not take this job because *you* were black?"

"You should have been honest. Direct. 'Yeah, I know this is shit for you and it's not what you expected. I'm not here to step on your toes.' Something like that. Instead, you came all slick and sly, buddying up to everyone like you were the answer to our prayers."

"Wow. And *you* were honest? And direct?" he challenged.

She turned away, rattled momentarily, but recomposed herself.

"OK, yes. I was sneaky, but I did what I had to do..."

"As did I."

He held her eyes. She was thrown by the honesty there and the flash of, what, *vulnerability?* Needing to guard herself, she mirrored his folded arms and crossed her legs. It worked—he leaned back, and a stiff silence fell.

A child's howl broke the stalemate.

"Well, it could be worse than sharing a villa." Lani made a wry face. "We could be sharing with Kike's boys."

The crying intensified in pitch and volume.

"Her boys? No, they're angels," Dara deadpanned.

Lani smiled. "I found Timini in my room yesterday—I have no idea how he got there."

"Which one's Timini?" Dara frowned.

"The older one. Tife's the baby. Anyway, the destruction the little beast caused in the short amount of time he was in there was pretty impressive. I promised not to tell Kike—think I've got a friend for life now."

"Kike's definitely getting fed up with them." Dara nodded, bemused.

"I've got a five-year-old niece who's a handful, but nothing like those boys. She's practically a rocket scientist compared to them."

"Girls are generally brighter and more precocious than boys."

"You mean at that age?"

"At every age," Dara retorted, and he laughed. The man was indestructible; no matter how much hostility she threw at him, he transferred the negative energy and sloughed it off. It was actually...impressive somehow. He must also have had a gift for reading other people's energy, because suddenly his elbows were on his knees, his eyes boring into hers.

"Look," he said. "There are conferences all over Africa—Mauritius, Nigeria, South Africa—conferences that Ian doesn't bother going to because he's got a fat Asian practice and he doesn't need to. We could go together, get new clients for him. I'm talking about oil, commodities, shipping across different industries. We network and market together, widen the pool. So, when new disputes come up, we've got a chance. Ian gets new clients, and we get our names out there. If we work as a team," he exhaled at the possibilities. "We're selling the Nigeria angle, the London angle, the Singapore angle. There's one in Lagos coming up soon, actually."

"You want me to market with you? Why?" she asked, her curiosity fully stirred.

"I do. You're a fantastic lawyer. I get why you don't like me, but the advantages I've been given are on a par with those of most white lawyers in my position. I respect you, I respect how hard you've worked, and I want to work *with* you."

Thinking hard, Dara tried to look nonchalant. She shuffled in the chair and drummed her fingers against her arm. Talking to Jan about the Lagos of her childhood was one thing; returning there as an adult for work made her nervous. An African was the first thing people saw when they looked at her, but every interaction she'd ever had with a Nigerian—or African—had confirmed how un-African she was. The thought of returning with Lani, who would show her up without even trying, was too much.

"We both know that Ian's decision isn't going to come down to who bills the most hours, or who does the best work, but who can bring in fresh meat," she hedged.

"And we have the best chance of bringing that in together. Think about it." Lani's face shone with excitement.

For a second, she was drawn in—she saw the vision he was painting, and from a logical perspective, it made sense. It would give her a valid, low-risk reason to return to Nigeria. She could even try to see her grandparents' house again. She still remembered the address...

Kike's words returned, reminding her of Lani's advantages. Lagos would be his home turf—and he would use every opportunity to keep his edge over her.

She made up her mind. "I'm sorry. No. I don't trust you."

"Why not?" He looked thoroughly ticked off now. "Is this about that American girl? Did one of your friends say something?"

"Her name is Lillian, and no, it's not about her, why would you think that? What friend?" Dara asked.

Lani sat up, his body tense now as their exchange drew to a

close. "I don't know what you've heard about me and her, but it's not true, and I find it a little insulting that you think I'd get myself mixed up with some random American and her thug husband, especially when I've gone out my way to stay away from her. I guess it's clear what you think about me. I'm glad I know now."

"Good, glad we're clear about that," Dara shot back, rising snappily and taking great satisfaction in being the first to leave.

When she got back to her room, she sat on her bed, unsettled. It was easy to push Lani away, but harder to deny how enticing his offer was. The thought of returning to Nigeria—of maybe even seeing her childhood home again—gave her butterflies. If it was a work trip, it would be all expenses paid, and she would have the added benefit of having someone to show her around, someone who knew Lagos like the back of his hand.

Caught between her head and her heart, she drew the curtains and began to change for dinner.

Amaka

Amaka panted as she rushed through Changi Airport, her carry-on luggage echoing on the marble floor. Rohit chased behind her and then they split, searching both ends of the departure hall for the right check-in desk. She found it first and bolted for the budget-airline desk, cutting around the long queue of passengers for the desk on the corner.

"Flight FD377?" she wheezed, waving to catch the nearest check-in officer's eye.

The couple next in line hesitated as she edged past them. "Sorry, sorry. FD377 to Seminyak."

He tapped some keys and shook his head. "Boarding for the 8:55 to Bali is closed now, madam."

"Please . . . if the gate's still open, I can be there in five minutes," she pleaded.

The officer leaned over to talk to his colleague on the next desk. As they spoke softly, Amaka thought she saw his eyes dart down to the green passport in her hand.

Rohit touched her waist behind her, breathing heavily. "Is it too late?"

"I'm sorry, ma'am. The gate is closed," the officer said.

Rohit made a clucking sound that was more sympathetic than annoyed and put his arm around her shoulders. "Sorry. We tried."

They moved over so the next couple could step forward.

"He looked at my passport," she fumed. "Before you came—he looked at it and *then* told me the gate was closed."

Rohit peered at it quizzically. "Why? What for?"

Seething, she dragged her luggage around to the back of the queue.

"I'm booking the next flight," she said when he was next to her. "Foolish man."

"You want to go that badly?" Rohit stared at her.

"Why should I miss out because the Indonesian embassy released my passport three days late? Why should I be grateful that they gave me a visa at all—I work just like everyone else, and I'm going to spend my money just like the next tourist," she raged, edging forward as the queue moved. "And the audacity of that guy, discriminating against my passport. They act like every Nigerian's trying to flood their country with drugs. I paid for my flight like Kike and Bayo and Dara, and I'm paying for my share of the villa, so why am I the only one running around stressed?"

Rohit folded his arms and said nothing, which she took to be a sign that he didn't want to engage with her racism-fueled rant, even though she knew he'd had his fair share of negative experiences. She eyeballed a young white girl staring at her, but the next fifteen minutes passed uneventfully. They got to the front and were served by a different officer.

"Can I have a ticket for your next flight to Ngurah Rai Airport? I already have a return booked for Monday." She balanced her monogrammed backpack on the counter and unzipped it.

"There are no seats tonight, but we have availability on the 7:05 flight in the morning," the woman smiled.

"OK, fine, I'll take that." Amaka opened her passport so the Indonesian visa stamp was visible.

"That's $375."

Amaka flinched. It was nearly three times the amount she'd paid for her return.

"This is economy?"

"Yes, ma'am. If you're a member, you can also earn triple air miles with this flight."

Unappeased, Amaka touched her credit card to the card machine.

The woman's smile stretched. "I'm sorry, but your card has been declined."

Amaka squirmed. "Can you try again?" *This couldn't be happening.*

The machine asked her to present her card. *Declined.*

"I'm sorry. Do you have another card you can use?"

Amaka took out another card, refusing to make eye contact with Rohit or the officer. "Can you swipe this one?"

"Sure." She ran it through. Another low beep confirmed Amaka's worst fears. She'd been trying her hardest to curb her spending, but recently, money had been slipping away like water through a net. Ugo had started to ask more questions about the London house, so Amaka had been forced to transfer money back into the UK account when her mother requested the bank details and mortgage information.

"No, I'm sorry. There's an ATM nearby if you want to pay in cash?"

"Here." Rohit gave her a card. "Use this, please."

The officer ran it through, then smiled widely. She nodded in affirmation, then handed it back.

"Thank you," Amaka murmured, leaning into him.

He stuck his wallet in his back pocket and didn't respond.

Walking with Rohit to her condo lift, Amaka paused by her letter-box and pocketed her mail, which included a credit card statement and two letters from her UK mortgage provider. She squashed the letters in her handbag, making a mental note to open them when she returned from Bali.

Just before she reached for the light switch, Amaka remembered the state in which she'd left her apartment in her rush to collect her passport from the embassy and race down to Changi. As she and Rohit adjusted to the brightness, the mound of clothes on the sofa became clear. Worst of all, she'd left her shoe cabinet open, an invisible cave of illicit treasures with sixty pairs of shoes squeezed in.

"I didn't think I'd be back tonight," she said, shamefaced, parking her luggage by the door. She began gathering up the clothes as Rohit closed the door.

"Has that always been there?" He was staring at the shoe cabinet.

Amaka closed the cabinet door, which blended in with the walls, a pile of clothes in her arms. "This apartment has great storage. That's partly why I chose it."

She elbowed her bedroom door open and tossed the clothes onto the bed.

"I'm exhausted—what a stressful night. Do you want to order some food?" she asked on her second trip to clear the clothes.

"No, I'm going to head home," he said, but he hovered by the door like he was still making up his mind.

"Are you going into the office tomorrow morning? You can go from here," she offered tentatively. They hadn't talked in the taxi, and though she'd held his hand and rested her head on his shoulder, he hadn't reciprocated much.

"I'll pay you back. I overdid it this month, that's all," she said, trying to defuse the tension.

"Have you booked your ticket to Phuket?"

"Not yet. Sorry." She squirmed and lifted another armful of clothes, avoiding eye contact. "There are usually deals in the summer, so I don't need to book too early."

She had no idea where she was going to get the money for another flight so soon.

"The wedding planner said she's emailed you twice to remind you to book and you haven't replied."

"If you know I haven't booked, why are you asking me?"

"Because I want to understand why you care more about a weekend in Bali than coming to my sister's wedding."

"Who said I—?"

"You could have invited me to Bali." Rohit's voice was raised now. "We could have shared a room or booked our own hotel, but you didn't, Amaka. It didn't even occur to you."

"Rohit," she stuttered, at a loss as to which statement to address first. She was feeling rattled and blindsided.

"What? It's a girls' weekend? Or a Nigerian thing?" His face twisted in what could only be described as disdain, if it were possible for him to feel that way about her.

"I didn't know you wanted to come," she replied weakly.

Rohit turned away then whipped back. "Are you single?"

"What?"

"It's a simple question."

"No."

"Are you sure? You act like you're single. The minute we're not together, you act like I don't exist. You don't take me into consideration, you behave like people at work knowing we're an item would cause the world to end, you blow hot and cold—can you see where I'm going with this? Can you see why I've been going crazy trying to understand why the girl I'm with treats me like wallpaper? You don't act like you're in any way interested in...us!"

"Rohit, calm down. We've been hanging out. Things are moving slowly..."

"Hanging out—is that what this is? Are you serious?"

"Rohit..."

She knew she had to come clean to him. She hadn't planned to see Lani again—she'd been determined to ignore his messages, and she had for a while—but ever since she'd met Sanaa, she'd felt Rohit get distant. On the surface, things looked the same, but she didn't have the language to address what she knew was changing, and Lani was right there...she'd got a shock when she'd come face-to-face with that American girl, becoming completely tongue-tied. After she and Lani had had sex that night, she'd left and blocked his number. The old Amaka would have confronted Lani and demanded to know why Lillian was there, but she'd had no leg to stand on and felt like a complete fool. Not only was it confirmation that there'd been something going on with the American all along, but it was also a reminder of how easily Dara could find out.

"You know I've been dealing with a lot."

"What are you dealing with, Amaka? A family you refuse to share your father's money with? Or the fact that you're clearly struggling financially and won't admit it? That's what bothers me the most, that you can't just *communicate*!"

"Don't talk about my father—"

"Why not? Why are we never allowed to talk about anything that matters?" He came closer. "Like the way you never have enough money, but you have all these clothes and all those shoes?"

"It's none of your business, Rohit!" Amaka flared up. "If you want someone you can control, who's going to run after you and cling to you so you can mess with her head, that's not me!"

"That's bullshit, Amaka! Bullshit."

They glared at each other, breathing heavily.

"This is about your sister, isn't it?" she said tightly. "I'm not stupid. I know she didn't like me."

Rohit spoke after the briefest of hesitations. His coldness, more than his words, told her that this was already over. What she thought was a fight was actually an announcement.

"You're right. She didn't like you. She thought you were too materialistic, and she thought you wouldn't fit in with our family. My parents built their businesses from nothing. Sanaa works for them. Her fiancé is joining us, and one day, I'll go back. You'd know that if you cared enough to ask or listen. I thought, when we first met, that you might understand some of this: family, building together, relationships. But you're selfish and you're shallow and you have no idea what you want."

"Thank you for telling me who I am. You can get out now."

Rohit stared at her, something tugging beneath his anger and frustration. She saw a glimpse of the friend she used to have, the friend who knew her well enough to call her out, who recognized an ego-driven bluff when he saw one, but she didn't care. She was tired and she was finished; when he walked out her front door, they were finished, too.

"Look who made it!" Bayo hollered from the long wooden table where the whole party was eating breakfast.

Amaka pressed her cheek against Dara's. "Surprise!" Amaka cackled, her puffy eyes hidden under extra-heavy make-up. She didn't know how she was going to get through this breakfast without bursting into tears. She'd done her best to get it out of her system on the early-morning flight.

"When did you get here?" Dara looked confused. "I can't believe the visa came through!"

"She tried to slip in like a thief in the night." Bayo wagged his finger like he'd been in on it. "But Kadek had to wake me to sign her in. I promised to keep *mum* until the big reveal—which you just missed!"

"*Abeg*, let's sit down and eat." She led Dara to the table where she'd left a small space so they could sit side by side. "I'll give you all the gist once there are pancakes inside me."

She said hello to everyone at the table, waving at the children and Annie, air-kissing Kike, shaking hands with their friends Saffy and Tokunbo, and greeting Lani casually, as if she hadn't seen him since the barbecue. He nodded back coldly and turned away.

Amaka sat down at what looked like the scene of a natural disaster. The table was stained with dribbles of coffee, tea, juice, milkshakes and smoothies. Discarded bits of eggs, sausages, toast, tomato and soggy pieces of mushroom sat alongside creamy-coated wafers of prosciutto and salted fish, half-eaten mini-pots of fromage frais and a discarded child's breakfast bar, with bowls of porridge and boat-shaped slices of fruit overturned in the center. The plates were crammed on the table—one had to be cleared before another could be set down. Amaka gave her order of pancakes with honey butter, maple syrup and Chantilly cream; the children watched cartoons on an iPad, opening their mouths to receive spoonfuls of food fed by Annie, whose own breakfast remained untouched. The adults chatted about afternoon plans or surfed on their phones.

"So, are you going to tell us how you wangled the visa?" Kike broke into her thoughts, with that grating, English radio-broadcaster-courtesy-of-a-British-passport voice of hers. Nobody else on this trip had suffered to get here because none of them had needed to rely on their Nigerian passports. None of them had been forced to queue for hours at embassies and provide two copies of everything and carry yellow-fever-vaccination cards like an international leper. They hadn't been escorted to quiet rooms at airports and grilled about why they were in the country, even if they'd paid for the most expensive hotel in the hope of avoiding this exact treatment, and airline staff didn't eye their passports like they were unholy. And yet Amaka had to smile and flirt and pretend like they were all in the same boat.

"Yes, cough up, I want to hear this." Bayo grinned, settling himself in for a good story. "I was thrilled when you said you'd found someone who could do it, but so many have tried and failed. What did you get, a business visa?"

Everyone was listening now—everyone except Saffy, Kike's rail-thin, milky-skinned friend who was more interested in her phone and in rearranging her blonde braids. Her husband, Tokunbo, on the other hand, had his eyes locked on the deep V-shape of Amaka's breasts. She ignored him—his oversized white linen shirt, gold chain and three mobile phones were an irritating cliché of every married Nigerian man over forty.

"A friend at work helped me out," Amaka replied as nonchalantly as she could, but she was pissed, being grilled like this. "His family has a visa company they use, and he came through."

"A 'friend'?" Bayo teased. "The same guy from—"

"Yes, Rohit. The same guy I have lunch with sometimes," Amaka cut him off.

Bayo dug in with relish. "This is the same guy that you..."

"We broke up." The last thing she wanted was to tell Lani, but she couldn't tell one more lie.

"So you *were* dating him," Bayo said. "Why've you been pretending?"

Ignoring him, she turned to Dara, who hadn't reacted to the news about Rohit.

"Where's your friend, Lillian?" she asked pointedly.

"She arrives tonight. We've arranged for a car to pick her up," Dara replied.

"You, Amaka and Lillian are all in the same villa." Kike buttered a croissant. "Lani, too."

"I thought you were flying in together," Amaka pressed.

"She has to work on Saturdays." Dara still refused eye contact.

"I don't get that girl. Isn't she meant to be getting a divorce? Why is she still in Singapore?" Amaka frowned.

Kike kissed her teeth. "Wait until you get married," she pronounced cryptically.

"Why? What would I possibly understand then that I don't understand now?" Amaka made a face.

"She's enjoying her freedom. She's reclaiming her life," Kike asserted.

"The woman suffered, *sha*." Bayo shook his head in commiseration.

"You don't have to suffer to earn the right to reclaim your life," Kike snapped.

"Chill out, I never said you did," Bayo retorted. They glared at each other.

One of the boys began to fuss as Annie turned the iPad screen away and began to fiddle with it.

"You guys are so lucky to live so far from Nigeria." Saffy looked up from her phone, her accent more Nigerian than Amaka had been expecting. "I can't believe *this* is actually your life, and you don't have to deal with all the stress and other people's opinions."

Saffy's husband pointed his finger around the table. "And it's you women who oppress each other, *na*."

"I'm telling you!" Bayo laughed heartily. "It's women who hold each other to impossible standards. All this 'Nigerian men are this and that' is just a smokescreen for your own issues."

"Oh yeah, it's all in our heads." Amaka's sarcasm dripped. "That's why it's called patriarchy, right?"

"Oh my God, Amaka," Bayo bellowed. "This card-carrying feminism is too much."

His boys looked up from their tussle for the iPad, momentarily intrigued by their father's uncharacteristic change in tone.

"Next thing you're going to tell me is you don't want to get married," Bayo mocked.

"I don't," she snorted.

"And you don't want kids?"

"I *don't*. Seriously, aren't you embarrassed to be having this conversation in the twenty-first century? When are Nigerians going to catch up?" Amaka marveled that this was coming from Bayo, who had never shown this narrow-minded side before. Since when did he care about what other women did with their lives?

"Would you be saying that if... never mind." Bayo turned away, a knowing smile tugging at the side of his mouth.

"If what? Talk, talk, my friend!" Amaka clicked her fingers.

"You're only saying that because there are no guys in Singapore! I mean, there *are* guys, but even in London, it's hard for all my girlfriends. It's twice as hard here. You know what I mean." Bayo looked sheepish and kept his eyes away from Kike's glare.

"First of all, there are guys *everywhere*. What you mean is there are more Nigerian girls than guys." Amaka chortled at the irony of Bayo's words with Lani sitting right there.

"Much more." Bayo couldn't help himself. "Right, Lani?"

Lani's face was a wall. "*Bro*, don't."

"What?"

"Look, it's really simple." Kike cut in with uncharacteristic venom. "Just don't marry a Nigerian."

"Ouch!" Bayo reacted dramatically. "Bitter much?"

"Bitter?" Kike scoffed. "If someone removed the wool from Nigerian women's eyes and showed them how big the pond is, Nigerian men wouldn't get away with half the shit they do."

"How did we get into all this?" Tokunbo laughed uneasily.

"Me, I'm just minding my business," his wife giggled.

"You girls have been watching too many of those American women on YouTube," Bayo cracked.

"Compared to the antiquated, hate-spreading vitriol you watch online... yes, I can see how you would think that," Kike smarted.

"Careful, *Kiks*, big words," Bayo sneered.

"Hilarious," Kike deadpanned, but there was no mirth in her voice.

"Nigerian women and your grievances. Any excuse." Bayo tried to joke the tension away. "Not you, Dara."

There was no response from Dara, no riposte, which Bayo must have been relying on. Instead, she froze before reaching for her mimosa and sipping it silently.

Kike frowned. "What, she's not Nigerian?"

"Honorary," Bayo joked.

The mood turned now, snaking into a danger that was palpable, needle-like and abrasive.

"Nigerian men are so confused," Kike sneered. "The world has moved too fast for you—you're still trying to hold on to the way shit used to be, and you have no idea what you really want. It's probably hard for you guys to wrap your heads around, as pompous and puffed up as you are, but there are other men out there. It's not by force that we must marry Nigerians. So that's one reason. Secondly, marriage is not the be-all and end-all. It might sound incredible, but a woman can actually enjoy her life outside of marriage."

"Enjoyment—you'd know all about that, considering you've never had a job," Bayo snickered.

An awful silence followed, like a sickening, bony crunch.

The children began to argue, Timini yelling and trying to grab the iPad, Tife starting to whine.

"The battery dying, ma'am," Annie whispered apologetically, holding the iPad away from them.

"Can you take them away, please?" Kike gritted her teeth.

Annie tried to pull the boys out of their seats just as Kadek walked up the steps, a man in white pushing a wheeled tray behind her. She greeted the table with a smile, oblivious to the tension, and began to clear the empty, dirty plates onto the tray. As Kadek turned, the older boy propelled out of his chair, wriggling free of Annie's hands, and smacked right into her. The plates came crashing to the ground.

In a flash, Kike was up.

"Timini! When...will...you...listen!" She slapped him on the arm, shoulder and back. As each blow landed, the crack of skin-on-skin was worsened by the ugly, frustrated twist in her face.

It was over quickly, but the damage was done. Timini stared at the ground, his face a valiant yet soon-to-crumble mask.

Bayo stood up and, ignoring Kike, walked past her to pick the boy up in his arms. As they moved away from view, the table heard Timini's wretched cry, so distinct from any sound the children had made before—a cry soaked with shock and fear and disbelief. It crested over the guests, shattering any last pretense of enjoyment.

One by one, they started to disperse. Lani carried Tife behind Bayo, and Annie followed with their things. Kike apologized to Kadek, then moved around her as the hostess picked up the shattered plate pieces. Saffy and Tokunbo, sharing a feeble joke about the different names for spanking sticks when they were young, lagged behind, taking their time.

"Oh my God! What the hell was that?" Dara exclaimed when everyone was out of earshot. "Did you know things were that bad?"

Amaka shook her head, too emotional to speak, and slipped her sunglasses over her watery eyes. She'd finally made it to Bali and the trip was already a disaster. Like a broken cart hurtling at full speed, everything around her was disintegrating, one wheel at a time. Kike had voiced the anger she herself had carried for so long about her father, but hearing it out loud—and seeing the damage it was doing to the girl's marriage—was like a forewarning.

Walking back to their rooms in silence, Amaka couldn't stop thinking about Rohit. He was the one person who would have helped her find humor in this brunch from hell. She *should* have invited him. She should have had her fling with Lani, then brought Rohit with her, moving forward and building something solid. She should have talked to him about the shopping and the money, but once you pulled one thread, you needed the courage to face the whole thing unraveling, and she was a coward.

As they parted by the stairs, Amaka wanted so badly to reach for Dara's hand and spill everything that had happened with Rohit, but to do that, she would have to tell the truth about Lani. They were on the same flight back to Singapore; she decided she would do it then.

She closed her bedroom door behind her. A minute later, her phone buzzed with a message from Lani: *Can we talk?*

Lillian

The cool white dome of Ngurah Rai Airport arrival hall behind her, Lillian inched out nervously from under the small columns. Huddles of Balinese locals stood behind a metal railing holding boards with passengers' names. She thought she spied hers, but with one missing "l" and her surname misspelled, she wasn't sure. The holder, dressed in khakis and a baseball cap, caught her eye and visibly brightened. He greeted her warmly with a raised hand, took her luggage and beckoned her to follow him to a gray van with "Two Trees" printed on its side.

The sun began to set. Under it, the landscape changed from bare, sweeping stretches of road, with only the blur of a petrol station or makeshift shack, to narrow tracks clogged with traffic and back again. Her anxiety, which had skyrocketed over the past two months, began to surge. This was the first time she'd be seeing Lani and the Ibusuns since the barbecue. To calm herself, she leaned her head and arm on the door of the van, trying to relish the rushing gusts of evening air. Feisty as a playful child, she gave each changing scene a different musical score: Chopin's Ballade No. 1 in G minor as the car careered precariously around tight bends in the road; Liszt's "Un Sospiro" as it cruised in the open air.

It was a welcome change to be outdoors, away from Singapore's slow crawl and the worries that choked her thoughts. Almost every day since Amaka had seen her at Lani's, she'd wondered if that would be the day Dara would throw her out. As time passed, and life continued as normal, it occurred to her that she had caught Amaka just as much as she'd been caught. She was sure of this when Dara confirmed that both Lani and Amaka would be coming to Bali: Amaka wouldn't be saying a word. It became easier to pretend it had never happened. She hated herself for continuing to accept Dara's help. It was July—four months since she'd moved in—but she needed to save more, especially since the cost of renting in Singapore had shot up over the summer months.

As much as possible, without being rude, she'd found ways to stay out of Dara's apartment, taking on more students to tutor, which had paid for her flight. She'd been taking her laptop to cafés by the river to watch countless videos on proof of the existence of past lives. One video had led her to a tarot reading, and before she knew it, she'd started to watch psychics and astrologers, clicking on any video thumbnail that hinted at "spirit guides" or energies that had "passed over." She'd never believed in this stuff before, never even thought about spirituality, but the more she watched, the more she craved a miraculous explanation for what she was seeing and feeling.

Most nights she stayed up late watching these YouTube videos, feeling spikes of elation when the readers brought out cards about father figures or an "emperor" who would play a pivotal role in her life and help start a "new cycle," followed by despondency when none of the readings resonated at all. Everywhere she saw signs and synchronicities, as if the universe was telling her that Lani's appearance in her life was no coincidence. One day, she'd seen incense paper and orange rinds someone had left outside a Buddhist temple—an offering to their ancestors—so she'd bought a bag of oranges and placed them on the tray, saying a prayer for direction and guidance.

The car emerged onto a dark street and rolled to a stop, its headlights beaming onto bamboo-style gates. Automatically, the gates parted and both sides retreated into the wall; the driver shifted gears and drove inside, parking outside a small hut. Except for a few invisible crickets chirping, the silence was thick.

"Welcome to Two Trees..." a woman's voice greeted her.

Six slabs of stone created a stairway up to the hut, in front of which a small lady in a white blouse and linen trousers stood smiling. She pressed her palms together and bowed her head when Lillian reached the top, then introduced herself as Kadek. After placing a hot, wet towel in Lillian's hands, Kadek cupped a small stone mug of hot ginger tea in her palms; the steam tickled Lillian's nostrils and warmed her. She followed the hostess under a long veranda, sipping as she walked past solar lamps glowing in the grass.

"Villa One that way. You'll stay in Villa Two." Kadek stepped aside to reveal a half-lit glass and stone home, as well as a long, oval pool.

The sound of running water masked the deeper, heavier splash of a body in motion. Lani swam toward Lillian and Kadek, his head dipped low in the blue water, turning left and right with every stroke, eyes hidden behind black goggles. His movements were effortless, his limbs dark and strong, an extra-terrestrial being gliding in the fluorescent water. He ducked under—still unaware of their presence—and pushed against the wall with his feet, beginning another length.

"We will take your luggage upstairs and leave it outside your door," Kadek said.

"Thank you." Lillian sat on one of the deck chairs as Kadek and the driver went through a lounge and up some stairs. The frisson of excitement that danced inside her whenever she thought of Lani hit her hard now that he was so close. There was no way Lani being the first person she saw when she arrived was a coincidence. Staying in the same villa as him was all the plan of a large, invisible hand.

She waited for Lani to reach the other end, allowing herself to stare, uncensored, at his body dominating the water. She had never been a great swimmer—even if her parents had been able to find the time to take her to a public swimming pool, the thought of taking her to their swarming, oversubscribed recreation park would have filled her cautious parents with dread. A hose in a friend's backyard was the only way to cool down in those searing summers. So she had never seen Bem swim, but if she had, this is what she imagined her father would have looked like—tall and strong and dauntless.

When he turned around, she raised her hand shyly. His hand

was hard to see against the dark wall; she thought he raised it back. Slowly, he swam closer but his face looked straight ahead.

"You're a good swimmer," she said when he was close enough.

"Thanks." He turned his goggles inside out, wiped the fog from the lenses, and replaced them over his eyes. He floated by the edge, but she got the sense he was pausing out of politeness.

"I just got here...it's a beautiful place. We usually stayed at hotels," she stammered. "Have you been before?"

He sighed like he was answering the question for the umpteenth time. "First time."

His stiff reaction made her ramble on.

"Couldn't get here earlier cos of work; it's been really busy at the school. Are you still taking lessons in the evenings?"

"Yup."

"Great. It's a good school. I mean, it's not great for the teachers, but it's pretty good for students. No matter what, you always pass! That's a little inside joke with us."

"Right."

It was impossible to ignore his coolness now.

She glanced behind and around her. "Do you know where everyone is?"

"We're going to a club tonight, so they're probably getting ready." He pressed his legs against the wall and swam away, moving too fast for her to respond.

Feeling idiotic for hanging around but determined not to let this chance go to waste, Lillian shuffled to the front of the deck chair and waited. She tried to look as nonchalant as possible, taking in the dark navy of the starless sky that stretched above like a blanket, cloistering the villa from the rest of the world. Being under it comforted her and helped calm the thick, anxious taste that was starting to thicken her tongue.

After several lengths and a brief pause at the other end, Lani came to a stop in front of her once again. He seemed to get the message that she wasn't going anywhere.

Almost exasperated, he took off his goggles completely and wiped his eyes.

"Did you want something?"

Lillian was ready this time. "I wanted to apologize. I never got to say sorry about what Warren did. It was a huge misunderstanding and—"

"I know that because I didn't do anything," he practically snapped.

"Yes, I know, and I've made sure to tell everyone—"

"Is your husband going to be here?" Lani interrupted again. "Because if he turns up..."

"He won't, I promise," she blurted quickly. "We...we split up. And the police said the warning was more for him than for me. I'm sorry if I've made you uncomfortable. I don't want to ruin your weekend."

Lani let out a short, ironic bark. "Then why did you come? Why are you here? And have you been hiding outside my condo? Amaka told me today that she saw you outside my building. I had no idea what she was talking about. Is that true?"

"I...I..." Lillian stammered, close to tears.

"Yes or no?" he demanded.

"Yes. Yes, but..."

"Why?" he said, repulsed. "Why would you do that? What is *wrong* with you?"

He got out of the water and grabbed his towel, wrapping it around his waist. "I'm starting to wonder who's crazier: you or your husband. Just stay away from me. If you come to my house again, I'm definitely calling the police."

"Wait, please." Lillian jumped up. "It's not—there's a reason why...I'm not stalking you!"

She practically yelled the last words. She wasn't crazy; she *knew* she wasn't crazy.

"You're not?" Lani reacted in disbelief. "Then what do you call this? Turning up outside my apartment, coming to Bali, your husband assaulting me because he thought I was cheating with his wife?"

"He made a mistake. I didn't know how to explain it."

"Explain what? What are you talking about? I don't *know* you!"

"Yes, but I know you." She took a step forward. "The first time I met you; your face, your voice, everything about you. You're the carbon copy of my father, Lani. I thought I was imagining it because I've been under a lot of stress, but even Dara agreed. You look *just* like him."

"Dara? What the fuck? Are you telling me Dara knows about this?"

"I've been staying with her. I showed her pictures of my father, and she saw it too."

Lani stared up at the sky, one hand rubbing his head. "This is insane. Everyone has literally gone insane."

"It's not—it's true! I can show you." She went to grab her bag a split second before remembering her luggage had been taken upstairs. "If you would just let me show you..."

"Absolutely not. This is...this stops here. I don't know what you and Dara are playing at, but she will stop at nothing to undermine me. Fuck, I should have known this was her."

"You don't understand. My dad...my father..."

Lani groaned. "I just want a quiet weekend. Why does she have to be such a meddling *bitch*?"

He seemed suddenly weary. "Why does this matter? So I look like your father—I can't help what my face looks like. Why is this so important?"

"It's important because my father died when I was very young." She licked her dry lips, struggling to form the words.

"I'm sorry, but..." Lani left the words unspoken, but his gesture said *what does this have to do with me?*

Lillian tried to compose herself. She was really doing this.

"Do you believe in reincarnation?" she asked when she could finally speak. "Because I can't think of any other way this makes sense. I thought there might be some family relation, but I can't find anything. You turning up at my work, the connection with Kike...I wanted to get to know you, to see if there was some kind of link."

She was hearing music again. How could she explain that meeting him had made her hungry for music again?

Lani sliced through the air with his hand. "I'm sorry, but this isn't normal. I'm sorry about your father. I don't know what you're looking for, but this is too much. Seriously."

Lillian watched, horrified, as he leaned down to pick up his phone, a look of disgust marring his features. At the same time, a woman's legs appeared at the top of the stairs.

Lani fired a parting shot as he left. "And there is another possibility, Lillian. It's called a bloody coincidence."

As he neared one of the rooms a short distance from the pool, Amaka came down the stairs, dressed in a black-and-white body-con dress and ridiculously high purple heels, with tassels at the ankles. Like déjà vu, they stared at each other again, this time with Lani between them.

Lani didn't stop to speak to Amaka, but went into his room, and Amaka, after the slightest hesitation, turned in the opposite direction for the room on the other side of the stairs. Lillian turned her back so her crumbling face couldn't be seen. She didn't move until she heard Amaka's door close.

When Lillian was sure she was alone, she walked up the stairs and, using the key card she'd been given, opened her bedroom door.

"Hey, you made it!" Dara beamed from the dressing table where she was blow drying her hair, her white bath robe blending into the all-white room. She turned the setting to low and raised her voice. "How was your flight? I hope you've still got some energy tonight because we might be accidentally-on-purpose bumping into some Kiwis tonight, and I really need a wingman."

She turned the hairdryer off, turning serious as she took in Lillian's energy. "What happened?"

"What did you say to Lani?" Lillian burst into angry tears. "What did you say?"

"I didn't say anything." Dara held a hand up, confused. "I didn't mention you at all."

"He *hates* me and it's because of you, Dara. Why didn't you tell me things had got this bad? Why did you let me—"

"I didn't let you do anything." Dara put the dryer down. "I told you not to speak to him until I'd found out more. Clearly, you didn't listen."

Lillian slumped onto the bed, covering her face with a hand. "I just wanted to talk to him. I just wanted to see if he could… remember something. About a past life. I don't know."

"A lot happened today, none of it to do with you," Dara sighed. "We had an argument yesterday, and there was drama with Kike and Bayo at breakfast. It's been a really shitty day."

She felt Dara sit beside her and put an arm around her shoulder.

"Lillian, you've got so much going on. Don't you think you should focus on your divorce and negotiating with Warren? Neither of you have filed, but you're not speaking to each other. How are you going to move forward? Is Lani more important than sorting that out? Even if this reincarnation thing is true—and I'm not knocking your instincts—how is it going to help you now?"

Lillian shook her head. "You don't understand. I've *tried* to move forward, and I can't."

Dara's grip around her shoulder tightened and she heard an intake of breath.

"Did you know you have a patch of hair missing?" Dara gingerly raised a hand to Lillian's head.

"Don't." She shrugged Dara's arm off and went to the bathroom, locking the door.

Dinner at the villa was tense. Everyone overate, indulging in the luxury of authentic Thai food while trying not to stain their clothes. Grilled fish, tom yum soup, green papaya salad, pork omelet; in an hour, most of the plates were cleared. Little was said, the only real laughter induced by Tokunbo, who kept calling for more chili pepper to "make the food come to life."

Lillian didn't eat or say much and avoided looking at anyone in particular. She and Dara sat at the end of the table, near Kike's sons, and whenever the boys ran past Lillian's chair or dropped something near her, she tried to speak to them—they didn't give her a second glance. Kike was also very gentle with the boys, urging them to sing in Mandarin and letting them have extra dessert, but she didn't say much to Lillian. A strong wind whipping through the air drowned out the conversation at the other end of the table, but at one point, she heard Kike ask Dara about going to a hotel. Dara, subdued, shook her head.

As the villa staff began to clear the plates, she became slowly aware of the fact that everyone's attention had fallen on her.

Amaka, she noticed, kept her eyes down, and Lillian knew she was the one who'd said something.

"That's so cool" Saffy, said. "I used to play, too. I wish I'd kept it up. Can you play for us?"

Lillian went cold. She felt needles prickling her skin.

"What?"

"There's a piano here, *abi?*" Saffy asked Bayo then twisted round. "Yeah, I knew I saw one."

"If you'd like to. I don't mind," Bayo said. His manner was reserved but gracious.

Dara caught her eye. "You don't have to."

"Play, *na*! Why do people who play the piano never like playing?" Tokunbo complained good-naturedly. "Meanwhile, the tone-deaf keep inflicting themselves on us. Like those videos on Instagram where the child is destroying the violin and the parents are like, '*So good!*'"

"She doesn't 'play the piano,'" Dara retorted. "She's a pianist."

Tokunbo looked confused. "What's the difference?"

"I'll play!" Lillian hissed, her hands jerking out to quiet them.

The whole table fell silent, and she was glad—she was actually, shockingly, *pleased*. She would shut them up and show them they had no idea who she was. She glared at Amaka and then at Lani. He thought she was crazy? She would show him she had more talent in her two hands than all of them combined.

"Where is it?" she demanded to no one in particular. No one answered her.

She looked in the direction Saffy had indicated and stood.

They thought they knew her. She pulled the stool back and uncovered the keys: pearly-white teeth inviting her to devour them. It was an upright—nothing compared to her grand. The blend of sound was weaker, the tone shallower because of the thinner wood, but it was good enough for her current audience.

Rachmaninoff. *Yes.*

Her fingers rammed into the keys and, like a crash of waves against a rock, sound burst forth. Immediately, it melted to a melody that was deliberate and intense, a quiet agitation in every note. It rumbled, twinkled, then pounded again, a fierce rage biting to break free; she picked up speed, racing up the black keys like some demented chase. Thrilled at how easily it came, thrilled at the blur of her hands, Lillian stopped listening and watched the muscles in her arms bulge through her skin. Her hands moved up to where the notes were higher and sweeter, and then the key changed, the notes deeper and richer, then lower and darker, snarling and growling—

She stopped.

A solo clap multiplied into two, three, four hands raised in applause. When she finally turned around, the table was on their feet. Dara put two fingers in her mouth and whistled over the cheers. The last two sitting, Lani then Amaka, rose and slowly joined the clapping. Someone whistled, and the boys climbed onto two chairs to surf the wave of love.

The next day, Lillian sunbathed by the pool, weakened by a hangover. Saffy lay beside her, and Timini paddled in the shallow end. The sky was a sharp blue, with faint tracks of white clouds pressed against it.

"Do you guys mind keeping an eye on Timini?" Kike's shadow fell across Lillian, blocking out the glare of the sun. "Tife is refusing to nap."

Lillian squinted up at her, the shade a welcome respite for her throbbing head. The night had turned after her performance, and the Ibusuns had softened toward her, as if they'd recalculated her value. Dara had pulled her into a tight hug afterward, saying nothing more about Lani or her patch of missing hair; on the way to the club, Lillian had vaguely remembered Dara saying something about wanting to dance, but when they got there, Dara spent most of the night sitting. Lillian didn't want to worsen things by pushing her. With Amaka there, Dara had been quieter than usual, and Amaka had eventually joined Saffy and Kike on the dancefloor. The men disappeared to the opposite end of the club. When two random guys tried to chat Dara and Lillian up, Dara was polite but clearly uninterested. To compensate, Lillian ended up drinking too much, pretending to enjoy the hedonism that surrounded her when it was almost nightmarish: girls sliding down poles, waiters tossing bottles into the air, a monstrous chandelier, fluorescent blue fish swimming in a glass bar.

"Yeah, sure." She touched her hand to her forehead. It took so much effort to speak, and even those two words caused a surge of nausea.

"Why didn't you just leave them in Singapore?" Saffy exclaimed, tossing a yellow braid over her tanned, bony shoulder. "You'd be having so much more fun right now."

Kike ignored her. "I'll be just a moment. Don't say anything to Timini. By the time he notices I'm gone, I'll be back."

"Sure." Lillian peered at the little boy as he floated on a large, white unicorn, and scratched at her ankle, the beginnings of a mosquito bite rising into a hard lump.

Kike turned, walking down the white-hot pathway through Villa One's trestle veranda.

Saffy slid her sunglasses up her nose and scrolled on her phone. "Women are way too attached to the 'idea' of motherhood. Honestly, it's not that serious."

"Do you have kids?" Lillian asked, curious. She glanced at Timini, who had slid into the water and was now floating in a circular toy ring, then back at the door.

"Yup, and I left them with my mother-in-law in Lagos because that's what normal people do," Saffy boasted. "You buy them a fucking huge present, and that's it. We travel. At least, if you want to fuck your man more than once in a blue moon."

Saffy peered over at Lillian, showing real interest for the first time.

"Do *you* have kids?"

Lillian shook her head, waiting for the cut to burn through her. But nothing came. There was...nothing.

"*Ey, ey, ey*, incoming." Saffy nodded across the pool. "I thought he was at the beach."

A towel slung over his shoulder, Lani gestured a quick hello to Saffy before walking into his room. Lillian's chest tightened, like a band of iron had clamped around it.

Saffy leered behind a faux smile. "That boy is so fine."

Lillian didn't respond.

"You don't think so?" she asked.

"I guess." Lillian pulled her beach bag closer.

"Girl, do you have a pulse?" Saffy laughed and rose, slipping on her flip-flops. "Are there toilets near here?"

"Yes," Lillian said enthusiastically. "I'll show you."

She picked up her beach bag and walked Saffy around the pool, pointing out the outhouse.

When Saffy disappeared around the corner, Lillian took the photos she'd been carrying out of her bag. She would show Lani, and then he would see. He would *see* Bem, and he would finally understand why she'd been behaving as she had.

She walked to Lani's door, feeling like she was in a dream, like someone was calling her forward. Before she could slip a picture under his door, a stirring through the window caught her eye. One of the blinds had shifted to the side, leaving a gap—and a clear view of a naked woman standing by the bed. Lani, who was fully clothed and sitting on the bed, straddled her brown legs, and he gripped a full, fleshy buttock.

A scream ripped through the air. Lillian was knocked away by a hard shove in her back and as she fell, she heard a loud splash of water. She looked up and saw Kike beside Timini's little body in a floating ring. His legs stuck out of the ring, and his back peeked through the hole. He was face down in the water.

Kike shrieked her son's name and wrenched his head out of the water, tearing at the float around his waist.

A shock of electricity raced down Lillian's spine, and she began to shake on the floor, struggling to breathe.

She was meant to be watching him.

The door behind her burst open and a blur—Lani—flew out. He jumped into the pool and helped Kike pull Timini onto the side of the pool.

"No, no, no!" she wailed, her voice a terrifying sound: an ancient, angry plea in negotiation with an unseen force. She clung to Timini's legs with one hand and rubbed up and down his shin with the other. Her mouth began to quiver, mumbling words no one could hear. A knot of bodies surrounded them and someone— Dara—shouted Kadek's name. Numb, her throat unbearably hot, Lillian watched in horror as Bayo raced past. When he reached them, Lani wrestled Bayo aside and, cupping the boy's chin, started to blow into his mouth.

Everyone watched Lani push down on Timini's bare chest, wincing at his grunts, Kike's whimpers and the slackness of the boy's gray face.

Lillian couldn't watch anymore. For years, she'd been tortured by dreams that recreated the sound of her parents' last breaths and their drowned bodies. She saw them now.

A siren wailed, its cries growing louder as it approached. It triggered a fresh rush of adrenaline and Lillian choked back tears. She stared into the sky where the sun had begun to set, drawing its orange light down a dark hole. A breeze rustled against her; the air hinted at rain.

Dara

Dara crouched by the bed and switched on the lamp. Outside, electricity ripped across the sky, each shudder of thunder increasing in intensity. Shadows fell across the wall and bed of her guest bedroom, where Lillian was sleeping. She'd slept throughout the flight back to Changi Airport and in the taxi on the way back to Dara's. Ever since the paramedics had moved her from the pool, taken her into their ambulance and given her a sedative to calm her down, she'd been asleep more than she'd been awake.

The sky was dark again. Still no rain. Dara pulled the covers over her friend, even though the room was thick with the incoming storm. Lillian's somnolence was symbolic of the end of the trip, which had petered out, the mood turning as everyone in the group retreated to their own spaces. The Ibusuns, understandably, were not seen for the last two days, and neither Bayo nor Kike had asked about Lillian before they'd left. No one, including Dara, had actually noticed Lillian slumped a few feet away. The time between Lani administering CPR and Timini taking a breath had been so bleak and airless that the moment the little boy's face had twisted to life, Dara was so lightheaded she was in danger of fainting. The wet, dragging hack of water expelling from his throat was a sound she would never forget.

Kadek had called emergency services as Bayo and Kike clung to each other and wept, their son curled between them. It was while one of the Indonesian paramedics was trying to coax the crying boy from their arms to wrap a thermal blanket around him that the other spotted Lillian turned away from the pool, her hand clutching her chest. He repeatedly asked Dara and anyone else who approached to stand back, and after a few minutes, he helped her to the villa entrance. It was then that Dara had seen Amaka stumble backward, a white sheet clumsily wrapped around her naked body, and run into Lani's room.

After the ambulance took Lillian away, Dara had walked back up the stone steps, her body hot and burning in delayed reaction. She'd gone straight to Lani's room and pounded on the door. When Amaka opened it, fully dressed now and unable to look Dara in the eye, Dara had shoved the door open and slapped her so hard it felt like her palm had cracked open. Then she ran up to her own room and locked the door. She'd never felt more ashamed, gullible, furious and isolated.

A clap of thunder reverberated in the distance.

Dara let herself out and took Lillian's uneaten tray of food back into her dark, narrow kitchen. She tied up a plastic bag of rubbish and threw it down the chute.

As she washed her hands, her sadness broke through, and she cried quietly. She used her sleeves to dry her eyes and accepted, in that moment, that she could not carry Lillian any longer. She'd been pulled into something bigger than she'd realized and watching Lillian's mind and body break down without being able to do a thing about it triggered an overwhelming sense of powerlessness in her.

On top of the stress of the arbitration, she'd lost her closest friend and the only real support system she had in Singapore. The hurt and humiliation of seeing Amaka was the final, sickening twist to that disastrous day. It wasn't enough that Lillian had left Kike's child unsupervised to spy through Lani's window, proof that her fixation with Lani was a full-blown obsession that could have led to serious harm, but Dara now had to face the fact that her best friend had been lying to her for months. It was a new type of heartbreak, finding out that the person she'd trusted the most had thought so little of their friendship, that a man who Amaka must have known had little intention of making things serious was worth cheating on Rohit and fooling Dara over. It was enough to drive her crazy, trying to understand when it had started, how long they must have been laughing at her, how much Amaka might have been confiding in him.

On the flight back, with Lillian asleep beside her, it had dawned on Dara that Amaka must have told Lani about the slides. She had locked herself into the mercifully vacant toilet to vomit. Shaking, she'd stomped down the aisles looking for her, but even though they'd been booked on the same flight back, the lily-livered bitch wasn't on it. The last communication they'd had was a text Amaka had sent the next day, apologizing, swearing that it had been nothing but sex and warning Dara about seeing Lillian outside of Lani's apartment. Dara had deleted Amaka's number and erased all her texts.

As Dara changed into jeans and packed her laptop to work in a café, it was with great bitterness that she acknowledged that her mother had been right. She should never have got close to a girl she really didn't know, simply because they happened to be from a geographical region loosely drawn together by a bunch of white people a hundred years ago.

She decided it was time to ask Lillian to find a new place, but when she woke up in the morning, the guest room was empty.

Lillian was gone.

Three weeks later the Hakida hearing finally began. Dara and Lani sat in an arbitration chamber behind Charles Summers, the barrister Ian had flown in from London to argue the case; since the arbitration was the alternative to a court hearing, they'd needed a specialist litigator to represent both parties.

The opposing barrister for the Kenyan side sat on the other side of the room and the head arbiter, a Singaporean, sat at the narrow end of the table. A transcriber took notes in the corner. It was day three—still too early to call which way things would swing, or what impression each side was making.

Outside, a light rain drizzled against the windows. Although the sky stayed bright and blue, Dara could feel the increasing mugginess in her clammy palms.

She stifled a yawn and tried to stretch her aching neck without drawing attention; she hadn't stopped working before midnight for the past week. She'd been getting Summers everything he needed, keeping Hakida happy and been constantly at Ian's beck and call.

Behind her, Mr. Erikawa sat with his arms folded, a vacant expression on his face, but he was all smiles whenever they stepped out of the chamber. He was the picture of confidence, since Ian Breen never took cases to arbitration if he wasn't sure he could win. Ian would swoop in on the last day, shake every-one's hand and pocket a nice chunk of the three million dollars Hakida was suing the Kenyan government for. He hadn't come in today, which was a sign that the proceedings were progressing well. Aldrich Chambers, where the arbitration was being held, was state-of-the art and kitted out with every imaginable piece of technology one might need, but it was also incredibly expensive to rent, so keeping Ian and his astronomical hourly rates at bay made a difference to the final bill.

"As proven by article forty-three on page twelve of said docu-ment," the opposing counsel addressed the arbiter, "it is clear that in the run up to last year's general elections, the relationship between the Kikuyu chiefs and my client was a contentious one."

Dara scribbled in her yellow legal pad, taking notes. Lani did the same. They hadn't exchanged more than a few words since Bali. The usual coolness between them had sharpened to a knife edge, such that they barely even looked in the other's direction. After Timini's near-drowning, a new distance had formed between them that was as glum and resigned as their previous relationship had been tense and strained. It was as if the incident, revealing as it did so many hidden ties and infatuations, had also revealed sobering truths. Dara could only imagine what it must have been like to hold the limp, wet body of your best friend's son, trying to breathe life-saving air into his lungs. After she'd found out about him and Amaka, she'd waited for her animosity to rise ten-fold, but it never did. He didn't owe it to her to tell her about

Amaka—that was Dara's best friend's job—and he hadn't asked for Lillian to fixate on him. In fact, the one person he'd been clear and consistent about getting closer to was Dara. And she'd rejected him over and over again. She wasn't anywhere ready to be friendly, but if anyone had a right to be angry, it was him.

"As can be seen from the newspaper articles taken from that period, several meetings were arranged between the local chiefs and the governor of that region for the express purpose of resolving concerns about the bridge," the Kenyan's QC continued. "Although the resolution of those meetings was *ad idem*, there was no *actio pro socio*: the resolution was that of two separate parties."

Barely ten minutes passed without the Kenyans' QC using some unnecessary Latin phrase, probably for the benefit of the government representative sitting behind him more than anyone else. Recognizing that his analysis would be lengthy, Dara rested her hand and let her mind wander, remembering something Amaka had said months ago, something she'd thought of many times recently.

"Don't you think it's a little fucked up, two African lawyers working in an English firm, helping Japanese clients beat an African government, which is trying to screw over its own chiefs?"

It was business: economics, globalism, capitalism, whatever you wanted to call it. Tomorrow, Ian could take on an African client and sue a company much like Hakida. That's just the way it was.

And yet, in the six years she'd worked for him, he had never actually taken on an African client. Was there a reason why he should? Was it also a coincidence that there was no black partner in any of the firm's global offices? She was sure there was an explanation, but when it came down to it, what was it that siphoned black lawyers out before they made it anywhere near the bottleneck of the pyramid? No one was owed anything, and she more than anyone hated the idea of being put forward because it made her firm look good. Why couldn't she be made partner because she *was* good and had a solid business plan and worked well with clients?

There was a tap on the back of her hand and she looked up at

Lani. For a second, she thought he was reading her notes, but he was biting his lip, his fingers turning her pages over then pointing to the bottom right corner.

"Page 273," he whispered, a deep frown creasing his face.

She looked at the page on the left, then the one on the right. 272. 274.

Shit... Shit. Shit.

"I apologize. It seems we don't have quite the same referencing." Charles Summers turned back to Dara and Lani, stalling.

Dara shook her head, her heart sinking.

"Our numbers are also incorrect." The opposing counsel stopped squinting at the page and placed his glasses back on his nose.

The head arbiter nodded at his two colleagues on the panel, who acknowledged the same.

"Something has clearly gone wrong with the bundles. Our apologies," Mr. Summers continued smoothly. "Can I respond to this point after lunch? We'll need an hour or so to acquire the most up-to-date version."

The arbiters discussed briefly and agreed.

"In that case, could I request that the examination of our main witness be brought forward to before lunch?" the Kenyan QC suggested, seizing the opportunity. "We have him ready."

In the space of a few seconds, a small administrative error had left them wide open. No lawyer—not even one as good as Charles Summers—wanted to cross-examine a witness without notice.

"Yes, that's a fair request," the head arbiter decided. "The witness can be examined after the morning break."

"Is it dated the sixteenth?" Dara yelled into her phone, trying to hold an umbrella, hail a cab and balance her handbag at the same time.

The light drizzle had turned into a downpour so hard and fast that the road ahead looked like it was blocked by a gray screen of water. The trees, signboards and building names were blurred, and the streets were empty of pedestrians. Beside her, several people waited out of the rain in the taxi rank, and more sat in the lobby inside.

Irene's voice on the other end of the phone was muffled.

"What?" Dara shouted, pressing her phone so hard that her ear ached.

"Yes, it's dated the sixteenth!" Irene said more loudly.

"OK! I need three copies printed and bound *right now*! I'm trying to get a taxi." She waved furiously at one but its green light turned red.

"You want me to book a courier?" Irene said.

Dara hesitated. She had one chance to get this right. A courier could be faster, but if Irene had the wrong version, there would be no coming back from that. The last thing she wanted was to bump into Ian and have to explain why she wasn't at the arbitration, but she didn't trust anyone else to do this properly.

"I'm taking the MRT! I'm coming back now, so please get it ready. I need to be back here by lunchtime!" She hung up and ran around the side of the building.

The pedestrian crossing turned green, and she made a run for it, wincing under the full pelt of the storm.

A split second after her brain registered that running on wet ground with her hands full and wearing stiletto heels was a terrible idea, both of Dara's feet slid forwards and she smacked down, hard, on her back. It was the longest three seconds of her life. The rain thundered down onto her face, blinding her. Fumbling for her things, her back soaked and her umbrella turned inside out, she rushed to cross to the other side before the green man turned red.

Hot with embarrassment, aware of the eyes staring at her from both sides of the street, she dragged herself out of the hot, damp air and into the Siberian temperatures of the MRT. Shoving her umbrella into one of the plastic bags the station provided, she glared at the people parting to avoid her. Not a single person had offered to help.

"*Aiyoh!*" Irene gawped as Dara dripped past the secretary's desk and into her office.

"Is it ready?" Dara kicked off her heels and walked to the cupboard nearest the window. The streets of Raffles were completely dry, as though the storm a matter of meters away had never happened. She opened the cupboard and unhooked the skirt suit hanging on the inside.

"Yes. The last copy is being bound." Irene stood by the door. "I don't know what happened. Something must have gone wrong in the printing room."

"Can you book me a taxi?" Dara looked for something to wipe her hands on.

"Um, I think Ian prefers it to go by courier. There's one waiting downstairs."

"You spoke to Ian?" Dara froze. "Did I ask you to speak to him?"

"Eh, it's Ian's case. I must update him."

"At what point in the last half hour, when you were rectifying the mistake that *you* made, did you find time to speak to Ian?" Dara spoke softly to stop her head from exploding. "When, Irene? When you were exchanging lunch recommendations with the other secretaries? Or deciding what to eat for dinner after you leave here at five on the dot, no matter what we're working on or whether we need you or not?"

"Eh!" Irene gasped in shock. "You don't like my work, you can ask for someone else. I work here for nine years—never had any complaint."

"And yet, after nine years, you have no idea when to be discreet and when to move quickly! It's been over thirty minutes—the bundles should already be printed, bound and ready to go. That is all I'm interested in, so from now on, when I ask you to do something, do it!" Dara grabbed her fresh set of clothes and marched past Irene, who flinched and jumped back.

She changed in the toilets, fixed her hair and returned

to her office. Irene's desk was empty, and Lucy was back at her desk.

"What's going on?" Lucy stared at Dara as she entered.

"What?" Dara checked herself over quickly, worried something was sticking to her.

"Irene is bawling in Ian's office and your phone has been ringing non-stop for the last ten minutes."

Dara hurried to her desk. Six missed calls. All from Lani.

"Word for word." Ian barely moved. His eyes bore down on Dara and Lani as they sat behind his desk. His knuckles were pressed against his lips.

Dara had never felt so sorry for someone, even after the mess Lani had caused in her life. As he turned the pages of his yellow pad, rifling through his notes, she almost said a silent prayer.

Lani read out the conversation between the opposing counsel and the witness, Mr. Wachira:

"Can you describe the document?"

"It was an official document; it was white. It had the Local Housing Office logo at the top."

"And can you describe the contents of the document?"

"It was an internal memo. A memo from the head of the department giving instructions for tax deductions for the following tax year."

"And who was it addressed to?"

"I can't recall."

"You can't recall? In your sworn affidavit, you claim the memo was sent to the Kenyan Revenue Authority. Is this correct?"

"I believe so. As I said when I gave my statement to the lawyer for the Japanese, I looked at it briefly, so I can't really remember."

Lani paused, his lips pressed together. On the other side of the desk, Ian's eyes had closed. Lani kept reading:

"So how can you be sure the memo was regarding tax if you only read the document briefly?"

"*I saw the tax code—it's the internal code we use for branches of the government.*"

"*I see. But you can't remember which tribal group was mentioned in the memo?*"

"*I'm sorry, I don't recall. We have many tribes in Kenya. I don't remember which one.*"

"*I see. Thank you very much. Just to confirm once more, you do not recall which tribe this document pertained to, nor can you definitely confirm that it was addressed to the Kenyan Revenue Authority. Is that correct?*"

"*Yes.*"

"*So it could have been connected to any tribe and it could have been related to any local housing matter, not necessarily connected to tax?*"

Ian took a sullen breath and folded his arms. "Charles Summers's response?"

Lani turned the page of his pad:

"*Mr. Wachira, is it possible that the memo that you swore in your affidavit was addressed to the Kenyan Revenue Authority was indeed addressed to the agency and did refer to the Kiambu chiefs being given a tax deduction?*"

"*It is possible.*"

"We broke for lunch after that." Lani looked up at Ian.

A terrible pause followed and refused to end. Ian took off his glasses and pressed his fingers into his eyes, massaging his eye sockets.

"We flew a witness in from Kenya, put him up in a hotel, put him in front of the panel and he testified the exact opposite of his statement? Is that correct?"

"Ian, when I interviewed him, he said that—"

"Is that correct?" Ian looked down. His eyes were cold with rage.

"Yes. That's what happened."

"Thank you. Mabel is working on the Erwin case. She'll forward all the correspondence to you." Ian put his glasses back on and tapped on his screen.

And just like that, Lani was off Hakida. Stunned, Dara bit

back an involuntary smile. She couldn't believe how quickly the tables had turned.

Lani closed his notes and, swallowing hard, left the room. Ian sniffed irritably and folded his arms, thinking. Even though he wasn't speaking, Dara knew it was a positive sign that she was still in the room. She would never get another opportunity like this again.

"I can fix this," she said, goosebumps raising down her arm. "You always said that keeping the client happy was the number one rule, even more important than winning."

Ian stared at his screen, his temples bulging, but she knew she had his attention.

"What Hakida really wants is this bridge. It's what they've always wanted. They're not going to win the dispute after this. Mr. Wachira's...amnesia means that we no longer have a clear paper trail linking the chiefs and the Kenyan government together, only a tenuous connection between the government and one of the many tribes in the country. So not only can we not prove that the government breached their contract with Hakida—if we keep pursuing this angle, we appear incapable of distinguishing one group of chiefs from another.

"What Hakida really cares about is recuperating the costs it has incurred while its construction workers have sat idle for seven months. If this is really about the sacred, ancestral land, and not just about the terms of the contract, then we need an objective mediator to help us negotiate as quickly as we can, without prejudice to the proceedings. We need a win-win situation that makes both parties feel like they've got the upper hand. Let me speak to Patrick Ndoku and see what can be done."

Try me, she pleaded behind her stoic expression. *You're going to lose this case—a massive case—months before you retire.*

Ian sniffed again and took his cordless phone off its station.

"Irene. Dial Patrick Ndoku's private number in Nairobi." He waited a few seconds, then held the phone.

"Actually, Ian," Dara said quickly. "I think it would be better if this call wasn't made on that line. It's best if there aren't official calls to Mr. Ndoku today—anyone in his office could get hold of the phone records in the future."

Ian nodded grimly, but she could see he was impressed by her shrewdness.

"Bring me Mr. Ndoku's number."

A minute later, Irene came in with a Post-it note, stopping short at Dara's presence. Her eyes were red, and she held a wad of tissue in her other hand.

"Thank you." Dara stood to take the note from her. She tried to look conciliatory, but Irene ignored her and turned on her heel. Another burned bridge.

She dialed the number on her mobile, listening to the long, lazy ring of an international connection. She turned her wrist inwards and checked the time: 8 a.m. in Nairobi.

"Hello." Mr. Ndoku's voice sounded thick and sleepy.

"Hello, Mr. Ndoku. This is Dara Coker, the Morgan Corbett associate on the Hakida case." She fought the urge to turn away from Ian's eyes.

"Oh, Ms. Coker, yes. I've seen you on the emails. Does Mr. Breen need us to send something through? I was expecting an update from Lani."

"No, we don't require that. But we have a problem. Your revenue authority witness has just been examined and he's done a complete one-eighty." She stressed the *your* heavily.

"Our case has been significantly weakened, Mr. Ndoku, and we need to know why that is," she charged on.

"Well, your associate interviewed him..."

"With you present. You recommended this man as a witness."

"I assure you, my investigator—"

"Mr. Ndoku." She lightened her voice, letting her pitch rise to a girlish treble. "This is not your fault—I see that, and Mr. Breen sees that. It's more than likely that the witness was pressured to change his testimony. All we can do is rely on you. We need your help, Mr. Ndoku. Because really, you're our eyes and ears on the ground. You're the only one we can rely on to help with this problem."

There was silence on the other end.

"Perhaps another witness can be procured, but at such short notice..." Mr. Ndoku said.

It was an invitation for her to keep talking, for the request to come from her so he could feign ignorance about offering to conjure up a new witness if he needed to.

"Perhaps. But ultimately, what's important is that the future projects our clients want to commit to are able to go ahead. Hakida wants to build hydroelectric dams, Mr. Ndoku, power plants and irrigation dams in Kenya. These are ten-to-fifteen-year projects. If we could come to some kind of understanding with the chiefs, something that would be amenable to all parties—in the *interest* of all parties—this is work we can *all* benefit from."

Ndoku cleared his throat. "And the land? The sacred land?"

"We just need a number. Interest on increased costs of materials. In exchange for commitment to," she waited for Ian who held up three fingers. "Three more projects."

She let herself out after she and Ian discussed how to sell the new strategy to Hakida. Walking quietly past the closed door of Lani's office, she used every fiber and muscle to stop herself from exclaiming. She and she alone had solved their problem. Whatever happened, she was going to celebrate the fact that she'd annihilated Lani, even if she'd had to become a hyena in the process.

Amaka

"This one just arrived." The sales assistant hooked one gloved hand through the top handle and held the base of the bag in the other. "It's part of our Multicolor collection. It comes with a leather shoulder strap and our emblematic Double G motif."

Amaka held out her hands, transfixed, and stood up from the red velvet stool where she'd been waiting for nearly twenty minutes. She took the bag by its handles and found a sliver of mirror space to colonize. It was a fresh thrill to run her hands over the grained leather, press her palm against the cold metal buckle and release the catch. With time, the item would lose its intrigue and no longer present itself as the perfect solution to a problem she couldn't even articulate, but today it was pure joy.

Breathing heavily, she tried to control the frenetic energy building inside her. This bag was *her*, the Amaka that she used to be: cool, strong, fun and free-spirited. Not the mess she'd become. Not the mess everyone had witnessed in Bali. And this wasn't an impulsive buy—she'd seen the bag the week before and had held off, curbing her instinct until she was really sure she needed it. And if she needed further confirmation, the woman holding a different shoulder bag next to her was staring longingly at the one in Amaka's hands.

Relishing the attention, Amaka tried the bag on in different ways, electrified by the charged distance between wanting, imagining, buying and owning. The women around her understood. They recognized each other, heretics walking in open, unfiltered worship, making their pilgrimage down Orchard Road until they rediscovered their altar. Their eyes flicked down the sides of other women's torsos, looking for abbreviations, silver stamps, patterns, logos. They were hunters, hungry for new game: drawstrings, satchels, saddle bags, cross-body bags, statement bags, subtle bags, it-bags, the predictable and the purposefully unrecognizable. A woman could dress from head to toe in luxury, and the only thing that mattered was the nod of recognition from another. No amount of questioning the inherent value of these bags, or the cost–benefit of the materials, design and aesthetic, could change their minds. These women understood that they were manifesting their highest selves, aligning their best versions to what society's tastemakers had deemed the finest quality. From teenagers in Dolce & Gabbana fanny packs to old ladies in wheelchairs, croco-dile Birkins on their knees, age made no difference.

"We also have it in a blue and green," the sales assistant prodded, her hands interlaced in front of her.

Amaka had considered the blue and green, which was more understated and, arguably, more tasteful. The woman with the shoulder bag moved off, revealing a clear view of the store's window and the long line of Saturday worshippers waiting behind a red cord, some in transparent raincoats, others stuffing their umbrellas into the free waterproof sheaths hanging outside.

With a wide smile, the assistant blocked the window. "Please take your time. There's no rush."

"I'll take this one," Amaka decided. There was no point delaying—with her favorite sales associate off today, there would be no offer of champagne, nor an invitation to a private room.

The assistant took the bag and led her past pale-pink boudoir walls, with pouches hanging off them like fruit; shoes were arranged on tiers like cupcakes. They came to the till and waited behind three shoppers, all of whom were with their boyfriends. Beside them stood a row of turbanned mannequin heads bedecked in jeweled sunglasses and dangling earrings.

As they waited, Amaka considered whether to wear her new bag out of the store or get it boxed. She eyed it in the assistant's arms hungrily. Walking out with it always made her feel like a million dollars but opening the box at home felt like Christmas.

Thinking of unboxings reminded her of Kike, whose Instagram

page Amaka visited now. Kike's posts had become more sporadic since their trip. Her usual, teasing shots offering only the ceilings of impossible-to-book restaurants, stacked coffee table books and headless photos of her boys in matching linen short sets had been replaced by two cryptic quotes about forgiveness and the brevity of life, and then nothing.

Amaka went onto Dara's page, but she still hadn't been unblocked. She stared at Dara's profile picture, deliberating whether she should send another email. She'd thought her ending with Rohit had been painful but knowing that Dara hated her and that she'd humiliated her best friend was too much to process. It was too much to think about the look of betrayal on Dara's face or the astonishment of Kike's friends, or Lani's deep embarrassment as he physically distanced himself from her and refused to make eye contact. Why hadn't she told Dara when she had the chance? Why had she been such a coward, and why, instead of breaking things off, had she responded to Lani's text and gone to his room? Why couldn't she develop some self-control? Why did she have to push everything down and distract herself with fucking or shopping?

A text from her mother popped up on her screen. Amaka swiped it away, but something in the tone of the first line stopped her short.

She opened her inbox, preparing herself for the inevitable disappointment every message from her mother now carried.

Odim n'obi, my beautiful daughter. I want you to be ready when I arrive. I am boarding in one hour and then I have a short stopover in Dubai. I've attached my flight details so please be at the airport to meet me at 7:20 p.m. tomorrow (Singapore time).

We have a lot to discuss, Nne. It has been on my heart to talk with you about many things. I hope you won't be too busy with work.

Ka o di, my dear and see you soon.

The next twenty-four hours were an exclamation mark: a mad rush to clean her flat, stock her fridge and throw away the boxes of her recent purchases. It never stopped raining, even as the weak, pale sun peeked through, like a broken egg in washed-out clouds. Its yolk seeped into the sky, turning it a mustard gray.

Amaka's anxiety grew as the evening approached. When she could put it off no longer, she booked a taxi to Changi and waited in the arrival hall with a churning, unsettled gut. She saw her mother through the glass doors before Ugo saw her, and her insides twisted tenderly as she watched her pull a suitcase off the conveyor belt and struggle to haul it onto a trolley. Not only did she recognize that suitcase, but she could have sketched Ugo's royal blue blazer, wide pants and silk scarf from memory.

She flared, indignant, when Ugo was beckoned by security to pass her luggage through a separate detector by the exit. Unbeknownst to Ugo, Amaka and every black person she knew were regularly asked to do this.

Ugo pushed her trolley through the glass doors. As soon as her eyes met Amaka's, her mother grinned from ear to ear, and they hugged. Amaka's anxiety appeared absent in her mother, who pulled her into the type of full embrace that joined them from waist to cheek and left no gap. Amaka inhaled the full-bodied bouquet of her mother's Trésor perfume and let herself be rocked from side to side.

She took over the trolley and Ugo commented on the impressive airport, the speed with which they were ushered to a taxi and how the airport surpassed her expectations. It was dark and visibility was low in the heavy downpour, yet Ugo admired the drive, remarking that the streets from any airport were a solid representation of the rest of the country. She laced her fingers through Amaka's hand and cupped it. If her mother sensed her discomfort, she didn't say anything. Amaka wasn't sure either of them had the vocabulary to express anything close to what they were feeling.

As they drove by various landmarks, the rain eased and Ugo began to ask questions. Amaka found herself relaxing a little as she shared random trivia she'd picked up. She pointed out the Singapore Flyer illuminated against the dark sky, which was modeled after the London Eye, and according to a recent newspaper article was always half empty. She pointed out the iconic Marina Bay Sands hotel, part of the same group that owned the Las Vegas Sands. This prompted Ugo to gush about her favorite singer, Frank Sinatra, who she'd once nearly met in an airport. The mood lightened as Amaka went on with a list of potential tourist attractions for Ugo to visit. She realized she was embellishing the inherent value of these attractions (zoos, parks and cable cars were really all the same in major cities), and the effort was exhausting. This wasn't how she imagined her mother's first visit would be.

The taxi arrived downtown and pulled up to her building, a seventy-story skyscraper that looked no different to the office blocks around it. It was normally a brisk operation, navigating the four lobbies and elevators, but this time, Amaka scrutinized her home through Ugo's eyes. The 360-unit block offered state-of-the-art tennis courts, a swimming pool, a Jacuzzi and even its own restaurant, but the drawback was that its units were narrow and small.

Up in the lift they went, dragging Ugo's suitcase down a rabbit warren of indistinguishable corridors. At her front door, they slipped off their shoes and put them in the large plastic shoe rack. Amaka had cleared away the stack of shoes usually blocking her entrance, leaving only one pair of flip-flops, heels and sandals. Thankfully Ugo, who was normally eagle-eyed, must have been too tired to question why there were so few shoes in so much space.

Amaka turned on the lights. She didn't have the courage to turn and look her mother in the face. The apartment was so dreary—the rain and night sky made it more so. The walls were bare; there were no plants in the corners and no feminine touches. Being able to see the kitchen sink and front door from the sofa was the most depressing feature of all. The place was like a holding cell: a place to eat, sleep and change. Nothing more. Why had this never bothered her? How had an apartment like this suited her so perfectly for so long?

"Home sweet home. Thank God for journey mercies," Ugo said, and Amaka almost believed the cheer in the voice.

They parked Ugo's suitcase to one side and kneeled down, arms leaning on the sofa. Ugo said a short prayer with her rosary beads, as was her custom after every trip. Mercifully, Amaka wasn't asked to bring scarves to cover their heads.

"Do you want some tea, Mummy?" Amaka asked when they'd sat down.

The corners of Ugo's mouth came down as she considered the offer. "*Hmmm*, I drank so much tea on the plane. What do you have?"

"I've got some nettle tea and I bought some honey. The manuka one you like."

Ugo's smile was genuine. "Ah, then of course, thank you. They never have nettle tea on the plane."

Amaka switched on the kettle and watched her mother empty out her handbag. Another ritual.

"Your hair looks nice," Amaka remarked, taking out spoons. "Did you get it done at the salon?"

Ugo proudly ran her fingers through the corkscrew curls. "I just hired a fantastic new stylist. He used to do all the magazine and TV girls, but I snatched him. Our clientele has doubled. They love him because he takes such good care of the hair under the weave. In fact, he's trying to convince me to go natural. He wants us to start offering natural hair services. He's been showing me all these styles the young girls are wearing, and you won't believe it, but my hair has grown so much since he's been doing it."

"You're going natural?" Amaka couldn't believe her ears.

"*Ehn*, we'll see. If my hair continues growing like this..." Ugo continued unpacking her bag. "But I don't know who's going to teach me because I don't know anything about natural hair."

Amaka was skeptical as she took the jar of honey out the fridge and leaned it against the boiling kettle to melt.

"Natural hair is a..." She caught herself before she said *ball-ache*.

". . . lot more work than it looks. I haven't been able to find anyone to relax my hair since the one black hairdresser here left, and my hair's a mess under my wigs. I've also had to start ordering natural hair creams, and they're so expensive."

Ugo smacked the back of her hand into her palm—*oh well*. "The majority of our stylists focus on weave because that's what we Nigerians like, but the cost in the long-run is higher. No matter how beautiful we look, caring for weave is like putting cream on your clothes instead of your skin."

Amaka stopped taking out the tea bags, dumbstruck. *Who had her mother turned into? Was the most stylish woman she knew, the woman she'd modeled herself on for so long, about to start sporting an Afro?*

She made her mother's tea exactly the way Ugo liked it, warming the mug with hot water first, then filling it up three quarters of the way and adding two generous teaspoons of honey. Making it reminded her of Rohit and his mother's preference for turmeric and ginger tea. His sister's wedding invitation was still in her bedside drawer. She hadn't booked the flight to Phuket, and now she never would. He was answering her sporadic contact with silence. Their relationship—if you could call it that—was as dead as the dried-up lump of ginger she'd found at the back of her fridge.

"Thank you, *Obim*." Ugo pointed down. "Set it on the floor."

They sat side by side again, blowing into their tea. The silence was so achingly familiar that Amaka wasn't prepared for the urge to rest her head on her mother's shoulder. Ugo must have felt it too, because her next words were completely unexpected and slapped that urge away.

"Maybe I should cook pancakes in the morning?" Ugo smiled sleepily. "Just like for Papa after a trip."

"I don't eat pancakes anymore," Amaka bit back, crabbily. "But I can buy the ingredients if you want. That reminds me, I got you a gift."

She went into her bedroom and brought out the Gucci box, the only one she'd left in her sweep of the place.

Putting her tea down, Ugo wriggled forward.

"I got it for you as soon as I knew you were coming." Amaka

placed it on Ugo's lap. "They turn the air conditioning up indoors here, and I know you hate being cold."

Her mother's face dropped when she saw the brand name and the cream and black box. She opened the lid and peeled off the sticker holding the tissue paper down.

"Thank you, *Obim*." Ugo held the cream tweed cardigan up by the shoulders like it was a wet towel needing to be hung on a clothing line. "But you need to stop spending so much money." She frowned, as if trying to understand the need for so much red and blue ribbon, then folded it back in the box and closed the lid. "I've made a decision about the house. We will sell it and share the proceeds between the four of you."

"Mummy..."

Ugo held a hand up before Amaka could speak. "Enough. I've considered what you said, but this is my decision. We don't wait for others to do what is right. I am still your mother, so please respect me. Share it with them. It's what we should have done from the beginning."

She continued when she saw Amaka was listening, speaking more softly this time. "Emeka says Chinyere's mother has been seeking treatment in the UK and her children are bearing the cost. *Nne*, you would do the same for me. The money you've been collecting from the rent is yours, but we also need to sell the shares, *Nne*. The exchange rate has hit the naira hard, and the nail bar has been suffering. I had to close one of the salons, but all is well. With the shares I will manage."

Ugo gently pulled Amaka down to sit beside her. "You're doing well with your job. And with your part of the house, you will still have enough to buy property of your own." Her words were meant to be consoling, but they had the opposite effect.

The next week was like an elastic band pulled more tightly each day. Amaka was in a frenzy trying to replace the shares she'd sold.

Over that period, she took a cash advance from her three credit cards, sent the money to her current account and transferred it to the broker she shared with her mother in Lagos, authorizing him to purchase the shares back. The problem was that the share prices had shot up, so it was costing her more to put the same amount back in the account before she could tell her mother. Taking a cash advance also meant that all her other purchases cost more, so on top of the astronomical interest she was already paying, she was running out of money for basics.

Each morning, she would wake to her mother's tuneless singing, waiting fruitlessly for the warmth and security it used to cloak her in as a child. Very quickly, however, she would try to block out Ugo's voice. Next, something fishy and oily and bubbling on the stove would permeate through the walls. Then the TV would be switched on, and a constant news cycle would begin, mirroring her increasing anxiety. When she returned in the evening, they would eat the dinner Ugo had prepared or make a trip to Little India to buy ingredients for whatever Ugo wanted to cook: spinach, plantain, lady fingers or fresh fruit. The stalls would be half-closed, the ground covered in mucky yellow petals from the flower garlands hanging overhead. They had to duck to avoid the bees half-drunk on nectar, drawn to the rotting fruit, and while Ugo bartered, Amaka would feel the elastic band strain as she tried not to think of the interest piling up, the share prices sliding and the moment her mother would contact the broker. The worst part was not being able to talk to Dara about it, now that she finally felt ready to open up.

Almost two weeks after Ugo arrived, Amaka came home from work to find the TV turned off.

Ugo sat on the sofa, as hard and still as a rock. The tower of designer shoes in the cupboard behind her had been exposed, and every cupboard in Amaka's bedroom had been flung wide open.

Lillian

Lillian's bed was the safest place to be. Every thought of stepping out of her new bedroom or condo building was replaced with the fear of being forced to speak, of putting words to this swallowing sucking her down. This pillow was best and this duvet and this mattress. Staring up at the fan—watching as dust motes floated down and guessing where they would land—was how she could breathe.

Her tiny bedroom floor had been colonized by her books, her laptop, the contents of her handbag and countless other objects she'd shuffled from her old home to Dara's to this new purgatory. She'd moved in as soon as she'd signed the lease for the Yishun flat-share, the same morning she'd called the agent and the same day she'd moved out of Dara's apartment. For the first week after, she went to work like a zombie, dead from the neck down, and returned home as exhausted as if she'd run a marathon, dropped onto her bed and slept fully clothed without eating.

With each day it was harder to rise. Finally, she'd sent Marigold an email explaining that she was sick and asked for a few weeks off. As September was always a quiet month at SpeakNow!, Marigold had agreed, as long as Lillian agreed to the time being unpaid. The last string attaching her to the world and any sense of obligation loosened, even as she edged dangerously close to an abyss.

The cycle was the same: waves of disbelief, sadness and confusion roiled through her mind, agitating her in the middle of the night. Sorrow came next, trembling in her chest, and in it was a hopelessness that was so full it was frightening. When the despair came, she had to lie still or else lose herself in it, like water in a cup in danger of being spilled. When it passed, she would notice bruises she hadn't seen before, like a fingernail bent backward, swollen with blood, or a cut in her mouth. How had she let the past grip her so tightly that she'd allowed her life to disintegrate? Every time she shut her eyes, she heard Kike's little boy crying. She saw the water and struggled to breathe past the guilt that had resurfaced in full force, bloated with the guilt of her childhood.

She sat up and watched the wind sweep sheets of rain like the palm of a bored god playing with water, her body tensing at the sound of her housemates' feet walking past her door to the shared bathroom.

Lillian still wasn't sure what the Chinese girls did for a living, whether they were dancers or full-blown sex workers, but whatever they did, they were some kind of double act. On her days off, they were always home, watching Korean dramas on full blast and wolfing down chicken rice from the food court around the corner. They snored the afternoons away and then, as night fell, began their transformation. With their fake eyelashes and platform heels, their outfits were garish yet had an unpretentious openness, a *take me as you find me*. By early evening, they were gone. A couple of days after she'd moved in, she went downstairs to top up her phone credit, and the two girls had walked out at the same time. Li Rong had waved to her and Xian Xi had followed behind, both slipping inside a white twelve-seater pulled up outside the gate. She could hear the laughter and chatter of other girls inside it before the door slid shut and the car reversed away. Ever since they'd found out she taught English, they'd been dropping hints about her helping them, but Lillian rarely came out of her room when they were there.

Some days she'd surprise herself. She'd wake up with a clear mind and get up with a renewed sense of purpose, an unusual burst of energy. But within a few minutes of moving through the foreign space or reaching for the clothes she'd hung in the guest closet she would start to ruminate on the past few months and her thoughts would spiral. Drained and overwhelmed, she would return to bed, wanting to let it all out but needing to hold it all in, scared of what Dr. Geraldine would diagnose if she confessed all the tricks her mind was playing.

Lillian rolled over and pulled the bottom drawer of her bedside cabinet open. She took out the little envelope and fingered it gently. She'd brought it down from the shoebox in her bedroom and, over the years, when it had become worn and frayed, she had replaced it quickly, taking care not to look at the photos inside. Thinking about her parents was like holding a hot stone, speaking about them like putting the stone in her mouth. To look at them directly would be to squeeze the pebble in her fist and let it blister and burn her skin. But ignoring them, squashing them down, escaping into fantasy had nearly caused a boy's life to end.

"Try to relax. Get comfortable, and when you're ready, you can close your eyes," Dr. Geraldine said.

Lillian licked her lips and smoothed her palms over her jeans. She hadn't been back to see Dr. Geraldine since she'd left Warren. In hindsight, therapy shouldn't have been the first thing she'd cut to save money, now that she was desperate and no longer able to cope on her own.

She dropped back and down on the doctor's divan, trying to ignore how bulbous and uncomfortable the cushions behind her had become.

Dr. Geraldine's disembodied voice floated beside her. "Please, close your eyes."

Lillian obeyed and inhaled, shutting out what little light she could see in the shaded room. Instantly, her senses were overwhelmed by the too-soft velvety carpet curling between her toes; the floral, spicy incense; and the metallic rust of too many antiques. Her throat twinged with nausea. She was convinced she would be sick.

"Listen to the music," Dr. Geraldine soothed. "Let your mind rest on the music and on my voice."

It took several minutes, but at some point, Lillian found herself more aware of Geraldine's words than the room around her, especially on the words she kept repeating: "You are safe." The words entwined in Lillian's head until they became stronger than her own thoughts. Her anxiety about hypnotherapy remained, as did the gnawing fear over her own mental state, but as her breath deepened and lengthened, each thought was pushed back so that it no longer pounded against her skull. She was awake and she was asleep. Deeply relaxed but completely detached. Dr. Geraldine was close by, yet Lillian was in a cocoon that felt of her own making, with a closed door she felt she could open at any time.

Dr. Geraldine asked her a question, repeating it several times. She wanted to be taken to Lillian's proudest memory.

Lillian began to answer, speaking softly with her eyes closed. There was a piano on a raised church stage and her younger self stood at the bottom of the steps. Bem and Yahimba each had a hand on young Lillian and beamed into the camera that Mrs. Walsh, her music teacher, was holding. Her parents were exhausted from their hospital shifts, yet prouder than they'd ever been while girl-Lillian swung between euphoria and embarrassment, the adrenaline from her first school recital still pumping through her veins.

Then Mrs. Walsh was standing beside them, too close in their personal space, but forgiven because of her lavish praise.

Ain't you glad you listened to me—didn't I tell ya? She breathed out her thick accent, the lines around her mouth rivulets of delight. *We figured it out, didn't we!*

Bem and Yahimba were nodding, still in awe of the rapturous applause that had followed Lillian's performance, especially Bem, who had not heard the entire piece before. They left soon after, before the streets became too dark and before Mrs. Walsh could accompany them and force them to pretend to commiserate over how "the neighborhood had changed," which really meant too many of the "wrong kind" had moved in and there were too few Irish left. It was still warm, but the autumnal air had the beginnings of a pinch. On the way, they passed by neighborhood discount stores and empty lots where houses had once stood and stopped at a Dunkin' Donuts. They ordered and left quickly, no one commenting on the yellow police tape sectioning off the store next door.

Lillian told Dr. Geraldine what she could see: Bem was walking through the front door, taking off the cap that was wedged so tightly it left a deep groove on his forehead, blowing into his hands to warm them up. His green tunic and trousers that all the hospital orderlies wore were stiff as cardboard, and she could feel the pride seep through him as she sat by his feet and tugged at his boot laces.

She watched girl-Lillian circle behind the sofa to the kitchen, where she took two white boxes of food out of the fridge, poured them into the same container and stuck it in the microwave.

Put on the kettle while you're there, Yahimba said in Tiv. Already distracted, she was at the desk, her head bent over the medical encyclopedia she read more religiously than her Bible. The sofa, the TV, the old cabinet and a microwave. Home.

What did they serve in the canteen last night? Yahimba asked Bem. They hadn't seen each other properly for nearly a day.

Same as yesterday. I can't wait for your pounded yam and stew. Hospital food is turning me into a pencil. Bem rubbed his feet through his socks.

Yahimba laughed. *You'll be waiting a long time, my friend. But I fried some dun-dun. It's the last of the yam.*

The chewy white sticks of yam were already on a plate, and next to them, a small bowl of palm oil for dipping.

Mmm. The food in Bem's mouth threatened to spill out.

I hope you're not speaking Tiv to her all day. He wagged his finger at Yahimba after he'd swallowed.

She never speaks it back, so you should be happy.

I just want her English to be good.

You want her to be American. She already talks like them. Why can't she speak her own language when she's home?

Please, I'm tired. Let's not fight about this now.

Yahimba looked at Lillian. *Was it me that started or was it your father? You heard him?*

Bem spoke in English as he pulled Lillian into his lap. *Who was it? Was it me?*

Yeah, Dad, it was. She was laughing even before his fingers started digging into her ribs.

As Lillian slept on her mattress on the floor, her parents in the bed above, Bem's words were quiet but audible: *She will do better than us. No one will laugh at the way she speaks or ask to see a real American doctor. No one will make her start all over again.*

You're doing just fine, Yahimba's voice replied a minute later. *Just fine. Everyone has to retrain.*

Bem grunted. *Only foreign graduates.*

Well, what do you want them to do? Just let everyone in? Yahimba turned, the mattress creaking beneath her.

I would have trained as a nurse if I knew it would be this much headache. All those years practicing, and they're counting against me.

You—will—pass. Yahimba drew the words out in her weary-as-a-saint tone. *Did you not pay one thousand dollars for the exam? Do we have another thousand dollars hiding under the mattress? No. So you will pass.*

Pause. Lillian and girl-Lillian smiled as they waited for Yahimba to continue.

And didn't Dr. Cohn say he would help you—

Bem mimicked her, chuckling—he'd been waiting, too. *Dr. Cohn, Dr. Cohn. Where is a witness when you need one? Isn't this the same woman who was so suspicious of him?* "Why is he always trying to help us? Why is he being so friendly? What grown man offers his house and his piano to a Nigerian family because the father is working for him? Where is his wife? Where's his family?" *See you now.*

Yahimba's warm laugh shook the bed frame. *God bless, Dr. Cohn. And his family.*

She stopped laughing after those words and Lillian knew they were both saying a prayer for the doctor's wife and child.

Just as girl-Lillian drifted off to sleep, she heard Yahimba speak again.

I should warn you. I don't think it is medicine she'll be studying.

Bem laughed, baffled by his daughter's gift.

"Take me to their final day." Dr. Geraldine's voice floated into the bedroom and into Lillian's ear. "Where are you? Tell me what you see."

"I'm in the bedroom," Lillian murmured.

A thin, gray winter light filtered in. Bem and Yahimba's bed is made.

"The bedroom is empty. My parents are gone. They won't be back until lunchtime. I'm excited. I make myself breakfast and watch TV."

"Why are you excited?"

"They've gone for my piano. They've gone to bring it back. It's a Saturday. It's a long drive to Chestnut Hill, where Dr. Cohn lives. He's retired now; he's moving to New York and he's offered to loan us his piano."

"What else do you remember?"

"It's cold. I'm not allowed to turn the heat up, but now I can. Dr. Cohn says to keep the piano warm." Lillian smiles, eyes still closed. "So I'm warm and I'm happy.

"I finish my homework and fall asleep watching more TV. There's a knock on the door. It wakes me up. I know something is wrong. The clock says 3:45 p.m. They should be home." A moan cut off the last word.

"I look through the keyhole. There are two people, a man and a woman wearing black shirts with silver badges on their caps and chests. Police. I'm still in my pajamas, so I don't want to open the door. I feel so embarrassed—my mum would kill me. And I'm not allowed to open the door, but they never said what to do if it was a cop. The woman moves away from the door and I see another man's face—our super, who knocks and calls my name. I open the door.

"The woman cop asks for my full name, then asks if there is anyone living with me, like a friend or family member. I'm so scared I can't speak. I think I'm in trouble, or my parents are in trouble for leaving me on my own. Maybe there's something wrong with our papers and we have to leave, like my dad's friend in Ohio who was working on a fake green card.

"The cops wait outside while I change. Then we go down to their car. They're nice to me, but they don't say much. They take me to the station. I'm so scared." She swallowed. "Then I see Dr. Cohn and I think, maybe it's OK. Maybe everything's OK."

"But his eyes are red and his face is so white, and he can't speak. He sits me down on a hard wooden bench.

"'*Your parents had an accident,*' he says. '*They were driving on a bridge and their wheels skidded on ice. I'm sorry, but the car went over. By the time the ambulance got them out of the lake, it was too late.*'

"I couldn't understand what he was saying. I thought he was at the station because he was angry about the piano." Tears streamed down her face. "I said, '*I don't understand. Is the piano OK?*'

"That was the first thing I thought. *Is the piano* OK? But the piano, which was inside the removal van trailing them, didn't have a scratch. Not one scratch..."

There was an animal-like sound, a long, painful braying that shook her with anguish. It swallowed up the light in the station and pulled her into the guilt and shame that had followed her for two decades.

She didn't know how much time had passed, but somehow she was curled on her side, quivering, her wet cheek on a wet cushion. As Dr. Geraldine started to speak, Lillian's crying quieted.

"I want you to go into the police station and find Lillian. I want you to find her on that bench. Can you go in, Lillian?"

Lillian pushed her face into the cushion and nodded.

"Can you see her? I want you to sit next to her and talk to her."

Singapore Botanic Gardens was well lit with old-fashioned lamp-posts, and no path, wide or narrow, was empty of pedestrians. Despite the profusion of plants and trees, many marked with information signs and plaques, the air was scentless. Groups of tourists and families walked between the exits, stopping to peer at the location maps as the evening crept over them. Unlike most parks in major cities, this national park was completely safe, one of the ornamental jewels in Singapore's crown. A popular choice for glossy wedding photoshoots, it was polished, shaped and cut to perfection, teeming with plant life, real herb gardens, horticultural research centers, a children's park, an orchid garden and myriad historic monuments and buildings that mutely evidenced the colonial stamp of the British.

Lillian walked down a shaded trail under huge arbors, long tree trunks arching from one side of the path to the other. She followed the trail until it widened, taking her past restaurants, a gift shop and a waterfall, then up a little hill. Most of the visitors were going the opposite way, but she walked past several exits, taking the long route from her bus stop on the west side to Tanglin Gate on the east side of the gardens.

Her heart rate quickened as she reached the top of the hill. The vista opened up to Swan Lake, a greenish-brown body of water that held little of the romance of its name, but the rain had cooled the air and there was a light breeze rippling over the surface, so it had an unexpected charm. The setting sun was a liquid bronze that mirrored the giant sculpture of swans bursting mid-flight from the lake's center. It was the type of lazy light that weaved between branches in golden shards—light that made artists pick up brushes and cameras and pens—and it sparked Tchaikovsky's Kamarinskaya in her ear, the piece she'd played the day she met Warren. She breathed long and slow as she remembered the fast, jaunty piece, the only one that had concealed the noise of Warren's scraping chair.

He was waiting for her under the white gazebo, looking out onto the lake, just as they'd agreed. He rose stiffly, made some space for her, then sat down before she did.

"Listen. You should know that I've filed," he blurted out. "I had to go with unreasonable behavior. It was the only thing that made sense."

Lillian was silent. This wasn't how she'd expected the conversation to start.

"My lawyer didn't want me to tell you before we served...she wanted me to serve you at work but...I couldn't do that," he continued, playing with his hands. "I've been trying to work up the courage to ask for your address."

She nodded uselessly.

Warren went into business mode. "After you're served, you need to respond to the statement, and then we need to talk about money and assets and if you need any maintenance while..."

Lillian stopped him. "I know—I got it. I need a minute." She didn't need him to speak for her or help guide her anymore.

After a short pause, he spoke again. "There's something else. I've been seeing someone, and she's moved in."

A flurry of images shot through her mind, each of a different woman in different parts of her apartment, touching her things, enjoying the home she'd built. A sickening feeling overtook her as she thought of the nursery: would Warren paint it over and start again or would he one day install a different woman's child in that room? She didn't know which would be more painful. As much as she knew their relationship was over, it still hurt to see someone she'd once loved move on so fast.

Lillian took a painful breath. She had to focus on what she'd come for. There would be time to cry about all this later.

"Thank you for telling me. I've been seeing Dr. Geraldine again. I had a couple of sessions."

Warren still looked guarded, like he was surprised by her lack of reaction to his news.

"I wasn't...there was no cheating. There never was. I had an... infatuation, but it wasn't sexual. She thinks I have PTSD. It's... it's from when my parents died. It explains the flashbacks and the nightmares, the insomnia and anxiety. The numbness, too." She refused to look down at her hands or be overcome with shame.

"PTSD?" Warren scrunched his face and covered it with his hands. "Yes. Fuck, *yes*. Of course. Why didn't we see it?"

"I just couldn't...I couldn't talk about it. I still can't really talk about it now, except with her." She felt a moan rise in her belly like a low, tight ball.

Warren took her hand and held it. They sat there for a while, not speaking.

"I should have known." He jabbed a finger at his head. "Why didn't I realize?"

She squeezed his hand hard and struggled to speak. "There's no way you could have known. I couldn't talk about how I was feeling—nobody taught me how to talk about this stuff. We never had a hope in hell, Warren. It's not your fault. I knew you wanted kids; I knew you wanted a family. I lied to myself and I lied to you. I thought there was something wrong with me, that I had killed my parents because they went to collect the piano Dr. Cohn loaned us. It had snowed the night before and the roads were icy. They would never have gone out if they weren't so eager for me to have it. My dad must have lost control of the car because it crashed off a bridge. The piano was in the rental truck behind them.

"When we started having problems, I thought: *There, you see, I was right. There is something wrong with you.* I know what happened to them was an accident, but I've carried this weight, this worry, that I would pass on this...curse to my child. And when I wasn't scared of that, I was scared of what would happen to our kid if something happened to us. I let you go through the IVF and the adoption research and all the time I was praying it wouldn't work."

She covered her open mouth with her other palm as her chest heaved.

"God...did you even want to marry me? Did you ever really want a child?" he choked.

"I did. I just didn't think I deserved it."

He took her hand and pinched his lips together, trying not to cry. "I'm sorry you couldn't tell me. I'm sorry I pushed so hard. I wanted a family so bad I stopped caring how I got it, or if you were happy in the process. I could *see* you weren't—I could see it. It was just easier being angry with you than accepting it would never happen for us."

Lillian was crying freely now. "I've been carrying this guilt for so long. But I'm so tired, Warren. I'm so tired."

By the time she'd told him the full story, the lake and swans were covered in darkness, swallowed by the night. She told him how she'd gone to live with a friend of her parents, who wasn't really an aunt but who'd lied and said she was, and how her parents' friends scattered across the country had put some money together for their funeral. How the piano had been returned to Dr. Cohn but then a few years later, when she was a teenager, his lawyer had found her and her "aunt" and told them that the doctor had passed away, leaving her both the piano and a college fund, if she wanted to go. It turned out the piano was worth a lot of money and her parents had had no idea.

"His piano changed my life. I loved to play it as a child, but it took away everyone I loved. I've been stuck ever since, hating it so much that I couldn't even touch it. I kept it in storage throughout college and later when I was working, but I couldn't get rid of it, either. It's made me feel like I wasn't worth it, that I'll never be worth any of the sacrifices they made for me."

They walked side by side to the Tanglin Gate. On their way out, they passed a life-sized sculpture called "Joy." The iron mother raised her arms to the sky, her head flung back. Long, with a thin waist and exaggerated hips, her face was raised up to the baby she swung in the sky. Mother and child were fused into one and had no eyes, ears or mouth, but they were alive.

Warren and Lillian parted there. She handed him the copy of the deed for the piano she'd grabbed when she'd left their shared apartment, a copy of the original certificate stapled to the back. Manufactured in 1975. Original value: sixty-five thousand dollars. They agreed to split the sale and all their shared assets down the line. If she could walk away from her piano and let it go, she could finally be free.

Dara

"About done?" Ian was at Dara's door, briefcase in hand.

"Yes." She pushed up on her desk, trying not to look too nervous. Ian never came to her office.

"I just have to do a final read-through of the closing submissions," she said.

"Do you have five minutes?" He kept his hand on the door, as stiff and courteous as ever.

"Of course." Dara glanced through the glass behind him. The secretaries' desks were vacant and most of the firm had left for the day.

"It's Lucy's birthday today, isn't it?" Ian sat down in Lucy's chair. "Isn't that where everyone's gone?"

"Yes. To the Grand Hyatt. I'll head over there when I'm done." Dara crossed her legs and tapped a pen against her palm.

Stop. She put it down. *Relax.*

Since the Hakida arbitration had ended a month ago, she'd been in charge of all post-hearing admin, working side by side with Ian and taking over two new cases. Things had almost returned to normal, but now she was more confident and secure in her abilities. She no longer cared about trying to connect with Ian outside the office or being liked by the other lawyers in the firm. For the first time, she felt an assurance that didn't fluctuate.

"Should I send you the final draft?"

He dismissed that with a flick of his fingers. "No, go ahead. You've taken care of that before."

As if he was sitting in her office for the first time, he looked over the furniture, windows and files. Finally, he looked directly at her.

"I had a meeting with the senior partners today. I put your name forward for partnership and the vote went through. If London has no objections, we'll be announcing your junior partnership in April," he said.

Ian nodded at her silence, a small smile creasing his lips. "Congratulations."

Dara grinned widely. "I'm going to be a partner?"

"You *are* a partner. It won't come into effect immediately, but yes. HR will be scheduling a meeting."

"Thank you. Thank you, Ian."

As many times as she'd imagined this moment, it wasn't like this. She'd envisioned the entire firm gathered in the staff kitchen, glasses of champagne ready to toast as she was told the good news. As dramatic as that type of celebration appeared, the idea of being lauded in front of the whole firm made her jittery; receiving the news in private was much more satisfying.

Ian shrugged magnanimously. "You were the natural choice. Your work on the Hakida case, your quick thinking and calm head, and your loyalty to this firm have spoken volumes. Plus, the clients love working with you. You're an asset to the firm and we don't want to lose you."

Dara couldn't help it; his hard-won praise made her purr inside.

"And my team? Can I build my own team?" Her pragmatism kicked in.

"Yes, but the pool will be smaller, of course. I'm sure I can trust you to keep this in confidence. Lani won't be staying at the firm, but you can make your choice between Mabel and Lucy. Alternatively, you can manage them out and bring in someone new. Mabel lacks the killer instinct and Lucy the drive. From an HR point of view, it helps to keep a Singaporean on the team... but the choice is yours."

Dara felt her blood run cold. She had hoped it would come to this, so why was she so unnerved now that Lani was about to be cut? At the very least, she'd believed Ian had liked Lani and would keep him on.

"But I thought—"

Ian's face twitched with what: irritation? Disappointment?

"You both ran a good race," he said. "And, from what I saw, you're not afraid to do what it takes. 'Iron sharpens iron,' as my father used to say."

Dara nodded dispassionately. "You'll continue to head the team?"

Ian inhaled and opened his mouth to speak. A split second passed, and she knew he was saying the words for the first time. "I also announced my retirement at the meeting. Annabel and I have decided that it's time for us to return to the UK. She's been a saint, keeping her life on hold all these years. It's long overdue."

He glanced away and she knew: tucked away in this truth was a lie.

"I'll be leaving you my clients, Dara. I know they'll be in good hands." He was on his feet. "I know you value my advice, so take this as my final piece. Build your Asia practice. Lani was an attractive hire, but all the contacts in the world can't hide the fact that Africa is nowhere near where it should be. Let someone else take the risk; you have too much to prove to be able to bounce back from another Ndoku mess. You've broken into Asia—you, more than anyone, know how slim the odds of success are for any associate going for partnership. Don't look a gift horse in the mouth. You both worked hard and the experience was good for you. We've all had to fight our way through—it wouldn't be the top if everyone could fit."

Dara stared at him. "You hired Lani to *test* me?"

Ian chose his words carefully. "We had to be sure. Now we're sure."

Zeus. That's whose approval she'd been fighting for. An egotistical, selfish god who had played them against one another. This was who she'd spent six years sucking up to.

"Thank you, Ian," she said quietly. "When will you let Lani go?"

"An opportunity to work in-house with one of our clients has come up, so the timing is good. It'll give him time to look for something else."

She mounted the Grand Hyatt's decking steps toward the long table where Lucy and the other lawyers sat. She carried a plate from her quick stop at the Oasis buffet grilling station where stone slabs displayed thick, charred sausages and tender pink beef and steak. Glass cases offering up cold cuts, oysters and giant shrimp were flaunted on vats of ice with lemons and bushy heads of parsley. To her left, the ocean-green pool was deserted, and the ground was wet in patches.

"Ay!" Lucy cheered and the table's shiny, sweaty faces turned to her.

Around the table sat The Sirens—Ben, Chris and Tim—as well as Lucy, Lani, Mabel, Colin—the only senior partner there—and Gordon, a new trainee from London. There were eight greasy plates of blood-red meat, watery mollusks, powdery pizza crusts and wilted salad leaves slicked in oil. It was like a scene from Tantalus's feast: all bloody stains and chunks of flesh.

"Hi, everyone." She smiled as widely as she could. "Happy birthday, Lucy."

"Ian working you into the ground?" Colin gibed. "You see, this is what it takes: commitment."

Mortified, Dara sat on the only empty chair. If there had been any doubt about whether her confirmed promotion was an open secret, there wasn't now. She was the only one still in work clothes. Thankfully, Colin's deafening laugh smoothed over some of the awkwardness. When Dara looked up again, Chris was glaring at her. She eyeballed him back and felt gratified when he looked away—she'd come too far to back down now.

Lani sat on the other side of the table, listening to Mabel with a scowl on his face. Instinctively, she knew that Ian had told him about his secondment.

"Let's get you a drink." Colin raised an enormous arm to signal a waiter over. His puffy face looked like a blood-drained blowfish. "I know you ladies like your cocktails."

Picking at her food, Dara set a mental timer of one hour. Then she would make her exit. Everyone was drunk and loud, with the exception of Mabel, who was tipsy at best, and Lucy, who ordinarily couldn't stand these guys but looked like she was actually enjoying herself. The only other person who looked as uncomfortable as she felt was Lani.

"This is where I leave you, young'uns." Colin held out his arms like he was performing on a stage. "*Do* get into trouble, won't you? In fact…"

Colin held on to his chair to stop himself from falling on Chris, who instinctively put out his hands to help him. Several glances were exchanged over the table: amused, horrified, embarrassed.

"Waiter! Oi—over here!" Colin clicked his fingers in the direction of the gazebo. "Ever noticed how hard it is to get a waiter's attention in Singapore? It's like they're trained to avoid you. They look in exactly the opposite…oh."

A waiter stood at his elbow. "Yes, sir?"

"Good man!" Colin put both hands on the waiter's shoulders and gave him a hard squeeze. "What's your name?"

"Azeez, sir."

"Azeez, great. Azeez, can you get a drink for everyone at this table? On me." Colin emphasized every other word, as if this were a form of sign language necessary to communicate with someone very stupid or very foreign.

He rummaged so deeply into the pockets of his chinos it looked like he was searching for his balls.

"Have you got any absinthe?"

"Yes, sir."

"Then can you get…" Colin used his free hand to do a quick head count. "…eight Sazeracs. You know what a Sazerac is?"

"Yes, sir."

"Put it on this." Colin had finally retrieved his wallet and was holding out his bank card. "I need to take a leak. When I'm done, I'll come and get my card from the till. Don't bring it back to the table. Keep it at the till. I'll come there. OK?"

"Yes, sir."

"Don't bring it back here. I don't want to have to walk all the way back. I'll come to the till." Colin's hand finally came to a rest.

"Yes, sir."

Dara cringed at Colin's rudeness and threw Azeez a sympathetic glance. He deserved an Oscar for his performance of restraint.

"And you know what, one for yourself!" Colin decreed.

Azeez laughed uncomfortably. "No, thank you, sir."

"No, no, you must. Throw one more in. Or you can pocket the difference—we won't tell." Colin pretended to whisper, putting an arm around Azeez.

"It's not allowed, sir." Azeez shook his head.

"Go on! How long have you worked here? I've seen you here before."

"Twelve years, sir."

"Twelve years!" Colin whistled dramatically. "And they say you can't find good service in Singapore."

He pointed a finger around the table, becoming more unsteady on his feet. "You hear that? Twelve years. That's dedication. That's commitment. Go on, Azeez, have a drink."

"He doesn't want a drink, Colin," Dara snapped. Her voice was even but her tone was clear. It was one thing to be a dick to the juniors. This was something else.

"All right, all right," Colin shrugged, genuinely unbothered. "Good man. Good night, everyone. Happy birthday, Lucy."

He made eye contact with Dara and mouthed with a wink, "*Congratulations*."

"Bloody hell," Tim sneered after Colin left. "That was like watching a grizzly bear try to brush its teeth."

Mabel turned her head. "Dara, I've been meaning to ask you."

Her short bob was stiff and unmoving, her sleeveless dress scalloped with white lace; her face was gently powdered. Everything about Mabel was neat, slick and tidy.

"I've got a London trip coming up—we've got tickets for Wimbledon," Mabel said. "And I want to do some shopping while I'm there, but I never know where to go."

"Oh, right." Dara was astounded. Mabel, who never spoke to her if she could help it, was asking for fashion advice? "I mean, I'm not really a shopper. You could try some magazines?"

"I was hoping you might know some London designers or

boutiques?" Mabel still looked hopeful. "Londoners have such amazing style—so cool and laidback."

"You always look impeccable." Dara made a point of glancing down Mabel's outfit. "Was there anything in particular you wanted?"

"Oh, thank you. Shoes mainly, maybe some accessories. I just love that 'not trying too hard' thing. I really want to do it."

"Well, you could try some vintage stores, but it depends on what you like." Dara gazed down. "What are you wearing now?"

"Fendi." Mabel frowned at her own feet. "Is that passé in London?"

"Um, I think that translates everywhere in the world." Dara hid her smile. Was Mabel flattering her because she was now a partner or had the Singaporean's unfriendliness been a cover-up for her insecurities? Not having seasonal weather in Singapore meant that people wore the same clothes the whole year round. That, in combination with the fact that there was no Fashion Week, meant that anyone with a taste for trends had to look across the ocean, but it was amusing that Mabel assumed Dara had a clue about fashion simply because she was British.

"Actually, one of my best friends is really into..."

Talking about Amaka was like talking about your recently lost limb and pretending you were fine. Dara's anger had given way to a heartache she'd never experienced before.

She pressed on. "She loves fashion, so I'll ask her for some tips."

"Thank you," Mabel said, then dropped closer. "You heard about Ian, right?"

Dara nodded, but kept her body angled away to dissuade Mabel from going into too much detail. "I know he's moving back home."

"I heard Colin talking. His wife gave him an ultimatum to go back or get divorced. Apparently, she's been cheating with—"

Dara cut her off. "Mabel. Please. I don't want to know."

"All right, all right, all right!" Lucy held up her hands. "My birthday is over in a few hours and it's a family tradition to play at least one game on your birthday, especially when that game involves alcohol!"

Half the table groaned while the other half cheered.

"Since none of my family could be here, and today is my actual birthday, we're going to play one round of *something.*" Her voice wobbled.

"OK!" Chris submitted, gallantly. "One round. I have to take the boys to the trampoline park in the morning. If one of them breaks a leg because I'm hung-over tomorrow, it's your fault!"

"Great," Lucy beamed. "Charades?"

Azeez returned, skillfully balancing a tray of tulip-shaped glasses.

"Wonderful. Here comes Colin's disgusting drink," Tim clapped.

It went downhill fast. After their Sazeracs, Lucy ordered a bottle of tequila. Counting *A, B, A, B* over everyone's heads, she split the table into two groups: Lucy, Dara, Chris and Mabel were in one team; Gordon, Lani, Tim and Ben were in the other. Everyone wrote film and song titles on pieces of paper that were then deposited into two glasses. Each team member had ninety seconds to guess the correct title; if their answer was incorrect, they had to take a shot.

The score was 3–2 to Gordon's team. Chris reached for the last scrap in his group's glass, his team's final chance to equalize. Everyone said some version of a prayer that this one would actually have some sense to it—or be something someone had actually heard of. So far, they'd had film titles like *Dick* and *Kind Hearts and Coronets*, and songs like *De Do Do Do, De Da Da Da.*

It seemed the whole point of Lucy's family tradition was to get plastered.

"Oh crap," Chris slurred, sighing at the unfolded scrap.

"Time starts now!" Ben whooped.

"OK." Chris shook his arms out, full of adrenaline.

"No talking!" Ben and Tim yelled, their drunken double act refined with every round.

Chris made the projector sign.

"Movie," Lucy called out.

He held up six fingers.

"Six words." Lucy's face creased in concentration.

"Six words..." Dara murmured, feeling sick.

Chris held up four fingers then did the "T" sign.

"The! Fourth word 'the,'" Lucy yelled, and he nodded.

"Sixth word," Lucy raced on, her eyes glued to his hands. "Sixth word...Lion. Bear. Monster?"

She turned to Dara, baffled. They stared as Chris held the same pose—claws and bared teeth.

"Animal..."

"Beast..."

"Predator..."

Both girls were pantomimic in their confusion, hands stuck in the air, faces scrunched up.

"Tiger?" Mabel looked at Chris like he was the stupidest person on earth.

Jubilant, Chris clicked his fingers at her.

"Tiger!" Lucy clapped, then sat back deflated, no closer to working out the full title.

Tim let out a snicker and brought his thumb to his mouth.

Dara kept going, frowning at Chris's two fists, knuckles brought together. "Third word...against...fighting...boxing?"

Excited, Chris kept tapping his fists against each other.

"Try 'sounds like'!" Lucy ordered, but Chris gave up and moved on.

"Second word!" Dara yelled at Chris's two fingers. He spread his arms to the side like wings and with an open mouth, rolled and twisted his head at the table, with intense concentration.

"Dragon!" all three girls called out.

"Thirty seconds," Ben warned gleefully.

Chris looked panicked. He held a finger up.

"First word!"

Thinking hard, Chris gulped some air, then looked straight at Dara.

He pointed at her.

"Dara?" Lucy looked hopeful. "Sounds like Dara?"

Chris shook his head, pointed again. *At* Dara.

"Black?" Dara stared back at him. "The color black?"

Chris smirked and waited.

She felt everyone try not to look at her. She saw the horror on their faces, and that was when she knew how much she hated them. They couldn't believe they'd witnessed such a faux pas, such a toe-curling moment of epic proportions, and by Monday morning, this would be slobbered over by the rest of the firm.

"Seriously?" Lucy was indignant, shocked.

"Ten seconds..." Ben's voice was small and quiet.

Chris looked at Mabel, then thought better of it and held up three fingers. No one spoke, so he just stood there, holding them up.

"Time's up."

"Sorry," Chris exhaled. His glass was in his hand before he'd sat down, and he drained it. "Couldn't think of anything else..."

"*Black Dragon versus the Yellow Tiger!*" Gordon squealed. "It's a classic. Love Bruce Lee."

"Do you really think that was appropriate?" Lani's voice, full of ice and hard spikes, caused everyone to turn in surprise.

"Sorry, mate, I couldn't think of anything else." Chris made a face.

"That was completely out of order." Lani's top lip curled. "You owe her an apology."

"Come on!" Chris reacted melodramatically, but it was clear he was thrown by the fact that Lani was turning on him. "Don't you think you're all being a little oversensitive? That's the name of the film. It's not offensive."

"If you don't understand why that's offensive, I have no idea where to start with you," Lani growled.

"Why did you choose that title?" Lucy said to Tim quietly. "You were the only person writing with a red pen. That was your title."

"It's a classic kung fu movie. I didn't know he was going to do that," Tim pushed back.

"Black Dragon? Yellow Tiger? You couldn't choose any other title?"

"Yeah, was Chris supposed to point at me for 'yellow'?" Mabel piped up.

"It does have a little bit of blaxploitation," Gordon mused.

"Well, I didn't know that—I haven't even watched it," Tim snapped. "And I have no idea what 'blaxploitation' means. I wasn't *exploiting* anyone. I liked the title, so I chose it. End of."

"If you haven't watched it, why did you choose it?" Mabel asked.

"I just said—never mind. If you can't take a joke, don't play games." Tim laughed, took out his wallet and dropped two fifty-dollar notes on the table. "Come on, Chris. Let's get out of here."

"Which part of that was supposed to be funny?" Lani's voice raised. "Chris pointing at Dara or Chris almost pointing at Mabel?"

Oh God, Dara wanted to scream. *Let it go!*

She tried to think of something to say—anything to stop Lani from taking Tim head on so publicly, from being lured to The Siren's rocks, but came up empty. Why did she care? Why couldn't she just let Odysseus fall on his sword?

"You know, I'm really surprised at you, Lani." Tim shook his head as he stood up. "I didn't expect this from you. This is what's wrong with the world. Everyone's so bloody touchy, so easily offended. We know you're a bit sensitive at the moment—anyone would be—but jeez…"

The table fell silent.

"What was that?" Lani stared, unblinking.

"Hey, I'm not going to go there." Tim raised his eyebrows in mock surrender.

"Go there," Lani dared him.

"Look, all's fair in love and war. You gave it your best, and I'm on your side, remember? Here to help with any 'technical glitches,'" Tim smirked, making air quotation signs.

Tim gave Dara a knowing look. She drew a sharp intake of breath: *Lani had gone to Tim to delete her slides? He'd been willing to cross so far over the dark side to win?*

"Lick your wounds. In the morning, you can send Dara a nice bouquet of flowers—*woah, woah, woah!*"

If anyone had been foolish enough to get in Lani's way, it wouldn't have made a difference. He was round the table, flying at Tim. Tim yelled as they fell to the ground, rolling toward the steps. Amid screams and shattering glass, Tim pulled back to throw a punch a second too late: Lani's fist thwacked against the skin, bone and teeth of The Siren's jaw.

The gasps around them seemed to bring Lani to his senses. He held his fist and watched Tim struggle to his knees and then his feet, groaning and clutching his face. But then Tim took a step back and tumbled down the stairs.

Dara walked onto the streets of Raffles. A few minutes earlier, she'd been with Renée, the head of HR, who had disclosed the conclusion of the internal review into the fight at the Grand Hyatt. The hotel had dropped the complaint, but an article had appeared in an October column of "Tattle," a legal gossip website devoted to spreading rumors and reveling in the downfall of lawyers across the globe. Crediting anonymous sources, it shared the events of that night in toe-curling detail and hinted very strongly at Lani being the instigator. Dara had no idea who had contacted them, but when Renée asked Dara to sign a summary of her statement from their first interview, Dara found herself in the bewildering and unwanted position of defending her rival.

"Lani didn't push Tim down the stairs." Dara touched the paper with her fingertips like the thing had teeth.

Renée's look of contained surprise altered her expression. She took out an identical sheet, her gesture feeling rehearsed, like she had expected this.

"It should be the same." Renée unscrewed her fountain pen, hovering the nib over the paper.

"*As they wrestled on the floor,*" Renée read. "*Lani punched Tim, causing him to roll down the steps.*"

"That's not what I said. I said Lani hit Tim and then Tim fell down the stairs," Dara said. "They both got into a fight; they should both be disciplined."

"Lani is the only one who threw a punch. Isn't that right?" Renée looked down for confirmation. "These are your words. We recorded them in this room."

"Yes, but I explained at length what Tim did with the game and how that was the inciting incident. All it says here is that *'words were exchanged.'* I didn't phrase it that way."

Renée placed one hand on the statement, so her coral-pink manicured nail could follow the sentence Dara was referring to.

"It's not all that different." Renée gazed back at the sheet.

"But it makes it sound like—" Dara caught herself, her frustration rendering her inarticulate. She had to be careful. This wasn't her fight, but she was so angry with herself for not having the words she'd needed to stand up to Tim. She'd dealt with so many microaggressions, but when the chance to call out something blatant had come, she'd frozen. She couldn't let Tim win now.

"This statement sounds like Lani pushed him and he didn't. Tim definitely tripped," Dara insisted. "I can't sign this."

"Tim believes that Lani is the reason he fell down the stairs, and we have four statements confirming that Lani *knocked* Tim down the stairs." Renée's bafflement continued. "I thought your statement was in alignment."

Four statements. Whose? Ben, Chris and Gordon she expected, but who was the fourth? Not Mabel...Singaporeans preferred not to get involved in anything that could cast themselves or their reputations in a bad light; they were so paranoid about the government keeping tabs on them. She'd even heard of companies asking their employees not to offer witness statements for crimes as innocuous as pickpocketing, and she definitely wasn't imagining how carefully both women had avoided being alone with her or discussing anything about that night. Given the chance, they'd probably say they'd seen nothing, no matter how much they liked Lani.

But if it wasn't Mabel then it had to be Lucy.

"I just tried to record what I saw, rather than interpret it in any way," Dara smoothed over.

"I see."

Again, well-rehearsed. Nothing like the off-the-cuff tone it was meant to sound like.

Renée's sudden hardness made her plucked eyebrows and lined lips more pronounced. "The thing is, Dara, the firm has had some concerns about Lani for some time. I can't go into too much detail, but there have been questions raised about whether Morgan Corbett Shaw is a good fit for him. This is confidential. I'm sure you appreciate that. After this last incident, it's become clear that his behavior will continue to have a negative impact on the firm. There have been other issues—"

"Such as?" Dara pushed. If they were going to drag her into this, then she deserved to know.

Renée paused and Dara could see her recalibrating now that her flow had been interrupted.

"Aside from his conduct on the Hakida case and Ian's general discontent with the quality of his work, we've discovered a number of embellishments on his CV."

Dara could think of a counter-argument for every one of Renée's points: Hakida hadn't been Lani's fault; Ian had stopped feeding Lani work, so his billables had dropped; and for all her frustration with the nepotism he'd benefited from, she'd wager eighty percent of the people in the office had also exaggerated on their CV. She was more than ready to see the back of Lani, but not like this.

"And now, with disturbing the peace, he's brought the firm into disrepute." Renée wrinkled her nose at the displeasure of it all.

"Then why not just give him notice? Why do I have to change my statement if it's so clear-cut?"

"At our meeting, Lani hinted very strongly that he was not averse to taking legal action against the firm should he be terminated in the near future. However, the partners feel they've been left with no choice, so they want to make sure they've got all the facts clear."

Of course. They were worried about an unfair dismissal suit and were gearing up for a fight. With her statement supporting their preferred version of events, it would be hard for him to claim racial bias, and what other grounds did that leave? If he brought the case here in Singapore, the firm would have a strong chance: Singapore law was famously pro big business. But in the UK? That fight would be messy. No one would come out well, but Lani could win. Of course he could win.

The fucker. She didn't know if she should be impressed by his balls, thrilled he was finally out of the way, or incensed with the mess he'd caused in less than a year. If she changed her statement, then her transformation into full-blown hyena would be complete. But if she refused, they would come for her next. They'd twist every throwaway comment she'd ever made, sift through her emails, comb through every file she'd ever worked on so they could build a case against *her*.

This was how the firm worked. It was the hydra from which all the other heads sprung: poisonous, unyielding and vicious.

She tried one more time. "Renée, there were racial undertones to the fight. That isn't mentioned anywhere in this statement. Doesn't that matter?"

Renée looked apologetic. "Of course it does, and the partners have been made aware of that. But one person instigated a physical fight that resulted in another requiring medical attention. Tim's arm is broken. The firm has to send the right message.

"I'm sure you can see why the partners are very concerned. And as a future partner yourself..." Renée's eyes flicked to the door then back to Dara, a conspiratorial smile tugging at her lips. "...you understand how important it is to support and protect the firm. It's important to show everyone you're a team player."

Was this the cost of her reward? As a partner, she could control other people's futures, buy everyone cocktails on the company's credit card, but then what? The firm was already demanding blind loyalty, and her partnership hadn't even been announced yet.

"Your promotion won't be made official until next April... confidential, of course."

They would only confirm if she signed.

Years of loyal service and hard work had counted, in the end, for nothing.

Amaka

"*Kedu*, Mummy." Amaka entered warily and shut the front door.

Dressed in a royal blue Ankara blouse and mermaid skirt, Ugo had a grim face. She didn't ask Amaka to sit beside her on the sofa. When Amaka stood before her, her work bag still on her shoulder, Ugo began to speak in Igbo.

"For many years, I've been asking myself: why is Amaka like this? Why is she so stubborn? Why does she not want to be with her family or in her own country? Why does she prefer to be here with strangers?"

"Mummy, please." Amaka sighed, weariness and fear draining all her energy.

Ugo held her hand up. "We know that when a child is too stubborn, it's because he is knocking his own head against a wall. 'Which wall is Amaka knocking her head against?' OK, I will remove the wall. I removed all the walls, but still, after university, you made one excuse after another not to come home. When you finally moved back to Lagos, you did everything to keep away— *work, work, work*—no interest in starting a family and settling down. I thought, maybe I don't understand because I'm not as educated as she is, not like all her friends' mothers educated abroad.

"But look at me. My father refused to send me to university, but today I have my own business. Everything Chukwu left me, I have managed it well." Ugo's voice began to shake. "I started my own businesses. I've done it by myself. I've been an example.

"Chiamaka, I know your life has not been easy, but why are you trying to destroy it? You've always had a strong head, but what is this?" Ugo's voice raised and she threw her hand toward the open tower of shoes behind the sofa. "What *is* this? Who are you trying to be? Eh?"

"Mummy, I work hard." Amaka started to shake. "I can spend my money however—"

"You're lying to me!" Ugo screamed, wagging her finger violently before collapsing backward.

The force of it stopped Amaka's breath.

"You're throwing your money away and you're stealing! You're wasting your life!" Ugo snatched a piece of paper from beside her and threw it at Amaka's feet. "The broker told me that you emptied one of the accounts! Then I checked with the UK bank, and they said you've missed two mortgage payments! Are you trying to kill me? Are you trying to destroy my life?"

"Mummy, I just—it just got out of hand."

"Eh? What are you saying?"

Amaka covered her face. "Most of the shares are gone. I sold them. They're gone."

"Father God." Ugo stared up at her, her face a crumpled, baffled mess. "I've prayed for her, I've fasted for her...what more can I do? You have always been stubborn. You've always had a strong head. But this? Throwing away your money, your security? The sweat and suffering your father went through for you?"

"Mummy, please! Don't talk about him!" Amaka cried out. "I've made mistakes, but you don't have to mention his name."

"I should not mention his name?" Ugo stared. "Your father? You refuse to speak of him, you refuse to cry for him. Even the day we put him into the ground, you stood like a stone...He was not perfect, Chiamaka, but he was your father! Why can't you forgive him?"

Amaka sobbed, her arms wrapped around herself, her face turned away. Hot, angry tears poured down her face. "You don't know what you're asking me to forgive!"

She flung her bag to the floor and it crashed against the coffee table, its heavy oblique shape hitting the glass with a crack.

Ugo jerked back.

"This anger..." she said softly, frightened. "You trap the dirt in your eye and won't let me help you release it. You won't talk. Even before he died, something changed. Your father was your everything and then just like that…Is there something that he did? Please tell me."

Amaka looked slowly at her mother's face and saw the naked fear Ugo had been hiding, the fear that Chukwu had touched her or worse. She had never imagined that hiding the truth would torment Ugo this much. With a shudder, she slid down to the other end of the sofa.

"You remember when you first told me about Chinyere and his sisters? When I was seventeen? We went to his office for help with my American visa. You told me that he had three other children and another wife. I think you wanted to prepare me. You knew he would have photos in his office, or that they could come by."

"I remember." Ugo turned her face away.

"I already knew, Mummy. I pretended, but I knew he had other children. Four years before, you'd enrolled me in after-school lessons. He'd stayed with us just before, you remember? I wanted to help him unpack his suitcase, even though he never liked me doing that. I found the books and clothes he gave me before he left and there was a book of fairy tales and a remote-controlled helicopter that he said were for Uncle Emeka's kids. But there were also some shoes. Pink with a big buckle on the side, that jelly style—see-through with glitter."

She closed her eyes. "I thought they were for me. They were my size. I thought they were for my birthday, an extra-special gift because I'd waited for him so patiently. All those months he was gone. I was going to wear them to school and show all those girls who didn't believe I had a father. '*Show him! Show him!*' They used to make fun of me. And when he came, he was gone so soon I could never prove he existed.

"I put the shoes back and I waited for my birthday, and then I started lessons on the island. I was one of the only ones coming from the mainland—one of the only ones who didn't go to the British schools nearby, and I was always the last to be picked up waiting for you to come from work. And one day, at the end of lessons, when everyone was playing and waiting for their drivers to collect them, I saw a girl around the same age as me, sitting with her younger sister and calling her brother, Chinyere, to come because *Daddy is here.*"

Ugo began to rock, letting out a moan.

"I followed them because I saw her shoes. They were the same shoes." Amaka's throat was dry and hoarse, each word clawing its way out. "I followed them to the gate and they ran to a black Mercedes. His Mercedes. When they were getting in the car, he saw me. And I saw him. He looked confused and panicked. I was supposed to go to different lessons, remember, Mummy? You found the money to send me there."

Now it was Ugo's turn to cover her face.

"He got in the car and left me there. He pretended he didn't know me and he left."

A week later, Ugo flew back to Lagos. It was a week of late nights talking, crying and listening more keenly than mother and daughter ever had, as much to what was said in-between the words as the words themselves.

Ugo spoke about her teenage years growing up with Chukwu, who was her childhood sweetheart, and who she'd been in a relationship with throughout secondary school. Chukwu's parents came from more money and were respected in their village. While Ugo remained behind to attend secretarial college, Chukwu went to the University of Lagos; Nigeria was flush with newly discovered oil money in the late seventies and Chukwu had been convinced that he needed to be based in the then-capital. He returned to Umuahia just once in his first year, but never invited her to visit him on campus. Ugo could see something had changed in him; he would be distant and detached one day, then return to the boy she'd gone to primary school with the next.

At this point, Ugo's family had started to pressure him to set a date for the wedding. It was clear that his family—especially his mother—was not happy with Ugo as Chukwu's choice for marriage, believing he could do better now that he was in Lagos, but since everyone suspected that the couple had begun to have premarital sex, it was thought best that they be formally and socially recognized. They held their traditional wedding in 1977, a few months after Chukwu attended the lavish, ambitious FESTAC Festival of Black Arts and Culture, which drew musicians like Stevie Wonder, a cultural scene Ugo had been desperate to be a part of. Chukwu returned from Lagos a few times in his second year of university, but the plan to find her a job in the city, and for them to set up a family home, never materialized.

Representatives from Chukwu's family arrived at Ugo's home one morning in his third and final year. Sitting in her parents' front room, they returned her bride price, claiming they'd discovered a distant relative on Ugo's paternal side who was *Osu*—an untouchable outcast. Even though Ugo herself was not *Osu*, and that relative was long dead, there was nothing her family could do but accept the rejection. The return of her bride price was the symbolic dissolution of their union. They'd been married only three months.

Ugo then explained how her desperate letters to Chukwu had gone unanswered. Less than a year later, rumors began to spread that his family was preparing for another wedding, this time in another state. Uncle Emeka, Chukwu's younger brother, was the only one who cared enough to tell her the truth: Chukwu was marrying the daughter of a prominent Igbo businessman, one of the sponsors of FESTAC '77. Chukwu already had a job waiting for him when he graduated. Ugo spoke of her father's rage at the way she had been treated, and at Chukwu's parents' decision to seize an opportunity to advance their son rather than counsel him to do the honorable thing and preserve his marriage.

So, Ugo had finished her secretarial training. After working in Port Harcourt for two years, she went to live in Lagos with a family friend and got a job with an American oil company. She was twenty-four, Chukwu twenty-five, when they met at the birthday of a school friend.

The way the affair began was difficult for Ugo to admit and difficult for Amaka to hear. It was easy to blame Chukwu for pursuing her again, now that he was more financially stable. Seeing the stylish couple, him in a patterned shirt and bell-bottom jeans and his new wife in her belted mini-dress and platform soles, Ugo felt her bitterness bit into her principles and distracted her from her own search for a partner. Chukwu and his wife were hip and glamorous, surrounded by friends, and were wildly spending her father's money in the oil boom of 1982. But Chukwu was nostalgic for home and eager to show how remorseful he was. When he saw her at the party, he passed her a message through a friend and that was it—they began their affair. He pleaded for her forgiveness, explaining over and over how he had realized that no love would survive poverty; that he had to maintain his family and repay the huge loans they had borrowed to send him to school, so marrying a woman with money had been his best chance. He convinced her that he had never stopped loving her, that his marriage was an arrangement that helped present him as a family man in his business dealings, and that now, more than ever, he was in a position to support her financially.

Ugo was lonely, far from family and comforted by the explanation—however painful—she'd never thought she'd hear. Even though their love had been tainted by the humiliation of his rejection, and she knew he would never leave his wife.

That comfort came to an abrupt end when she fell pregnant. In 1983, Amaka was born; six months later, Chukwu's wife gave birth to a son. Ugo admitted everything to her parents, who insisted Chukwu's family and in-laws be told. A financial arrangement was agreed upon and, spearheaded by Uncle Onyekachi, it was decided that none of the children would be told until they were old enough to understand. Two or three times a year, using work trips as pretexts, Chukwu would spend time with Amaka. In the nineties, the military government's monopoly of the oil trade and the rise of the black market saw Chukwu's father-in-law's business fail, forcing him to develop his snail and chicken farms in the East.

Mother and daughter calculated that it was during this time, in 1996, that Amaka had seen her siblings for the first time. The shifts in her behavior and the rejection of her father suddenly made sense.

In this unburdening late into the night, Amaka saw the weight Ugo had been carrying, the consequences of one bad decision she would never be able to change. Ugo, who had never again married, who had never had the chance to explore what her life could have been, who had had to fight for her daughter to get the life she deserved while carefully handling the man who had the most power over that life. Amaka had luxuries Ugo had lost decades ago: her independence; the right to choose what she did. The more Amaka understood the narrow corridors of life Ugo had walked down, and the harsh judgment she'd suffered for deviating from the expected path, the more she grasped how important it was to Ugo that Amaka make careful choices.

After asking to see the empty bank accounts for herself, a more resigned and aged Ugo held Amaka tight and said that Chukwu's money must have been like his love: too slippery to be held down or counted on. Ugo, who had always clung to her faith, putting Jesus at the center of every difficulty and question mark, told her daughter that the outcome of her life was in her own hands. She, Ugo, would return home to figure out how to keep her businesses afloat without the money she'd been counting on, and would fully take over the accounts, shares and the decision over the London house. Amaka was now on her own.

After her mother left, Amaka began the process of cleaning and cataloging the items in her closet. As she worked, she traced the last ten years of her working life with every loafer, boot and heel. Here were the Prada peep-toes she'd bought after befriending a girl on the same table at a Lagos wedding, being shown a photo of the girl's fiancé and realizing it was the same guy she was sleeping with. And here were the Nicholas Kirkwood boots purchased soon after her mother's cousin joked that Amaka had inherited her father's dark coloring. She'd bought these Chanel ballet pumps when her very first boss invited her to his house party, only to find she was the only guest there. After a hasty exit, she knew she'd be blamed if she told anyone, so she channeled her rage and frustration into an overpriced session with a personal shopper. Her favorite Giuseppe Zanottis were acquired after a humiliating grilling at Charles de Gaulle Airport by a customs officer suspicious of her green passport, and these butterfly-winged Sophia Websters were purchased on her last London summer trip when she was thirty-one, the year her father had died.

Amaka had taken the bus from the center of the city, where she and her friends had been renting a flat on holiday, to Mill Hill, a quiet, green suburb in north London. She'd underestimated how cold the weather could be when wandering around in circles, and when she'd finally found the house and was let in, she'd been completely unprepared for the stacks of mail addressed to her father, some of which were warm from the heat of the hallway radiator where they'd been piled. Seeing his name, Mr. Charles Chukwu Okafor, so soon after his funeral, threw a gloominess over the whole trip that only lifted when she shopped. It was a reminder that she was no better than he had been—she knew his will was unfair to her half-siblings, yet she took his money and his house. She understood the secret guilt that drove him to change his will, the apology he was trying to extend and how much it would hurt him not to be forgiven. The only thing that helped her bear it was to spend the money as it came in, to treat it with the same level of unimportance she'd felt as his daughter when he was alive.

Amaka didn't know if it was even possible, but it was time to stop letting Chukwu control her. Her desire to chase after men like Lani—unavailable men like her father who dangled shiny objects while slicing her up into tiny, invisible pieces—did nothing but leave her wanting more.

Her father was never coming back, and he would never be able to right his wrongs. No one would ever make this burden easier to bear or help her make better choices. She would never have a childhood with Chukwu, and it would never be fair, but she had to stop letting one chapter of her life control the rest of it.

Weeping, she sent out emails to the luxury consignment stores she'd been a loyal customer of, replying to the regular requests they sent to buy back her pieces. Selling her bags and shoes was more than clearing out her cupboard; it was dismantling the mask she'd been hiding behind.

After the last email had gone through, she sat on the couch and dialed Dara's number. It rang until the call cut off.

A few heads rolled up as she walked through the bank. Hardly anyone was in yet, but she knew Rohit would be at his desk early. Her legs were weighed down, but she fought the urge to run. Instead, like a robot, she walked to her desk, her handbag swinging and thudding against her thigh. She held the strap to keep it still. The knock of the hard box against her hip had once felt like a reassuring piece of armor, but now it was just a heavy wrecking ball. She dumped it on her desk and walked across the floor to Rohit's partition, where he had moved desks after the Bali trip.

"Hi," she said tentatively.

For a split second, surprise flashed across Rohit's face, but he recovered well and continued typing.

"Can we talk?" Amaka tried again, drawing closer and picking at her nails. There was no point hiding her nerves—she *wanted* him to see how nervous she felt.

His response and hostility were expected.

"I'm busy, as you can see," he replied coldly, taking out an earphone.

"Rohit." She stared at him until he eventually looked back at her, exasperated.

"I. Am. Busy."

"When can we . . . can we talk later? At lunch?"

"Is this a game to you? You all of a sudden want to talk—why? You woke up today and decided this is the day I suddenly have time for this? I'm busy, Amaka. I'm at *work*. If you haven't got something work-related to talk to me about, then you need to go."

"It's not about work," Amaka admitted, though a part of her was tempted to pretend it was. Lying would make things worse, although seeing how fed up Rohit was, it was hard to believe anything could make things between them deteriorate even more.

"A lot has happened, and I wanted to talk to you. I know I owe you..."

Rohit's eyes deadened and he put his earphone back in.

Amaka drifted away, hoping he might call her back. When she returned to her desk, she tried to settle into work, but every few minutes, she couldn't help but look at him. It had been so easy before to pretend he wasn't there—that she was unaffected by the way things had ended—but now that everything was out in the open, now that she had nothing more to hide, she couldn't stand leaving things the way they were any longer. She wasn't deluded enough to believe that the mess she'd made could be cleaned up enough to get him back—she even found herself wondering if wanting him back came from the right place. This was the sort of question Dara would have asked her, if Dara wasn't one more relationship she'd lost.

I need to make things right. She marched toward the stationery room. *All I can do is say sorry and tell the truth.* He'd once loved her directness; she had to take the risk that he loved it still.

One of the admin staff helped her find what she was looking for in the cupboards: a board, some cord and a marker pen. She worked carefully, taking her time with each word. When she was done with the sign, she stuck two drawing pins into the exterior of her partition and hung it up.

It took an hour but felt twice as long, especially now that she no longer had sales alerts and brand email notifications to distract her. Gradually, the traffic increased as people walked by her desk. Some did a double take, some openly gawked and others stared at her questioningly.

Holding her breath, she watched as one of the analysts from their team walked past her desk and straight to Rohit. With his back to her, she couldn't see anything, but then miraculously, he moved aside and Rohit rose, a baffled frown on his face.

"Amaka, do you have a minute?" Indira's silky drawl said behind her.

"Yes, of course." Amaka jumped, startled that Indira was in this early. "I'm not busy."

She tried to get to her boss before she could look down at the sign, but a step before she reached her side, Indira's eyes lowered.

"What's this?" Indira took the sign off.

"It's just a joke," Amaka laughed nervously. She hadn't bargained for this extra level of humiliation.

"A joke? You're playing jokes at work?"

Amaka tried to get her mouth to respond, but her tongue wouldn't move. To her mortification, Indira began to read the card.

"I'm a dick. I got scared. I'm asking for one more—"

"Indira, sorry," Rohit jogged up to them. "It's my fault—it's a stupid prank. A dare. I actually left it on Amaka's desk last night and I forgot to take it off. I really apologize, you weren't meant to see that. Could I?"

Astounded, Amaka watched as Rohit held out his hands apologetically. Indira didn't look like she believed him for a second, but she squinted her eyes in a way that hinted at amusement.

"Try to stay focused." Indira gave him the sign. "Amaka, my office."

Amaka delayed, torn in both directions. Locking eyes with Rohit, she felt like bursting. She wanted to thank him, kiss him, tear the sign out of his hands. His expression was unreadable, but his actions said so much.

"Amaka."

Turning away from Rohit, she followed Indira, who shut the door and gestured to a chair, her face as austere as her gray blouse and silk trouser suit.

"What was that about?" Indira's tone was gentler than Amaka had expected.

When Amaka shrugged helplessly, Indira sat back in her chair and took in her protégée.

"I'm glad you have someone in your corner," Indira said lightly. "Although, I'd prefer it if you kept your lover's tiff out of the office, which, I have to say, you've done pretty well so far."

Amaka tried to smile but her eyes filled with tears the more she blinked them back.

Indira sighed. "I wanted to speak to you before you found out. I asked HR not to tell you yet. I wish there was more we could do, but it doesn't look likely that another appeal will be successful."

"Sorry? An appeal?"

"Your employment pass was rejected. It's usually a standard procedure. We appealed, but there was no change, and with the ministry...you don't get any explanation, and there's no one you can really speak to."

"But...why?" Amaka stammered.

The breath Indira took was so awkward and prolonged that it told Amaka everything her boss didn't want to say.

"Because I'm Nigerian? But I got the EP the first-time round. What changed?" Amaka couldn't believe it.

"Sometimes they do this," Indira said apologetically. "They have quotas and they can cancel or decide not to renew. It's shameful, but it's always been this way. I'm sorry. I promise you, I will do everything I can to help you..."

Amaka burst out laughing. It was too much to think she'd been looking in the wrong direction, digging a hole between who she was and who she wanted to be when the ground beneath her had been shifting the whole time. The irony of the timing was bittersweet.

They sat at a wooden table in the office kitchen at the end of lunch, waiting for one of the compliance officers to warm their dinner in the microwave. It was the slow lull before the crash of trading began again, and it would soon cease to be her life.

"What are you going to do?" Rohit asked guardedly when they had the place to themselves.

"There's nothing I can do. I just had a meeting with HR, and they said I have until my employment pass runs out," she replied, relishing his presence and attention. The recent news underlined just how precious being with him was.

"This is insane. And you had no idea?"

"I knew my EP was up for renewal at the end of the summer. I think I got a reminder, but I completely forgot to chase it. It's my fault; I can't blame anyone."

"How long do you have?"

"One month." She chewed one of her nails. "Indira says I might be able to get an extension. I have to find someone to take over my apartment. I have to find a job—I have to go back to Lagos. I'm going to miss Sanaa's wedding next month, if I'm still even invited."

She covered her face. Unable to stop herself any longer, she reached for his hand and gripped it. "Rohit, I'm sorry. I fucked up. I was selfish and fucking stupid. I just lost control. I should have been honest with you from the beginning."

He moved his hand away. "You were seeing someone?"

She wrung her hands and nodded.

"The guy you went to Bali with," Rohit said flatly.

Amaka nodded again. "I didn't go *with* him, but I knew he'd be there."

"Why? If that's what you wanted, why didn't you just end it with me? Why treat me like a fool, meet my sister, pretend like you cared? Did you feel sorry for me?"

"I do care. I just don't know how to...I don't know how to do *this* without protecting myself, without setting up fail-safes, and I didn't want to be alone." She wiped the tear dripping down the side of her nose.

Rohit glared at her like she was a stranger. "So you used me? I've spent months trying to get you to open up. I've tried to show you over and over that I was here for you."

"I know."

"You just didn't have the guts to say it wasn't me you wanted." He glared at her.

She looked at him sadly. "How do you know what you want in love when you've never seen it? When you've never believed in it?"

"You're going to have to come up with something better than

that. I'm talking about behaving like a decent human being, not someone who lies and deceives people like it's their second job."

"I love you, Rohit. That's the truth." She opened her hands, helpless. "I just don't know what to do about it."

His face, when she looked up, was full of disappointment, but he believed her. She could see it, but he also saw her clearly, too. He'd thought they were the same, that she was just like him—funny, bright, a rule-breaker who grabbed life with both hands, honest and whole. Now, he saw the truth.

"This version of love I can't do, Amaka. I can't move forward constantly looking over my shoulder, wondering if you're seeing someone else, trying to make things work with someone you really want." He didn't meet her eyes. "Whatever you need, it's not with me. And I just—I want something different now."

They sat in silence until the kitchen door opened.

On her first attempt, the call rang until it cut off, but the second time she tried, a gruff voice answered.

"Nigerian High Commission."

"Good afternoon." Amaka twisted to the edge of her seat in the corner of a café near work. It was a French café, usually popular, but the lunchtime crowd had emptied now. She pushed her half-eaten croissant and latte away.

"Good afternoon."

"I need some help, please. I'm a Nigerian citizen living here in Singapore, and I've just been informed that my employment pass won't be renewed. I work in a bank, and they don't know why my renewal was rejected. I keep getting an automated machine when I call the Ministry of Manpower, and I'm waiting for them to respond to my email—"

"We don't deal with employment matters. You will have to go through your place of work."

"I spoke to them, and they said if I can get someone to write a letter, that can sometimes help. They suggested I try you." Her stomach started to ache.

"Miss, we cannot help with employment. You must speak to MOM directly."

"Is there someone I can speak to? I'd like to arrange an appointment with the ambassador or an official," Amaka retorted stubbornly.

"There's no ambassador or embassy here."

"The high commissioner then," she pushed back, desperation creeping in.

"There is currently no longer an appointed high commissioner posted here."

"So...who am I supposed to call?" *What was the point of an embassy with no ambassador?*

"For all consulate matters, including passports and emergency certificates, you must report to the High Commission in Malaysia."

She cut the call and wrenched open the handles of her bag, retching into it a sticky brown sludge.

Lillian

The food court near Lillian's new apartment was open air, naked under the evening sky, with stalls and tables curving around an open center. Almost every seat was full of families reluctant to handle a Sunday night dinner alone on their helper's night off. Packets of tissue, rolled-up pashminas and umbrellas held the owners' spots until they returned.

Ravenous from watching trays of food pass by, she and Amaka found a vacant table and sat down, past caring about the splashes of soy sauce and scattered grains of rice around them. They split up and wandered around the stalls, eventually choosing spicy Yong Tau Foo with fish balls and kai lan swimming in a film of red, oily soup, and chili crab with sweet fried bread to dip in the sauce.

Lillian ate her soup quietly, eyeing Amaka as she ate. She'd agreed to meet, but only if Amaka came to Yishun and only if they went somewhere she could afford. Her recent therapy sessions had unlocked a channel from her heart to her mouth—she was no longer holding her tongue or inconveniencing herself for people she didn't like. And if there was one person she didn't like, it was Amaka.

But Amaka's fight was gone. It was strange to watch someone so gusty and obnoxious now try to muster smiles and make pleasant small talk about the food, even if it was a welcome change from her usual domination of conversations. Dressed in a hoodie that she must have been boiling in, with her braids pulled up and no makeup, for once, there was no trace of any of the sheen and shine that usually adorned her. With a jolt, Lillian realized that she recognized the docile spirit she was witnessing in Amaka: it used to be hers. Long before she'd collapsed in Bali, she had carried this same broken, numb pain. The only difference was that she had done it for so much of her life, and so convincingly, too. It made her angry how much repressing herself had suited everyone around her.

They ate, pretending the two of them being together was the most natural thing in the world. Or maybe Amaka was waiting for her to say something first? When they finished, they washed their hands in one of the white basins nearby and bought a coconut each, plastic straws sticking out.

As she leaned in to drink, Lillian stretched the fingers of each hand, one after the other, trying to be as inconspicuous as possible. The phantom aches she used to get before a performance had returned, as had the perfect mix of excitement and anxiety she hadn't experienced in so long, like nerves before seeing an old flame.

She'd started listening to music again, watching YouTube recordings of her old performances. The last time she'd taught at SpeakNow! she'd watched an administrator lick and peel stacks of paper. It had reminded her of the crisp mechanics of warming her scales, running her fingers up and down with a light, firm touch, connecting one note to another, as though she were checking in with a younger, separate part of herself. "I don't know how I can help you," she finally broke the silence. "Dara and I aren't speaking either, as I told you last week."

Amaka stopped sipping, and her body collapsed in on itself, like a wind musician who had run out of air.

"If you're not speaking because of me, because of what happened in Bali—" Amaka had the decency to look embarrassed.

"Not everything is about you," Lillian said archly. "Why would we stop speaking because you were fucking the one person she can't stand? Why would you being the worst friend possible be the reason?" She played with her straw. "Besides, *I'm* not talking to *her*, not the other way around."

It was obvious Amaka was dying to ask why, but instead she looked up at Lillian, almost shyly.

"Why didn't you tell her you saw me at Lani's? You could have made trouble, but you didn't."

"I should have told her. I wish I had told her. I definitely didn't do it for *you*. And you told Lani."

"I'm not trying to be a hypocrite. I just want to know why."

Lillian took a moment to think. As much as she had the upper hand here, she had to make a decision: speak frankly with this girl or leave now. Her curiosity had caused her to answer Amaka's call, but the humility in Amaka's tone had been what brought her down here.

"The first time I met Lani, I was in a bad place. Things were hard with my husband—we'd been trying for a baby for three years. I was having all these dreams; I wasn't sleeping, and Lani... He looked so much like my dad, who died when I was a child." She let it all out. "Everything about him reminded me of my father. It wasn't a sexual thing, he just...I just felt so much better around him."

She laughed humorlessly. "Lani had zero time for me, but I wanted to believe it was possible to speak to my father again—to ask for his guidance. I started to believe in reincarnation. I showed my father's pictures to Dara, and she pretended she could see the resemblance. So we both lied to each other, I guess."

Amaka was quiet, reflecting on Lillian's words until she made her own confession.

"I have to leave Singapore next month. I don't want to leave without talking to her. I've called, sent voice notes—she won't answer. I deserve it, and maybe she thinks it's for the best, but... if I keep walking away, I'll literally end up an angry, bitter woman, without any friends. Or shoes."

"Shoes?" Lillian tried to work that one out.

"Never mind. I'm sorry I've been a bitch to you. Dara only ever wanted to help you, and I put all kinds of suspicious ideas in her head. If she had ulterior motives, it's because she was wrapped up in work, and she let this stupid rivalry with Lani get out of hand. I'm not sleeping with him anymore..."

"I should hope not, after Bali."

"Yes, and in Bali we *both* made mistakes because we were focused on the wrong things," Amaka said seriously. Though there was no accusation in her eyes, Lillian squirmed at the memory of Kike's son being pulled from the water.

"Is Timini OK?"

Amaka nodded. "He's fine. They got him checked out when they got home. I saw Kike post recently about moving back to Lagos. I don't know if it's connected to what happened..."

Amaka paused. "We both made mistakes, Lillian. I need your help fixing mine."

Not yet ready to answer, Lillian drank her coconut water and Amaka did the same. At the far end of the food court, a light rain had started to fall, scattering families from the tables and chairs, but where they sat it was dry. Lillian had seen heavy rain on a sunny day many times in Singapore but had never witnessed the legendary localized weather up close.

"Insane." Lillian stared, using the top of her coconut to scoop and eat the white flesh. "How can two people be in the same place and experience such different weather?"

Amaka eyed her munching. "Coconut meat is really high in calories, you know?"

"I'll take my chances," Lillian replied sarcastically, digging out another chunk.

They approached the residence entrance of Dara's condo. Music from the riverside restaurants blared round the corner and two migrant workers sat on the curb, using free Wi-Fi.

Lillian punched in the code and the door clicked open.

"We'll have to take the stairs," she told Amaka. "Without a key card, the elevator won't work. It's only four floors."

"Do you think she'll be pissed?" Amaka asked nervously, following Lillian to the stairwell. "With us just turning up?"

"I thought you liked a little drama?" Lillian teased, but she was also on edge. She didn't feel proud of the way she'd left Dara's apartment, but she was still hurt about being treated like a fool.

Mixed with that was the undeniable fact that she missed her friend and she'd loved being her roommate.

They got to Dara's door and Lillian pressed the doorbell. She imagined, as they waited, Dara muting the TV, putting her bowl of cereal to one side and slipping her feet into her rabbit-shaped house slippers. The pang for their former intimacy snuck up on her and she was unprepared when the door opened, unlocked.

Dara's eyes bulged and she did a double take. "What are you doing here?"

"Can we talk?" Lillian asked.

"How did you get in?"

"I still remember your code," Lillian admitted. "Amaka wanted to talk to you, and you're not answering her calls."

After a brief second, Dara stepped back for them to enter. She sat at the dining table, tensely folding her arms.

She stared pointedly at Amaka, who came to stand behind a chair.

"I'm sorry I didn't tell you about Lani," Amaka started.

"You said that already, many times. If that was enough, you wouldn't have had to come here," Dara retorted.

"Give her a break, Dara," Lillian said.

"I will *not* give her a break! She's been fucking him this whole time! The very person who came to take my job, the person she was meant to be *helping me get rid of*."

Dara barrelled on. "What is it about this guy? Is he the best ass in the world or something? You completely destroyed our friendship for *that*?"

Lillian reached over and put her hand on Dara's. "Girl, take it down a notch. Please."

Dara lowered her voice, but it made her anger even more intense.

"You were the one person I shared everything with. You were like family to me." Her voice trembled. "Are you really that desperate? Because of *him*?"

"OK, stop." Lillian had had enough. "Seriously."

Dara kept raging. "I'm just so fucking tired of the people who are supposed to care about me treating me like shit! You could have told me *at any time*, and I wouldn't have liked it, but it wouldn't have made you a liar!"

"Maybe she had a good reason for not telling you!" Lillian argued.

"Oh really? So what's the reason, Amaka? Why didn't you tell me?"

"Dara, all you cared about was your job. That's all you thought about and all you talked about, constantly," Amaka said tearfully. "I should have told you, but I've been dealing with a lot, and you didn't notice! I've been struggling and I didn't know how to talk about it, but you took everything personally—me not calling you and not being there for you. But how about you being there for me? It's been all about you."

"Excuse me?" Dara looked stunned. "All about *me?*"

"She slept with Lani, OK, but this is bigger than that," Lillian snapped.

"I'm surprised at you, Lillian," Dara bit back. "You're like a dog with a bone every time someone mentions Lani's name, and now you don't care?"

Lillian recoiled, hurt. "A dog with a bone?"

"Stop, please," Amaka pleaded. "Dara's right, OK? I lied and I fucked up, but I didn't tell him anything about your presentation, I swear."

"We all make mistakes." Lillian glared at Dara. "You've made mistakes, too, right?"

Dara huffed. "What are you talking about?"

"You went behind your colleague's back to poach his client and you wiped out Lani's slides *before* he deleted yours. You're not perfect," Lillian rattled off.

"Well fuck me, Miss Lillian, have you been keeping a list?" Dara scoffed.

"It's not OK for friends to throw your mistakes back in your face, is it? *Kinda* makes you wonder if they're going to throw all the things they've done for you in your face too."

"When have I—"

Lillian interjected. "Friends can't always live up to your

expectations, you know? You can't only be there for them when you think they deserve it."

"Bloody hell!" Dara spluttered, still looking shocked that Lillian was deigning to speak to her like this. "Then forgive me for helping you when you were depressed and giving you a place to stay."

"You offered," Lillian replied defensively.

"Great! So you can pay me back." Dara's awkwardness in extricating her long legs from under the glass table bought Lillian a few seconds.

"There we go." Lillian pointed straight at her. "I knew it was coming. You think we don't see you looking down on us? Yeah, you got your shit together, you make good money, you're doing your thing. You didn't give up your life for some guy and you don't need to impress nobody with nothing. You don't get to say shit about anyone else's shit till you know their story, and then you sure as hell don't get to throw it back in their face!"

Dara stared at Lillian like she'd been punched in the gut, like her friend's words were needles lancing an inflamed boil.

"Is that what you've been thinking about me... all this time?" Dara whispered. "That I have a martyr complex?"

She stabbed the table with her finger. "I know what it's like to have the very people who are supposed to care about you not give a *fucking* penny, so I helped someone who was making a complete mess of her life because I—"

"You felt sorry for me," Lillian flared.

"Yes, I felt sorry for you! Is that so bad, feeling sorry for a complete stranger? You could have said no at any time, but you're the one throwing it in my face!" Dara hissed. "The very thing you're accusing me of!"

"Stop!" Amaka pounded her fist down. "Stop. This is insane. I'm the reason for this mess. Stop ripping into each other! Please!"

The sight of Amaka so worn out and close to tears was like a bucket of cold water bringing Lillian and Dara to their senses.

Amaka dried her face with the sleeve of her hoodie, her voice hard but her cheeks wet and puffy. "I'm broke. I've run up more credit card debt than I can afford to pay back and now I've lost my work pass and I don't know how I'm going to pay for my moving fees and pay off the debt. I've totally messed things up and I've messed things up for my mother too."

Dara looked shocked, both by what she was hearing and the sight of Amaka crying. "Is this all the bags you've been buying?"

"And the shoes and the clothes and the shades and the jewelry," Amaka exhaled.

"I don't understand—why do you need all that crap? Why did you let it get to this point?" Dara looked genuinely baffled.

"I couldn't stop. The more I bought the more I wanted. There was always more, and it was always perfect... always just what I needed to make me feel like exactly who I wanted to be." Amaka picked at the paper napkin she'd folded in her hands and began tearing little rips in it.

"For him?" Lillian asked softly. "For Lani?"

Amaka shook her head sadly. "I wanted him the way I wanted a new bag. I had to have him. With him, I was exactly the type of woman who my father would have wanted me to be: sophisticated and elegant. Someone to chase, not someone who chases. Nothing like my mother."

Seconds passed before she spoke again, but Dara and Lillian waited, hanging on every word.

"When I was born, my father was married to another woman. He married my mother first, but traditionally, not legally, then abandoned her. When she moved to Lagos, he got her pregnant. He had another family in a nicer part of town, and he put us in the shittier part. She loved him. I think he loved her, too, but it was a selfish love.

"The first time I saw my half-siblings, my father blanked me. The next time I met them was at his funeral. No one spoke to us. When my mother tried to see his coffin, we were thrown out of the room, and we spent the rest of the day near the kitchen. But the worst part was seeing his wife and children dressed in clothes that were more expensive than anything I'd ever seen while we looked like the house help. His wife wouldn't even let us wear the traditional family cloth."

Lillian touched her arm gently. "That's terrible. No one should treat family like that. It wasn't your fault, you hear me? You've spent all this money, but it'll never make you good enough in their eyes. You've got to be good enough in yours."

Dara struggled to hold back her tears. "Why didn't you tell me about your dad? I would have understood. I would have *understood*, Amaka."

They dabbed at their eyes with the corners of their shirts. Lillian reached for a packet of tissues in her bag, offering it to them.

"I never knew my father." Dara stared at the table. "My mother got pregnant when she was a teenager, and she never told my grandparents who he was. That's why I have her maiden name."

She dabbed her cheeks with a square of tissue. "I never felt like I was missing anything until I left Nigeria. I was too young to really understand. But I asked her about my father when I was a teenager and she refused to tell me. I haven't spoken to her since I moved here. Even before that."

Amaka stared at her. "What? I didn't know this."

Dara shrugged, but more tears spilled out. "It's better this way, trust me. I'm on my own, and it feels better being honest about it. Hoping and waiting for her to act like a real mother is more painful."

Amaka wiped under her red eyes. "Holy St. Francis, I need a drink."

"That's not the answer," Dara said quickly.

"I know, I know." A hopeful smiled played on Amaka's lips, then vanished.

"I didn't tell Lani anything about your presentation, Dara. I'm telling the truth, I *swear*."

"I know," Dara nodded. "I know it wasn't you. Tim admitted it was him, the fucking bitch. I hope he breaks his other arm."

Lillian and Amaka looked at each other, completely lost.

"It's a long story. Actually, it's really juicy." A chuckle bubbled out of Dara. "But that's for another day."

She blew her nose. "The important part is the end...I made partner."

"What? Are you messing around?" Amaka covered her mouth. "What?"

"Mm-hmm. It's not official until the new tax year in April, but I've been made an offer...and Lani is out."

The smiles on her friends' faces drained away.

Dara continued nonchalantly, but her expression was tight. "But they want me to sign a statement confirming that he started a fight with another lawyer and violated his probationary period."

"What?" Lillian exclaimed. "Did he?"

"No. Yes...somewhere in between," Dara groaned. "I lit a flame and it turned into a forest fire."

"What are you going to do?" Amaka asked quietly.

Dara shrugged. "I don't know. But now I've finally got what I wanted, I can't stop thinking about why I became a lawyer in the first place and what my grandfather would think about me 'winning' this way," she said quietly, gazing into the space between the two girls.

Amaka touched her hand lightly. "I'm probably the worst person to give advice right now..."

"Agreed," Dara quipped, and Lillian bit her lip to stop herself from smiling.

Amaka made a face. "Clap for yourselves. Sometimes the best person to listen to is the person who did exactly what you don't want to do. Don't let what your grandparents or your mother or anyone else wants or wanted influence you now. I mean, history is important and all that, but at some point, you have to stop blaming other people. Sink or swim. Whether it works out or not, what do you actually want? And if you're not ready, then fine, but it's up to you."

"I agree," Lillian nodded, her eyes shining. "Forget who he is and forget me and Amaka. Don't be scared to go for what you want, but don't let them play you, either. I know exactly what Amaka's talking about. It's why...I've been looking at flights back to Philadelphia and talking to a couple friends about jobs, mostly teaching piano, maybe going back to school. It's time."

She met both girls' eyes and took in their surprise. "It's not going to solve all my problems, but I've got to stop running. I've just got to stop."

"Look at you, Miss Lillian," Dara marveled. "You've come a long way."

Lillian gave a side smile. "It's that or keep watching tarot videos to tell me what to do with my life."

Amaka recoiled in horror. "Eh?!"

Dara burst out laughing at the look on her face.

Two months later, in December, Lillian stretched out on the bed in Dara's guest room, watching a performance of a Clara Schumann piece she loved. The anticipation of her flight in a few hours and the last-minute panic of buying winter clothes (and then trying to fit all her things into three suitcases) had wiped her out. Drowsy from the rich, creamy pasta Dara had cobbled together as her official last supper, she closed her eyes and listened to the quiet of her own thoughts, thankful that their friendship had rebounded to the point where Dara was comfortable letting her stay one more night. For the first time in her life, she felt a spirited, healthy excitement about the future, tinged with just the right amount of trepidation. Things had come together. An old friend from Curtis who played with an internationally acclaimed bassist had helped her get a job teaching music in a conservatory in Brooklyn—not Philly, after all.

It would be her first Christmas in the U.S. in more than four years.

Her share of the sale of the piano had bought her a plane ticket home and a deposit for a shared room, but with little change to spare. Warren had agreed to withdraw his divorce petition and let her file in the U.S., which would not only come through a lot faster, but also meant that neither of them would have to blame the other. She'd unfriended him on social media, but not before she'd seen a photo of him and his new Indonesian American girlfriend, who fitted snugly under his arm. In the last photo Lillian had seen, his girlfriend's hand was cupped around the small, hard bulge of her belly, and both of them were grinning from ear to ear. She stared at the photo for a full minute before closing the browser.

Surprisingly, Lillian missed Yishun, despite being there only a short time. She'd started to get used to the stares, and Orchard's flashiness was non-existent there. It had felt like real life. There were no futuristic robots chirping to themselves as they zig-zagged around, cleaning the streets. Instead, hunchbacked old men wiped and swept and shuffled away, their necks bowed down to the ground. Teenagers in school uniforms were more boisterous, less restrained. She saw more glimpses in Yishun of murky, human truth: flashes of violence, like a jogger kicking at his dog in the reservoir park; a father slapping his toddler at a taxi stand to stop him from crying; a helper pinching the child she was caring for at a bus stop; a middle-aged white man strolling down the street, while his young Asian partner and her Asian son followed miserably behind him; a drunk couple declaring their profound, frustrated love in the early hours of the morning, then tearfully striking each other's faces. Yet there was community, too. Many times, she'd seen strangers gently steer a distressed older person to a nearby bench as a local business owner made a phone call to a helpline.

It's time to return to real life. Bem was no longer a trainee doctor waiting for the residency program that would change their lives; Yahimba would never walk beside her or listen to her play. It was time to stop torturing herself with who she might have been with their guidance, if they'd been there to water the seeds and shade her from the harshness of the sun. Maybe they weren't behind her but waiting ahead, ready for her to hurry up and live using everything they'd given her.

Voices roused her. Amaka had left Singapore the month before, and Dara never had guests. Realizing she hadn't heard the bell ring, Lillian sat up, intrigued.

As soon as she recognized his voice, she felt like she was on a rollercoaster that had dropped straight down.

There was a knock on the door and Lillian paused the video. It opened and Dara's face appeared—sheepish and guilty-looking, but determined.

"Don't panic."

"What is he doing here?" Lillian started.

"I'm sorry I didn't do this for you properly before." Dara's words rushed out, full of adrenaline. "I did ask Kike something, just before the accident, and she told me that Lani's mother wasn't Yoruba. It turns out she's half Tiv."

Lillian gasped. "What?"

"I couldn't let you go without talking to him. He owes me now, and you've got to talk to him properly to find out once and for all."

Lillian kneeled on the bed, her feet together. "Owes you? For what?"

"It doesn't matter."

Lillian folded her arms, refusing to drop it.

"I had the chance to throw him under the bus, but instead... I don't know, we're going to build a bridge. Maybe. It doesn't matter right now, Lillian. Go talk to him."

"Dara," Lillian stammered. "He doesn't want to know. He made that clear."

"Show him the pictures. Please. Just show him. Then you can get on the plane and never have to wonder about it again."

Taking long breaths to steady herself, Lillian finally nodded and, opening her hand luggage, took out the faded envelope.

Lani was in the kitchen. Trembling, Lillian showed him the photo from the recital, and then another and another.

The look on Lani's face was indescribable. He took a screenshot of one of the pictures and sent it to his mother, phoning to wake her at 6 a.m. in London. He put her on speaker and they listened, their hearts in their mouths.

"Yes, that was Bem... Bem Ajuwa... my second cousin—we had the same great-grandfather... Bem was a gynecologist... he moved to the U.S. in the 1990s... we heard he passed away over there... a car accident... and the wife passed, too..."

And just like that, a piece of Lani's family thread knotted itself to hers.

Amaka

In January, a year after Lani first arrived, a grimy fog descended on Singapore, as it did almost every year. Despite being labeled an "act of nature," it was man-made, blown in from hundreds of forest fires raging in the Sumatra region of Indonesia. It was impossible to get anyone to accept blame or responsibility for the annual affliction created by companies razing trees and expelling hundreds of animals in their never-ending thirst for palm oil. Countries pointed fingers at each other while citizens staggered through the mist, wearing white masks across their mouths, dry eyes blinking like the gashes of extra-terrestrial mouths. Outdoor events were cancelled, and the Pollutant Standards Index, the computerized reading that tested air quality (and curiously always gave better results from within Singapore than independent sources outside) was refreshed and shared hourly. The very things that made Singapore what it was—the rooftop bars, the beach clubs, the alfresco dining—were all closed up.

For Amaka, nine thousand miles away in London, this was a small compensation. Winter dug into her, stinging her cheeks raw, driving against her chest and neck. No matter how tightly she wrapped her coat around herself or tugged her scarf, the cold won. The ground, thank Jesus, was dry, so there were no devilish puddles to turn her feet into numb bricks. Stamping herself warm and tugging a beanie over her ears, she paced on the pavement. Each stone square was mismatched in brown, gray and mossy green, and leafless trees jutted their knobby branches into the sky.

She settled on the wall below the "For Sale" sign. As with so much of London, the wall was uneven and low; it forced her to sit like a child, her knees reaching up past her waist. Slipping the keys back into her pocket, she waited, twisting her head up to stare at her father's house, at the brown brick and white columns straddling the yellow door. Both tenants were at work and Amaka had both sets of keys, but she didn't want to go in until Chinyere arrived. Outside felt like safer, neutral ground. So much could go wrong between now and completion. Ugo personally extending an olive branch by selling the house was a momentous first step, but until the papers were signed and the money was split four ways, Amaka knew her siblings would not fully trust them. Their mother was still undergoing treatment, so they were eager to move quickly. Everything had been done over the phone between her and Chinyere, and today was the first day they would meet. Her youngest sister had sent her an Instagram request just the day before, and conversations with Chinyere had started to become less tense. Amaka had already decided that her share of the sale would be used to revive Ugo's businesses before thinking of anything else. If Ugo could finally come to a place of peace and security, then Amaka hoped her mother could finally start to live her life for herself.

A woman carried hefty Tesco bags past Amaka. Somewhere to her right, children's voices laughed from a small, gated park. She wondered if this was where she and Chukwu would have stayed had he ever made good on his promise to bring her to England all those years ago.

She reached behind her and took a photo of the house, texting the image to her mother, who was probably stuck in Lagos traffic on her way back home. Only Ugo would understand the mix of emotions she was feeling, standing outside the last link to Chukwu she was about to let go of.

The last two months staying with her mother in Lagos had not been easy. What was left of Amaka's things from Singapore had remained unpacked in a spare room, and she'd spent her time applying and being rejected from multiple jobs. Deliberately secluding herself, she'd kept her return home quiet, staying more connected with Dara and Lillian thousands of miles away than with the people around her. There had been no farewell parties—there never were when you lost your job and got kicked out of a country so many people were desperate to get into. Hardly anyone from Singapore got in touch at all, though she'd got one text from Lani, who'd apologized for things getting as bad as they had and wished her luck. That, in the end, was all their mess had been worth.

So she was overwhelmed when Bayo called just before her flight out, telling her he'd heard about her financial troubles and that he and Kike wanted to give her the Ndidi Emefiele painting of the floating head she liked so much. It was worth quite a bit, he'd said, and they could sell it for her or let her have it and try to find a buyer. Of course she'd agreed, but for a split second, that old demon had breathed in her ear, whispering what she could do with the cash rather than pay off her credit card debt.

It was only then that she admitted the depth of her addiction.

In Lagos, she made a weekly ten-minute walk to 1004, the housing estate where her therapist lived. Once a week, the counselor—who she'd picked from the top of a Google search—opened a book of self-penned poetry and asked Amaka to use her own words to complete the emotive and theatrical verses. Each session began with Amaka struggling to hide her smirks and ended with her sniveling and sometimes full-on weeping. Though a little cringey at first, the poetry was strangely effective.

Many times, the first thing she did in the morning was reopen the online retail websites she'd deleted and fill up her shopping basket. Nausea would overcome her, and with shaking hands, she'd close her laptop and force herself to move away.

One day she opened her emails to find one from her old bank. From its London branch, to be exact, informing her of an opening in its risk management team and inviting her to apply for the position. When she got the job a week later, she was left in no doubt that Indira's fingers had been all over the appointment. She'd been convinced she would be unemployed for at least a year; she would never forget the difference the right boss could make. From that point on, the way she saw herself changed. She couldn't be completely worthless after all.

The next day, she and Ugo sat down, and her mother's undisguised joy at having Amaka home came to an end. It was hard to explain the hunger that had been gnawing at her for years, to confess the need to be near Chinyere and his sisters, and to admit that Ugo's love and sacrifice alone were not enough. They spoke late into the night, taking small steps to close the last, unspoken rift between them. In the morning, they'd decided to make a trip to Umuahia, her parents' hometown, when Amaka was next home.

She'd sold her bags and the rest of her shoes in the run up to Christmas, making more of a profit than she would have in the pre-owned luxury market in Singapore. This was deeply ironic, given the fact that holidays were *exactly* the seasons in which Nigerians from around the world flew back home, using the clothes they wore to peacock how well they were doing abroad. Using the money she'd made, she bought herself a ticket to London once her work visa came through, and then used the last of her savings on a deposit for a room in a flat-share in Ealing.

A crisp wind whipped the stiff branches above and bent the twigs below. Shivering, she went on to Rohit's Instagram page and scrolled through the images of Sanaa's wedding—they'd been etched in her mind for months, but she still couldn't help herself. She stared at her favorite one, taken in a huge marquee with candy-colored stripes, flower petals and origami birds billowing above the wedding guests. Everyone was dressed in light, silk saris, pastel-colored tunics and panama hats, and they clapped and cheered for Rohit's sister and her new husband, who sat on a little stage. In the foreground, Rohit stood with a group of his male cousins, captured at what must have been the end of their choreographed dance. The smile on Rohit's face was contained, his body straighter than his relatives who were doubled over, some exhilarated, some animated, all beaming. Amaka was glad the camera was too far away to see his eyes.

Sometimes, she imagined she'd gone to Phuket. She imagined she'd been brave enough to try again, and whole enough to be fully herself. Eventually, Rohit would have been won over and he'd have introduced her to his Bangkok friends and, like one of the pictures of them swimming in the ocean, she'd have stopped complaining about messing up her hair and joined them in the water.

A nervous swimmer, she would have clung to his back once the ocean bed dissolved, and he would have stayed close to the shore, not teasing her for once. She'd have held on to his slippery, bare shoulders, slowing him down in the racing games and laughing so hard that her ribs ached. After a while, they would have grown quiet and floated away from the group. She would have tilted her head up to a sky empty of planes or birds. The moment would be pure but fleeting, like a gold coin flashing then slipping into deeper water.

Footsteps approached to her left. She was standing when Chinyere's brisk thud came to a stop. Like her, he was dressed in work clothes.

"Hi," she said nervously.

"Hi," he said gruffly, keeping his hands in his coat pockets. He wasn't as tall as he'd looked on the video call, and she noticed his acne had cleared up.

"The estate agent isn't here yet, but I've got a key." She gestured to the door. "Should we wait inside?"

"Yes, we can go in." He stepped back to let her lead the way, his eyes falling briefly on her boots.

"Nice shoes," he commented as she turned the keys in the door.

"Thanks." She held back the true extent of her delight, twisting a red ankle boot to one side. "They're Gucci."

She'd held on to just one pair.

Lillian

"Damn, Miss Lillian," Andre whistled, taking off his puffer jacket and hanging it on the coat-rack. "All dressed up for me?"

Lillian chuckled and put her phone back in her handbag. A PSI email alert updating her about the air quality in Singapore had momentarily taken her out the room and back onto the island. "You wish. You're a little early."

"That OK?" Andre peeled off his gloves and stuffed them into his jacket pockets.

"Sure. You can warm up first. Let's start with the minors." She wheeled her chair closer to the piano stool. "How was school?"

"It was *aight*. I try to think about it as little as I can once I leave," he quipped, running his right and then left hand down the F minor key. "Man, the subway is whack today. I ditched last period and it still took me over an hour to get here. I was hoping I could get some extra practice in."

"On Lexington Avenue?" Lillian's heart was in her throat.

"No, the Broadway Express. Lots of traffic 'cos of the Lunar New Year parade. You going into the city?" Andre grinned. "You look good, Miss Lillian, real talk. You look *hawt*."

"Andre, you're fifteen. Stop it. And you shouldn't be skipping class—you know the deal we have with your mom. Now, are you sure the delays weren't on Lexington?"

"I'm sure. Can I stop with the scales now? I really want to get into the music."

"All right, let's go over the last few pieces."

The lesson went by quickly. Andre had started playing only a year before, transferring from another teacher when she'd joined the conservatory, but he was a quick learner with an excellent ear. They ended the session with a new piece.

Her young student slid his hands up the notes, the second and fifth fingers of his right hand fumbling from one chord to the next. He took his foot off the pedal a little too early, cutting off the chime effect instead of letting it fade.

"Awesome," she grinned, shaking him by his shoulders. "Andre, that was *so* good!"

"You think so?" He squeezed his hands between his knees, but a hopeful smile showed he dared to believe her.

"So good. Your tempo was excellent: slow and sweet. And you sight-read really well. A couple things. Remember to keep your wrist soft—floppy, like this." She let hers hang, shaking them to demonstrate. "If you stay stiff, your hands will ache after you play this piece a couple times. And then, remember your fingering, here and here. It'll make it much easier to find the inverted chords, which are, don't forget, exactly the same notes, just turned upside down. Let's try playing the right hand an octave higher, like the book suggests. You'll really be able to hear the bells that way. Try it."

She settled back in her chair and let Andre find his new opening. This time, he used the pedals throughout, his long feet in black winter boots pressing down with greater ease. The high-pitched tinkle of *The Westminster Chimes* filled the practice room. Languid and gentle, almost romantic in its innocence and simplicity, it was a piece she'd taught countless times, but she would never tire of its ability to charm her students.

"What do you think?" Lillian asked Andre when the last chord faded away.

"Not bad." His eyes shone.

Lillian smiled and picked up his book of sheet music. She flipped past the next three pages and circled the page number of his next piece.

Andre took the book back and stared at it. "Oh, shit."

"It's a little more challenging, but you're ready. I'll send you a YouTube performance before our next lesson. Take a look at the fingering for the left hand. The right's pretty straightforward." She rose as Andre stuffed the book into his backpack.

"Cool, cool. Then can I play something from, like, this century?" he cracked.

"I got you," she chuckled. "Go on. I'll see you next week."

"Wait, I was going to ask," he said as he pulled on his coat. "Could you play something? You said you might last time."

"Yeah, sure." She smiled, deciding on Dvorak's Humoresque in G flat, a short piece that came to her quickly, though it had been years since she'd played it. As her fingers skipped across the keys, the light, sweet tune sang through the room, and she pictured a village fair where little children, safe and happy, capered and bounced in step with a merry-go-round. It was a tune for fathers to pull their children onto their knee as they hummed along; for mothers, round and soft, with hands coated in flour; for kitchens aired with orange peel and cocoa pods; for apple trees to drop their fruit of cloying, wrinkled skin and browning pits. The melody ended, and in its place, darker, wistful chords chimed, as though the Czech recalled a loss, a love made sweeter because it was gone.

As she looped to the beginning, the music pulled her back so she was in the church hall, both her parents watching, and then in Dr. Cohn's home, Yahimba sitting beside her. Lillian felt her mother's stockinged calf leaning on hers, her arm resting on the stool behind her. She was riveted by the small miracle of her eleven-year-old fingers speaking a language she couldn't understand. The wind rattled the bay windows of the alcove, frosting the glass panes with its icy breath, drawing mother closer to child. When the piece was done, it hung in the air; her mother, and the warmth and weight of her leg, evaporated too.

She walked down the opposite end of the corridor, swiping herself into the staff room. It was empty, as it always was in the late afternoon. She'd timed her last lesson the way she had today because she wasn't ready to field questions about why she was dressed smarter than usual. She'd been working at the conservatory less than two months, but it already felt as familiar and comfortable as the old winter coat she'd dug out of storage which now hung on the rack by the door. She loved the worn sofa, the burp of air bubbles in the water dispenser, the smell of day-old coffee and cigarettes. Most of the teachers were older and full of gossip about tours and shows, every day dangling juicy morsels in response to news stories about this artist or that musician. She loved sitting, listening and laughing, and they loved having an audience. Then, volleying one or two more bitchy barbs over their shoulders, they would roll out to their next class, teaching drums, clarinet, piano and voice. Between the teachers and the students, most of whom were on some kind of financial assistance, she was surrounded by people who lived and breathed music.

Lillian finally felt at home.

After printing out the instrumental sheet music for *Fallin'* by Alicia Keys, she slipped it into a plastic sleeve, writing Andre's name on a label before sticking it on and setting it aside for next week. She swapped her flats for a smart pair of boots and shrugged her coat on, wrapping and knotting her scarf.

On the subway into the city, she hummed *The Westminster Chimes* under her breath, thinking of Amaka and wondering if they would ever reunite in London and regain the surprising intimacy of that last month together. Somehow, they'd found themselves at the same juncture in life. On a tight budget, packing, unsure of where they'd be moving on to next, they'd clung to each other, texting first thing in the morning and last thing at night, rarely going a day without a phone call. They were careful at first, eager not to hurt or pass judgment, but with each day, the spark of who they were was relit, and they allowed the truth of their personalities to breathe. They gave their opinions, they gave advice and helped each other when they could. Twice a week, they had met outside Amaka's building and run around the bay, across the Helix Bridge, past the Formula 1 grandstand and back around over the Esplanade bridge. Each time they spoke less and walked more. They completed their last run in bittersweet silence, watching the sun set in a flaming-red sky.

Amaka had been the one to leave first, having less time allowed by her Nigerian passport. Their farewell dinner the night before had been an extravagant one on top of Marina Bay Sands and paid for, of course, by Dara, the only one of them still with a job at that point. Lillian had wondered if the choice had been a wise one. The cinematic view and super-realism of the city below would have been a painful reminder of what Amaka was leaving behind. From the bar, the three women had looked out at the skyscrapers hedging around the dark basin of water, like protective shards of glass. The roads and bridges were rods of gold light, rich tunnels of wealth from the banks to the rest of the city-state. Women in loose, silk shift dresses—so many carrying Chanel Boy Bags and YSL chain clutches that it was practically a uniform—let their men steer them gently by the small of their backs. On the hotel side of the bar, night swimmers floated at the edge of a mile-long infinity pool, hovering like fish over the steep drop.

There had been nothing to fear. They'd laughed at themselves, the people around them and each other, and Lillian knew they'd be OK. She still worried about Amaka, but it seemed like her friend had made peace with the place her life had come to and her fall in fortune. Comforted by each other's presence, they'd focused on Dara, lapping up every detail of her new business plan, praying that the risk she was about to take wouldn't end with her in the same boat they were in.

Her phone buzzed as she walked up the subway steps and onto the street.

Good luck! Lani's message read. *My mother says she feels in her "spirit" that it's going to go well.* X

It was just what she needed to hear, just what she needed to hook her faith on. She'd reply later and explain that it was a long application process, sometimes taking up to two years, and that there were many hurdles ahead. She had to complete a profile; there would be interviews and workshops and then a wait to see if someone liked her and wanted a single black woman to raise their child. And even afterward there would be more inspections before it became legal and final.

There was no need to worry about that now. It was enough to simply find the adoption center, walk up the steps, press the bell and go in.

Dara

Dara walked past the seafood restaurants in Boat Quay, ignoring the water tanks displaying monstrous, prehistoric crustaceans squirming sluggishly, promoters badgering her to eat them. The streets were half-empty. The gray, ghostly pall from the bird's-eye view of her office window was less visible now that she was on the ground. Several people threw her odd glances because she was maskless. She'd tried wearing a mask, but she found it hard to breathe through; she preferred to brave the haze's charred odor for the short walk down the quay to her condo.

She ducked under the short tunnels, their tiled walls covered in government-sanctioned graffiti that captured a colorful and inoffensive passage through history, from the Malay kingdom of Singapura to present day. There was a grumble behind her as a river boat cruise drove past and approached the next jetty.

She made a split-second decision to buy a ticket to Robertson Quay. As the only person on the boat, the space was a luxury. The evening breeze was cool and the ride was quiet; the city looked older and more worn, reminding her of the parts of the island that were frozen in time and could only be accessed by boat. *Kampongs*, they were called then: rustic huts with chickens pecking at your feet.

A faint memory returned to her of a trip she'd taken to Ibadan with her grandparents. Perhaps they'd been going to a wedding or some type of formal ceremony, because she remembered everyone being formally dressed and the itchy torture of one of those dresses with an underlayer of netting that Granee loved to put her in. Sitting between them, she'd slept for most of the journey, leaning against Grandad's arm or in Granee's lap so that her dreams were perfumed with his freshly laundered suit and the aftershave he used to dab on the red silk handkerchief in his breast pocket, and Granee's thick French scent. She remembered this journey because every time the car hit a bump and woke her, or her grandfather asked Godwin, their driver, how much fuel was left, she felt a tightness in their bodies and heard it in his voice. She felt it, too, in her grandmother's silence, because Granee never stopped talking. She usually had an opinion on everything: how the cook should cut the meat, how often the gardener should water the plants, how the houseboy should iron her husband's black trousers (inside out, then along the crease, not flat from the front). They were talkers, her grandparents. They talked and they argued and they laughed. But every time a car sped past them, Granee tensed and clutched a hand on her knee, took a deep breath and exhaled.

Fear was something she'd never associated with her grandparents before, but now she vividly remembered their constant need to keep her safe from accidents, from sickness, from pain. Their fear had made her so afraid of making a mistake she hadn't realized how few risks she'd actually taken in her life.

"Boarding pass, please."

Dara took out the slip of paper and handed it over.

"Is this enough?" She put two ten-dollar notes down.

The barista at Dubai Airport handed her change back in dirhams and Dara found an empty table to wait at for her breakfast. Yawning, she found her place in *The Fishermen*, a novel with a blood-red cover and sinister hooks hanging in a tangled knot. She had pushed for this book about four brothers destroyed by an oracle's prophecy in the last book club vote and won. Ironically, after Amaka, Lillian and Kike had left, Dara had continued to attend and had hosted a few times at her place;

in the last meeting, Nana had announced her move to Paris, and Dara found herself volunteering to take over. It was funny how things had changed.

After twenty minutes, she put the book down. She was fascinated by its mythic symbolism, the Yoruba and Igbo mythology she was still learning about, but there was too much swimming inside her head to concentrate right now. She unzipped her laptop and opened her slides for the legal conference she and Lani would be speaking at, proofreading them again before reading the latest welcome email from her hotel. There was another email from the conference organizer, giving adjusted timings for the presentation. There was nothing more to do.

Lani's aluminum case came to a noisy stop beside her. He put his tray down and unhooked the bulging white shopping bags.

"Could you have done any more shopping?" Dara teased, sliding her laptop away to make space on the table.

"I'm very good at giving gifts. It's one of my love languages," Lani grinned, sitting down. He stretched his legs out to the side of the table and draped his arm round the back of the chair beside him. "And my family has expensive taste."

"So you said." Dara frowned at his position. "You're going to trip someone if you sit like that."

"Who?"

"Whoever might be walking past."

He threw his head back and laughed. "You worry too much about other people. Let them take care of themselves and leave my legs alone."

He held one of his bags out. "Here."

"What's this?"

"Open it."

Half-embarrassed, Dara took it and peered inside.

"Yoruba?" She took the box out.

"It's a USB stick with lessons pre-loaded." He looked pleased with himself as he sipped his latte. "They had lots of languages. Of course, you don't really need it to get about, but I thought since this was your first trip back, and you'll have down time…"

"Did you get one for yourself?" Dara covered up how touched she was.

"No, I speak Yoruba."

Dara scoffed, disbelievingly. "*You* speak Yoruba? Yeah, right. You're the whitest black guy I know."

"Bloody hell, you finally said it," Lani chuckled. "Well, you're going to get a bit of a shock when we get there because I'm fluent. All my nannies spoke Yoruba or Tiv."

"I'm impressed. And…dumbfounded." Dara turned the box in her hands. She'd learned quite a bit about him in the last two months, but clearly there were still surprises. The man was very comfortable talking about himself now: she knew all about his great-grandfather setting up one of the first law firms in Nigeria, his secret love of rock music, his love for his five-year-old niece who knew every player's name in the current Arsenal team and the mother who split her time between London and Lagos but never entered Nigeria without a return ticket already booked.

Lani got a glimpse of her laptop screen. "Let's have one more look at the slides."

She turned it around and they clicked through it.

"I'm not sure about the end," she frowned.

"You mean you're not sure if *I* should end." Lani's smile was a little unconvincing. "You're going to have to trust me, you know, if this is going to work."

Doubt must have been written on her face because he turned serious.

"Are you having second thoughts?"

"And third and fourth and fifth…"

"No, really. Do you not want this?"

"Lani, we're too far down the road for this."

"But that's not the same thing as wanting it. Doing something because you think you have to and doing it because you believe in it are two different things."

They'd had this conversation many times. They'd gone over the risks, but they'd also been clear about their whys. They were tired of waiting for the powers that be to deem them good enough.

They had swum upstream, but it got even harder the higher up you got, and so much more complicated when you had to prove yourself in so many more ways than everyone else. They wanted to do their own thing, to work for themselves. They sorted through various arguments, bringing up examples from the past, personal ones and cautionary tales, weighing up the mental and emotional costs of working for a firm versus setting up their own. In the end, they'd come up with the perfect solution: a Singapore-based legal consultancy for Asian and African companies looking to invest in one another. Dara stayed in Singapore; Lani was now based in London. It had worked on paper so far—they'd generated a huge amount of interest—but now they were doing it for real.

"Do you regret giving up partner?" Lani stared at her.

She knew he still wondered if he would have done the same. It wasn't a question worth probing too much since deep down, they knew the answer. After less than a year on his CV at Morgan Corbett Shaw, and having narrowly avoided a legal dispute, going into business with Dara had been a heaven-sent solution for him. Dara was the one with the most to lose and Kike's warning the year before about Lani's habit of leaving destruction in his wake was never far from her mind.

Dara shook her head. She'd taken a calculated risk. There was no backing out now. "Making partner would never have been the finish line, just the beginning. It would never have been enough. The moves would have been different, but the game would have stayed the same. I couldn't give another decade of my life to that."

"So, you're in? Fully?" Lani's face brightened.

She pretended to think about it for second, enjoying making him wait. "You know all those classical stories I like telling?"

"Oh God, not another one," Lani groaned, eating his croissant.

"My grandfather used to read them to me from this huge book—it's out of print now. One of my favorites was about Hercules and the hydra. It's a mythical creature. A snake-like monster with three heads."

"I know what a hydra is; I read a book once." He performed one of her exaggerated eye-rolls and they laughed.

"Anyway, Hercules cut each of the hydra's heads and then his nephew, Iolaus, burned the wounds. They buried the heads and then they used the blood, which was poisonous, to make these deadly arrows to kill other monsters. They took the very thing that was trying to destroy them and used it to their advantage, becoming this incredible killing machine. Did they want to kill? No. But they did what they had to do, and it made them stronger. That's how I feel. Plus—" She tried not to choke up. "Setting up my own company that's doing business in Nigeria? I know my grandfather would be really fucking proud of me, but more importantly, *I'm* proud of me."

Lani nodded and they shared a smile.

"You know, I could introduce you to a few friends while we're in Lagos." Lani looked impish. "I've got a mate who would really dig your whole independent woman, cutting hydras' heads off thing."

Dara allowed herself a good, long laugh.

"Lani Idowu, I would rather cut my own head off than date one of your friends," she said when she was done. "And not that it's any of your business, but I'm seeing someone, so you can take that particular burden off your plate."

"*Oh...*" Lani made a show of pretending to be impressed. "Please tell me it's not a lawyer."

"No. If you must know, he's a teacher, although he would make an excellent private detective." She sniggered, enjoying how irritated Lani was, and picked up her book again.

Turning the page, she grew warm at the memory of Adam's first Instagram message. She'd been genuinely flabbergasted that a stranger she'd flirted with in a random hotel in Bali had gone to the trouble of looking for her online with the scant information she'd given him. Somehow, being one of a handful of black, female lawyers in Singapore had paid off. As they moved from texting to calling to Zooming, Adam's sweetness and uncomplicated interest had become sexier and more appealing: no games, no ego, no competition. She'd explained how her concern for Lillian had kept her from showing up that night at the hotel, and that was all it had taken for them to start afresh.

She'd booked a flight to Wellington for when she returned from Lagos, and from there, he'd organized different stops around the country. She knew she was moving fast, but she was way overdue to take a big, fat risk. Their first trip together would either be the best of her life or a complete disaster, but she would *live* this perilous journey, not just read about it.

"How long until Jan's plane arrives?" Lani checked his phone.

"Another hour," Dara murmured.

"Are you going to ask him not to speak pidgin when we get there or am I going to have to do it?"

"Yes, please, offend the director of our company and the Singaporean permanent resident it's registered under, why don't you?" she retorted.

"Not happy about that. It's really not good for optics for a German to be a major shareholder in a Nigerian company, not with what we're trying to do."

"It was the only way, and if it wasn't for Jan, I wouldn't know it was harmattan season in Lagos right now and that I'd need a jacket, so that's thanks to him and not thanks to you." She put her earphones on to put an end to their conversation and eased back into her seat. "I'm going to take a nap. Let me know when they announce our gate."

Closing her eyes, she returned to the Lagos she'd once known, willing the fragments she remembered to survive—the dragonflies, the butterflies, the blossoms—all the while knowing that nothing was ever meant to stay the same.

Acknowledgments

Thank you so much to my literary agent, Hayley Steed. I've loved working on this book with you and I've learned a lot from you. Thank you for helping me whip it into shape and for making me take my time.

Thank you, Amy Baxter, for your love of this book, for caring deeply about the details and the women and the world. Thank you, Rachael Kelly, for the bird's-eye scrutiny and for powerfully guiding the manuscript toward a finished, polished book. The journey became so fun and real when we came together—the margin comments still make me laugh.

Thank you to my parents, Dr. Charles Fadipe and Mrs. Morayo Fadipe, for the best gift you can give a young girl—an excellent education—for supporting choices they didn't always understand and for reminding me how long I've dreamed of this. I know you're both so proud.

Thank you to my twin sister, Taiye Fadipe-Brown, for letting me steal books I didn't pay for and not getting annoyed at me for reading them first, and to all my siblings and family for their love and support.

Thank you especially to my older sister, Charlotte Fadipe, and Uncle Femi Adenuga for your help with researching Bem's medical training in the U.S. Thank you, Sam Koiki, for your help with Amaka's role as a credit officer, Ify Bamigboye and Mrs. Esther Madu for helping me with Amaka's Igbo and Divya Batra for helping me flesh Rohit out and sharpen the dynamics between Rohit and Sanaa. I hope it was authentic enough!

Thank you to my amazing beta readers and friends who read

this book or gave up precious time trying to help me choose a title without getting fed up: Yomi Wilcox, Amy Hii, Shola Asante, Rebecca Scroggs, Vanessa De Hamza.

Thank you to Ms. Sefi Atta for so graciously giving me feedback and spurring me on.

Thank you to Alice Clark Platts and the Singapore Writers Group for being my training ground and for showing me that publishing a book was truly possible.

Thank you to my first heroes, my English teachers—Ms. Michelle Crawford and the late Ms. Sally Dugan.

Thank you to Suzannah Dunn and the team at the Curtis Brown Edit and Pitch Course for the excellent critiques and for connecting me to other writers all trying to wrestle their way into writing professionally.

Thank you to all the coffee shops and restaurants that let me overstay my empty coffee cup: The Book Café, Kith Café, Beviamo, The Dempsey Project, Claymore Connect.

Thank you to the amazing Book YouTubers who helped demystify and democratize the business of publishing: Alexa Donne, iWriterly, Ellen Brock and ShaelinWrites.

Thank you Singapore for the ride. It was wild (especially the end).

Thank you Lord Jesus for your grace.

The Singapore Book Club's Reading List

Purple Hibiscus, Chimamanda Ngozi Adichie
Homegoing, Yaa Gyasi
The Sympathizer, Viet Thanh Nguyen
The Seven Husbands of Evelyn Hugo, Taylor Jenkins Reid
Love in Colour, Bolu Babalola
The Joys of Motherhood, Buchi Emecheta
The Bride Test, Helen Hoang
Americanah, Chimamanda Ngozi Adichie
The Vegetarian, Han Kang
Nothing to Envy, Barbara Demick
The Fishermen, Chigozie Obioma

Lillian's Music List

Ballade No. 1 in G minor, Opus 23, Frederic Chopin
"Un Sospiro," Franz Liszt
Kamarinskaya, Opus 39 No. 14, Pyotr Ilyich Tchaikovsky
Prelude in C sharp minor (Op. 3 No. 2), Sergei Rachmaninoff
The Westminster Chimes, Duncan S. Miller
Humoresque in G flat, Antonin Dvorak
Fallin', Alicia Keys

Art

Vietnamese Woman, oil painting on canvas, Iryna Khmelevska
Painting by Ndidi Emefiele, title unknown